Dear Readers,

Welcome to my School for Young Ladies! My name is Charlotte Harris, and I founded this institution to help impressionable girls make wise decisions about their marital prospects. As a widow who traveled a rocky road in that area myself, I would like them to learn from my mistakes. My late husband, Jimmy Harris, wasn't a *bad* man—he just had a way of spending all my inheritance that was rather annoying. When he left me destitute after fighting some silly duel, I was forced to fend for myself. I do not wish to see my girls suffer the same misfortune.

That is why my curriculum now emphasizes lessons for avoiding fortune-hunters. I know the more vulgar in society call my academy "The School for Heiresses" due to my success in that area, but we do offer all the standard courses for young women, as well. My ladies can dance, play the pianoforte, and sing with the best of them (just ask Lady Venetia, who once softened up a kidnapper by singing him ballads).

Fortunately, I'm not alone in my endeavor. I have a wonderful benefactor who ferrets out gossip about potential husbands for my girls and who advises me in business matters concerning the school. Since he wishes to keep his anonymity, he will only say that he's a distant cousin of my late husband. He goes by the name Michael, but between you and me, I doubt that he's related to the Harrises. No one in Jimmy's family ever showed an ounce of the wit "Cousin Michael" shows in his letters.

Truth be told, I'd very much like to know who Michael is, but he's not saying—and, in exchange for his help, I agreed not to pursue it. However, that grows more difficult by the day. Especially since I think I have a bit of a crush on him (shhh, don't tell my pupils). Nonetheless, thanks to him, several of my young ladies have successfully navigated the treacherous waters of society to find husbands who not only suit them very well but who also love them very well.

I hope you'll enjoy their stories!

> Respectfully,
> Charlotte Harris
> Owner and Headmistress
> Mrs. Harris's School for Young Ladies

New York Times Bestselling Author

Sabrina Jeffries

QUEEN OF THE SEXY REGENCY ROMANCE

The Summer

of the

School for Heiresses

Parlor Games / Regency Trivia
Excerpts / Author Video

Monthly Drawing for $50
National Department Store
Gift Card / April-Aug. 2009
(One prize each month for 5 months
— a prize fit for an heiress!)

Inside scoop on two new
Heiress books for 2009

Summer
2009

Join the
fun at:

www. SabrinaJeffries.com

Sabrina Jeffries

Never Seduce a Scoundrel

POCKET BOOKS

New York   London   Toronto   Sydney

Pocket Books
A Division of Simon & Schuster, Inc.
1230 Avenue of the Americas
New York, NY 10020

This book is a work of fiction. Names, characters, places, and incidents either are products of the author's imagination or are used fictitiously. Any resemblance to actual events or locales or persons, living or dead, is entirely coincidental.

This Pocket Books paperback edition May 2009

POCKET and colophon are registered trademarks of Simon & Schuster, Inc.

For information about special discounts for bulk purchases, please contact Simon & Schuster Special Sales at 1-866-506-1949 or business@simonandschuster.com

The Simon & Schuster Speakers Bureau can bring authors to your live event. For more information or to book an event contact the Simon & Schuster Speakers Bureau at 1-866-248-3049 or visit our website at www.simonspeakers.com.

Cover photography by Alan Ayers; hand lettering by David Gatti

Manufactured in the United States of America

10 9 8 7 6 5 4 3 2 1

ISBN-13: 978-1-4391-4018-5
ISBN-10:   1-4391-4018-9

To Suse the Wonderful—I couldn't have
done it without you!

Chapter One

London
June 1818

Dear Cousin Michael,
For the next few weeks, I shan't be at the school, but in
London chaperoning Lady Amelia while her father and
stepmother are in the country. Do continue to send
your missives. I'll need your sage advice, for Lady
Amelia is high-spirited (dare I say, almost as much as
I?) and liable to land us both in trouble before the
season ends.
Yours sincerely,
Charlotte

*W*ho would ever guess balls could be boring?

Certainly not Lady Amelia Plume. When she'd
first come to London from the tiny seaside town of
Torquay, every tea, every ball, every soiree had been a
wonder.

But that was two years ago, before she'd realized they
were all alike. And the Dowager Viscountess Kirkwood's
annual spring ball was no exception, judging from the
crowd Amelia surveyed as she entered the rose-
bedecked ballroom. It was the same dull people—the
same prancing fops and gossipy matrons and frivolous

young misses. No aspiring lady adventurer with an ounce of self-respect would stay.

Unfortunately, she'd promised her Scottish friend, Lady Venetia Campbell, that she would. At least Venetia, whom she spotted a short distance away, knew how to enliven a tedious evening.

"Thank heaven you've come," Venetia said as she approached. "I swear I shall die of boredom. There's hardly anybody interesting here."

"*Nobody?*" Amelia asked, her disappointment acute. "No Spanish ambassadors or explorers newly arrived from the Pacific, or even an opera singer?"

Venetia laughed. "I was thinking more in terms of eligible men."

For Venetia, that meant clever men. Not that she couldn't have her pick of the male crop, clever or otherwise. Besides being obscenely wealthy, she had the sort of beauty men slobbered over, with raven tresses and creamy skin and rather . . . enormous breasts.

Next to Venetia, Amelia was abominably average—of average height, with average skin, of average tone. Her average figure would never inspire rhapsodies, and her medium brown hair vacillated between being curly and straight.

But she had quite a lot of hair, thank goodness, and kept it lustrous with pomatum and her American stepmother's honeysuckle water. Amelia's eyes might not be the siren's green of Venetia's, but men described them as "sparkling," and her breasts generally commanded attention.

In short, Amelia possessed her share of modest attractions . . . and modest suitors. Granted, most men only cared about her not-so-modest inheritance and her position as the Earl of Tovey's daughter. But she didn't intend to marry any of them, anyway—neither the Marquess of Pomeroy, an aging general who fancied her and her fortune, nor their hostess's son, the Viscount Kirkwood himself, who'd made overtures to her last year.

She aspired to a more adventurous life—touring Turkey like Lady Mary Wortley Montagu, or living in Syria like the legendary Lady Hester Stanhope.

"Actually," Venetia said, "there's one person here we'd both find 'interesting': Lord Kirkwood's American cousin." She nodded to a spot beyond Amelia. "Major Lucas Winter is apparently in England on assignment with the United States Marine Guard."

Expecting some weather-grizzled older fellow, Amelia followed Venetia's gaze. Then stared. Good Lord, how had she missed *him* when she'd come in?

Major Winter stuck out in the cramped ballroom like a hawk among pigeons. He wore quite the dashing blue-coated uniform, which bristled with gold braid, and a wide, bloodred sash around his trim waist. Her heart raced just to look at it.

And not only his uniform, either. His inky hair matched his inky boots, and though far from grizzled, his sun-browned skin made the other gentlemen look positively anemic. It hinted at days spent at sea, at battles on the Mediterranean. Oh, the adventures he must have had!

"Now *that* is a man," Venetia remarked. "They do grow them tall and well built in America, don't they? Even if his features are somewhat rough."

True. The man's jaw was a bit too angular and his nose a touch too narrow for handsome. And any English lord would ruthlessly pluck those thick, unruly eyebrows. But even if his appearance were changed, as long as the man wore that brooding scowl, he would continue to look "rough."

And fascinating.

"He hasn't yet asked a single lady to dance." Mischief glinted in Venetia's eyes. "But you'll adore this—they say he travels with a veritable arsenal. If he keeps insulting the officers, he may even have to use it."

"He insulted them?" Drat it, she'd missed *everything* by coming late.

"He told Lord Pomeroy that the Americans won their recent conflict with us because English officers are 'more interested in promenades than pistols.'"

Amelia laughed. She could only imagine how the general had taken *that* pronouncement. Especially from a man like the major, who clearly saw this as enemy territory, even though the war had ended three years ago. As Major Winter sipped champagne, he scanned the ballroom with the barely leashed contempt of a spy doing reconnaissance.

"Is he married?" Amelia asked.

Venetia frowned. "Come to think of it, no one's actually said."

"I do hope he isn't." Amelia slid another glance his way. "He must be remarkably brave to face his old enemies in their own territory."

"And he must have something more than deadwood under his kilt," Venetia added, her Scottish burr faintly evident.

Amelia eyed her askance. "You've been reading the chapbook of harem tales again, haven't you?"

"It's quite informative." Venetia lowered her voice to a whisper. "What do you think? Does the major have a 'sword' worth worshipping with one's mouth?"

"Goodness, even *I'm* not shameless enough to speculate on the major's 'sword.'"

Venetia chuckled. "Your stepmother will be delighted to hear it."

Amelia laughed. "Lord knows Dolly despairs of me enough as it is, poor thing. She hated being dragged across the world by her late husband, so she can't understand why I would jump at the chance to travel."

Her gaze drifted back to the major. The American marines were famous for battling the Barbary pirates in years past. Was he too young to have experienced that? Did she dare wangle an introduction to him to find out?

Lord Kirkwood glanced in her direction and murmured something to his cousin, who followed his gaze. It was the first time the American had looked her way, so she flashed him an inviting smile.

He didn't return it. His eyes narrowed on her with a sudden predatory intensity, then drifted rather impudently down her gown of yellow Chinese silk with its Oriental red flounces. By the time they trailed back up to fix on her face, hot color was rising in her cheeks.

Goodness gracious, the man was bold. No Englishman had ever looked at her as if she stood there stark naked. How very intriguing. It sent a delicious chill right down her spine.

Then he ruined it with a curt nod and returned his gaze to his cousin.

Well! What was she to make of that?

"Where's your stepmother tonight, anyway?" Venetia asked.

"She and Papa left for Torquay yesterday," Amelia said absently. Now that Dolly was expecting her first child, Papa was determined to coddle her in the country. "They nearly made me go, too, but Mrs. Harris fortunately agreed to come to town and chaperone me while she's not needed at the school."

Amelia and Venetia had graduated from Mrs. Harris's School for Young Ladies two years ago, and their schoolmistress still bore a strong affection for them—as they did for her. That's why they rode out there monthly for tea and her "lessons for heiresses." Not to mention the wealth of information she received regularly from her mysterious benefactor, "Cousin Michael."

"Much as I adore Mrs. Harris," Venetia said, "I wouldn't want her for a chaperone. She'd never allow you a private moment with a gentleman."

"What gentleman is Amelia having a private moment with?" a querulous voice asked behind them.

Amelia stifled a groan. It was Miss Sarah Linley, another schoolmate. Amelia had tried to like her, but Silly Sarah's petulance and snobbery made even Amelia clench her teeth.

"Hello, Sarah." She pasted a polite smile on her face. "We were just talking about the lack of eligible men here."

"What lack?" Sarah said. "I see several. Lord Kirkwood, for example."

"Who I hear is trying to marry a fortune," Venetia pointed out.

Sarah twirled one of her golden ringlets about her finger. "And I *have* a fortune, don't I?"

The banker's daughter also had the exquisite features of a porcelain doll. A pity she had nothing resembling a brain.

"Lord Kirkwood would never show an interest in *you*," Venetia bit out, not bothering to hide her loathing. Thanks to Sarah's frequent mentions of "those dirty Scots," the two of them were always at daggers drawn.

"Ah, but he has already done so," Sarah said, in a voice dripping condescension. Then she sighed dramatically. "Unfortunately, my parents disapprove. Papa calls Lord Kirkwood a 'titled wastrel' and wants me to marry some tea merchant with pots of money. They only let me attend tonight because the merchant was coming here, too. *Me*, married to a tea merchant! Can you imagine? When I could be *Lady* Kirkwood?"

"I'm sure the viscount is brokenhearted," Venetia said sarcastically.

"Oh, the tale isn't over yet." Sarah flashed them a secretive smile.

Amelia knew better than to encourage her, but Venetia clearly couldn't stand having Sarah know something she didn't. "Really?" Venetia prodded.

Sarah leaned close. "Promise you won't tell anyone?"

Venetia exchanged a glance with Amelia. "Certainly not."

"He slipped me a letter at the last assembly declaring his intentions."

Amelia barely disguised her shock. She'd thought Lord Kirkwood sensible, but if he would seriously contemplate marriage to Silly Sarah, he was clearly mad . . . or more desperate for funds than society realized.

"I wrote him a response, too." Sarah assumed a tragic air. "But it's likely to remain in my reticule forever. Mama watches the mail closely and has threatened to take away all my jewels if I even dance with Lord Kirkwood." She glared across the room. "Still, he could manage a word with me if not for his awful cousin."

Their gazes turned to the American major just as he exchanged words with two male guests. As tempers erupted, Lord Kirkwood stepped in to douse the flames.

Sarah sighed. "Every time his lordship heads toward me, his ruffian of a cousin annoys someone else. And it's not as if I can just walk up and hand my note to him. Someone might see, and Papa will have my hide."

"Give it to a servant then," Venetia said dismissively.

"And if Mama notices? Or the servant tattles? My parents will probably lock me in my room or do something equally horrible."

"You could leave it somewhere he's sure to find it," Amelia suggested. "Like his study."

"Men are playing cards in there," Sarah said, with a petulant frown.

"Then put the letter on his bed," Amelia said. "Or better yet, his pillow. No servant would dare remove it until his master saw it."

As Sarah stared at her aghast, Venetia added, eyes gleaming, "Yes, Sarah, why don't you trot upstairs and put it on his bed?"

"Very funny," Sarah said with a pout. "You both just want to see me get into trouble so you can have Lord Kirkwood for yourself."

Amelia nearly retorted that Lord Kirkwood had approached *her* before he'd even thought of Sarah, but she couldn't be that mean. "I'm only pointing out," she said tersely, "that the house is small, and there are servant's stairs. You could sneak up and do it before anyone even noticed you were gone."

"If it's so easy, why don't *you* do it?" Sarah snapped. "You're the one who craves adventure."

Amelia started to retort, then paused. She did like a good adventure. The stealth of it, the sheer excitement of sneaking about . . . why *not* do it? Not for Sarah, of course, but just to see if she could get away with it.

It wasn't as if anything else exciting would happen tonight. Besides, the major's room was probably up there, too—she might even get a glimpse of the "arsenal" Venetia had mentioned.

"All right," Amelia said. "I'll take the letter up myself."

Sarah looked surprised, but Venetia scowled. "Don't be absurd. You can't go into the man's bedchamber."

"It's the best way to make sure he reads Sarah's letter."

"It's the best way to be ruined if anyone sees you," Venetia snapped. "Might as well walk over and hand him the letter, for pity's sake. The gossips would tear you apart either way."

"If Amelia wants to help me," Sarah protested, "why shouldn't she?"

"Because she'll get herself caught, you little fool."

"If I get caught, I'll play dumb," Amelia said. "I'll bat my eyelashes and pretend to be a flibbertigibbet wandering the house in search of the retiring room."

"The flibbertigibbet act won't work with everyone," Venetia warned.

"Then I'll be sure not to get caught." Amelia turned to Sarah. "Give me the letter." Sarah slipped it out of her reticule and into Amelia's hand.

Ignoring Venetia's continuing protests, Amelia shoved the envelope into her own reticule, then hurried off toward the hallway. All right, so this wasn't exactly the sort of wildly exotic adventure she dreamed of, but it was better than nothing. Now if she could just reach the door to the back stairs without being seen . . .

She was in luck. The stairway was next to the retiring room, so it was easy to choose one door over the other when no one was watching. Upstairs, her luck continued, for the floor with the bedchambers was deserted.

But which room was his lordship's? Listening for approaching servants, she opened doors in rapid succession, dismissing the one smelling of rosewater as belonging to the Dowager Viscountess, and the second as belonging to the lady's maid. Just as Amelia opened one across the hall, voices came from the stairs. With her blood thundering in her ears, she slipped inside the room and closed the door.

As someone passed by out in the hall, she glanced about her. This room was certainly a man's. A pair of polished boots sat at the foot of the bed, and a sword belt with an oddly shaped sword in its scabbard hung from a chair's post. Lord Kirkwood's sword would be kept in a cabinet downstairs, so this must be . . .

Major Winter's room.

A forbidden thrill tingled along her skin. This was her chance to see his arsenal. And find out more about him—where he'd been, where he was going.

Whether he was married.

As excitement spiked her blood, she crept over to examine his shaving stand. Like most military men, he was scrupulously neat, his brushes and comb kept quite clean. The same was true of his orderly dressing table. She found no jewelry, but did discover a wicked-looking ivory-handled dagger tucked in the single drawer.

A peek inside the hanging wardrobe revealed clothing that was well made but not dandyish, serviceable gloves and boots, and two well-worn beaver hats. She found more of his arsenal, too—a locked pistol case, another dagger, and even a rifle, for goodness sake. But nothing to show whether he had a wife, drat it.

Then she spotted the opened letters on the writing table. She hesitated, her blood running high. Did she dare? It would be going rather far, wouldn't it?

Oh, but that was the reason she *should* do it. No adventure was without risk.

Hurrying over, she peered down at the topmost sheet. The letter from the Navy Board to the American consul gave Major Lucas Winter permission to view the Deptford shipyards. Interesting, but not terribly informative. She thumbed through the others. More boring correspondence, no wifely letters.

Then she reached the bottom sheet, which contained a curious list of names with comments scrawled beside them. "Mrs. Dorothy Taylor" was annotated with a series of French addresses, a date, and a terse description. "Miss Dorothy Jackson" had no description, but the French addresses and mention of a brother. "Mrs. Dorothy Winthrop"—goodness, the man had a penchant for Dorothys—had only a date and one address, along with a reference to her American husband.

The last name was underlined twice: "Mrs. Dorothy Smith." Amelia froze. Before Dolly had married Papa, her name had been Dolly—Dorothy—Smith. Amelia swallowed. It meant nothing. There must be a hundred Dorothy Smiths in London alone.

But as she scanned the comments beside Mrs. Dorothy Smith, her heart sank:

> *270 Rue de la Sonne, Paris*
> *May have had companion in Rouen in Nov. 1815?*
> *Departed Calais for Plymouth alone on Feb. 1816*
> *Fair-skinned, green eyes, reddish hair, short*

Amelia stared blankly at the paper. The description certainly fit Dolly. And Dolly had visited both Paris *and* Rouen before arriving in Plymouth in 1816, when Papa had swept her off her feet and married her. "May have had a companion"—of course she'd had a companion. Her now deceased merchant husband.

But why would Major Winter be interested in Dolly? Clearly her name was what triggered his interest, so he probably hadn't known her personally.

Turning the sheet over, she found more chilling notes:

Dorothy Frier alias Dorothy Smith?
Times match when Frier fled US to escape capture

Dolly? Trying to "escape capture"? By whom? And why? The word *alias* sounded perfectly criminal. Did Major Winter's involvement mean that the American government was part of it, too?

Perhaps the Dorothy whom Major Winter sought had been a British spy. But the war was over—who cared about spies now? Anyway, it couldn't be timid Dolly, who flinched when people argued, who bent over backward to please Amelia and Papa, who'd been eager to marry Papa and give him full use of her fortune when she could easily have married a rich—

A sick apprehension settled in her belly. What if Dolly had come by her fortune dishonestly?

When Amelia's widowed father had met Dolly in Plymouth, the two had fallen in love almost instantly. Dolly had been so sad, so delicate, that Amelia's big, gruff Papa had wanted nothing more than to protect her. And who wouldn't? Dolly was a sweet-natured darling.

But it was Dolly's fortune that changed their lives. Dolly's money had paid for Mrs. Harris's expensive school. Dolly's money had provided Amelia's dowry and come out in London. And Dolly's money had allowed Papa to bring the estate into good working order after their years of frugality.

Amelia searched the papers, hoping for other information, but found none. What now? Dolly had never mentioned the name Frier, but then, she'd said little about her past. Could Dolly have had another sort of life? Dolly did enjoy card playing—could she have been a gambler? Or the wife of a gambler or a card cheat?

No, it was absurd. Dolly would never participate in any sort of criminal scheme. She lacked the temperament for it. She couldn't even deny Amelia the smallest request, and she cried over the deaths of goldfish, for goodness sake. The idea of her doing something criminal was ludicrous. That her recent life mirrored this other Dorothy Smith's was merely a horrible chain of coincidences.

But the major wouldn't think so. She could tell he was the sort to be a thorough investigator. Indeed, he might already know about Dolly. It would explain why he'd stared at Amelia in the ballroom.

So how long before the major traveled down to Devon and spoke to Papa? Or tried to haul Dolly off to America for something she was surely innocent of?

Amelia had to warn her, but how? And about what? She didn't know what he was after—it might be nothing. She wasn't even sure he'd connected Dorothy Smith with Dolly. And upsetting Dolly in her delicate condition was out of the question. Besides, wouldn't it be better to find out why the man was there first?

A pop nearby made her jump. It was only a log in the fireplace, but still . . . she had to escape. The room had taken on a distinctly threatening cast, with its boldly displayed sword and hidden weapons and ominous notes hinting at treachery. If the major caught her here, no telling what he'd do.

She carefully restored his papers to the way she'd found them, then hurried out the door. Thank goodness the hall was deserted. She still had to deliver

Sarah's letter, a task she now wanted to be rid of as swiftly as possible.

As she hastened toward the only remaining bedroom, she retrieved Sarah's letter from her reticule. But she couldn't get it closed again, which was why she didn't notice until too late that someone had ascended the stairs.

"What the hell are you doing up here?" snapped an unfamiliar male voice with a distinctive accent.

She nearly had heart failure. Thrusting the letter and her reticule behind her back, she jerked her head up, only to come face-to-face with the one man she should avoid.

Major Lucas Winter.

Chapter Two

Dear Charlotte,
A little high spirits never hurt anyone. Nonetheless I
shall be happy to advise you, and if trouble does attend
you, I stand ready to aid you both. Do try to give me
ample notice, however. I shall need time to prepare for
any escapes from Newgate.
Your faithful servant,
Michael

Lucas watched as the blood drained from the young woman's face. Good. A fearful Englishwoman was a truthful one. When he'd come up to grab his dagger, he hadn't expected to stumble across the stepdaughter of the woman he was investigating. Clearly enemies lurked in more than just the ballroom downstairs full of redcoats. And this particular enemy was hiding something behind her back.

"Well?" he demanded. "Tell me why you're outside my room."

A sudden change came over her face, and she fluttered her eyelashes at him. "*Your* room? I don't even know who you are. I was looking for the retiring room."

He snorted. "In the family quarters on the second floor? Try another tale. That one won't wash."

Although she was even prettier up close than in the

ballroom, her pout showed her to be the kind of spoiled female he hated. "Really, sir, I don't know why you make such a fuss. How was *I* to know the family rooms were here? I'll just go downstairs—"

"First show me what's behind your back," he demanded.

"You mean my reticule?" she said, a bit too quickly, and held it out.

"And in the other hand?"

"Nothing to concern you," she snapped. The shift from petulant young miss to lofty lady of rank made his eyes narrow, and she immediately softened her tone. "It's private."

Stepping forward, he took her by the arm. "Maybe we should just continue this downstairs."

"No!" She jerked her arm from his grip, and something fell to the floor. As she reached for it, he stepped on it. Her head snapped up to meet his gaze, her eyes blazing. "Remove your foot at once!"

Had the lady actually stolen papers from his room? Swiftly, he picked up what he'd pinned under his boot. A sealed letter addressed to "Lord Kirkwood." Hellfire and damnation. One look at her blushing cheeks told him what *that* meant—though Kirkwood hadn't mentioned the girl having a liking for him.

Damn her for sneaking about where she shouldn't. Now that he'd insulted and embarrassed her, he'd never get the truth out of her.

He gritted his teeth. Better change tacks. He held out the letter. "I believe this is yours, ma'am."

She took it from him with a sniff. "I *told* you it was private."

"A soldier's bound to think the worst when a woman's prowling about by herself. In America, a female sneaking about a soldier's quarters is generally up to nothing good. Or nothing respectable, anyway."

Her fiery blush deepened. "Is that your idea of an apology?"

Damn. He couldn't say the right thing tonight to save his life. "Of course not." He forced civility into his voice. "I beg your pardon, ma'am. I'll tell my cousin you tried to protect his privacy."

"Lord Kirkwood is your cousin?" she said, with wide-eyed innocence.

"I should introduce myself. I'm Major Lucas Winter."

"I'm Lady Amelia Plume." She flashed him another pretty smile, the kind that could get a man into trouble.

But not him—not until he confirmed that she wasn't sunk up to that pretty smile in her stepmother's affairs. "If you want," he said tersely, "I'll deliver your letter to my cousin myself. It's the least I can do."

"Oh, no, you've already done your least," she quipped, waving the battered letter before him. "I think it would be safer if I just do what I came up here to do and put it in his room myself. Before you shoot it for 'lurking about.'"

Her clever remarks were strangely at odds with the silly filly she'd appeared to be earlier. But then, her kind—wealthy and well connected—was like that, flighty and fickle. He should know; he'd been raised by her kind.

The reminder darkened his humor. "Don't worry, Lady Amelia, a little dirt on your letter won't affect my cousin's interest in your fortune."

"It isn't *my* correspondence, but a friend's," she protested.

"Right." He opened the door to his cousin's room with a flourish. "Go on then—deliver your 'friend's' letter. I'll wait here while you do."

By standing in the doorway he forced her to walk past him to enter, and he caught a whiff of her perfumed hair. It reminded him of something. Honeysuckle. Like the soap all the ladies seemed to favor in the town where he'd grown up in Virginia, before his father had moved them to Baltimore.

The faint scent of home made him want to howl his frustration. He'd been hunting Theodore and Dorothy Frier for over two long years. When other marines had returned home to enjoy the peace, he'd had neither a home nor peace. And now, thanks to the Friers, he'd been forced back to the country he loathed. It was one more thing he'd hold them accountable for, once he brought them to ground.

Lady Amelia returned to the doorway, and he moved aside so she could exit and close the door herself. He didn't want to smell her scent again, to be reminded of all he'd lost . . . or to notice how damned attractive she was.

To his irritation, instead of running off right away, she faced him. "Thank you for letting me complete my task. And I'd appreciate it, sir, if you would not . . . That is, if anyone were to know that I—"

"You want me to keep this little encounter between us."

Eyes the color of rich chocolate met his. "That would be lovely, thank you."

So the lady wanted a favor, did she? He could use that. "Don't be too quick to thank me, ma'am. I'll expect something in return."

She tensed. "Oh?"

Asking his questions right out would arouse her suspicions, and he didn't want her alerting her stepmother. But she'd handed him a way to get closer to her so he could investigate more discreetly. "I want a waltz from you."

"A-A waltz?"

"The man takes the lady's hand in his, puts his other hand—"

"I know what a waltz is," she said dryly.

"Then I want one in exchange for my silence."

She blinked, then flashed him a flirtatious smile. "Why, Major, you aren't trying to blackmail me, are you?"

The flirting put him on his guard. "That about sums it up."

"It's not very nice of you."

"I'm a soldier, ma'am, not a courtier. I use whatever's at hand to get what I want." He let his gaze trail down her. "And what I want tonight is a waltz."

Coyly, she lowered her eyes. "When you put it like that, how can I refuse?"

She turned, and her gown, weighted by its flounces, clung to her backside, outlining her curves before settling into place. He tensed. When was the last time he'd bedded a woman? Paris, probably. But that French whore's heavily rouged cheeks and unwashed body bore no resemblance to the silky attractions of the perfumed creature undulating down the hall before him.

He couldn't tear his eyes away. God have mercy, she had a walk that would heat a man's blood to boiling. He'd noticed it even in the ballroom.

Before he could douse the fire in his veins, she turned to cast him a smile so blazing it lit up her whole face. "Just so you'll know, Major Winter, I would have danced with you without the blackmail." Then she sashayed to the back stairs and disappeared.

For a second, all he could do was stare after her. What a little tease! First his cousin, then him. If he didn't know better, he'd think she was after something—

He scowled. Damnation, maybe she'd been inside his room after all.

Swiftly he entered it and examined everything. He scanned the surfaces, searched the carpet for stray threads, even sniffed the air. Nothing looked out of place. Even his papers sat exactly where he'd left them. Though he thought he smelled honeysuckle, he couldn't be sure, with so many bowls of flowers lying around. Kirkwood's servants must think he was a damned Prissy Pantaloons, like their English masters.

Still, he doubted a society female would come in here. Lady Amelia might be bold enough to leave a letter on a suitor's pillow, but she'd never search a stranger's room. Hell, unless she knew his real reason for coming to England—and she couldn't— she'd never even think to look. If she knew how to think at all.

She was just a flirt. Good, he'd use that, too. If she wanted entertainment, he'd happily oblige her. How better to get information from the little lady?

If he could manage a flirtation when he was so on edge. Damned redcoats—they always did this to him. The war might be over, but they still plagued him.

Fine. Let them come at him. And in case they did . . .

He found his dagger in the drawer. He should have carried the damned thing with him in the first place.

Hiding it inside his wide sash where it made a reassuringly firm bulge, he headed out and down the stairs. Before he reached the bottom, two drunken redcoats approached.

He tensed. "Gentlemen," he said with a tight nod.

He continued down, but they blocked his path. As the old anger settled hard in his belly, he felt instinctively for his dagger. *Steady, man, they're only young fools in their cups.* But that didn't quell the clamor in his gut.

One of them nudged the other. "Will you look who it is—one of them American savages who fled at Bladensburg while we burned their puny capital to the ground."

It was the wrong battle to mention. The American militia *had* run from the British, but not the Marine Guard.

"You're mistaken, sir." Lucas fought to restrain his temper. "I'm one of the savages who stood firm with Commodore Barney." He couldn't suppress a sneer. "Not that you green lads would know that—you were probably cowering in a barracks somewhere."

He knew he'd struck a nerve when both men flushed to their ears.

"Now if you'll excuse me . . ." He shouldered past them.

One man grabbed his right arm. "See here, you insolent Yankee—"

With instincts honed from years in battle, Lucas whipped out his dagger with his left hand to press it to the man's ribs. "Unless you want a blade in the gut, boy, you'd best let go."

The other soldier lunged at him drunkenly, but Lucas crossed his right arm over his left to grab the man by the throat. "Go ahead: two to one odds are nothing to me." He squeezed until the man began to choke. "All I need is a reason."

He didn't even need that. Fueled by the sight of red-coats, a dark haze filled his vision, whirling him back to an airless tunnel and the screams of—

"Major Winter!" came a sharp voice beyond them. "Release those men!"

It took a second for the haze to lift and another for Lucas to remember where he was. Then he saw Kirkwood hurrying up the hall, alarm in his face.

Smothering his remaining rage, Lucas smiled coldly. "Certainly, cousin." He let go of the one man's throat, but had to force himself to sheathe his dagger. His breath came fast and hard, parching his throat. "I was just explaining some things. But we understand each other now, don't we, boys?"

The one he'd held by the throat fell to his knees gasping. The other fellow gaped at him. "You're mad, you are!"

Lucas regarded him with contempt. "See that you remember it."

Stiffening, the man growled. "Someone should teach you some manners."

Lucas laid his hand on the dagger's hilt. "I'd be happy to oblige anytime—"

"Enough, both of you," Kirkwood said, sounding harried. He turned to the soldier. "Go on with you, before I tell my mother you accosted our guest."

Sullenly the man relented. As he weaved down the hall, Kirkwood glanced at the gasping soldier on the floor and called for a servant to bring water. While the servant attended the man, Kirkwood motioned to Lucas to follow him into his study.

As soon as they'd entered, Kirkwood shut the door. "Good God, Winter, are you *trying* to get yourself killed?"

Lucas went to pour himself brandy from the decanter on Kirkwood's desk. "Trust me, those two asses could hardly walk, much less kill anybody."

"True, they're better known for their prowess at the tables than in battle. But that wouldn't stop them from trying."

"And dying," Lucas said calmly, though his hands had begun to shake so hard he could barely clasp the brandy glass. Now that the blood rush of battle was subsiding, it alarmed him how close he'd come to killing them. That was *not* why he was in England.

He forced his glass to his lips and drank deeply, needing the burn to bring him back from a distant hell. What a cruel joke—having his quest take him to the one place he couldn't stand to be, the one place he couldn't be easy.

Kirkwood gazed at him warily. "I should have discouraged you from wearing your uniform tonight, but with the war having ended so long ago, I foolishly believed you gentlemen would have put it behind you by now."

"I can't speak for your soldier friends," Lucas snapped, "but I have a bit of trouble letting bygones be bygones. What was done to me and my men was beyond the rules of war and common human decency."

"I realize that," Kirkwood bit out. "And if I'd known Mother meant to invite so many officers, I would have nipped it in the bud. But a number of them have sisters who are heiresses, and she hoped to coax the females here—"

"She's determined to marry you off, isn't she?" Lucas said, desperate to get off the subject of English officers, desperate to forget how close he'd come to murder. Kirkwood had once helped Lucas at great cost and trouble to himself, but some matters they would never agree on.

His cousin wasn't to be put off. "It doesn't serve your purpose to make enemies here. No one will talk to you about Lady Tovey if you keep causing trouble."

Lucas swallowed more brandy. "They're not going to talk to me about Lady Tovey regardless. Because I'm not one of them, and my father was in 'trade.'"

"Whatever the reason, your behavior hampers your investigation."

With a grim smile, Lucas thought of Lady Amelia. "Not necessarily."

Kirkwood stared at him. "What's happened? Have you learned something?"

"I will once I claim my waltz with Lady Amelia."

"Someone introduced you to her?"

"Not exactly." Lucas watched his cousin's face carefully. "I caught her upstairs with a letter for you."

Kirkwood's surprise looked genuine. "For me? Are you sure?"

"Your name was on the envelope, and she put it on your pillow."

He seemed vaguely shocked. "I can't imagine why."

"There's nothing between you?"

"I expressed interest once, but she rebuffed it. Lady Amelia is choosy. She came to the marriage mart late, and doesn't seem to mind if she leaves it late."

Interesting. *Choosy* wasn't a word he'd have used for the lady, with her flirting smile and swinging hips. "Why did she come late?"

"How should I know? But she had her first season only after her father married."

Maybe because she hadn't had the money for it before? No, her father was a damned earl, for God's sake. Kirkwood needed money, yet continued to live at a level far beyond the average American. Lack of money might have nothing to do with Lady Amelia's late entry into society.

"Lady Amelia must have changed her mind about you," he told his cousin. "I watched her put that letter on your pillow myself."

Kirkwood shook his head. "Frankly, I'm astonished. According to Miss Linley, the woman has repeatedly said she isn't certain she even *wants* to marry."

"Miss Linley?"

"One of Lady Amelia's former classmates from Mrs. Harris's very prestigious School for Young Ladies. Privately, we call it Mrs. Harris's School for Heiresses. Taken together, the families of her students probably own half of England." He gave a wan smile. "Tonight

Mother invited every female who'd ever graduated from there. Most of them accepted."

"Don't they care that you're after their money?" Lucas asked, incredulous. He would never understand this English marriage barter system. Though Americans had it, too, most considered it undemocratic, which was why the high-class ones tried to disguise it.

"Some of the ladies care, but they attend anyway to meet other gentlemen. Other ladies are willing to make the bargain. Like Miss Linley, who has a fortune, but craves the position I can offer. Or at least I think she does—she hasn't answered my letter." His eyes narrowed. "Could Lady Amelia have been delivering a letter for Miss Linley?"

"Lady Amelia did claim she was doing it for a friend."

"Ah." He turned for the door. "Perhaps I should take a look—"

Lucas stopped him. "Not yet. I need you to introduce me officially to Lady Amelia. She agreed to a waltz, and I mean to claim it."

"How did you get her to agree to a waltz?"

"I put the fear of God into her."

Kirkwood scowled. "I hope you didn't draw your dagger on *her,* too."

"Of course not," Lucas said irritably. "I can handle women like her."

"If you say so." Kirkwood walked to the door. "Come on then, I'll introduce you. But try not to offend the chit, will you? Her friends are all gossipy as the very devil, and I still have to marry one of them."

Setting down his glass, Lucas followed his cousin. "Surely a man of your intelligence and connections can do something else to get money."

Kirkwood opened the door. "Not at my rank and not in England. Here, an eldest son has obligations. I have two sisters and a younger brother. If I marry an heiress, they're taken care of. If I don't . . ." He sighed as he ushered Lucas through the door.

Poor bastard. Though Kirkwood might not mind a wife who was about as useful as a ship's masthead, Lucas couldn't imagine using marriage to support his family. If he ever got around to finding a wife, *he* would be the one putting food on the table, not her.

Thankfully, the hall was deserted as they headed for the ballroom. "What if you can't get anything out of Lady Amelia?" his cousin asked.

"Don't worry, I will." How hard could it be to get a frivolous flirt to reveal what he needed to know?

"Why not ride down to Devon and confront her stepmother?"

"If Lady Tovey *is* Dorothy Frier, then the minute some American soldier shows up at her husband's estate asking to speak to her, she'll smell a rat. She's liable to alert Theodore Frier or run off before I can get past her butler. And this time, they'll make sure I never find them."

"Only if she's really who you think she is. If you're right about her, then she's a bigamist, for God's sake."

"Assuming that she and Frier were legally married in the first place. It may have been a common law marriage. Clearly she got tired of being dragged from pillar to post by him, because I lost his trail after they separated in France. And how better to hide from the authorities than to marry a titled lord like Tovey?"

"Yes, but—"

"If she's not who I'm looking for, then why did she have Tovey carry her off to the country the minute your mother started telling her friends about her visiting American cousin? She decided not to take any chances, that's why. You said that she prefers the country; what else would a woman hiding from the law prefer?"

"So she sent her stepdaughter to my mother's ball to be accosted by you?" Kirkwood asked skeptically.

"Look here," Lucas said, growing exasperated, "I don't know how the woman's mind works. All I know is that Lady Tovey is the only lead I have left. I'm not going to risk alarming her or having her warn Frier until I'm sure I have the right woman." He glared at Kirkwood. "Why all the questions? Do you have some problem with introducing me to that flighty wench, Lady Amelia?"

Kirkwood arched one eyebrow. "If you're going to call her a 'wench,' I do. She's not a bloody taproom maid, you know, whom you can bully into—"

"Fine," Lucas growled, "I'll claim my waltz without an introduction." He walked away from his cousin.

"Stop, damn you!" Kirkwood called out irritably behind him. As Lucas halted, he came up alongside him. "I didn't say I wouldn't do it, for God's sake. I just want to be sure you behave like a gentleman. Might you at least *attempt* to be circumspect and polite?"

"I'll be the soul of discretion," he drawled.

"Why don't I find that reassuring?" Kirkwood sighed. "Perhaps luck will shine on us, and you'll learn what you need to know in one encounter."

"I hope so. Because the quicker I finish this, the quicker I go home to Baltimore—far away from all you damned English."

Chapter Three

Dear Cousin,
Although I hope Newgate isn't in my future, I would
trust no one but you to break me out. Now for a more
serious matter: Should I encourage Miss Linley to
marry Lord Kirkwood despite his lack of fortune? She
needs a husband of intelligence to make up for her lack
of it, and I fear that her parents' choice, Mr. Chambers,
would indulge her silliness even more than they do.
Your always inquisitive relation,
Charlotte

Amelia paced the retiring room, her pulse wildly clamoring. Major Winter had given her quite a fright. Goodness! She wanted adventure—not heart failure!

Not that she cared about adventure if it meant Dolly was in trouble. But was she? Just because the major made a lot of notes about a woman with a similar name didn't necessarily mean anything. It certainly didn't mean he knew of Amelia's connection to a Dorothy Smith.

She had to find out what he *did* know, and that meant more encounters with him. Amelia wiped her clammy hands on her skirts. She could do this. She'd handled that disaster in the hall well. Never mind that she'd had to behave like a silly flirt; at least she'd fooled him. Or he wouldn't have asked for a waltz.

I'm a soldier, ma'am, not a courtier. I use whatever's at hand to get what I want. And what I want tonight is a waltz.

Lord, but the man made blackmail sound enticing.

But beneath his seductive, slow-as-honey drawl was an iron will. He wasn't some simpering lordling she could control with a smile here and a sharp word there—he was a seasoned officer of obvious intelligence. How would a true lady adventurer persuade him to divulge his secrets?

Her flibbertigibbet act might work: men said things to a stupid girl they'd never say to a clever one. But she needed something more to distract him.

A slew of scandalous fantasies born of reading the harem tales swirled through her head. She frowned. Not *that*. She wanted adventure, not ruin. Still, he *had* responded to her flirting. And even a suspicious marine might let something slip when a pretty woman turned his head.

A little trill of excitement rippled over her, and she squelched it ruthlessly. What was the matter with her? Yes, the man exuded the most intoxicating air of danger, but until she knew if Dolly was in trouble, she dared not let that sway her.

Heading toward the door of the retiring room, she stopped at the mirror to fluff her curls and pinch her pale cheeks. When Major Winter came for his waltz, she would play the wide-eyed miss to perfection, full of innocent remarks and teasing smiles meant to lull him into revealing everything.

She sailed out the door in a spirit of bold bravado. Then nearly lost her nerve when she spotted the major himself standing with Lord Kirkwood and her chaperone.

Her pulse broke into a gallop. Some lady adventurer *she* was. At this rate, she'd never find out what she needed to know.

Forget that this concerns Dolly. You're a spy on a mission. The American has secrets you must uncover for the good of your country.

Her pulse settled. That was better.

Their host glanced her way as she neared the group. "Ah, Lady Amelia, we were just asking Mrs. Harris about you. I'd like to introduce my cousin."

"Of course." As the sounds of a quadrille wafted out to her, she forced a smile to her face. The waltz was next. Goodness gracious.

Lord Kirkwood swiftly performed the introductions. When he mentioned that Amelia's stepmother was American, she had to suppress a groan, but the major merely smiled in response. Then he asked for the waltz in a perfectly appropriate manner. If she hadn't known he might be investigating Dolly, she would have been flattered.

For a moment, she feared that Mrs. Harris, a petite thirtyish woman with incongruously flaming hair, might protest, since the major hadn't exactly made the best impression. The widow did seem to regard both Lord Kirkwood and Major Winter with some wariness. But thankfully she only said, "Enjoy yourself, my dear," and flipped open her fan.

As the major led her into the crowded ballroom, Amelia felt his gaze bore into her. "Is Mrs. Harris your relation?" he asked.

"No. My schoolmistress."

"I thought young ladies were generally chaperoned by family."

Did he mean anything by that? She couldn't tell. "Yes, but my parents aren't in town right now." She watched for his reaction.

He showed no sign of concern or surprise, just polite curiosity. "Oh?"

"Papa and Dolly left for the country today—"

"Dolly? The American stepmother Kirkwood mentioned?"

Drat it, if he hadn't known before of her connection to someone named Dorothy, he did now. What should she say? He could easily find out the truth, and if he caught her lying about something that simple, it might rouse his suspicions. "Yes."

"I reckon Dolly's short for Dorothy." He led her to the floor.

She faced him with a bright smile. "We've always called her Dolly. I believe that's actually her Christian name. In England plenty of women are named Dolly, you know, and it isn't short for Dorothy at all. Why, only last week—"

The waltz began, cutting off her babbling. Thank goodness. At this rate, he'd guess what she was about long before she learned anything from him.

As he took her hand and laid his other on her waist, she forced herself to relax. Spies acted their roles with unruffled efficiency. They didn't babble.

Then he swept her into the waltz, and she focused on the dancing instead of her nervousness. But that only made it worse. Because now she was aware of him as more than just an investigator. Unlike the other men she'd met, he attracted her. His shoulder flexed beneath her fingers, his hand rode her waist intimately, and he smelled of brandy and steel, if that were possible.

The critics were right—the waltz *was* too intimate, especially here beneath the romantic glow of argand lamps, with Lady Kirkwood's roses scenting the air and the tiny orchestra filling the room with the most exquisitely sensual—

"Why did your family go to the country without you?"

Thankfully, the question jerked her out of her silly, girlish thoughts. Then she realized that while his question was perfectly understandable, his tone was almost too casual.

She made her own tone match his. "They didn't want to ruin my fun by forcing me to leave town in the middle of the season. But Papa felt it best that Dolly spend her confinement at our estate."

He looked surprised. "Confinement?"

"Do Americans not practice such a thing?" she said with a look of wide-eyed innocence. "In England, when a lady is *enceinte*—"

"I know what confinement is." He took several deep breaths as if trying to calm himself. "I just didn't realize that you English retire to the country for it."

"Dolly's in fragile health."

"I see," He sounded skeptical. "Is it their first child?"

"Yes." Fearing any other truths he might elicit, she changed the subject. "You dance well, Major Winter." Actually, he danced like a soldier, masterfully taking control of every step. No one would ever have trouble following *his* lead.

"You sound surprised," he said. "Did you think Americans don't dance?"

Remember, be a silly flirt. "Of course not. But I *am* surprised a big, strong soldier like you ever bothered to spend time waltzing." She ran her hand over his powerful shoulder provocatively, then leaned close enough in the turn to give him a glimpse of her bosom. Men always seemed to like that.

His gaze dipped unerringly to her chest and stuck there. "I've navigated a few ballrooms in my day," he drawled.

His bold gaze thrilled her. Her skin tingled beneath her gown, as if she'd exposed far more than the swells of her breasts, and she could scarcely keep her breathing steady, not to mention her steps.

She dearly wished he'd stop looking at her as if she were naked. Aside from the annoying furor it roused in her blood, it made it awfully hard for her to concentrate on the task at hand.

Only after he brought his gaze back up to lock with hers was she able to think what to say. She flashed him a smile. "I heard you were more interested in pistols than in promenades."

He eyed her closely. "Upstairs, you acted as if you didn't know who I was."

Drat it, she'd slipped up again. "I hadn't connected you with the man everyone's been gossiping about. Not until you introduced yourself."

"Ah." His wary expression didn't abate. His eyes searched her face from beneath incredibly long, sooty lashes. "What other gossip did you hear about me?"

"Not much. No one seems to know anything." She cast him a coy glance. "Speculation has run high. Everyone wonders why a man who so clearly dislikes the English would be in England visiting his cousin."

He scowled. "What makes you think I dislike the English?"

"Come now, Major Winter, you're less than cordial to the gentlemen, and you haven't danced with any of the ladies—"

"Because I had nothing to blackmail them with. Not because they're English." The smile he flashed her would have sent her pulse into a tizzy . . . if his eyes hadn't remained as wintry as his name.

"So your stay in England is just a social visit." Just to provoke him, she added, "And you wore your dress uniform to a ball bristling with English officers because you thought it would help you make friends?"

A muscle worked in his jaw as he whirled her into a turn with surprising competence. "All right, I admit it. I'm not just visiting my cousin. I'm here consulting with the British about the treaty they're brokering with Algeria."

Her heart sank. He hadn't mentioned looking for a Dorothy Frier *or* Smith, which meant his investigation was secret. That couldn't be good.

She probed further. "But why *you*? You're not a diplomat."

"I've had plenty of experience dealing with the Barbary pirates."

Her pulse leaped. "You were with Lieutenant Decatur at Tripoli?" she blurted out.

His eyes narrowed. "You *know* about that?"

Drat her quick tongue. But why did he have to mention the one subject she found utterly fascinating?

Oh well, a flibbertigibbet could have a passion for pirates, couldn't she? "Everyone knows about Tripoli," she said lightly. "The newspapers covered it extensively, you know."

"But you couldn't have been more than a girl when it happened."

"A very bored girl in a very dull town. So I read the papers." She'd kept clippings of every engagement of the Americans against the Barbary pirates.

Tossing her head girlishly, she added, "If there'd been any decent shops, I wouldn't have resorted to such tedium, but a girl can only embroider so long." She fluttered her lashes. "And what girl isn't swept away by tales of corsairs?"

"Ruthless corsairs who kidnap men, women, and children for money. Have you any idea—" He broke off with a sneer. "No, of course you don't. You think corsairs are a subject for entertainment."

"Try living in Torquay for weeks on end with only a brooding father for company," she said petulantly, "and see what entertains *you*."

"What about your stepmother? Wasn't she around then?"

She tensed. *Tread carefully.*

"Dolly and Papa didn't marry until a few years ago." Should she say more? Might he then reveal why he was interested? Or what if she told him the *wrong* information? His reaction might tell her if it was her own Dolly he sought.

She shot him a vacant smile. "They met right in

Devon. England was Dolly's last stop after her tour of the Continent, and her ship from Italy—"

"Italy?" he broke in, clearly surprised.

As a horrible fear settled in her belly, she forced her tone to sound breezy. "Florence, if I remember right. She visited all sorts of places after her American husband died—Spain and Italy—"

"During the war?" he interrupted, both eyebrows raised.

Drat it, she wasn't good at this lying business. She could hardly admit Dolly had come to England after the war, for the timing would coincide too neatly with the dates he had for Dorothy Smith leaving France. "Oh. No . . . that is, she was in Italy at the end of the war, but before that . . . well, I could be wrong about Spain. It might have been Greece. I'm not sure." She shrugged. "I can never keep all those foreign countries straight, can you?"

He gritted his teeth. "It's my job to keep them straight."

"Oh, of course." She made herself giggle. "Do you travel a great deal? You must have been to Tripoli at least if you have experience with Barbary pirates." She cut her eyes up at him in what she hoped was a teasing glance. "Unless, of course, you were a pirate yourself."

She could well imagine him as a corsair, black hair tossed by the wind, a shining gold loop dangling from one ear, bare chest—

Stop that. You're trying to determine if he really is here to help with some treaty.

"I wasn't at Tripoli with Decatur—I'd only just been commissioned as a midshipman. But I was with

O'Bannon at Tripoli the next year, marching across the desert to Derna."

He'd accompanied the valiant O'Bannon? She couldn't believe it! She was dancing with a man who'd actually been inside the fort at Derna, who might have freed slaves and even entered a harem—

Drat him, none of that mattered. And he was probably lying anyway. "You'd have been only a boy."

"Someone of seventeen is more a man than a boy."

She didn't have to feign her surprise. "But now you'd be—"

"Really old," he said dryly. "Almost thirty."

"You don't look thirty."

"Ah, but I am," he said, in an amused rumble of a voice that resonated through her body more seductively than the music of the waltz. "And if you don't believe I was at Derna, I can give you details."

Her curiosity warred with her prudence. Curiosity won out. "Like what?"

"We were four hundred strong—Arab cavalry, Greeks, mercenaries, and a handful of American navy and marines. It took us fifty days to cross the desert. The khamsin winds whipped the sand into storms that blotted out the sun even at midday. When we ran out of food, the Arabs butchered some pack camels, and that's what we ate until we reached our supply ships waiting at the coast near Derna."

"You ate a camel?" she said, fascinated.

He shrugged. "Had to. We were half-starved."

"Yet you and your companions still subdued the fort and forced the town to surrender in less than two hours," she said in a breathless rush.

That brought him up short. He cocked one brow.

"You certainly paid close attention to what you read in the papers, didn't you?"

She blinked. There she went again. "Oh, yes, I paid attention to it all," she said blithely. "Especially the part about the marzipan sword."

His gaze turned contemptuous again. "You mean the *mameluke* sword."

"Mameluke?" She cast him a vacant glance, though she had to bite her tongue to keep from asking if it was the strange sword in his room. "They didn't give you Americans marzipan treats shaped like a sword?"

"No, it was an actual sword." Then he added in a patronizing tone, "It has a blade and everything. If you like, I can show you mine sometime."

She wanted to slap him for his condescension . . . and kiss him for offering to show her the sword. The rascal certainly knew how to tempt a lady adventurer. "You carry it around with you?" She tried not to sound too excited. "Do you expect to have to subdue the enemy by force?"

His gaze drifted to her lips, and his voice turned husky. "If that's what it takes."

Her breathing quickened, and her stomach went all trembly. "Are we still talking about swords, Major?"

"Absolutely," he drawled. Something intoxicating flickered in the inky depths of his eyes. "What else would I speak of to a well-bred young Englishwoman?"

The words leaped from her lips before she could stop them. "Your wife, perhaps?" *That* was certainly something a flirtatious flibbertigibbet would say. And she merely asked as part of her investigation. That's all. Truly.

He blinked. "I'm not married."

She ignored the errant thrill that coursed through her. "Thirty is old to be still unmarried, isn't it?"

"I've been kind of busy the past ten years, ma'am. I was too young for a wife before the war with England, and during it, I didn't have time for courtship."

"But the war has long been over. What have you been doing since then?"

His gaze grew shuttered. "Diplomatic missions." The waltz was ending, so he led her from the floor.

"Where?" she prodded, hoping he'd reveal his real purpose. "Somewhere you couldn't find a wife? It seems to me—" She broke off as she spotted a gentleman pushing his way through the crowd toward them. "Oh, no, *he's* here."

Thoughts of eliciting information vanished in the wake of her need for self-preservation. "Pardon me." She released his arm. "I have to go."

He hurried after her as she swept toward the nearest glass door that led out onto the gallery. "Go where?"

"Away from the marquess," she hissed. "And please don't follow me. You're hard to miss, Major Winter; you'll lead him right to me."

Thankfully, he heeded her request. Once outside, she peered back through the door. Major Winter had vanished, but the Marquess of Pomeroy had halted to scan the area. When his sharp blue eyes fixed on the glass doors, she jumped back.

Spotting a nearby pillar, she slid behind it. She fixed her gaze on the crack between the pillar and the wall, through which she could just see the glass doors.

"What did I miss?" came a voice at her elbow.

She nearly jumped two feet. Whirling to find the major standing there, she cried, "You beast! You gave me the most horrid fright! What are you doing?"

"Joining you. I came through another door." His eyes gleamed at her. "Too bad you couldn't find a pillar to hide behind upstairs, or you could have—"

"Shh," she hissed.

Just in time, too, for they both heard the glass door opening. She tensed as a voice called out, "Lady Amelia?"

Her gaze shot to Major Winter. As if to protect her, he edged closer. A smile touched her lips. It was rather thrilling, hiding out here with the major.

A long silence ensued, during which she envisioned Lord Pomeroy surveying the gallery with his supercilious stare. When she heard the click of his heels on the stone, she flattened herself against the cold marble, struggling to keep her breathing quiet.

That was no small feat with the major standing inches away. His hand had found her waist, and he stroked it silkily, enticingly. She swallowed hard.

His gaze fixed on her throat, and again there was that delicious flicker in his eyes. But Lord Pomeroy's muttered curse broke the moment. As Amelia held her breath, the footsteps receded, and the door closed.

"Do you mind telling me what that was about?" Major Winter asked.

"I don't wish to speak to Lord Pompous . . . I mean, Pomeroy," she breathed, worried that the man might come out again and find them.

"I guessed that much. Who is he?"

"The man you met earlier, the one to whom you made the comment about promenades and pistols."

"General Paxton?"

"Try calling him that instead of Lord Pomeroy, and he'll bite your head off."

"I did. Call him that." The moon illuminated the major's lips as they quirked up in a wry smile. "And he did bite my head off. Self-important old goat, isn't he?"

She cast him a chastening glance. "We English consider him a war hero for routing Boney. That's why the prince honored him with the title of marquess."

"Then why are you hiding behind pillars to avoid him?"

She sighed. "He wants to marry me, curse him. Me and my fortune."

"Doesn't he have his own?"

"Not really. They gave him lands and the title, but he has to maintain it."

His gaze probed hers. "And you don't want to marry a fortune hunter."

His hand still rested on her waist. She knew she should move away, but she couldn't bring herself to do so. "Who does?"

He leaned his forearm against the pillar, his expression calculating. "I guess that means I don't have a chance with you."

"Don't you have money?"

"I did once." His voice now held an icy edge. "But it vanished years ago."

"You should have been more careful," she said lightly, though her blood pounded in her ears. Had his money "vanished" because of Dolly?

Anger flashed in his eyes. "Care had nothing to do with it." Dropping his hand from her waist, he pivoted on his heel and marched off.

She followed him down the gallery. She had to know more, which meant not antagonizing him. "You have other advantages that make up for your lack of fortune, Major Winter."

"Do I?" he growled.

She slanted her gaze up at him. "What woman could resist a handsome, strapping marine like you, who's had such exciting adventures? Hearing your tales would keep a woman entertained when other duller husbands would not."

He paused to regard her with obvious skepticism. "And you would marry a man because he'd had adventures?"

"Certainly! It would be great fun." With a flirtatious smile, she continued down the gallery. "Especially if my husband took me on adventures, too."

"So why not marry General . . . Lord Pomeroy?"

"He's *old*, for goodness sake!" she said in her best flighty manner.

"Well then, why not one of the other English officers?"

"Most of them only want my fortune to fund their retirement." Sadly enough, that was true. "And the few adventurous officers either don't want wives or are already married." She turned to him with a pout. "Even the married ones expect their wives to stay home like good little girls and never see the world, while they sail to the West Indies and beyond."

"Trust me, Lady Amelia, you wouldn't enjoy seeing the world if it meant spending your days in a cramped ship's cabin or long hours on a camel's back."

"Oh, what's it like to ride a camel? Can they run like horses, or is it more like a trot? Do they really go for hours without water?"

He stared at her. "Camels are smelly and dirty and cantankerous. You wouldn't like riding one. You certainly wouldn't like eating one."

Goodness, she was giving herself away again. "Of course not," she said primly. "I imagine camel meat is rather tough."

"Tough and stringy. Not food for a lady." He shifted his gaze to the gardens below. "I suppose you got this interest in adventure from your stepmother."

He kept turning the conversation back to Dolly. He *must* suspect her somehow. Walking over to the gallery rail, she stared down into the bushes to hide her agitation. "Why do you say that?"

He came up to lean against the rail beside her. "I'm sure she told you all about her own travels in France and—"

"Not France, Major Winter." Her blood pounded in her ears. "It was Spain, remember?"

"Right, during the war. I forgot." He searched her face. "You must be very close to your stepmother if you adopted her love of travel."

"I can't imagine what you mean," she hedged. He must be after her Dolly. Until she knew why, she didn't know how to answer his questions safely. She had to get him off the subject.

"I gather she and your father haven't been married long, yet you seem to share her interests. How long *have* they been married, anyway?"

"Major Winter," she said, desperate to change the subject, "are you going to just stand there babbling about my relations? Or are you going to kiss me?"

He frowned. "Beg pardon?"

Turn his head, she reminded herself. *Away from Dolly.*

Her heart thundering wildly, she walked her fingers up the gold braid of his coat. "When a man follows a young lady onto a gallery and talks to her of suitors and such, he generally has something other than conversation in mind. We're alone, and the stars are out. You couldn't ask for a better opportunity." She tugged his hand to her waist.

He didn't remove it and dragged in a sharp breath. "How old are you?"

"Nearly twenty-one."

"Too young for me," he said hoarsely.

"Nonsense. Lord Kirkwood is your age, and Lord Pomeroy is over fifty. It didn't stop either of them from pursuing me." She lowered her eyelashes in what she hoped was a provocative manner. "Of course, if you find me unattractive—"

"No man in his right mind would find you unattractive," he ground out. "But that doesn't mean I'm fool enough to kiss you."

Some insane and reckless instinct possessed her. "Then I'll have to kiss *you*."

Chapter Four

Dear Charlotte,
You and I are in perfect agreement. The spoiled Miss
Linley needs a husband with a firm hand. Besides, Mr.
Chambers secretly frequents the sort of establishment
no gentleman should visit, which shows a definite lack
of character.
Your opinionated cousin,
Michael

Every muscle in Lucas's body went as taut as a full sail. God have mercy. The flirt actually rose up on tiptoe to press her lips to his. Hell, she was young enough to be . . . well, at least a younger sister.

But she didn't kiss like a younger sister, that was for damned sure. She had the most tempting lips he'd ever tasted. Not to mention her pretty little treat of a body that made him want to run his hands over every inch.

Before he even got the chance to enjoy himself, however, she broke the kiss, drawing back with a knowing smile.

His temper flared. She was just like her countrymen, baiting and tormenting him, thinking she could escape unscathed because he was a crass American and she was the highfalutin English. But she'd been the one to start this, and she was damned well going to finish it.

He snared her around the waist and dragged her

against him. "If that's your idea of a kiss, it's no wonder you crave adventure." Seizing her chin, he growled, "*This,* Lady Amelia, is a kiss." Then he covered her mouth with his.

Although she froze, she didn't fight him, so he took advantage. He moved his lips on hers, testing, tasting, enjoying. Then, splaying his fingers over her silk-clad back, he thrust his tongue inside—

She jerked back, but didn't pull out of his embrace, just stared up at him with those luminous, chocolate-hued eyes. "What are you doing?"

"Kissing you."

She colored. "Yes, but you . . . that is . . . your—"

"That's how we savage Americans kiss." Her reaction irritated him. Given her flirting, she had to know what he was doing. "But I suppose you don't like a plain soldier daring to kiss you with his whole mouth."

"I-I didn't say that," she protested.

"Good. Then you won't mind if I continue where I left off."

Without giving her a chance to resist, he kissed her again. He didn't know which drove him harder—her obvious shock at his insolence or the fact that she'd meant only to tease him—but he wasn't letting some lofty English lady get the better of him. Not tonight, not when his blood still ran hot and furious after his encounter with the soldiers.

He took her mouth as insolently as any marauding army, half-expecting her to fight off the attack with the same ferocity. To his shock, she not only refused to fight, but when he probed between her lips, she even let him in.

Hellfire and damnation. It was like sinking into warm molasses—silky-smooth and so damned sweet it twisted his anger into something more dangerous. Intoxicated, he plunged his tongue deeply inside her mouth, then again and again. With every thrust, she melted a little more until she was as soft as freshly churned butter in his arms.

It would drive any hot-blooded soldier crazy. What luscious lips she had, tender as a Virginia peach. And the honeysuckle smell of her was so like home that for a second he forgot she was English, forgot whose stepdaughter she was. He just wanted more. A lot more. He wanted to conquer her, consume her.

When she looped her arms about his neck, crushing her soft breasts against his chest, he took it for an invitation and let his hands roam . . . up her back, then down over her shapely hips, then up along her ribs until his thumbs brushed the undersides of her—

"We must stop this," she drew back to murmur, her face flushed and her breath coming quickly. "Someone will soon notice that we're both gone from the ballroom, and if anyone catches us here together, I'll be called 'fast' or worse."

His mind struggled to assimilate her words. Then he scowled. "That's the price you pay for adventure, darlin'," he rasped, fighting the powerful urge to throw her over his shoulder and carry her down into the bushes.

She didn't seem to realize she skirted the near side of danger, for she cast him a cold glance. "You wouldn't be so flippant if you knew the price they'd try to make *you* pay if we were caught together."

"Flippant is a hell of a long way from what I feel just now."

Though her expression warmed, she tried to leave his arms. But he wasn't ready to release her. What she'd said had sunk in, and he wanted answers.

"Exactly what price do you think 'they' would try to make me pay?" he asked as he fought to rein in his reckless lust.

"Marriage, of course. A gentlemen isn't supposed to kiss an unmarried lady unless he's courting her. And you aren't, are you?"

The words "hell, no," rose to his lips, but he caught himself. He had let himself get carried away by her honeyed mouth, but he wasn't there to annoy some slip of an Englishwoman. He was there for justice. Which he couldn't get without dealing with her.

And how better to deal with her than to court her? Courtship was the perfect disguise for his purpose. If he played his cards right, she might even bring him home to meet her parents.

Lowering his gaze to her reddened lips, he said, "I could be."

She blinked. "Could be what?"

"Courting you."

It was perfectly safe. Kirkwood had already said the lady wasn't interested in marrying, and she'd as much as admitted it herself. Besides, she wouldn't want anything to do with him after he apprehended her stepmother and Theodore Frier—which he meant to do once he was sure he had the right woman.

She watched him uneasily. "You 'could be' courting me? After one kiss?"

He lifted his hand to cup her cheek, running his thumb over her sultry lower lip. "More than one kiss. And sometimes that's all it takes."

"Really?" Her voice was oddly brittle. "I thought you were here on business."

"Business?" he said warily.

"The treaty with the Algerians."

"Oh. Right." It was at least partly true. His superiors had agreed that it would provide him with a suitable cover while he tracked down the Friers. "Doesn't mean I can't look for a wife while I'm going about my business."

He thought he saw anger flash in her eyes, but then it was gone. He must have imagined it—why would she be angry? Females like her collected suitors like so many jewels. She wouldn't care if one more hung around.

"So now you're looking for a wife." She slid her hands down to his waist, then froze as she felt his dagger. "What's this?" She thrust her hand inside his sash, then pulled out the knife and held it up with an arch glance. "Do you always carry a dagger when you're courting?"

"Do you always check your suitors for weapons?" he countered, snatching it from her and shoving it back in his sash.

She hesitated, then cast him a smile more in keeping with the flighty flirt she'd seemed earlier than the woman he'd just been kissing. "Of course not, you silly man. It was accidental." She wagged her finger at him. "But this is exactly the problem with your courting me. You don't know the rules."

"What rules?" he clipped out, annoyed by her abrupt change in personality.

This time when she pushed him away, he let go.

"Of proper English society." She flashed him a teasing smile. "In England, arming oneself for a ball is considered terribly rude, Major."

"Lucas," he said tightly, bothered by her silly propriety after those hot kisses. "Call me Lucas. It's my Christian name."

She lowered her lashes demurely. "We aren't engaged yet, sir. And we aren't likely to be if you continue to flout the rules of proper society."

To hell with the rules of proper society. He just wanted the chance to find out what he needed to know.

Then again . . .

"You could teach me not to. Flout the rules, I mean." Yes, that would work. He couldn't continue his investigation if she wouldn't see him because of his "rude" behavior. "You could give me society lessons." Unable to keep the sarcasm from his voice, he added, "Make me worthy to be your suitor."

An oddly calculating gleam appeared in her eyes. "That's a brilliant idea."

He sure hoped so. "Who can teach me better than you?" The one woman who might lead him to Dorothy Frier, and from there to Theodore Frier.

"Who indeed?" She fluttered her lashes at him. "Although I'm not sure it's worth my effort, when plenty of other gentlemen court me who already know the rules of English society."

He gritted his teeth. If she thought to make him beg for the "privilege" of courting her, she was in for a surprise. But he did have something she wanted. "Ah, but none of those other fellows can feed you the tales of adventure you crave."

She stared at him. "You have a point."

"I can even give you adventures of your own, if you want."

Her gaze grew steely. "What sort of adventures? Your kisses?"

His blood ran high. *That* would certainly make up for his having to endure "society lessons." "If that's what you want, darlin'."

Her expression turned coy. "We'll see. If you prove yourself 'worthy' to be my suitor, then perhaps a few of those adventures might be in order."

So the little tease meant to practice her wiles on him, did she? Fine, let her practice all she wants. "Then we have a bargain. You give me society lessons, and I give you adventures. Of whatever kind you want."

She hesitated, then flashed him an arch smile. "Very well. Feel free to call on me at Papa's town house. Lord Kirkwood can give you the direction." She glanced back toward the glass doors. "Now I'd best go in before someone comes looking for me."

When she walked off, he started to follow. She stopped short. "We can't enter together or people will assume—"

"That we were out here doing something we shouldn't?"

"Exactly." She gazed back at him from beneath seductively lowered lashes. "And let this be your first lesson: no one ever lets on to other people that they've been doing something they shouldn't."

"In that case—" He brushed his hand down the back of her dress.

She leaped away with a blush. "What are you doing?"

"There's dirt from the railing on your gown. And if you don't want anybody knowing what we were doing . . ."

"Oh." She dusted off her gown. "In future, you really should tell me what to do, not take it upon yourself."

"All right. Next time I'll let you touch your own backside." Her shapely, fits-perfectly-in-a-man's-hands backside.

A laugh bubbled out of her. "And you certainly shouldn't say the word 'backside' in society."

He bristled at the instruction. "You'd rather I said 'ass'?"

She cast him a reproachful glance. "You're not supposed to refer to any part of a person's body at all."

"So I can't offer to give you a hand? Or take your arm? Or lend you an ear?"

"You know very well what I mean, you silly man."

"Don't be too sure. According to you English, I'm a savage."

"Even savages can learn to behave."

"If that's what they want."

She raised one eyebrow. "I thought you did."

He forced a smile. "As long as you don't try to turn me into one of your fancy milk-fed gentlemen."

"Oh, I doubt there's any danger of that," she said, in a voice that could only be called sarcastic. But just as he wondered about that glimpse of another side to her, she gave him an inane little wave, and added, "I hope to see you sometime soon . . . Lucas. I can't wait until our next adventure."

Then she sashayed down the gallery with her hips swinging, leaving him to stare after her with blood afire. Oh, he'd give the little flirt an adventure all right. Just let him alone with her somewhere he could lay her down and—

He cursed under his breath. *Don't be a fool.* This "courtship" was meant to elicit information, nothing more. Let her tease and bat her eyelashes. While she played at taming the American savage, he'd be interrogating her, not making love to her. Because no matter what, he meant to get answers.

As Amelia entered the ballroom, her inane smile turned into a scowl. Court her, indeed! The scoundrel meant to use a courtship to find out what he needed to know about Dolly. And probably even wangle an invitation to the estate.

Impossible though it seemed, Dolly *was* the focus of his investigation. He'd asked too many pointed questions, had tried to trip Amelia up too often.

Not to mention this scurrilous courtship. The cad would pretend to court a woman just to get what he wanted? How dare he?

Well, two could play that game. While he tried to kiss her into giving him information, she'd tease him into revealing why he was after Dolly. His foolish suspicions couldn't possibly be based on anything substantial. And she'd prove it, even if she had to play the flirty flibbertigibbet until she batted her eyelashes off.

"Have you been outside all this time?" came a familiar female voice at her elbow.

She started, then faced her chaperone. "Yes. I needed to clear my head."

Mrs. Harris looked more concerned than disapproving. "He didn't bother you, did he?"

Her heart pounded. "Who?"

"Lord Pomeroy. I saw him go out after you, but before I could intervene, he was back inside. So I figured you'd dealt with him sufficiently on your own."

"Oh." She smiled in relief. "Actually, I hid. He never even saw me."

Mrs. Harris let out a breath. "Thank heaven. I would have felt very remiss as a chaperone if he'd laid one hand on you. But I didn't realize you'd stayed out there. Someone engaged me in conversation, and by the time it was done—" She broke off, her gaze fixing on something to the left of Amelia.

Amelia turned to see Lucas enter the ballroom just one door over from where she had come in. Oh no.

Catching their eyes on him, he nodded and went on, leaving Amelia to face Mrs. Harris. Even as her chaperone's sharp blue gaze swung to her, she said hastily, "It's not what you think."

"You were with *him*? On the gallery, alone?"

"Yes, but we were only talking. He came out to make sure Lord Pomeroy didn't bother me."

"Did he, now?" She eyed Amelia closely. "Be careful, my dear. When a man of Major Winter's age—"

"He's no older than you," she protested.

"That's quite a bit older than *you*. Not to mention he's merely a soldier, and you're an heiress."

"So he must be after my fortune, right?"

Mrs. Harris hesitated. "Possibly."

Amelia tensed. Should she confess everything she'd discovered in the major's room?

Probably not. Conscious of her duty to her charge, Mrs. Harris might try to pack her off to the country. Amelia didn't want to alarm Dolly unnecessarily—or cause Papa to regard his wife with suspicion. Best that she keep this knowledge to herself until she knew more.

"I seriously doubt Major Winter is interested in my fortune," Amelia said.

"Why not? We know little about him beyond his connection to Lord Kirkwood. We don't know his family background or his income—"

"All of which would be good to know, wouldn't it?" Yes, such knowledge might help her figure out why Lucas was after Dolly.

"You're interested in him?" Mrs. Harris asked.

"You might say that."

Mrs. Harris's heavy sigh made her brazen red curls shake. "I'm not entirely surprised. He *is* the sort of man who would appeal to you." Her voice grew brittle. "He's of the right age to be worldly without being old. He wears a dashing uniform and lives a dashing life and is exactly what every young girl thinks she wants. Until she gets it."

Amelia lifted an eyebrow. "Are we still talking about the major?"

Mrs. Harris blinked, then chuckled. "Forgive me, my dear. I do tend to let my own experience color my perceptions, don't I?"

"Occasionally, yes," Amelia said, with a smile.

Not that she blamed Mrs. Harris. A baron's daughter, the woman had eloped in her youth with a reckless cavalry officer, who'd run through every pound of her inheritance within two years of their marriage. Fortunately, he'd possessed the good sense to die in a duel, leaving Mrs. Harris free to resume her life. But the widow had been understandably cautious about men ever since, both for herself and her charges.

Mrs. Harris stared across the room to where Lucas helped himself to some punch. "So you like the American major, do you?"

"I like his tales about fighting Barbary pirates. I like his exciting profession." She liked his kisses, which were every bit as enthralling as those in the harem tales. Like the one where the corsair captured an English widow and kissed her so deeply and passionately that—

She groaned. Drat Lucas for using his corsair's kisses against her. She mustn't think about them. They were merely part of his strategy, the tactics of a scoundrel—nothing more. Easily forgotten.

Like a comet in the night sky was forgotten. Or an eclipse of the sun. Or the Thames freezing over when she was sixteen.

She scowled. Curse the man for not meaning his kisses. "Whether I like him will depend on what I can learn about him." She fixed her gaze on Lucas's strong, broad back and smiled grimly. "As a certain wise woman I know always says, 'information is more valuable than gold.'"

"Nice to see that some of my instructions took root," Mrs. Harris said.

"Don't worry, they all did." She tore her gaze from her adversary. "And I know just the person we should consult about Major Winter."

"Cousin Michael?" Mrs. Harris said.

"Oh. I hadn't thought of him, but yes, you should certainly write him. I was thinking of Lady Kirkwood. Who better to reveal his secrets than the man's own relations?"

"If she'll tell us," Mrs. Harris pointed out.

Amelia smiled. "She wants an heiress for her son, doesn't she? Valuable information can travel both ways."

Mrs. Harris gave a reluctant chuckle. "You are more devious than I gave you credit for."

"I learned from a master." With an impish grin, Amelia squeezed her chaperone's hand. "Come on. Let me watch you work."

Though Mrs. Harris rolled her eyes, she went with Amelia to seek out Lady Kirkwood.

Fortunately, they found the Dowager Viscountess standing alone by the orchestra. As they approached, Lady Kirkwood smiled cautiously. "Mrs. Harris. How good to see you."

"Thank you," Mrs. Harris answered. "Amelia and I want to ask about your relation, Major Winter."

"I'm not sure what I can tell you. Our families aren't close."

"A pity," Amelia broke in. "My dear friend Sarah Linley said you'd be the perfect one to ask."

Lady Kirkwood thawed considerably. "Ah yes, Miss Linley. A lovely girl."

Mrs. Harris pressed the advantage. "And very admiring of your son, I hear."

If anyone knew how the game was played, it was Lady Kirkwood. "He certainly admires her greatly as well." She touched a hand to her silver hair. "I do hope you'll tell her that I said as much."

"Of course," Amelia said smoothly. "She'll be delighted to hear it." Ecstatic, more like. "Now, about Major Winter—"

"Ah, yes. My cousin." Lady Kirkwood leaned closer. "Distant cousin, I should say. His mother is descended from the fourth Viscount Kirkwood."

"And what about his father?" Mrs. Harris asked.

"Why do you wish to know?" Lady Kirkwood countered.

"Major Winter has shown an interest in Lady Amelia."

Amelia held her breath, praying that Lady Kirkwood didn't know about the overtures her son had made to Amelia a year ago. Otherwise, their questions could be awkward.

Apparently she didn't, for she smiled. "Has he? I confess I'm surprised. Not that Lady Amelia isn't a lovely young woman, perfectly capable of attracting any young man, but . . ." She sighed. "Major Winter doesn't really like the English. He's rather vocal about it."

"I suppose the war brought about this prejudice of his," Mrs. Harris said.

Lady Kirkwood shook her head. "It's more than that, though I don't know the whole of it. My son David knows, but he won't say. Something happened when Major Winter was in England right after the end of the war—"

"He's been in England before?" Amelia broke in.

"Yes. I'm not sure why. I assume it had to do with

the peace treaty. I do know David helped him with his passage to America."

How very strange. What would an American be doing in England so soon after the war? Could he have been a spy? Connected to Dolly?

That made no sense. Lord Kirkwood would never have aided a spy. Besides, back then Dolly hadn't reached England yet, and Lucas clearly hadn't even known which "Dorothy" she was until recently.

"Well, regardless of how he feels about other English ladies," Mrs. Harris said, "he's shown a clear partiality for my charge. I was hoping you might tell me something of his family and prospects."

"What little I know." Lady Kirkwood cast them a thin smile. "I can tell you this. Though his mother was from one of the finest families in Richmond, Virginia, his father was a common sailor. Apparently the father was personable enough to turn heads, which is how he enticed the mother into marrying him."

"So how did the major gain a commission?" Amelia asked. "Through his mother's family?"

"Not exactly. Though I believe Major Winter grew up poor—sailors in America aren't paid any better than sailors here—the family later came into money. The father quit the navy when Major Winter was a boy to start a munitions company. He invented some special cannon for ships that made him rich. By the time Major Winter was sixteen, his father had the connections to gain his son a commission in the American Marine Guard."

Mrs. Harris looked pleased. "Is he the only son, then? Or at least the eldest?"

"The only son, fortunately." Lady Kirkwood's voice turned contemptuous. "If he were the eldest, he'd have to share the estate with his siblings. Those mad Americans actually allow all the children to inherit. It's unconscionable. How can families remain strong when they parcel out their assets?"

Amelia bit back a retort. Personally, she'd always found the English system rather unfair to daughters and younger sons.

"So he'll inherit his father's company," Mrs. Harris said.

"He already has. His parents died three years ago, while he was abroad."

The bald statement hit Amelia like a blow. Lucas's parents had died in his absence? How awful!

"Poor man," Mrs. Harris said with a tsk of sympathy. "I suppose he's been forced to take over the running of his father's business concern as well. Is that why he's here? Something to do with the munitions company?"

"No, no . . . he's here about some treaty. He's still in the Marine Guard." Lady Kirkwood seemed a little confused. "I suppose he has someone who manages Baltimore Maritime for him. Yes, I'm sure that's right."

Amelia was still fixed on the incredible sadness of Lucas's losing his parents when he was only . . . what . . . twenty-seven? He couldn't have been more than that if it had been only three years ago—

Three years ago. A chill shook Amelia. Wasn't that when Dolly had left America for Canada? "Both of his parents died at the same time?" Amelia asked shakily, afraid to even consider the horrible possibility that rose in her mind.

"Yes." A sudden shutter came down over Lady Kirkwood's face. "I don't know all the details, but it was very tragic." And clearly her ladyship had just reached the limit of her willingness to reveal secrets.

Still, Amelia had to know one thing. "They weren't murdered, were they?"

"Murdered!" Lady Kirkwood snorted. "Of course not. Those Americans are rough, but I'm sure they don't go about murdering perfectly respectable people."

"Forgive Lady Amelia," Mrs. Harris put in hastily. "She has a wild imagination."

"I should say so. Murdered, indeed." Lady Kirkwood drew herself up. "If you'll excuse me, I have other guests to attend to."

As soon as the woman had stalked off, Mrs. Harris whirled on her. "What on earth was *that* all about? Murdered? Really, Amelia—"

"I'm sorry. You know me—always dramatic."

Amelia could barely hide her relief. Thank goodness Lucas didn't suspect Dolly of involvement with his parents' deaths. That would be awful.

Mrs. Harris searched her face, but dropped the matter. "At least now you can be sure that Major Winter is not a fortune-hunter."

"Yes." But he'd said something on the gallery about losing all his money. Had that been a lie, or did Lady Kirkwood simply not know? And did it have anything to do with Dolly? Probably not, or surely he wouldn't have mentioned it to Amelia in the first place.

Mrs. Harris eyed her consideringly. "You don't look terribly reassured."

"A woman should always be cautious. Before I become involved with Major Winter, I have to assess how serious his intentions might be. And behave accordingly."

"A wise course of action, my dear." Mrs. Harris smiled broadly.

What an understatement. Lucas Winter's calculating kisses were clearly meant only to distract her from his secretive investigation.

And before this was all over, she meant to make him pay for that.

Chapter Five

Dear Cousin,

What shocking news about Mr. Chambers! I should never have guessed. He has such a sweet face. Wherever do you learn these things? And what do your sources say about Lord Kirkwood's cousin, Major Lucas Winter? He has shown an interest in Lady Amelia, which concerns me. He does not *have a sweet face.*

Your always grateful friend,

Charlotte

The lamp in the tunnel went out. Footsteps stamped on the floors above, covering Lucas's own shouts. He couldn't be heard, couldn't see . . . it was so dark in the tunnel, so damned dark and cold.

On hands and knees he scrabbled along the damp dirt to the shaft, only to look up and find the entrance blocked by its heavy stone. He climbed up to shove at it, but it didn't budge. And he couldn't make himself heard over the noise.

Then musket shots, half-muffled by the stone. The redcoats were firing, damn it!

Screams sounded above him, terrible cries of dying men, *his* men. This shouldn't happen! The redcoats had no right to fire, none at all! He bloodied his hands pounding the stone, but it did him no good. His men were being murdered above him . . .

The cold seeped into his bones, making him shiver in his thin rags. The foul air clogged his throat, and he began breathing heavily. How much air did he have? How long could he last before it ran out?

He tried to think, but the screaming went on and on—

Lucas shot up in bed, drenched in a cold sweat, his heart clamoring so loud in his ears that it took a while to remember that he was safe now. He wasn't huddled half-naked and starving in the lightless tunnel, waiting to die.

He'd just kicked off the covers with his thrashing, that's all. And since he wore only his drawers to sleep in, he'd gotten cold. Everything was fine.

Fine. Right. Throwing his legs over the side of the bed, he sat there gulping air, struggling to still his frantically beating heart.

As his pulse slowed, he dragged the coverlet around him, then rose to go to the window, where the faint wash of light on the horizon signaled approaching dawn. Greedily, he drank it in to banish his lingering ghosts.

Damned nightmares. He hadn't had one in months, not since he'd been closeted belowdecks on his passage from Canada to France. That horrific voyage made him fear that he'd never again be able to spend weeks at sea. A marine who started gasping for breath the second he went below was useless to his ship.

But the dreams had ended in France, and he'd started to hope . . .

He pounded his fist on the sill. It only took seeing the redcoats at a ball to bring the nightmares back. Christ, he couldn't wait to leave this damned country.

He took one last look at the brightening sky, then raked his fingers through his tangled hair. Turning to the washbasin, he poured icy water in it to splash on his face. Judging from the dead embers in the fireplace, the servants would be slipping in soon to light the fires.

No point in trying to return to sleep. He was too agitated, too on edge. What he needed was to work off his tension with a round of swordplay, or a hard ride or a frenzied bout of lovemaking . . .

Damnation, where had that come from?

But he knew: Amelia. Pretty, flirty, infuriating Amelia. Who wanted to ride a camel and had a luscious honey of a mouth that stirred needs he'd suppressed for month upon lonely month. Too bad she was English and the stepdaughter of a criminal's wife, because just the thought of losing himself in that silky body—

He snorted. As if that frivolous female, who wouldn't even let him court her without "society lessons," would take him into her bed. She claimed to want "adventures," but she'd probably faint if she ever got one.

He stared into the mirror at his face, shadowed by morning whiskers and drawn from lack of sleep. Hell, she'd probably faint if she got near *him* right now. And since he meant to call on her this morning . . .

He shaved and dressed with care. Never mind that the flirt only put up with his "courtship" because she was bored—he needed information. And if that meant he had to look halfway civilized and dance to her tune, then he'd do it, by God, even if he had to grit his teeth the whole time.

An hour later, he headed down to the dining room. He was surprised to find his cousin already there.

"Kind of early for you, isn't it?" Lucas strode to the sideboard, where the servants had laid out cold bread, cheese, and fruit just for him. "I thought none of you ate breakfast until after ten."

"I haven't been to bed yet," Kirkwood mumbled.

Lucas surveyed his cousin, who was hunched over a cup of hot tea. Sure enough, Kirkwood still wore his evening clothes. "Balls go late here, do they?" He finished piling food on his plate, then took a seat at the table opposite his cousin.

"It ended at three. But I went out to my club afterward. I just got home."

"That explains it. I didn't wait until the end. Went to bed as soon as Lady Amelia left at midnight."

"I noticed."

His cousin's acid tone put Lucas on his guard.

"I also noticed Lady Amelia and her chaperone speaking to my mother." Kirkwood settled his red-rimmed gaze on Lucas. "They seem to think that you're seeking a wife. And that you've fixed your hopes on Lady Amelia."

Stifling his irritation, Lucas poured himself some tea from the pot in the center of the table. "You know women. They think what they want."

"Not all women. Not Mrs. Harris, for example. And not without reason." He glared at Lucas. "What did you do? I noticed that both you and Lady Amelia vanished from the ballroom for a while, and I have to wonder—"

"Go to bed," Lucas growled. "Before you start fooling with things that don't concern you."

"Take care, Winter. You may be a guest in my home, but—"

"—you're the only one allowed to court a woman for the wrong reasons, right?" When his cousin bristled, he added, "It's a flirtation, nothing more. And don't be thinking I started it, because I didn't. *She* did. So if the flighty female has a hankering to flirt with an American savage, I'm sure not going to stop her." He scowled at Kirkwood. "And neither are you."

But his cousin's expression had softened. "Flighty female? Lady Amelia?"

"Don't worry about me taking advantage of that featherbrain." He rolled a slice of bread around a hunk of cheese and took a bite. "I swear, every time Amelia calls me 'a big, strapping soldier' and bats her eyelashes, I want to throttle her."

When his cousin made a choking sound, Lucas glanced up to see Kirkwood fighting a laugh, his eyes overly bright.

"What?" Lucas asked.

"You are speaking of Lady Amelia, right? The Earl of Tovey's daughter?"

"Why wouldn't I be?"

"No reason." Laughter sputtered out of Kirkwood. "I'm merely trying to envision the woman calling you a 'strapping soldier' and batting her eyelashes."

Lucas scowled. "You think I'm lying?"

"No, of course not," his cousin said, managing an even expression, which he then ruined by breaking into laughter.

"I'm not an ogre, you know."

"Absolutely not," Kirkwood responded in a suitably sober tone.

"Women do find me attractive," Lucas grumbled. "They do flirt with me."

"Even featherbrains like Lady Amelia." Amusement danced in his cousin's eyes.

"Sure. Why not?"

Kirkwood held his hands up in mock surrender. "Why not indeed?" He rose. "I think I'll head off to bed and leave you to your plotting."

"Wait." Lucas picked up his tea. "I need directions to Lady Amelia's."

Kirkwood halted in the doorway. "So that's why you're looking so dapper. You plan to call on the 'flighty female.'"

"In a few hours." Lucas said. "I want to give her and Mrs. Harris a chance to have breakfast. Besides, I need to polish my sword before I leave." He leaned back in his chair. "I promised to show Lady Amelia my mameluke sword." He snorted. "*She* thinks it's made of marzipan."

Kirkwood laughed heartily. "Does she indeed?"

"I tell you, I don't know how you put up with these silly English heiresses."

"It's a trial." His eyes gleamed with renewed humor. "Better not take too long with that sword. You don't want to pay your call too late."

"You're right. I should catch them before they leave to go shopping, or whatever they do all day. I'll just give the sword a quick wipe."

"Or go on over and let the lady polish it herself," Kirkwood joked. "That'll teach her to think it's made of marzipan."

Lucas flashed on a vision of the flirt rubbing his sword, and a whole different image came to his mind. "Trust me, if I thought Lady Amelia would polish my 'sword,' I'd be over there right now."

His cousin blinked, then scowled. "You know perfectly well I didn't mean that how it sounded. A gentleman shouldn't even think such things about a lady, much less say them."

"Good thing I'm not a gentleman." Lucas drained his cup. "Don't worry. I'd never say it to *her*. Not that she'd understand it, anyway."

"You might be surprised," Kirkwood muttered, and left.

Lucas scowled after him. Nothing about Amelia would surprise him. The woman was as changeable as the wind.

But it didn't matter. As long as he got what he needed from her, she could change fifty times an hour. *This* time, Theodore Frier wouldn't escape him.

Despite not going to bed until one, Amelia rose early. She generally preferred to sleep late, but concern for Dolly had her entering the breakfast room of her father's town house the next morning long before eight.

She'd tossed all night, examining her brief two years with her stepmother, searching for clues. And now she wondered if she might find them in her travel journals. She kept several, full of clippings and sketches and whatever tales she could coax from Dolly about the woman's travels. Until Amelia could travel herself, her journals were all she had.

Hurrying to the writing table by the window where

they were stacked up, she pulled out her latest and read through it. Nothing leaped out at her that told her why Lucas was interested in Dolly.

With a sigh, she inserted in her journal an article Venetia had given her last night about some Scottish Scourge fellow who robbed English nobility on the highways. Apparently he hated Venetia's father, Lord Duncannon, for he always mentioned the man to his victims, although Venetia didn't know why.

Then Amelia transcribed Lucas's description of the march to Derna. He'd captured the essence of the experience so fully, she could practically taste the sand. And had he *really* eaten a camel?

She scanned a loose clipping. A camel had to be better than what this pasha in Algeria ate. One of the man's wives had tried to poison him, but had merely given him a bad case of indigestion.

He'd probably driven her to it with his roving eye and insatiable appetites. Perhaps she'd grown tired of watching concubines parade in and out of his chambers to do what the harem tales described:

> We captives were taught how to worship the pasha's body, how to excite him with kisses we spread over his massive chest and his taut belly. Next we were instructed to caress that "sword" men carry between their thighs, first with our hands and then with our mouths.

A blush crawled up Amelia's cheeks. When she and Venetia had first read that, they'd laughed wildly. The very idea! How did women keep from giggling?

Now it didn't seem quite so odd. If a man like . . . say, Lucas . . . were to lie naked before her and demand that she worship his body—

"You're up early, my dear," Mrs. Harris said from the doorway.

Amelia jumped. Lord, the woman was as bad as Lucas, creeping up on a person. Summoning a smile, she turned to greet her chaperone. "So are you."

Mrs. Harris went to the sideboard. "I thought I had better write that letter to Cousin Michael about Major Winter as soon as possible." She picked up a plate and filled it with stewed pears, cold tongue, and thickly sliced brown bread.

"If anyone can ferret out information, it's your cousin." Perhaps he could even shed light on what the major wanted from Dolly.

"I don't know how I would manage without his support."

The comment roused Amelia's curiosity. "Is it true he gave you the money to start your school?"

"Yes." Taking a seat at the breakfast table, Mrs. Harris buttered her bread lavishly. "I could never have afforded to launch it on my own."

"Yet you've never met him. I don't understand. If he's your cousin, why—"

"My late husband's cousin, my dear, not mine. And my husband was very evasive about his family." She ate some bread, then wiped her lips with ladylike delicacy. "I confess I have not pursued the matter too hard. Cousin Michael only requested one favor in exchange for helping me—that I allow him anonymity. He said it would help shield me from gossip. He did not wish to ruin my reputation after my husband—his own relation—had ruined my life. Since that was an excellent point, I acquiesced to his condition."

"Whoever he is, he's certainly well connected. How else could he know so much gossip? Unless—" A delicious possibility occurred to her. "Might he be a Bow Street runner?"

Mrs. Harris chuckled. "Leave it to you to imagine such a thing. No, I don't think it's anything as romantic as that. I rather suspect from his penmanship that he's an elderly man. His writing is very shaky."

"Perhaps he's trying to disguise it," Amelia speculated, but Mrs. Harris's answering laugh didn't lend credence to that either.

She and the other girls had spun many a fanciful tale about Mrs. Harris's mysterious benefactor: a secret admirer, a lost love, a wealthy sultan who yearned for the pretty widow from afar.

A sudden knock at the front door made Amelia bolt upright. "Are you expecting someone?"

"No."

When the new footman, John, came down the hall to ask if they were home to a Major Lucas Winter, they exchanged startled glances.

"He's come to call at *this* hour?" Mrs. Harris asked.

"Yes, madam. He says Lady Amelia agreed to give him lessons."

Amelia groaned. "I forgot about that." When Mrs. Harris shot her a quizzical look, she said, "I promised to help him learn how to behave in English society."

"Shall I show the gentleman in, then?" John asked.

"By all means," Mrs. Harris said with a smile. "*This* should be interesting."

Only after the footman had gone did Amelia remember that her travel journals were spread out everywhere. Hastily, she began to stack them up.

"What are you doing, my dear?" Mrs. Harris asked.

"Just tidying up." She could hardly explain that her journals might reveal she had a brain. Mrs. Harris wouldn't approve of her masquerade as a flibberti-gibbet.

Mrs. Harris laughed. "He won't notice if you're untidy—he's a man."

Before Amelia could finish putting her journals away, John announced her caller, and the major entered.

As she turned from the table, and Mrs. Harris rose, Amelia's heart lurched in her chest. Lord help her—men that attractive shouldn't be allowed to roam society. It simply wasn't fair.

"Good morning, Major." Amelia moved to block his view of her writing table.

"Morning, ma'am." He tipped his head toward her, then greeted Mrs. Harris. "You both look well."

"So do you," Amelia said.

More than well, curse him. The fierce corsair's features that suited his uniform so well also suited his dark brown morning coat, doeskin riding breeches, and gleaming top boots. She knew, from having searched his wardrobe, that it was his finest clothing, apart from his uniform. She might be flattered . . . if it weren't part of his strategy to get information out of her.

That made her snap, "And what brings you out at this ungodly hour, Major?"

Mrs. Harris looked startled by her rude remark, but returned to her seat at the breakfast table.

"What's ungodly about it?" he drawled. "I've been up since dawn."

"That may be so, but no one in London ever pays a call before noon."

"I didn't realize you English were such lie-abeds."

"Mrs. Harris and I are both up, aren't we? We're simply unprepared for visitors. You should remember that next time."

"I'll surely try," he said through gritted teeth. Clearly Lucas wasn't used to being "instructed" in anything.

She hid a smile. She would make him rue the day he ever tangled with the daughter of the Earl of Tovey. Gesturing to his sheathed sword, she said, "I thought we agreed last night that you shouldn't arm yourself for social affairs."

He laid his hand on the hilt. "It's the mameluke sword I offered to show you."

A thrill shot through her, unbidden. All right, so the scoundrel had brought her the one thing guaranteed to spark her interest. That didn't mean she should fall down at his feet in a swoon.

"How kind of you," she said coolly, though she ruined the effect by hurrying over to clear a space for it on the end of the table opposite where Mrs. Harris continued to eat her breakfast. "Bring it over here so I can see it."

He did as she asked, unsheathing the sword and laying it before her. With her heart in her throat, she examined it thoroughly, imagining him wielding it in battle. The curved hilt of gold-plated brass shone gembright, even in the foggy-morning light.

But the blade itself was what most interested her. "What are these?" She indicated the black, Eastern-looking symbols etched along the nearly three feet of tempered steel.

"I don't know what they all mean, but this one is the Star of Damascus." He pointed to a six-pointed star. "Damascus sword craftsmen use two triangles joined as a sign of their guild."

"May I touch the symbols?" she asked.

"Be careful, my dear," Mrs. Harris called from the other end of the table.

"Yes," he said, "don't cut yourself. This *is* a working sword."

"A very hardworking sword, I'm sure." Its numerous nicks and worn spots attested to that. Amelia fingered each one, wondering where it had been acquired. "Did you carry it at Derna?"

"No. My government only issued the mameluke to the rest of us after Hamet presented O'Bannon with his."

"It's astonishing." She skimmed her fingers down the blade. "You keep your sword in excellent condition, Major Winter."

"I do my best." His voice sounded rather choked.

She glanced up to find him staring at her hand as she stroked down the blade, then up again. What was wrong with him? It wasn't as if she could hurt the steel by touching it. From the way he stared, she'd have thought the sword was a living thing, for goodness sake.

Next we were instructed to caress that "sword" men carry between their thighs, first with our hands and then our mouths.

Surely he was not . . . he did not imagine that she . . .

She started to jerk her hand back, but something stopped her. The harem book had said that a man became uncomfortable when he was aroused. And Lord knew she wanted to make the major uncomfortable.

Deciding to test that possibility, she caressed the sword again, this time with a lingering, loving touch. "It's truly magnificent," she gushed.

He went rigid, a muscle working in his jaw. "Thank you."

"I've never seen such a fine piece of work." Delighted by the results of her experiment, she stroked the weapon up and down.

His hand shot out to halt hers. "You might hurt yourself. The blade *is* sharp."

"It certainly is," she said coyly. She moved her hand away . . . only to clasp the hilt.

His audible groan made her want to crow aloud.

She fondled the hilt. "Would you let me do a rubbing of it?"

His gaze shot to hers, and the heat in his eyes gave her pause. "A rubbing?" he said hoarsely. "Of my . . . er . . . sword?"

"Yes. I'd take care not to use too much pressure." She smiled sweetly, though his smoldering gaze made it difficult for her to breathe. "But I doubt I could harm it, as hard as it is."

"You have no idea." Without warning, he sat down rather stiffly in a chair and pulled it up to the table.

"Major Winter," Amelia admonished him, managing a frown, "it's impolite to sit before all the ladies are seated."

"You can't blame the poor man, Amelia," Mrs. Harris broke in. "You kept him standing too long after his ride over here."

Her chaperone was watching her with one eyebrow raised, but Amelia was having too much fun to stop. "Nonsense, a short ride is nothing to a big, strapping fellow like him. Right, Major Winter?"

He opened his mouth to retort, but Mrs. Harris intervened again. "Show him your travel journals, dear. He might find them interesting."

Amelia sighed. There was no way to hide them now. But she wasn't ready to give up on this delightful game quite yet.

Chapter Six

Dear Charlotte,
Alas, few men of character have sweet faces. Life's trials
show up first in a person's features. But I shall see what
I can discover about Major Winter, even if I must pry
the information from his family's closed lips.
Your obedient servant,
Michael

As if through a fog, Lucas heard Amelia say, "We should probably sheathe your sword. Will you do it, sir, or shall I?"

Sweat broke out on his forehead. God, yes. Give him a minute alone with the little tease, and he'd have his sword sheathed so quick and deep that—

"I'm sure the major can *put it away* later," Mrs. Harris snapped.

Amelia cast a bright-eyed glance at her chaperone that he noticed even in his lust-induced fever. If he didn't know better, he'd think the damned female was tormenting him on purpose. But how could a flighty virgin turn a discussion of a mameluke sword into sensual torture?

"If we're not going to sheathe it," she said in a suspiciously innocent voice, "then I could do the rubbing—"

"Didn't you mention travel journals?" he ground out. If the lady said another word about rubbing or sheathing, he'd be panting at her feet like a hound. "I'd like to see those."

Amelia turned a cool smile on him. "Oh, it's just something silly I do. A big, strong marine like you would find it tedious."

"I daresay being big and strong has naught to do with it," Mrs. Harris put in. With a stern glance at her charge, the widow rose and went to the table Amelia seemed bent on shielding from his gaze. Picking up a stack of strange-looking books, she brought them over and set them in front of him.

While Amelia fidgeted, he opened the first, a collection of rough paper sheets bound with string between two thin boards. Each sheet held something different affixed with glue—a newspaper clipping, a theater ticket, a feather.

But along with the usual female things—pressed flowers and sketches of French gowns—she'd included maps, articles about battles, and sketches of unusual characters. Amazingly, the flighty lady had put in facts about every item. She'd even commented on the articles.

Then there was page after page of Barbary pirates—clippings about captures, accounts by captives, descriptions of their culture. Most of it concerned the naval battles, including the march on Derna. She'd even written down his own account.

She sure was a strange little female, wasn't she?

He turned the page, and a sketch arrested him. "Where did you get this?"

"The Indian chief?" She smiled proudly. "My stepmother drew him."

Lucas's pulse quickened. "His fur-lined hide boots show him to be Maliseet." Lucas stared at her hard. "And the Maliseet live in New Brunswick."

Her smile faltered. "That can't be. They don't have Indians in Brunswick; the Germans would never allow it."

"No, dear. He's talking about Canada." Mrs. Harris poured herself some tea.

"I'm sorry to correct you," Lady Amelia said petulantly, "but Brunswick isn't in Canada, wherever that is—it's in Germany."

"*New* Brunswick is in Canada," he said tersely, refusing to let her confuse the matter. And could any woman who'd put together journals like these really be as half-witted as Lady Amelia seemed? "From looking at this picture, I'd say that your stepmother has definitely been to Canada."

"Do you think so? She probably just copied the picture from a book."

"I don't know, Amelia." Mrs. Harris stared hard at her charge. "Your stepmother might very well have visited Canada. She's quite the world traveler. I daresay that is why Lord Tovey became so enamored of her, that and her for—"

"Major Winter," Amelia interrupted, "I'm so sorry, but we're forgetting entirely about your lessons."

"I reckon we'll get to it eventually." He wanted to know what Mrs. Harris had been about to say.

But Amelia was having none of it. "No, really, we wouldn't want to waste your time. Besides, it's too perfect a day to stand in here discussing my silly journals. Why don't we take a turn about the garden? We can talk about the rules of society and enjoy the damask roses at the same time."

He stared at her another long moment, but she merely looked at him with that inane smile he never knew how to read. "If that's what you want." He tipped his head to Mrs. Harris. "Pardon us, ma'am."

"Certainly," the widow said, though she gazed at her charge as if Lady Amelia had sprouted donkey ears.

He offered Amelia his arm, and they headed down the hall. He noticed the many rooms, thick rugs, marble fireplaces, and beeswax candles. His cousin's house didn't have this many fancy paintings on the wall, and it smelled of tallow candles. Amelia's family had money, that was for damned sure.

But everything looked new, as if it had been bought in the past few years. If he was right, and the money to buy all this had come from—

"Lucas, slow down!"

Amelia's voice dragged him from his thoughts, and he realized he'd been striding so fast she was having to run to keep up with him.

"Pardon me, ma'am," he bit out as he slowed his pace.

"You're awfully eager to see our roses," she teased.

"I sure am," he lied. "Nice house. Expensive-looking." They headed down the back stairs into the big garden. "No wonder the fortune hunters are beating down your door. Have you lived here long?"

Her steps slowed along the garden path. "Long enough. And here's another lesson for you—it's horribly rude to talk about money and how much things cost." She arched one brow. "Even Americans probably follow that rule."

"You're the one who brought up fortune hunters last night." When she eyed him askance, he added, "You should practice what you preach."

She pouted at him. "And you should take these lessons seriously, sir, or I shan't even bother to give them to you."

"I promise you, I'm taking them very seriously." *More seriously than you can possibly know.*

"Oh? I daresay you brought your dagger, even after what I said last night."

In London, with footpads roaming every street? Damned right he had. But he'd stowed it where she wouldn't notice. "No, ma'am," he lied, figuring she'd never know the difference.

"You're just saying that to appease me."

Eyes gleaming, he halted to open his coat. "Feel free to search if you want."

When her gaze dropped to survey his chest, then turned admiring, his blood ran hot. As if she could see right through his waistcoat, her eyes did a slow crawl up to his face that sent his pulse galloping. Hellfire and damnation—where had the woman learned to be such a little seductress?

Then she gazed at him from beneath flirtatiously lowered lashes. "Much as I'm dying to find out just how big and strong you really are, Lucas, I had better not." She glanced beyond him. "And you'd better close your coat before Mrs. Harris puts a swift end to this lesson."

Sucking in a harsh breath, he followed her gaze. Through an upstairs window, he could see her chaperone sitting at a desk, keeping an eye on them as she wrote something. Damnation. That would make it hard to kiss Amelia into telling him what he needed.

He let his coat fall back into place. "I guess opening my coat is something else I shouldn't do in good society."

"Absolutely not." She continued down the path. "Don't ever remove it, either."

He fell into step beside her. "Not even in the card room?"

"Not if ladies are around." She cut her eyes up at him. "Do you play cards?"

"Once in a while. But I've never gotten myself into trouble with them, if that's what you're asking."

"I suppose you meet a lot of card cheats."

That was a strange comment. He glanced over to find her watching him closely. "Not too many, why?"

She looked relieved. "I was just wondering, that's all."

"You think Americans are more likely to be card cheats, is that it?"

"Really, sir," she protested, "you mustn't take every innocent remark and turn it into a criticism of your countrymen."

"Have I been doing that?"

"You certainly did last night at the ball. The soldiers were quite put out."

"Then they shouldn't talk about battles they damned well never fought in."

"And you shouldn't use such foul language."

He bit back a hot retort. "Beg pardon, ma'am. I've spent nearly half my life with soldiers. I sometimes forget how to behave around a lady."

She tipped her head. "As long as you reform your behavior."

He snorted. He'd reform his behavior for an English-woman when the moon fell into the Atlantic. "I don't know what your stepmother told you about Americans, but we don't make a fuss if a man cusses sometimes." That wasn't completely true, but he had to turn the conversation back to his quarry.

"Dolly hasn't mentioned it, no."

He took a risk. "Kirkwood tells me that her parents were English, not American."

Amelia increased her pace along the path. "Yes, they emigrated to your country before she was born."

That fit with what he'd learned about Dorothy Frier. "Where'd she grow up?"

"I have no idea," she said lightly. "She rarely mentions her life there. It reminds her too much of her late husband, whom she dearly loved."

"Who was he?" When she raised an eyebrow at him, he added, "Maybe I know him."

"His name was Obadiah Smith. He owned a trading concern in Boston."

He frowned. When Theodore Frier had headed north from Baltimore, he'd joined Dorothy in Rhinebeck, New York, not in Boston. And from there, the Friers had crossed the border into Canada.

So was Dorothy Smith *not* Dorothy Frier? Or had she simply lied to her new family? "I don't recognize the name, but then I don't know Boston. Are you sure that's where she lived?"

"Of course I'm sure." She pouted at him. "And don't try to tell me it was Brunswick just because they both start with a B. I know it wasn't."

"We've established that," he said dryly. "So where in Boston did they live?"

"How should *I* know?"

"Well then, how long did they live there?"

She slowed her pace along the path. "She hasn't told me every detail of her life. Why are you so interested in my stepmother, anyway?"

He had to be more careful. "No reason."

She batted her eyelashes at him. "Because if your idea of courtship is to talk about my boring old family, we're not going to progress very far."

"You're right, of course." Gritting his teeth at the reemergence of her flirtatious side, he stopped to pluck a bud from a rosebush, then held it out to her. "Please accept my apology."

Her eyes suspiciously bright, she stopped to sniff it. "Your apologies need work, sir. Our gardener would have your head if he caught you stealing a bud from his prize rosebushes."

He reached up to tuck the bud in her hair, then let his hand trail down her cheek in a lingering caress. "Your gardener's not here, darlin'," he rasped.

She dragged in a breath as her gaze met his, and last night's kisses loomed up between them, a tantalizing specter that made his blood roar in his veins. When she licked her lips, he lowered his head.

But before he could kiss her, she jerked back. Casting a glance at the upstairs window, she murmured, "He might not be here, but Mrs. Harris certainly is."

"You English make it dam—darned hard to court a woman. In America, people give a man room to talk to females. They don't breathe down his neck every minute."

"There *are* ways to get around that."

She laid her hand on his arm and his blood heated right up again. "You could take me riding, for example. Then I need only bring a groom with me."

Riding. What good would that do? He could hardly distract her with kisses if they were on horses with a groom at their heels.

Then another idea occurred to him. "How would you like to see a genuine Barbary pirate ship?"

Her face lit up. "Really?"

"Really." That would give him plenty of chances to be alone with her. "There's a captured one at the royal naval shipyard in Deptford, and I'm allowed the run of it."

"Then Mrs. Harris will have to come along, of course," she said.

He scowled. "Why?"

"We'll have to go in my carriage. It's too dangerous at the docks for an open gig, and I can't go off alone with you in a closed carriage."

Damn—he'd been figuring on a groom riding outside. He should have known better.

Still, a ship was a big place, and he might be able to do *something* once he had her on board.

"All right, we'll make it an outing for three."

Chapter Seven

Dear Cousin,
Forgive me for my many notes, but this matter about
Major Winter requires haste. He has the oddest effect on
Lady Amelia: she turns into a pea goose whenever he
enters a room. And I can assure you that she is never a
pea goose around men.
Your anxious friend,
Charlotte

*L*ucas was surprised by how speedily Amelia talked
her chaperone into the outing. The ladies changed
their clothes, and in less than an hour they all headed
for His Majesty's Royal Dockyard in Deptford.

"What we're going to see is called a xebec, isn't it?"
Amelia asked from her seat next to Mrs. Harris across the
carriage from him.

He narrowed his gaze on her. "How did you know
that?"

"An English xebec docked at Torquay once. I heard
that the French later sank it."

"The *Arrow*, yes. That's why the navy wants to refit this
one for their own use. Xebecs can be very handy ships."

"How did they acquire it?"

"A squadron headed home captured it off the coast
of Spain."

Mrs. Harris lifted a gloved hand to her throat. "Did it have captives?"

"No. The pirates had just headed out to sea."

"Thank goodness," Amelia said softly.

His gaze locked with hers. "Aye. The Barbary pirates are none too kind to captives."

They fell silent as the carriage rumbled out of St. James's Square. Lucas wanted to ask more questions about her stepmother, but Mrs. Harris made him wary. The flighty Amelia might not notice he was interrogating her, but Mrs. Harris sure would.

After a while, the stench of the Thames filtered into the carriage as they approached Westminster Bridge. Amelia craned her head toward the window, drinking in the sights with a lively expression while they crossed the river.

He looked out to see a bristling army of masts beneath them, each fighting for purchase on a river choked with watercraft. Barges shouldered their way past penny boats, as merchantmen sailed by with their prows in the air like fancy ladies' noses turned up in disdain. Skiffs skidded past the lumbering ferries that dared to cross the paths of the massive frigates, with pilots cussing at oarsmen and sailors with every turn.

He noticed that Mrs. Harris sat rigid in her seat, her hands fisted in her lap like cannonballs. "Are you all right, ma'am?"

Her gaze flew to his. "Fine." She managed a wan smile. "Perfectly fine."

The hell she was. But he wouldn't press her, especially when Amelia seemed to be having the time of her life.

"There are so many boats," Amelia breathed. "Just imagine where they've been, and what exotic places they're going to from here."

It wasn't something he pondered much, having seen plenty of docks in his life. "Have you never been to the riverfront?"

"No. No one I know ever travels abroad. I've seen the docks at home and in Plymouth, of course, but they're nothing like this."

"You mean, noisy and reeking of human filth?" As they left the river, he gazed out to where a scruffy flood of raw male humanity surged along the streets, with the only women a few whores floating in their midst like rouged lifeboats.

She eyed him askance. "I see a fascinating array of colorful creatures bent on wrestling a living from the river."

He snorted. "If that's what you call them. I call them sailors and wherrymen and the lowest sort of water rat."

"Have you no romance in your soul, Major, no sense of adventure?"

Mrs. Harris, who seemed to have relaxed now that they'd crossed the Thames, smothered a smile.

"If this is what you consider romance and adventure, then no," he snapped. "Ships are for taking people where they want to go, that's all."

"Strange words from a man who spends his life on the water," she retorted.

"It's because of how I spend my life that I see it for what it is and not as a romantic adventure."

"I quite agree," Mrs. Harris put in, "but you'll never

convince Amelia. The first thing she asked when her stepmother enrolled her in my school was if we ever took outings anywhere interesting."

Her stepmother had enrolled her? "And when was that?" Maybe he could get something useful out of Mrs. Harris after all. "How young are English girls when they go off to school?"

"Well, in Amelia's case—"

"It was before my come out, of course." Amelia fluttered her eyelashes at him. "Surely you could figure that out, you silly man."

He scowled. The lady was as mercurial as an actress. She was like two different people.

He went still. *Yes. Exactly.*

"You have no idea how complicated a girl's debut can be," she chattered on. "You have to walk a certain way, and stand a certain way—I could hardly keep track of all the rules."

"You seemed to manage it splendidly," Mrs. Harris said, with lifted eyebrow.

Amelia twirled her bonnet ribbon about her finger like some coquette. "A girl has to learn everything if she wants to have fun in society."

"I'm sure she does," Lucas muttered. The more he got to know Amelia, the more her frivolous side annoyed him. One minute she was talking about xebecs and putting things so clever-like, it made a man take notice. The next she'd give him a vacant stare, and nonsense would fly out of her mouth. It just didn't fit.

Especially when her chaperone seemed just as surprised by her flighty self. Was it a role Amelia took on? If so, why?

It gave him something to ponder the rest of the ride, while she babbled about dances and fan language and other gibberish. Whoever heard of a fan talking, anyway?

Soon they were approaching the docks at Deptford. Trying to get back the sensible Amelia, he glanced out the window and drew her attention to a frigate with a Spanish flag. The lightermen were toting barrels down the gangway. "They must have just started to unload that old girl there. With her sitting so low in the water, her hold's probably full to bursting."

Amelia followed his gaze. "What do you think it's carrying?"

"I don't know." He said something deliberately stupid. "Maybe cotton."

She snorted. "Why would anyone import cotton from Spain, and in barrels, too? It's wine, more like, or even olives."

"What makes you think it's a Spanish ship?" he drawled.

"Well, of course it is. It's flying—" She caught herself, then cast him a silly smile. "It's flying what I assume is the Spanish flag. With so many bright colors, it has to be Spanish. Then again, it could be French and carrying silks."

"Could be," he said noncommittally. And she really *could* be as stupid as she seemed. But he began to doubt it.

The carriage halted. "We're here." Leaping from the carriage, Lucas turned to help Mrs. Harris dismount, then Amelia.

His hands practically spanned her slender waist. His pulse quickened as her honeysuckle scent sweetened the air around her, and she gazed at him with sparkling eyes and flushed cheeks.

He set her down on the dusty road, fighting to keep his sudden surge of lust in check. Hellfire and damnation, she was pretty. Under other circumstances, he might even consider making this a real courtship.

He snorted. Right. With an English lady whose favorite entertainment was probably spending her inheritance. Which he was pretty damned sure was stolen.

He gave Mrs. Harris his other arm. "There she sits," he said as he led them to the dock. "It's the black one anchored about a hundred yards out with the lateen rigging."

"But it's so small!" Amelia exclaimed.

"That's big for a xebec. It's really a xebec frigate, but the draught's still too shallow to hold much weight. That's why there's so little cannon. You can't see it from here, but it only has thirty-four guns, when the average warship carries twice that. The pirates rely on swiftness and maneuverability instead. To capture her the navy had to bring down two sails with broadsides."

He gazed down at Amelia. "You want to board her? We could row out in that dinghy—"

"Yes!" she exclaimed, just as Mrs. Harris said, "Absolutely not!"

Amelia shot her chaperone a pleading glance. "Oh, surely we must go aboard. I want to see it up close."

Eyes wide with horror, Mrs. Harris released his arm to back away from the dock. "I shall not, will not, get in any dinghy."

Disappointment suffused Amelia's face as she met his gaze. "I forgot. Mrs. Harris doesn't . . . like boats. Or being out on the water."

Judging from the widow's panicked expression, it was more than a simple dislike. If anybody could recognize an irrational fear, he could.

He gentled his voice. "I could still take Lady Amelia out to it, Mrs. Harris. You'd be fine here with the coachman."

"Oh, yes, please!" Amelia released his arm to go to her chaperone's side. "I would dearly love to see it."

"But, my dear, if something were to happen, if a squall were to come up—"

"There's not a cloud for miles, and it's only a few yards out," Lucas said indulgently. "I won't let any harm come to her. I'll look after the lady like she was my own flesh and blood."

"You see?" Amelia chirped. "With such a strapping fellow to protect me, I have nothing to fear."

Mrs. Harris glanced from him to the dinghy to Amelia, whose face was so pleading that she sighed. "I suppose it can't hurt."

"Oh, thank you!" Amelia cried with a squeeze of the widow's hand.

As Amelia seized his arm and they headed down the dock, Mrs. Harris called out after them, "But be careful, Amelia! You know how reckless you can be—do not go anywhere the major says not to!"

"I'll be fine!" Amelia called back, grinning at him from beneath her bonnet.

Mrs. Harris stood far behind them, wringing her hands.

Lucas got into the dinghy first, then handed Amelia down into it.

"Don't lean too far either way, or you'll overset it!" Mrs. Harris cried.

Eyes twinkling, Amelia took a seat across from him with the balance of a born sailor. "I'll be very careful!" she called back.

With a shake of his head, Lucas sat down and took up the oars.

As they pulled away from the dock, Mrs. Harris was still shouting, "And stay above deck! There might be rats down below!"

"I can't hear you!" Amelia called back cheerily. "We won't be long!"

Smothering a laugh, he rowed toward the xebec. "She's got a right strong dislike of the water, doesn't she?"

Amelia nodded. "She nearly drowned when she was a girl, and it made a great impression upon her. She won't go near boats, and she tenses up whenever she crosses a bridge."

"I noticed." He smiled. "But boats don't seem to bother you."

She threw her head back with an expression of sheer delight. "Never. I love the water. Papa even used to take me fishing when I was a girl."

"I take it you and your father were close."

"As close as a girl can be to a man who spends most of his time buried in a book." She eyed him curiously. "And you?"

"You could say we were close. Father was a military man like me. Served in the revolution."

"What revolution?"

He arched one eyebrow. "The one against England."

Laughter trilled from her lips. "Oh. Right. I forgot about that."

"Believe me, I didn't," he said bitterly.

Her smile faded, and she gazed out over the water with a pensive expression. "Is that how your father died? In battle?"

"No," he said tersely. He wasn't about to tell her how his father died. Bad enough that the entire population of Baltimore knew it. And that he hadn't learned of it himself until it was too late for him to stop it.

They'd reached the xebec now. He sent her up the rope ladder first so that he'd be below to catch her if she fell, but she climbed up nimbly as a cat. In fact, she moved so quickly he didn't have time to dwell on the tempting swing of her hips or the glimpses he got of her stockinged ankles. As soon as she reached the top, she sat on the rail and swung her legs over, then disappeared.

With a curse, he clambered up to the top. "Damnation, Amelia, wait for—"

"Oh, Lucas!" she cried. "It's amazing!"

He climbed aboard, then glanced around. It really was. Sweet, clean lines, and almost delicate timbers. A gazelle where most warships were elephants. "You still have to watch where you're going on it. Those lady boots of yours can get caught in the gratings, and there's hatchways and oars—"

"Oars! It's a sailing ship."

"Yes, but it can turn quicker with both. That's why a xebec can attack a warship armed with twice the cannon. A xebec doesn't stay still long enough to take a broadside, or it would be blown out of the water. It's too flimsy to handle that kind of assault."

She stared down at the deck. "I can see that. The timbers aren't oak—or at least not English oak. They could be evergreen oak, since that grows near the Mediterranean. I don't suppose olive wood is strong enough—"

"Not being an expert on Algerian woods," he said, unable to hide his amusement, "I couldn't say for sure, but I doubt it."

She stiffened, then flashed him an inane smile. "Balsa wood, perhaps? That floats very well."

The return of the flighty Amelia was too much for him. "Don't," he growled.

"Don't what?"

"Don't play that ninny act with me."

"I-I beg your pardon?"

"The fluttery eyelashes and the silly smiles and the ridiculous remarks. They're not you, and we both know it. So you can stop it for good. There's no need for it—I know what you're up to."

Chapter Eight

Dear Charlotte,
I shall proceed with all due haste. Remember, however,
that gaining information about Americans is more
difficult. Fortunately, I have a friend on the Navy
Board. He might know more.
Eager to oblige your every request,
Michael

"U-Up to?" Amelia's heart beat faster than the ship's flags flapping in the wind. "I can't imagine what you mean," she said, attempting to regain lost ground.

He fixed her with his unnerving stare. "I've heard Englishmen talk about their women. They think you all lack sense, and the truth is, they prefer that. So you females believe you can only catch husbands by pretending to be idiots."

She gaped at him. *That* was what he thought she was "up to"? Trying to snare a husband?

"But you don't have to do that with me," he went on. "I like a woman with a brain. So don't pretend that yours shriveled up the minute you turned fifteen."

She sucked in a breath of relief. She might as well use his explanation. Besides, it didn't mean she had to give up playing the flirt.

"Eighteen." She smiled to cover the lie. "I was eighteen when I started pretending not to have a brain."

With a self-satisfied look, he offered her his arm. "I knew it. Nobody could have your knowledge of flags and ships and be as stupid as you pretended."

She let him lead her along the deck. "Thank you. I think."

She let him have his moment of triumph. Perhaps then he wouldn't notice that her silly self had only shown up when he'd asked probing questions.

A pity she couldn't confront *him,* too. But as long as he didn't realize how much she *did* know, she'd have an easier time questioning him.

"Why has the navy allowed you access to the xebec?" she asked, as they skirted the side of the ship facing away from land. They passed several cannon set into wooden blocks before rounding the mainmast. "Surely they didn't think it would help you in your treaty efforts."

"They thought I could suggest modifications. My father's company used to design cannon for ships, you see."

"Used to?" she prodded.

"Now that he's dead, the company is rudderless. So to speak."

"And you have no interest in designing cannon."

He smiled ruefully. "Actually, I have no aptitude for it. While Father was building his company, I was off fighting the Barbary pirates. After I came home, I did try my hand at it, but . . ." He shrugged. "I'd rather fire a cannon than make one. Then the war with England began, and I—"

"Jumped at the chance to fight again."

He arched one eyebrow. "You could say that."

"Yet you're no longer fighting." She ventured a probing comment. "These days you deal with villains."

His gaze shot to her, sharply focused and intent. "What do you mean?"

"The pirates, of course. And the treaties."

"Right." His expression grew shuttered. "But negotiating a treaty is a battle, too."

"So how long have you been negotiating these treaties? I thought the British routed most of the Barbarys in Algeria a couple of years ago. Yet if this xebec-frigate showed up near Spain—"

"You sure are fascinated by those damned pirates."

She refused to let him change the subject. "I'm fascinated by anything more exciting than my own tedious life. Like your treaties."

"And my 'adventures.'" Eyes darkening, he caught her by the hand and tried to pull her into his embrace.

As her pulse beat erratically, she broke free of him. "Not here. Mrs. Harris can see us."

"No, she can't. This side of the frigate is hidden from the docks."

A little thrill skittered down her spine. Though he was only trying to distract her from her questions, she couldn't help being tempted. And being aboard this dratted pirate ship actually enhanced the gruff major's romantic appeal.

She backed away along the deck. "Nonetheless, we must limit ourselves to the right sort of adventures."

"What sort might that be?"

"The ride to the docks. The little jaunt out here by dinghy." She managed a teasing smile. "The tour of the xebec."

He hunted her like a corsair running down a brig at sea. "Pretty tame adventures, wouldn't you say?"

Spotting a hatch nearby, she darted toward it. "You haven't finished showing me the frigate, and I'm dying to see what it's like belowdecks."

"I thought your chaperone told you not to go below," he said, but his voice held an odd edge.

She reached the hatch and opened it. "I didn't hear her say a thing," she joked. "It was far too windy."

He didn't laugh. "Stay right there, Amelia." He strode across the deck toward her. "Don't you dare climb down that ladder."

She peered into the dark hatchway. "Come now, Lucas, I just want to—"

Grabbing her arm, he yanked her back from the gaping hole. "No. You're not going down there, damn it!"

"Whyever not?" She swung around to face him, but her words died on her lips.

His face was the ash white of the ship's sails, and his eyes were fixed on the black hole as if it represented the gates to hell.

"Lucas?" she said in a low voice.

He didn't seem to hear her, and his fingers dug into her arm like talons.

"Lucas!" she said more sharply. "You're hurting me."

He jerked, then hastily released her arm. "We're not going below." Pivoting on his heel, he strode toward the quarterdeck. "But I'll show you the rest of the ship up here if you want."

She followed him. "Why don't you want to go belowdecks?"

"I just don't want *you* going down there," he

snapped as he passed through the door beneath the quarterdeck.

She hurried in after him. They stood in a modest half circle of a room that had probably served as the captain's cabin.

"That's balderdash," she said. As he whirled to face her, she added, "I saw the expression on your face. You looked as if you thought the devil himself lived belowdecks."

His jaw went taut. "You're imagining things."

"I most certainly am not. I could plainly see that you—"

He marched up to her and kissed her hard.

When he drew back, her blood pounded fast and furious. She stared at him in dazed surprise. "What was that for?"

"To shut you up." Then, with eyes smoldering, he caught her head in his powerful hands, sending her bonnet tumbling. "But *this*," he growled, "is for me."

The kiss wasn't so much hard as thorough. And searing. And demanding. He took control of her lips as if they belonged to him, as if he was laying claim to her.

She tried to remind herself that he wasn't, but Lord, the man could kiss! He conquered her mouth as surely as any corsair, plunging his tongue deep inside in the intimate way he'd shown her last night, then repeating the outrageous motion with bold, eager strokes.

She kissed him back, tangling her tongue wildly with his. He tasted of coffee and smelled of the sea, an irresistibly exotic combination.

But as his kiss grew more fierce, she tore free and turned her head away in an attempt to catch her breath . . . and regain her sanity. That's when she saw Mrs. Harris pacing the shore through an open porthole.

Mrs. Harris couldn't see *them* in the darkened cabin, but that didn't register until after Amelia muttered a hoarse cry and wriggled from his grasp.

Trying to restore control over her reckless impulses, she backed away from him. "I did not give you permission to kiss me."

He stalked her mercilessly, his intention amply clear. "You gave me permission last night."

"That was different."

Anger flared in his face. "Because we're truly alone, and you can't call out for an Englishman to protect you from the American savage if he gets too rowdy?"

She came up hard against the cabin wall and groaned. Before she could escape, he was on her, his arms bracketing her body. "You claimed to want adventures, and I'm happy to oblige." He leaned in close, his eyes alight. "But that was just hogwash, wasn't it? You only want what you can control. And you can't control *me*."

She glared at him. "Are you sure about that?"

Oh, dear, not the thing to say to a furious male who imagined that she and her countrymen were trying to subjugate him.

Then again, he seemed to reveal more when he was under the influence of his temper . . . or his passions.

With a toss of her head that she hoped looked nonchalant, she added, "I think I've controlled you fairly well until now."

She held her breath for his answer, wondering if taunting a "savage" was sheer madness.

But instead of looking angry, he looked thoughtful. "Well, I'll be damned."

"There's no doubt about that," she shot back.

To her shock, he actually smiled before bending in close to press his mouth to her ear. "The sword. You *did* do it on purpose, didn't you?"

"What are you talking about?"

"This morning in your breakfast room, when you started stroking my mameluke. All that talk about how hard my sword was—you knew the whole time what your sly words were doing to me."

Her stomach sank. "I can't imagine what you mean."

"You deliberately caressed my sword and talked about rubbings and sheaths to arouse me and then leave me in that state with no hope of relief."

"Don't be ridic—"

"And I reacted like any man. The way you knew I would, didn't you?" He breathed heavily in her ear, but since she couldn't see his eyes, she didn't know if it was with anger . . . or something else. Whatever it was, having him so close—and so threatening—thrilled her.

And made her bold. She turned her head to meet his gaze. "If you were affected, it's only because your mind is sunk in depravity."

His eyes glittered. "You started it, so you're the one whose mind is sunk in depravity." He lifted his hand to stroke her hair. "You're quite the little Delilah, aren't you? Yet I'd swear you've never had a man in your bed."

"Certainly not!" She tried to push free, but he held her fast against the wall.

"Then how did you know just what to do this morning, to bring a man to his knees without so much as touching him?"

"I . . . I guessed, that's all."

"You guessed," he said skeptically. He kissed her ear, then nibbled the lobe. When he had the audacity to lave the inside with his tongue, she shivered delightfully. Lord, to think that ears could be so sensitive!

Then he was skating his mouth along her neck, down to the furiously beating pulse at her throat, which he kissed into a fever pitch. "Come now, Amelia, you're too much an innocent to have guessed any such thing. So how did you know what to do? Did that stepmother of yours teach you how to—"

"Hardly," she said with a shaky laugh. The very idea of Dolly teaching her how to seduce a man was outrageous.

He pressed a kiss into the hollow of her throat, then moved lower. "Someone taught you. And since she's a widow—"

"I read a book," she blurted out.

He drew back to stare at her. "A book?"

She blushed. "About the Barbary harems. And what goes on in them."

He arched one thick eyebrow. "You mean one of those silly collections some Englishman cobbled together to titillate fools? Why would you read such claptrap?"

She thrust out her chin. "Curiosity, of course. How else is a sheltered young woman supposed to learn the truth about . . . certain matters?"

He laughed outright. "You think you can get the truth from harem tales? Half of them are lies, and the other half, wild exaggerations."

Having him laugh at her was infuriating. "They were certainly truthful about how to rouse a man's 'sword,' judging from how easy I found it to tease *you*."

His amusement faded to a sudden dark intent. "Good point." He bent his head to her mouth, but halted a breath away. "So you're curious about what goes on in a harem, are you?"

"Yes," she cautiously admitted.

"Then you should have your curiosity satisfied."

That put her on her guard. "What do you mean?"

Eyes gleaming, he dropped his hand to rest on her waist. "Seems to me you've been awfully obliging today. You've been downright generous with the society lessons—telling me not to cuss or open my coat, and not to sit down even when you deliberately provoked me into . . . exposing myself, if you will."

The edge in his voice set loose a thousand butterflies in her belly.

His hand slid up along her ribs. "And since our agreement was that I'd give you adventures in exchange for your lessons, I should take care of that right now."

Her heart raced, and she had to struggle to answer. "It's fine, really. Showing me this ship is adventure enough."

"To repay you for all your many kindnesses?" he said, definite sarcasm in his voice. "Hardly."

To her utter shock, he covered her breast with his hand.

"Lucas!" She grabbed his hand. "What do you think you're doing?"

"You're curious about what the Barbarys do with their captives, so I'm showing you."

"If you think I'll let you ruin me—"

"It doesn't have to go that far." A provoking smile played about his lips. "You can keep your innocence and still taste what a captive experiences." He moved his hand over her breast, slowly, sensually.

"But—"

He sealed her mouth with his, kissing her with all the fervor and intensity of a man devouring his last meal. And she could no more resist the kiss than the earth could resist the pull of the sun.

Especially when he caressed her breast with a delicious deftness that shattered all her resistance into bits.

Lord help her. She'd imagined this very thing a hundred times. From the moment she first became aware that parts of her body were rather pleasurable to touch, she'd thought about what it would be like to have a man touch them.

She'd even touched herself a few times, which had only whetted her appetite for more. But she'd known she wouldn't get more until she married, because no English gentleman would ever dare. Perhaps that was why Lucas's doing it seemed so exciting and reckless.

"Let me give you a real adventure," he said in a guttural voice, "not one you'd have to read about."

The prospect of having him touch her even more intimately set loose a flurry of wild emotions—fear, excitement . . . anticipation. Oh, she was truly wicked.

Not to mention reckless. In here, he could do anything to her that he wanted. Especially now that they'd moved out of Mrs. Harris's line of sight.

"I don't think that's wise," she said breathlessly, though she didn't stay his hand.

"Would any adventure worth its salt be wise?"

"I suppose not." She had trouble thinking with his fondling her, with his hot mouth brushing kisses along her neck . . . And really, would it be so bad to engage in one measly . . . intimate . . . adventure?

She glanced toward the porthole. If she screamed, Mrs. Harris would surely rescue her, fear of water or no.

He must have taken her silence as consent, because he tugged loose the opaque fichu she wore tucked into her day dress.

"Lucas, I haven't yet agreed—"

"But you want to. I can see it in your face." The devilishly clever scoundrel smiled. "I know how much you like having control. So when you say stop, I'll stop. The adventure will end there."

He was offering her a safe adventure. Or the safest one she was likely to have. And if he broke the rules he was setting forth, she'd fight him tooth and nail while screaming for Mrs. Harris.

How could she possibly lose?

Chapter Nine

Dear Cousin,
Have you seen the enclosed newspaper account of last
night's ball? It mentions the major most unfavorably. I
didn't realize he had such volatile emotions. Under the
circumstances, it's very worrying. Amelia isn't exactly
the calmest of individuals herself.
Gratefully yours,
Charlotte

All right." Amelia prayed she hadn't gone insane.
"Give me an adventure. Show me how a Barbary pirate
would treat his captive."

Fire leaped in his face seconds before he seized her
mouth again, kissing her with slow, marauding thrusts
of his tongue. Then he drew back. "Turn around."

"Why?"

He raised an eyebrow. "Awfully insolent for a captive, aren't you?"

Although she scowled, she did as he'd asked. But
when she felt him knot her own fichu around her
wrists, she panicked. "I did not agree to—"

"I have to secure my captive," he said in that honeyed drawl that always made her stomach flip over.
"Any self-respecting Barbary pirate would."

The instant thrill that shot through her annoyed
her. "So help me, Lucas," she retorted, as he turned her

to face him, "if you ruin me, I'll make you regret you ever came near me."

"I've no doubt of that, darlin'. But there's a hell of a lot of room for adventure between kissing and ruin." He smiled. "Besides, it's not even tight."

Skeptical, she tested her bonds. Sure enough, he'd tied it so loosely that a little wriggling would free her.

If she wanted to be free. Which she didn't. Because the surge of excitement flowing through her at the thought of being bound and at his mercy was like a drug searing her veins.

She forcibly reminded herself of her purpose. "Have you ever done this before?" she asked, struggling to control her wayward breathing.

"What do you mean?" He stripped off his gloves with a ruthless efficiency that would make any captor proud.

Her blood pounded in her ears. "Tried to take a woman captive." She kept her tone light, though she well remembered the words "escape capture" in his notes about Dolly.

He looked bemused. "Sorry, but it's my first time playing the Barbary pirate. Why? Am I doing it wrong?"

"No. You seem very adept at imprisoning a woman." That was as close as she dared come to referring to Dolly's possible "escape."

He gave her a wicked smile. "I'm sailing uncharted waters." His voice roughened. "I've been sailing uncharted waters from the minute I met you, darlin'."

The man certainly had a way with words. And when he tossed his gloves aside, a shiver of anticipation rippled down her spine.

"But I'm pretty sure of what a pirate should do next," he said as he reached to untie her bodice ribbons. "He'd want to examine his spoils."

"His s-spoils?" She gave a nervous laugh.

He arched one eyebrow. "You made me take your lessons seriously. Now you have to take the adventure seriously."

If he only knew how "seriously" this adventure was affecting her! "Go on. The pirate is examining his 'spoils'—which I apparently am."

"Damned right. But he'd want a better view."

When he thrust his hand scandalously inside her bodice to unknot the upper ties of her corset and her chemise, she swallowed hard. Then he dragged her gown, corset, and chemise off her shoulders, restraining her further but freeing her breasts from their confines. His heated gaze dropped to her breasts.

Goodness gracious! She stood before a man bare-breasted for the first time in her life. She didn't know whether to be outraged . . . or delighted.

Having her hands behind her back lifted her bosom even farther out of her corset, and as her breath grew ragged, her breasts rose and fell in a motion that seemed to tantalize him.

"You'd be a fine prize for any Barbary pirate," he said hoarsely.

His frankly admiring tone tantalized *her*, and his rampantly carnal expression made it clear that right now he wanted her for one thing only. And it wasn't her money or even the information he sought about Dolly.

Men looked at Venetia this way, but never her. As the object of a man's desire, she'd always been the second choice.

Lucas made her feel like the first choice.

The remnants of her resistance vanished, and she lost herself in his fantasy . . . her fantasy. She even thrust her breasts up for his gaze, and was rewarded by the covetous hunger shining in his eyes.

"But a pirate would do more than one kind of examination." he said huskily.

"Oh?" she breathed, then blushed to hear the eagerness in her voice.

He apparently heard it, too, for his gaze shot to hers, thrilling her with its fiery intensity. "He'd have to assess by touch." Then he covered her breast—her *bare* breast!—with his hands.

And it was *wonderful.*

He slid his other hand about her waist to pull her close so he could scatter feverish kisses over her neck and throat, kneading her breast with his bare palm and sending wild sensations along every nerve. She was such a brazen hussy. But it felt so glorious, so . . . exquisite.

When he thumbed her nipple into a fine, aching point, she practically shoved her breast into his hand, she was that eager for more. Yes, she was shameless . . . shameless! And she didn't even care. She rose to his caresses, sweetly, eagerly, refusing to deny herself this luscious moment.

"Is this enough adventure for you, darlin'?" he rasped against her throat. "Or do you want more?"

He pressed a searing, openmouthed kiss to the

upper swell of one breast, and she caught her breath. More? *More?*

"Let me show you . . . taste you . . ." Then he lowered his head to seize her breast in his mouth.

Lord help her. This was certainly more . . . more delicious, more enticing, more everything! Mouths could do so much . . . suck and tease and oh, Lord, *that*. He was laving her nipple with sensuous rasps of his tongue that sent a wild rush of sensation coursing through her, tightening her belly, rousing her blood.

When he scraped her nipple with his teeth, she nearly went insane, squirming against the fichu pinioning her hands, sure that she would die of pleasure before he was done.

How did female spies manage it? How did they use the sensual arts to elicit information, when the sensual arts were so very . . . distracting?

He transformed her into a strange carnal creature beyond her control. Everything above her navel tingled; everything below it burned.

As if he'd guessed what she felt, he reached behind her to unfasten her gown until it hung loosely on her, then slipped his hand inside the front, down past her corseted belly to the juncture between her legs. To her utter shock, he boldly rubbed her soft flesh through her chemise.

She squirmed beneath the intimate caress. "Are you . . . sure a corsair would feel the need to examine his captive . . . there?"

He lifted his head, his breath coming in rough, staccato gasps. "Hell, yes. Especially when his captive has been so naughty."

"What?" she gasped. "How have I been naughty?"

"You've teased me for two days now. Only a few hours ago, you amused yourself by priming my 'sword' for an encounter you planned to deny me." He brought his lips to her mouth, but stopped a breath away to add in a ragged whisper, "Well, darlin', I'm going to give you a taste of what that's like."

Then he took her mouth again, thrusting his tongue deep even as his devilish fingers stroked her hard below. The fierce thrill of it made her arch up on her toes and strain against him, craving more. Oh, Lord . . . goodness gracious . . . what on earth was he doing to her?

His brazen fingers mimicked his brazen kisses until she felt a shameful dampness seeping into her chemise. Surely he could feel it, too.

If he did, it only made him caress her more blatantly, until a curious sensation built between her thighs, swelling in her most private place, making her undulate against his hand in mad, heedless thrusts.

Abruptly, he brought his hand up to fondle her breast. Moments ago, she would have welcomed it, but now it wasn't enough.

She ripped her mouth from his to beg, "Lucas, please . . . ," not sure what she wanted, but knowing unerringly he could provide it. "Please . . . I . . . I want—"

"What?" he murmured against her cheek. "What do you want?"

"I-I don't know," she breathed, mortified.

"I'll tell you what you want." He nipped her earlobe. "You want release. Or as we coarse Americans put it, you want 'to come.'"

"Whatever it's called," she said, turning a pleading gaze to him, "I want it."

He gave a husky chuckle. "So do I. I'll give it to you if you give it to me."

She stared at him, dumbstruck.

He slipped her wrists free of the fichu binding them, then drew back to unbutton his breeches. That's when she noticed the bulge in them. The very large bulge in them.

She swallowed hard as he unbuttoned his drawers. With his eyes brooding over her like a corsair over his captive, he rasped, "It's time for that 'rubbing' you wanted to do of my sword, darlin'." He stripped off her gloves, then slid her hand inside his drawers to close it around his "sword." "You give me a rubbing, and I'll give you one."

As she stood there, her hand inside his breeches, fascinated but appalled by her own curiosity, he reached inside her gown and dragged the hem of her chemise up to her corset, then cupped her again between her thighs.

Except this time she was bare to his fingers.

He rubbed the aching flesh hotly, silkily. With his free hand he showed her how to caress him, how to tug the flesh in long, firm strokes.

"Oh, God, yes," he moaned as she took control, though it was hard to concentrate on pleasing him when he made her insane with his own strokes.

He strained against her as their hands moved in tandem between them. "You're so damned wet and sweet . . ." he whispered into her ear.

"And you're so . . . big," she whispered back, half in wonder. "And hard."

He managed a choked laugh. "Now do you . . . understand why you . . . drove me crazy earlier? With all your . . . talk of rubbing my . . . sword?"

"I understood it then, too," she teased him.

"You're a virgin Delilah, learning how to torture a man from naughty books."

Her face flamed, and she opened her mouth to retort, but another sound shattered the near stillness of waves lapping against the ship. "Amelia!" called a sharp voice across the water. "Amelia, where are you? What's going on?"

"Damnation," he growled, as they both recognized Mrs. Harris's voice.

Amelia tried to pull away, but he held her fast. "We're not finished," he protested.

"I have to answer her, or she'll convince some oarsman to come out here after us." Wriggling free, she sidled around the curved wall to the porthole that faced toward land, being sure to let her head fill it as she worked frantically to restore her clothing. "We're touring beneath the quarterdeck!" she called out.

Mrs. Harris caught sight of her bare head and frowned. "Where's your bonnet?"

Lucas came up behind her and muttered, "Tell her the wind blew it under here."

As she repeated his brilliant excuse in a carrying voice, he slid his hand around to fondle her breast. She nearly choked. Though she knew Mrs. Harris could see only her face, there was something terribly unnerving about having her chaperone staring at her while he was touching her so wickedly.

Unnerving . . . and strangely titillating. She pressed her breast into his hand.

"Get rid of her, damn it," he commanded. "Tell her we're looking for your bonnet." His other hand dragged up her skirts in front so he could resume his more scandalous caresses. "Tell her we'll be out as soon as we find it."

She caught his hand, but that only prompted him to move hers back inside his drawers to stroke his "sword." His boldly rampant "sword."

She tugged hard on him, thinking it might make him behave, but instead he choked out, "Yes, like that . . . please, darlin' . . ."

It was the "please" that decided her. She knew he'd rather eat nails than say it to an Englishwoman. As her blood roared in her ears, she called out his excuse to her chaperone, praying her flushed cheeks wouldn't give her away.

Mrs. Harris cried, "Are you all right, dear?"

"Fine!" she called back, desperate to get away from the porthole. Lucas was doing the wickedest things to her, and the excitement building in her down below was too exquisite to ignore. "It's just a bit warm . . . in here."

Warm wasn't the word for it. Blazing. Searing. Engulfed in flames. She thought she'd die if she didn't get relief soon.

She didn't wait to see if Mrs. Harris accepted her tale. Sliding away from the porthole, she released Lucas's "sword" and pivoted to face him. He was on her at once, devouring her mouth as he dragged her hand back inside his drawers.

Then he returned to caressing her, but this time he was even more outrageous. He actually had the audacity to thrust his finger inside her. Inside her!

She tore her mouth free to murmur, "Lucas . . . you shouldn't . . ."

"Hush, darlin'," he whispered as he branded her neck with fiery, openmouthed kisses. "It's just my finger, nothing more. But you have to let me . . . drive you as crazy . . . as you're driving me."

She exulted in those words. "Am I?" she whispered, though speech grew more difficult by the second.

"You know you are," he groaned. "Faster . . . stroke me . . . faster . . . I beg you, my sweet Delilah . . ."

She liked the begging, oh yes. And the way his kisses grew wilder and more frantic when she did as he begged. Gone was the calculated, controlling major. In its place was a man who needed a woman, who needed *her*.

This would be the perfect time to ask him what she wanted to know. But she couldn't. Not with this amazing pressure building inside her down below . . . swelling . . . arching . . . tearing a scream from deep inside her throat—

Thank goodness he caught it with his mouth. Because she could no more have stopped it than she could have stopped the tempest of pleasure rocking her limbs, gushing hotly and sweetly through her veins, sending her to a glorious place where nothing existed but the man bringing her to ecstasy . . .

And finding his own, for moments later, she felt rather than saw him yank something from his pocket and jam it inside his breeches. She felt the something—a handkerchief perhaps?—wrap around her hand right before he groaned against her lips, and a sticky wetness seeped into the cloth engulfing her hand.

She'd learned enough about relations between men and women to know that it was his seed. A fierce delight seized her. He'd found pleasure in her arms, too.

But as they both quaked in the aftermath of their shared enjoyment, as their fervent kisses settled into a rapidly cooling embrace, the reality of what she'd just done sank in. They had . . . she had . . .

Lord help her. This had gone too far. She'd be banished to hell for such debauchery, no matter what her purpose.

Her purpose—hah! She'd forgotten about her purpose the moment the man began his cursed seductions.

She drew her hand from his breeches and slipped out of his arms, struggling to calm her raging pulse. What was she to do now? He would expect more "adventures," now that they'd indulged themselves to this dangerous degree. And if he were really courting her, she might even be eager to supply them.

But he wasn't, drat it all. Like any man, he was merely seeking his own pleasure. She stole a glance at him to find him watching her with that brooding gaze of his. He probably thought her a wanton and considered that enough excuse to indulge himself while pretending to court her.

She tamped down her anger at the thought. She'd brought this on herself, with her cursed fascination for the forbidden. But she wasn't a fool: any more adventures like this and she'd find herself ruined. She wouldn't risk shaming her family.

Turning her back to him, she carefully restored her clothing, trying not to remember the myriad thrills of having him kiss her neck, gaze at her bare breasts . . . fondle her into ecstasy.

She choked down a sigh. Oh, she was truly wicked. There was nothing else for it—their private encounters must end. She was useless at balancing her new reckless urge for passion with her duty to find out about Dolly's secret past, and that was dangerous. Not only for herself, but for Dolly. For some reason, he hadn't used their sensual encounter to question her, but that didn't mean he wouldn't in the future.

So from now on, she must keep their "courtship" public. She must never let him guess how much his "adventures" affected her, or he wouldn't rest until he got another chance to take advantage of her weakness.

And that could only lead to disaster.

Chapter Ten

Dear Charlotte,
I had indeed read the newspaper's account. I dare say,
however, that you need not worry about Lady Amelia.
I'm sure she can handle Major Winter if he proves
troublesome. You have well inoculated her—indeed, all
of your young ladies—against scoundrels.
Sincerely,
Michael

Damnation. What the hell have I done?

As reason seeped back into his fevered brain, Lucas
groaned. He'd really lost his mind this time. He'd
ruined everything.

And nothing proved it more than the way Amelia had
slid away from him. No tender final kisses, no clinging,
no lingering in his embrace. Here he stood, struggling
for breath, her honeysuckle scent around him and the
taste of her still on his tongue, and she was withdrawing.

Not that he blamed her. He'd bound her hands.
Pleasured her. Made her pleasure him. Christ, he'd
nearly done the unthinkable.

But damn it, when she'd plagued him about going
belowdecks, having her witness his weakness had
goaded him into blotting it from her mind. And once
he'd realized that she'd *deliberately* performed that bit
of sensual torture with the mameluke this morning,

he'd been seized by the urge to conquer her, to show her she couldn't tease and taunt him like she undoubtedly did those Prissy Pantaloon lords.

He'd conquered her all right. And now she'd make him suffer for it.

After tossing his soiled handkerchief aside, he buttoned his drawers and breeches with the quick efficiency born of years hurrying to meet the call of duty. He glanced furtively at Amelia, but she wouldn't even look at him as she straightened her own clothing. Damn, damn, damn.

Amelia was young and inexperienced, not to mention a very eligible heiress with a titled father. She wasn't some merry widow he could play at pirates and maidens with, binding and stripping her for their mutual pleasure. Or a dockside whore he could shove up against a wall and fondle after paying her a few coins.

Amelia would punish him for this. Even though she'd agreed to everything he'd done, even though she'd willingly participated, had even made him forget for a short while—

He gritted his teeth. When he should have been interrogating her, he'd been enjoying her instead. And he'd probably angered Amelia, ruining his future chances.

The worst part was that he'd do it again in a second if she'd let him. Because being intimate with her had been the closest he'd come to heaven in three years.

God have mercy.

She faced him, her clothing back in place and her fichu covering her pretty breasts. If not for the trembling of her hands as she drew on the gloves he'd stripped off her, he would've thought nothing had happened between them.

"That was certainly an interesting adventure," she said evenly.

An interesting *adventure*? That's all she could say? He eyed her warily. "Are you all right?"

"I'm fine. Why wouldn't I be after your . . . rousing efforts?"

He struggled to take in her reaction. The English were reserved, but *this*—"I should apologize."

"For what? You promised me an adventure, and that's what you gave me. Now it's done."

Done? *Done*, damn her?

Smiling coolly, she tucked a few stray hairs into place. She'd never looked more English.

She'd also never looked more desirable. He wanted to thrust her back against the wall and make love to her until she'd lost her cool smile and aloofness, until he'd reduced her hair and clothes to a shambles, and had her panting and sighing beneath him—

Careful, man. By some miracle he'd been handed a reprieve, and he'd better grab it while he could.

"We should return to shore," he said, determined to match her calm.

"Yes." She bent to pick up her bonnet with such nonchalance, it made him grit his teeth. "And Mrs. Harris must never guess what we were doing."

"Why not?"

Her horrified gaze shot to him. "You can't possibly think she should know!"

"Not about all of it. But surely even you English kiss when you're courting."

Was that anger in her face? It was gone too quickly for him to be sure. Besides, why would she be angry over that, when she hadn't been over the other?

"We aren't formally courting." She tied her bonnet with stiff motions. "So until things are more settled between us, I'd prefer you not say anything to Mrs. Harris about it."

His eyes narrowed. The longer this went on, the more chance for Dorothy to find out who he really was. She and Frier could be two countries away by the time Lady Delilah deigned to let Lucas into the inner family circle.

"Then let's settle matters now." He tried to sound as unmoved as she looked. "I don't have much time in England. I haven't even met your parents yet." Inspiration struck. "And we can't keep our hands off each other. Truthfully, we might find ourselves forced to marry anyway if we keep meeting like this."

"Truthfully," she countered with a hint of sarcasm, "I see no reason to rush. We only met yesterday, Lucas. A short courtship is generally considered six months, and a long one a year or two."

Her remote tone chilled him. Did she mean to keep him dangling after her for weeks while she made him dance to her tune? "If you think I'll extend my stay in England until—"

"No, of course not." She stuck out her chin with a sudden imperious expression. "But surely it wouldn't hurt to spend a few days getting better acquainted with each other before we let others know your intentions."

Determined to rattle her, he let his gaze trail slowly, covetously down the body he'd been caressing only minutes ago. "I thought we'd gotten pretty well acquainted already, darlin'."

Instead of the blush he'd hoped to provoke, she shot him a look of such fury that it gave him pause. She wasn't as calm or aloof as she pretended. Strangely enough, that pleased him.

"I'm talking about a different kind of acquaintance, Major Winter."

"So we're back to 'Major Winter' and 'Lady Amelia,' are we?" he taunted her. "That's the kind of formal acquaintance you mean?"

"Yes, the proper kind, where people converse instead of—"

"Driving each other crazy with desire?" He lowered his voice to a husky murmur. "Arousing each other for their mutual enjoyment?"

She searched his face. "The kind where people reveal more to each other than just their bodies. Where they share their fears—like why they become immobilized with terror at the sight of an open hatchway leading belowdecks."

The words hit him like a poleax to the gut. Damn her and all her curiosity.

"When we can share *that* sort of connection," she added softly, "when you can be honest and truthful with me, then, and only then, will you meet my parents." Whirling on her heel, she marched out from beneath the quarterdeck.

For the entire journey home in the carriage, Amelia regretted her hasty words. It wasn't just the gut-wrenching horror of his expression after she'd said them. Or the fact that he'd barely spoken two words to her during their exit from the xebec or their tense ride in the dinghy.

It was the sinking feeling that she'd gone too far. Whatever demons had made Lucas react so powerfully to an open hatchway couldn't be easy ones, and a man with his pride would hate having them noticed, much less discussed.

What if her cruelty drove him to act rashly—to haul Dolly off to America with him? Since he hadn't yet, did that mean he didn't really suspect Dolly of anything criminal? Or just that there were laws preventing it? Even if there were, clearly Lucas was sufficiently on edge to act out of wounded pride.

But drat it, she had pride, too. And every time he mentioned their "courtship" as if he truly wished to marry her, she wanted to slap him. He was merely trying to press her into bringing him to meet Dolly. Sly scoundrel. Two-faced devil. She would keep him chomping at the bit until she was sure he couldn't hurt her stepmother.

"You are both very quiet," Mrs. Harris said from beside her. "Was the ship not to your liking?"

Certain parts of it disturbed Major Winter enormously, she nearly said, but one look at his rigid expression killed the words in her throat. "It was fine."

"Lady Amelia found it . . . dirty." Lucas taunted her with a glance, curse him.

"I can't imagine that a little dirt would bother Amelia," Mrs. Harris said.

"You see, Major?" she shot back. "You should have let me go belowdecks as I asked, instead of protesting how dirty it would be."

When he glowered at her, Mrs. Harris jumped in. "In such a situation, caution was appropriate. I'm sure there were rats. And though Amelia might not care about dirt, she would care quite a bit about having rats nibble her toes."

That didn't seem to mollify Lucas. "I'll remember that when choosing our next outing. Maybe we should do something more tame—visit a museum or go for a ride in the park."

"A ride in the park sounds wonderful," Amelia said in a sugary voice. "I'm sure Mrs. Harris would enjoy it, too."

"Tomorrow then?" he countered, though the icy glint in his eyes showed he didn't like being trapped into including the widow.

"Certainly," Amelia said, glaring back at him.

"No, dear, not tomorrow." Mrs. Harris turned to Amelia. "Have you forgotten the meeting of the London Ladies Society? Miss North is counting on you to support her new cause, and you promised her you'd go."

Louisa North was a viscount's daughter who'd served as lady-in-waiting to the late Princess Charlotte. To escape her grief after the princess's untimely death a year ago, Louisa had kept busy by helping prepare Mrs. Harris's girls for their presentations at court.

But recently she'd turned her efforts to prison reform, the subject of the scheduled meeting. After everything Louisa had done for the school, Amelia had happily agreed to attend. She couldn't go back on her word now. "Yes, I'm afraid I had forgotten," Amelia said. "I must go."

"And the day after tomorrow is the graduates' tea," Mrs. Harris said. "You can hardly miss that, since it's being held at your house."

Amelia sighed. Annoyed as she was at Lucas, she still needed to spend time with him to learn more about his plans. But if she started canceling her plans with friends to please him, Mrs. Harris might decide things were already progressing to the point where she should write Papa or Dolly about it. Amelia dared not risk their rushing back to London prematurely.

"Perhaps an evening event, then," Lucas said tersely.

"Tomorrow night I already have an obligation," she said, adding as he frowned, "but I have no engagement for the following evening, after the tea."

He eyed her assessingly. "Then I'll see what play we can attend."

"Oh, the theaters aren't open on that night," Mrs. Harris put in.

Lucas settled back against the squabs, leveling a frown on both of them. "You ladies make it darned hard for a man to court a woman."

A stunned silence fell over the carriage. He'd as much as made a formal declaration of his intentions—after Amelia had requested that he wait to do so.

She struggled to restrain her temper. He was exacting his revenge for her comments about the hatchway and her seeming refusal to see him. He was also forcing her hand, which created problems for her.

That was evident from Mrs. Harris's response. "Well! You Americans are blunt, aren't you?"

"And presumptuous," Amelia added. She'd have to convince Mrs. Harris there was no reason to write Papa and Dolly about her "courtship" just yet.

"We discussed this," he retorted. "You didn't say no."

Amelia felt the widow's gaze on her. "I didn't say yes, either. I said you could court me, and we'd see how it went." Her eyes narrowed. "As I recall, I also asked you to keep the matter private until we were more sure of . . . each other."

His gaze bore into hers. "I'm sure of you."

Liar! You don't even want me!

"Major Winter." Mrs. Harris laid a calming hand on Amelia's arm. "You Americans may be aggressive in achieving your aims, but we English tend to be cautious. We do not leap willy-nilly into important decisions concerning our futures."

"I don't have time for caution, ma'am," he drawled. "At this rate, I'll see Amelia once a week, and that's not enough. I'll be moving on soon, you see."

"Oh?" Amelia retorted. Let him be the one uncomfortable for a change. "And what pressing business do you have to deal with next? You're consulting on a treaty. Won't your government allow you all the time you need?"

A muscle worked in his jaw. "I'm waiting to hear about the possibility of an impending appointment as a consul. Since certain personal difficulties prevent my continuing in the Marine Guard, I would hate to be unable to pursue it."

If he could be blunt, so could she. "What sort of personal difficulties?"

"Amelia, that's rude," Mrs. Harris said in a low voice.

Lucas's gaze locked with hers. "The sort that make it difficult for me to live on board a ship for months on end."

Then it hit her: he couldn't or wouldn't go belowdecks. That would certainly create difficulties for a marine.

As he jerked his gaze to the window, staring grimly at the docks, a surge of sympathy made her regret her hasty words. Poor, proud Lucas. How she wished she could reach over and kiss away the harsh lines of his rigid expression.

No wonder he took his mission to find Dorothy Frier so seriously. He could no longer protect his ship as a marine was supposed to, so he was serving his country another way. Though he was surely misinformed about Dolly and certainly shouldn't be pretending to court Amelia to further his aims, at least she understood the fierceness of his intent.

"I'll leave the night of the tea free for you, Major," she said softly. "When you decide on our plans, you may send me a note to inform me."

His gaze met hers, dark and vulnerable. "Thank you," he said gruffly.

They rode a while in silence, with only the creak of the carriage and the clopping of the horse's hooves on cobblestone making any sound. They were now approaching St. James's Square.

To her chagrin, she found herself loath to say goodbye. Granted, the next two days would give Cousin Michael time to find out more about Lucas's mission, and that could only help her. But she would miss Lucas. *Him*, the most infuriating, secretive, arrogant fellow she'd ever met!

And the only one who'd ever sent her pulse racing, the only one who'd ever made her feel desirable. If he proved to be a true scoundrel when this was done, how would she ever endure it?

Mrs. Harris suddenly went rigid beside her. "Oh, dear," she muttered. "You were right, Amelia—that man is indeed a pest."

Confused, Amelia looked over to find the widow staring out the window, then saw what she meant. A carriage sporting a marquess's coronet on its crest was situated two doors down from her town house.

Just what she needed to make her day complete. Lord Pomeroy.

Chapter Eleven

Dear Cousin,
Thank you, kind sir! I do my best to "inoculate" my
ladies, as you put it so drolly. No disease is more
dangerous than a bad husband, for if a woman catches
that pox, she'll languish from it her entire life.
Your friend,
Charlotte

"Please, Lucas, leave the man be," Amelia said a short time later, heartily wishing Mrs. Harris hadn't noticed Lord Pomeroy's carriage in the street. She explained to Lucas what it meant.

They now stood in the stables, since Amelia had insisted that the coachman carry them back here to disembark. The last thing she needed was Lord Pomeroy seeing the major with them.

She blocked Lucas's path as he headed toward the stable door. "Lord Pomeroy doesn't concern you."

He glared down at her. "Like hell he doesn't. Mrs. Harris has just been telling me that the man used to sit in his carriage outside your house to intimidate your suitors. And you expect me to leave him be?"

Though his unexpected protectiveness was rather endearing, his interference would only worsen matters. "He stopped hanging about after Papa refused to contemplate any marriage between us. Today he probably tried to call on me, was told I wasn't home, and decided to wait. That's all."

"Or," Mrs. Harris interjected, "with your father gone to the country, Lord Pomeroy has returned to his old tricks. Especially after seeing the major's marked attentions to you last night."

Amelia shot Mrs. Harris a frustrated glance. The woman was *not* helping.

Lucas looked fit to be tied. "Then somebody should remind Pomeroy his attentions aren't welcome. And not just in words, either." Reaching inside his breeches pocket, he pulled out his sheathed dagger.

"Dear Lord," Mrs. Harris muttered.

"You told me you didn't have it with you!" Amelia exclaimed.

"I lied." He calmly removed the dagger from its sheath. "No decent soldier leaves his quarters unarmed."

Amelia glanced around to find the grooms casting surreptitious, wide-eyed glances at Lucas's dagger as they unhitched the horses and began rubbing them down. "I won't let you use that."

Lucas's gaze met hers, glittering with anger. "A military man like Pomeroy only understands one thing. And it takes another man to explain it to him."

"He's a former general—do you think he'll simply roll over and play dead?"

"When the choice is to *be* dead, he will."

"It'll only make him more determined to plague me with his suit. He'll see it as 'saving' me from you." When Lucas merely tucked his dagger into the front of his breeches, prominently displayed, she added, "If you threaten a lord, you'll be arrested, no matter the reason. And how will that help me?"

Lucas's jaw tightened. "Then tell me what to do. Because I'm not leaving until I'm sure you'll be all right."

"We'll be fine, really. Lord Pompous is nothing but bluster. He wouldn't dare do more than scowl at suitors from his carriage."

"Some men will do anything to get money," Lucas bit out.

His fierce conviction gave her pause. Was he talking about himself? Or someone else? Because surely it wasn't just Lord Pompous that had him agitated.

Fine. Let the hotheaded idiot attack Lord Pompous. He'd probably injure the man, get himself arrested, and eliminate both her problems. Lord Pompous would leave her be, and Lucas would be safely in jail away from Dolly.

Except that she couldn't bear to think of Lucas in jail. Not after seeing his ashen face as he'd stared into that hatchway. And certainly not after he'd touched her so intimately.

For better or worse, their battle must stay between them. So she had to calm his fears. She summoned a blithe smile. "Really, Lucas, I'm sure he'll tire of this tactic when he sees it isn't working."

Lucas clenched his fist. "He's not one of your soft-skinned lords. If this doesn't work, he'll take more drastic steps."

"Like what? Anything else would create a scandal, and he wouldn't want his reputation as a war hero besmirched. Besides, he knows I won't marry him under any circumstances. And since he has to have my consent for a wedding, and my father's consent in order to access my fortune—"

"But if he knows that," Lucas said, clearly frustrated, "why is he lurking outside your town house instead of wooing a more malleable heiress?"

"Because it's not just Amelia's money that interests him," Mrs. Harris put in, "no matter what she says."

Amelia frowned at her.

"It's true, and you know it, dear. When you first went into society, you were so eager to hear his tales of war and he was so flattered by your interest that he decided you were the only young lady for him."

"Yes," she protested, "but I long ago realized my error, and I've made it clear to him a thousand times that my interest was merely academic. He thinks that since I'm in my second season already, my lack of offers will eventually make me accept his suit. In time, he'll realize he's wrong."

Lucas turned his skeptical gaze on Mrs. Harris. "What do you think?"

"I agree with Amelia. Though his avid interest is troublesome, I doubt he'll act on it beyond what he's doing now. He wouldn't risk the scandal."

"Lord Pompous may be a general," Amelia added, "but he's also a marquess and very conscious of his own importance."

"Right," he said with disgust. "I keep forgetting how highly you English regard titles." But at least he'd sheathed his dagger and returned it to his pocket.

"Besides," she went on, "do you honestly believe that my father would leave me alone in London if he thought I was in any danger?"

His gaze locked with hers. "I'm not sure *what* your father might do."

He was referring to Dolly somehow—she was sure of it, but she couldn't figure out what he meant. "He would never let me be hurt, I promise you. So you might as well return to the Kirkwoods.'" She took his arm and added more firmly, "Come, I shall walk you to the gate."

"I'll meet you inside," Mrs. Harris murmured.

Amelia cast her a grateful smile, glad for the chance to tell Lucas a private good-bye. She had things to say to him that couldn't be said before an audience.

They left the stables, but Lucas stopped short just outside, a calculating gleam flickering in his eyes. "I must get my sword from your breakfast room."

When he turned as if to follow Mrs. Harris, she tugged him in the other direction. "Oh, no, you don't," she said, laughing. "You're just hoping to run into Lord Pomeroy." She cast him a coy smile. "Besides, you can't have your sword back until I do my rubbing of it."

His eyes darkened. "Teasing wench. That's the real reason Pomeroy haunts your door. He wants you to do a rubbing of *his* sword."

She blushed. "Balderdash. He merely wants my fortune." They'd reached the gate. "And you, sir, are going to let him be, and return to the Kirkwoods' by the back way so he doesn't see you."

"Actually, I think a friendly word soldier to soldier might be in order."

"Drat it, Lucas—" she began.

"No weapons, I promise."

"Not good enough." She glared at him. "Promise me you won't speak to Lord Pomeroy."

A half smile played over his lips. "And why would I be fool enough to promise that?"

"Because if you don't, I'll refuse to see you again." She pushed against his chest lightly with her gloved hand. "Now go on with you."

He caught her hand against his chest before she could withdraw it. "I'll promise not to speak to Pomeroy if you'll promise that if the man keeps annoying you, you'll let me handle matters my own way."

"By shooting at him? Provoking him? Fighting him?"

"Whatever it takes to make him leave you alone."

She'd be flattered by his concern if she weren't suspicious of what prompted it. He probably feared that Pomeroy would do something precipitous that would make it difficult for him to complete his own plans.

Tamping down her hurt at the thought, she tried for a light tone. "I promise that if I find myself in grave mortal danger, I'll summon you to dispatch my enemies."

"I'm serious, damn it." His hand tightened on hers. "Promise me. For once, just indulge me."

"It seems to me I spent most of the afternoon indulging you."

He gave a harsh laugh. "If you'd indulged me, darlin', you wouldn't have left that ship a maiden." With a brooding glance, he lifted her hand to plant a kiss in the center of her palm. "Next time I won't show such gentlemanly restraint." Drawing down the top of her short glove, he pressed another kiss to the pulse beating madly in her wrist. "Because when a man wants a woman, he doesn't stop until he gets what he wants."

She caught her breath. How she wished she could believe the fierce intent in his gaze, the yearning in his voice. How she wished this was a real courtship, that Lucas really would want to marry her.

But when he spoke of wanting, he meant only her body, nothing else. The courtship was simply a means to an end. He hoped to gain something from it as surely as Lord Pomeroy hoped to gain her fortune. Lucas was just better at hiding his true intentions.

She swallowed the lump in her throat. As soon as he'd finished his investigation, the "courtship" would end, so she mustn't indulge any foolish fancies otherwise. Not if she wanted to protect her heart.

With a wan smile, she extricated her hand from his. "Mrs. Harris is signaling that I must go in," she lied as she opened the gate. "Thank you for showing me the xebec."

He dragged his gaze down her body in a look as intimate as any physical caress. "Thank you for showing me . . . everything."

Her temper flared. "Be careful, Lucas, or *you* may be the one forced to sit outside my town house in a carriage." She hurried up toward the house.

Lucas watched her go, his blood pounding in his ears. Hunker down in a carriage waiting for Lady Delilah to grace him with her favors? Not a chance. If she ever closed the door to him, he wouldn't wait around for her to change her mind. No woman was worth that humiliation, not even Lady Delilah.

Except when she sashayed down the path with that walk that boiled a man's blood. Or let a man kiss her damned fine mouth. Or fondle her downy-skinned breasts. Or tease the sweet little pearl between her legs until she sighed and turned a man's cock so hard that even the strokes of her warm hand weren't enough to—

He tore his gaze from her backside with a curse. She was a Delilah, all right. She could drain the strength out of a man just by sauntering away from him.

He reached into his pocket for his handkerchief to wipe the sweat from his brow, then remembered he'd left the soiled linen on the ship. He should have left his lustful thoughts there, too, because the more he indulged them, the more they distracted him. And that wasn't good.

Not when he was finally getting somewhere. By purposely declaring his intentions in front of Mrs. Harris, he'd guaranteed one of two reactions. Either the widow would promote his suit and encourage Amelia to summon her parents to London for a meeting. Or, if she didn't approve of the match, she'd write them herself with her concerns, and that would bring them running to London.

So if he played this right, he'd soon be meeting Lady Tovey. He couldn't let his randy cock ruin that.

He started down the back way to Lord Kirkwood's, then paused as he passed the alley beside the Tovey town house that led to the street. Hellfire and damnation, it didn't sit well to leave that general situated out front.

You promised not to speak to him.

True, but that didn't mean he couldn't do some reconnaissance. Striding up the alley to the street, he rounded the corner just in time to see Pomeroy stalk down the steps of the town house. The general had probably tried to pay his call again without any success.

As Pomeroy crossed to his carriage, Lucas looked over his rival from behind. For a man of fifty-odd years, he was pretty agile, with a brisk walk and the erect posture common to soldiers. As best Lucas could remember from the ball, the man was attractive enough to please a woman, despite his jowls and pug nose. His graying hair was still thick, and his status as a war hero would cover most ills. He could probably find a wife with ease, so why pursue Amelia so hotly? It had to be for more than her fortune.

He watched to see if the man drove away, to see if Amelia was right and Pomeroy had just been waiting for their return. But the marquess got into his carriage without a word to his dozing coachman. It took only a short wait to determine that he wasn't going anywhere.

Lucas frowned. Damned idiot.

Pomeroy thought to intimidate other suitors? Fine. He wasn't the only one who could use intimidation as a strategy. Lucas might have promised not to speak to Pomeroy, but he hadn't promised not to be seen.

Strolling into the street, Lucas began to whistle. Sure enough, Pomeroy's grizzled features appeared in the carriage window. Lucas walked right up to the town house. Pretending not to notice the general glaring at him, Lucas reached into his pocket for his whetstone, then took out his dagger.

He sat down on the steps and began to sharpen his knife with long, slow strokes, wiping the blade off on his boot leather periodically. And all the time, he whistled as if he had nothing better to do while late afternoon edged toward dusk.

After a few minutes, he glanced at the carriage. Lord Pomeroy was still watching him, but he looked uneasy. When their gazes met, Lucas deliberately tipped his hat to the general. Pomeroy frowned.

Come on, you old bastard, Lucas thought. *I dare you. Get out of the damned carriage, and we can have this out right now.* He couldn't think of anything more satisfying than beating an English general to a bloody pulp.

But after glaring at Lucas, Pomeroy drew back from the window.

Gritting his teeth, Lucas returned to sharpening his knife. *Snick, snick, snick, snick,* wipe. The motion helped calm his temper, which was a good thing. Because he was fairly itching to bury the blade between Pomeroy's ribs.

It wasn't just because the man was English or even a general. He told himself it was because Pomeroy's antics complicated his own plans, but deep down, he knew that was a lie. He just couldn't stand the thought of *any* other man hanging after Amelia, even a puffed-up warhorse like Pomeroy.

He forced that unsettling thought from his mind, forced himself to concentrate on sharpening his blade. *Snick, snick, snick, snick,* wipe. *Snick, snick, snick, snick,* wipe.

The motion continued long after Lord Pomeroy's carriage finally trundled off into the dusk.

Chapter Twelve

❧

Dear Charlotte,
At last I have the information on Major Winter that
you've been awaiting. I'm attaching a thorough report,
courtesy of my friend at the Navy Board.
Your helpful cousin,
Michael

"Perhaps we should move the sarcophagus into the hall, my lady."

Amelia scarcely heard her footman. A week ago, she would have protested the very idea of removing her pride and joy from the drawing room that Papa and Dolly had allowed her to decorate herself. A week ago, she'd have delighted at the chance to show off to her schoolmates her new Egyptian-styled furnishings.

A week ago, she hadn't met Lucas.

In the two days since the outing to the xebec, he and Dolly had absorbed her thoughts. She'd convinced Mrs. Harris not to write Papa about her "courtship" until matters progressed further, but how long could she put the woman off?

Now, as she and Mrs. Harris readied the drawing room for the tea, she examined everything Dolly had ever revealed: every scrap of information, every mention of her past, every reaction to every comment.

As the druggets were removed from the floors, she remembered Dolly's shock the first time she'd seen Amelia cover up the expensive Axminster carpet with protective baize. As the butler brought out Amelia's precious Wedgwood black basalt tea service to replace the everyday one, she remembered Dolly's surprise at the idea of owning more than one tea service.

Either Americans were much less extravagant with their money than the English . . . or Dolly had never had quite the life Amelia had assumed, given her marriage to a wealthy merchant.

So with an hour left before the girls arrived for their monthly "lessons for heiresses," only one thought consumed her. What if Lucas was right? What if Dorothy Smith wasn't who Amelia had thought her to be?

"Has the mail come?" she asked the footman.

"No, my lady," he answered. "Not yet."

"Didn't you already send your acceptance to the Kirkwoods?" Mrs. Harris asked. Yesterday, Amelia and Mrs. Harris had received an invitation to dine with Major Winter and the Kirkwoods tonight. "And explain why I cannot attend?"

"Yes, I gave it to Hopkins early this morning to send over."

"Are you sure you don't mind that I am not accompanying you?" Mrs. Harris persisted. "I had already promised my friend—"

"No, it's fine. I'll be perfectly safe with a footman for the short carriage ride over. It's only a family dinner, nothing formal. With Lady Kirkwood there, no one should find it improper."

"Then why are you so anxious about the mail?"

"We still haven't heard from Cousin Michael about Major Winter."

"Ah." An indulgent smile touched Mrs. Harris's lips. "Do not fret yourself; my cousin will send us information soon. But he said it would take time."

I don't have time for caution, ma'am.

That's what Lucas had told Mrs. Harris. And if he didn't have time, neither did Amelia. Yet she was forced to go on with these meaningless social affairs until circumstances were right. It was enough to make a woman scream.

How did female spies bide their time asking questions while pretending not to know things? She was far too impatient for such slow maneuvers. Clearly, she would have made an awful spy.

"My lady?" the footman prodded her. "Shall we move the sarcophagus?"

"As much as I . . . er . . . admire your signature piece," Mrs. Harris put in, "it does take up quite a bit of room. It would be just as striking in the hall, don't you think? And the ladies would still see it as they enter."

"That's fine," Amelia said dismissively.

She paid no attention as footmen moved the sarcophagus out and three chairs in. Until she could see Lucas again, she couldn't rest easy. But she'd feel a little better if she heard from Cousin Michael.

Restlessly, she walked over to the bay window to watch for the postman. Instead, she saw another irritating sight. "Oh, Lord, he's back," she muttered, and left the window at once.

"Lord Pomeroy?" Mrs. Harris asked.

"Yes." When Mrs. Harris headed over to look, Amelia said, "Don't let him see you. It only encourages him to come in and seek an audience with me."

Mrs. Harris peeked out. "Where is Major Winter when we need him?"

"Don't say that; this is all *his* fault. His knife-sharpening display ran Lord Pompous off temporarily. But when the marquess returned yesterday, he came earlier and situated his carriage closer."

"And Major Winter ran him off again then, too."

They'd returned from Louisa's meeting to find Lord Pomeroy's carriage parked on one side of the street and Lucas sitting on their steps on the other.

This time the major had brought a pistol to clean.

"Now he's back, curse him," Amelia pointed out, "with his carriage practically on our front step. Lord only knows what the major will do this time to try running the man off."

"Polish a cannon perhaps?" Mrs. Harris quipped.

Amelia shot her a pained glance. "You laugh, but I wouldn't be surprised. They're mad, both of them."

But Mrs. Harris's attention had strayed. "There's the postman, dear."

Moments later, a footman entered with their letters. Mrs. Harris thumbed through them, then held up one with a triumphant smile. "It's thick, and that's a good sign." She strode to the escritoire and broke the seal with a letter opener.

After skimming the letter, she offered Amelia the second sheet. "He sent along a report from his friend at the Navy Board." Her eyes gleamed. "Suffice it to say, our major is not all that he seems."

Amelia took the report in shaky hands, then read it with her stomach roiling:

According to my superiors, Major Lucas Winter is on special assignment with the Marine Guard to capture a criminal and return him to the United States to stand trial. At the end of our late war with America, a British citizen named Theodore Frier embezzled $150,000 from Jones Shipping Company, a contractor to the American navy. The man apparently fled to Canada with the money. Since then, Major Winter has been tracking Frier. Although Frier was last seen in France, Major Winter has good cause to believe he is now hiding in England. That is what Major Winter is investigating.

Mrs. Harris smiled. "You should be flattered the major is taking time from his important duties to court and defend you."

"Yes," Amelia choked out. She could hardly reveal that courting and defending her were part of his "important duties."

Because Theodore Frier was probably related to Dorothy Frier, alias Dorothy Smith. Her stepmother.

She clutched the report to her chest in a vain attempt to still the wild beating of her heart. Dolly knew an embezzler. No, Lucas must suspect her of something more damning, or he would have already traveled to Torquay to question Dolly. And he wouldn't have kept his real purpose secret. Clearly he didn't want to alarm Dolly, so he probably believed that she'd helped Theodore Frier, either in his escape from America or in the embezzlement itself.

A chill iced her veins. Did Lucas actually consider Dolly an accomplice? Dolly *had* come to England with a fortune. Was that just coincidence?

It had to be. It must.

And if it wasn't?

The ramifications knocked the breath from her throat. Amelia's dowry might really belong to this Jones Shipping, and possibly even the American navy itself. Why else was Lucas the one investigating? Besides being a decorated officer of their Marine Guard— a branch of their navy—he had a knowledge of shipping companies from his father's work with ship cannon.

So they'd sent him to retrieve Theodore Frier. And the money, too.

It explained so many things Lucas had said. The interest in Canada, the questions about when Dorothy had arrived here and where she'd come from, the comments about Amelia's inheritance.

Nice house. Expensive-looking. . . . Have you lived here long?

Some men will do anything to get money.

Lord help her. What if Dolly *had* been part of this embezzlement?

No, timid, soft-spoken Dolly a criminal? Never! Amelia read the report again more carefully, but Dolly wasn't even mentioned. Yet the major's notes had focused only on her.

Amelia set her shoulders. That could easily be explained. Pigheaded, arrogant Lucas couldn't bear not to catch his man, so he'd fixed on Dorothy Frier as a last resort. If he'd been searching ever since the war's end, he was bound to be frustrated. So he'd seen a few similarities between Dorothy Frier and Dorothy Smith and had assumed Dolly was Theodore Frier's accomplice.

Well, he was wrong. And she'd tell him so the minute she was alone with him again.

You don't know everything he knows. What if he has irrefutable proof?

Very well, she would make him show it to her. She was tired of dancing around the issue. When she saw him at dinner, she would demand that he lay out every bit of evidence leading to Dolly, so she could refute each one. Then she could thrust the tempting scoundrel from her life once and for all.

"Are you all right, dear?" Mrs. Harris asked. "You seem upset by this news."

She was sorely tempted to tell Mrs. Harris everything. Surely she could depend upon the widow's discretion.

But what if the whole thing turned out to be nothing more than Lucas's overzealousness? Mrs. Harris would forever look at Dolly—indeed, at the whole family—differently. Besides, alarmed by Lucas's intentions, Mrs. Harris might insist upon writing to Papa and Dolly, no matter how much Amelia protested. And Amelia would feel awful if Dolly lost the baby over what proved to be nothing.

No, best to keep quiet until she spoke to Lucas. Then she could determine an appropriate course of action. If the major's evidence *did* seem significant, she might need to hurry to Torquay to speak to Papa about the situation.

"I'm fine," she told Mrs. Harris. "I'm just disappointed that Lucas has been so secretive."

Mrs. Harris put her arm around her shoulders. "He

only met you a few days ago. You can't expect him to trust you overnight. These things take time."

"I know." The motherly gesture brought a lump to Amelia's throat. She laid her head briefly on the widow's breast, then moved out of her kind embrace.

She'd just run out of time. Clearly, Lucas had mentioned a lack of it for a reason. Was there pressure from his government to accost Theodore Frier soon? Or was he merely trying to force the courtship along so he could get to Dolly?

Probably the latter, knowing Lucas and his impatience. Witness how he'd behaved on the xebec.

She winced. And how she'd behaved, too. It shamed her to think of it now. She'd been as reckless as he, throwing herself headlong into his arms even knowing that his interest in her was pretend.

Yet it certainly hadn't felt pretend. When he'd whispered, "please, darlin'" or "I beg you, my sweet Delilah," it had felt very, very real.

She stiffened. *Don't lie to yourself, Amelia. If it had been real, he would have told you about Dolly. He didn't. And still hasn't.*

But tonight he would.

Unless she saw him before then, when he came to annoy Pomeroy as part of his cursed program to ingratiate himself with her. If he did, should she confront him? No, there'd be no privacy with her fellow classmates milling about and Mrs. Harris watching. Besides, his evidence was at the Kirkwoods'.

Though if he did show up here, she'd have trouble restraining her tongue and her temper. Dolly, an embezzler's accomplice—hah!

She frowned at Mrs. Harris. "I now perfectly understand your cynicism about men. Sometimes they're nothing but a curse."

Mrs. Harris laughed. "For proof, you need only look out your front door."

"One of my clippings mentioned a pasha whose wife poisoned him. A pity I can't do the same to Lord Pompous." An almost hysterical laugh bubbled to her lips. Only imagine poor Papa, with a supposed thief for a wife and a murderess for a daughter.

"If I remember the clipping correctly, the man survived the poisoning," Mrs. Harris pointed out, "so what good was that?"

"Ah, but the poison gave him a great deal of indigestion." She smiled grimly. "I'll wager he reconsidered his arrogant behavior toward her after spending a few hours in a . . . forcible purge."

"I'll wager he had his wife executed for it," Mrs. Harris said dryly.

Amelia only half heard her. What if she were to . . .

She headed for the door and called for a maid. As soon as the girl appeared, she said, "Have Cook prepare a tray with a nice selection of cake and biscuits, a pot of strong tea, and a flask of brandy. I know Papa keeps some somewhere."

"B-Brandy?" the maid asked.

"Not for me, for Lord Pomeroy." The girl started to leave, and Amelia added, "But bring the tray to me when it's prepared. I want to add something to the presentation before we send it out to him. And do tell Cook to hurry." She wanted Pomeroy gone before her friends arrived.

As the maid scurried off, Amelia headed for the still-room cabinet upstairs.

Mrs. Harris hurried after her. "Amelia, what are you planning?"

"To purge myself of the annoying Lord Pomeroy."

The widow groaned. "You cannot possibly mean to—"

"Why not?" Lifting her skirts, Amelia ran up the stairs with Mrs. Harris at her heels. "It would make him think twice about stationing himself outside my door. And it will certainly get rid of him during the tea."

"Are you sure this will work?" Mrs. Harris asked as they reached the next floor. "That it won't merely prompt the marquess into more drastic behavior?"

"At this point, I don't care." Amelia cast a frustrated glance down the stairs. "For today, at least, I'd like to be free of the little drama in our street. Can you imagine what everyone will say if they arrive to find not one, but *two* men at daggers drawn on my doorstep? I'm merely providing Lord Pompous with an incentive to move on. That way, if Major Winter does happen by, he won't settle himself on my steps polishing a cannon."

Mrs. Harris hesitated before turning toward her bedchamber. "Then I have a purge that will make any man take off at a run directly after ingesting it."

Amelia laughed. "Why, Mrs. Harris, I would never have guessed you could be so wicked."

Mrs. Harris flashed Amelia a rueful smile. "You have no idea, my dear. At times I am just as tempted by mischief as you."

"Good," Amelia said stoutly. "We lady adventurers must stick together."

Before the so-called gentlemen adventurers—Lucas and Lord Pompous and yes, the mysterious Theodore Frier—trampled them underfoot.

Chapter Thirteen

Dear Cousin,
Lord Pomeroy has become such an annoyance that he
has forced us to resort to drastic action. I shall keep you
informed of the results. Newgate may be in our future
yet.
Your shameless friend,
Charlotte

Lucas walked briskly toward Amelia's carrying today's
"tool of intimidation"—his Springfield rifle with bayo-
net—along with his cleaning gear. He was getting
damned tired of the general's standard battle maneuvers. Advance on enemy territory. Stake his claim. Wait
for the enemy to strike.

Which Lucas couldn't do if he was to honor his
promise to Amelia. He didn't know how much longer
he could bide his time, however. Every time he saw that
damned general, it riled him up.

Suddenly, a coach clattered down the street in front
of him at breakneck speed. It was Pomeroy's—racing
away from Amelia's street as if the devil nipped at its
heels. A niggling unease settled in Lucas's gut. What
had set the general off before Lucas had even arrived to
stand guard?

He got his answer when he turned onto Amelia's
street to enter a scene of pure society mayhem. Coach-

men shouted, grooms scurried, and horses stamped as fancy coaches with ornate crests descended on Amelia's house. Liveried footmen handed out young ladies and their maids. Judging by the costly look of their carriages and clothing, these were Amelia's classmates.

Damnation, he'd forgotten. She was holding a tea today.

No wonder the general had raced off. Seeing this many lofty young ladies swarming about, all rich, all noble, and all probably virginal, would send *any* man running for the hills.

Any man except Lucas. He'd come to see her, and no society tea would stop him. Because Amelia hadn't accepted his invitation to dine tonight. Was she balking at the courtship? Punishing him for trying to run off that ass Pomeroy? Whatever the reason, he meant to get to the bottom of it.

But he didn't aim to have an audience for their discussion. He'd wait until her friends were settled inside, then have the butler summon her for a private word.

Once the street cleared, he approached the house, climbed the front steps, and rapped at the door. The butler himself answered, and the warmth in his features showed that he recognized Lucas as the man who'd run off Pomeroy for the past few days.

Lucas smiled. "I'd be much obliged if you'd tell Lady Amelia that Major Winter is here to see her."

"I'm sorry, sir, but Lady Amelia is engaged at present."

"I know. I just want a quick word with her." Lucas heard laughter spilling down the stairs. "At least tell her I'm here."

The butler nodded and showed him inside, then climbed the stairs. Setting his rifle and gear by the door, Lucas began to pace the foyer.

Amelia was his only remaining lead. Between his stints on Amelia's doorstep, he'd pursued other, more flimsy leads. In the interests of improving relations between their two countries, the British government had happily opened up records about Frier's parents and their emigration to America. But they'd downright refused to provide information about the Earl of Tovey.

All he'd learned was the date of the earl's marriage. Though it fit nicely with the dates of Dorothy Frier's movements, it really only proved that she might be using the alias "Dorothy Smith," which he already knew.

But he planned to move forward in his investigation tonight at dinner. Kirkwood had promised to help; with two of them asking questions, it would look less suspicious. Lucas had to get Amelia there first, however. What was taking that damned butler so long, anyway?

No sooner had he thought it than the butler returned. "This way, sir." He gestured to the stairs.

She was meeting him upstairs? Fine.

He followed the butler to the next floor and down the hall past a big sarcophagus. Leave it to Amelia to furnish her house with a painted wooden coffin.

The butler stopped outside a room from which sounded noisy girlish chatter, and before Lucas even realized what he was up to, the man opened the door to announce, "Major Lucas Winter."

Hellfire and damnation. Just what he didn't need—to make his request before the whole hen party. But he was trapped now.

"Major Winter!" Amelia cried, as he walked in. With a brittle smile, she turned from helping the maids prepare tea. "Hopkins, take the major's coat and hat. He'll be joining us."

"I don't mean to intrude, ma'am." What game was she playing?

At least a dozen females packed the room, some of them perched on a couch of carved and gilded mahogany with sphinxes on the arms, others sitting in the matching armchairs, and all regarding him with avid curiosity.

"It's no intrusion, Major," said Mrs. Harris. Her eyes danced with merriment as she gestured for him to come sit in the empty chair next to her. "We took a vote. The ladies felt that we needed a man's perspective on our topic of discussion."

Uh-oh. Anytime a woman asked for a "man's perspective," she really meant she wanted him to state her own. But if he played this carefully, he might get Amelia's friends to tell him about Lady Tovey. And he could always talk to Amelia alone after the women left.

Giving the butler his hat and coat, Lucas seated himself in the black armchair Mrs. Harris had indicated. "I'll try to oblige you ladies, if the topic is one I know anything about."

That sent them into gales of laughter that Mrs. Harris silenced with a word. Then she introduced them. The only lady he took particular note of was Miss Sarah Linley, the woman Kirkwood meant to marry. Lucas understood why; anybody could see she was a beauty.

But he preferred brunettes to blondes any day. Plus she had that uppity society air that might suit Kirkwood fine but set his own temper to simmering. The air that Amelia usually lacked.

Not today, however. "We're so glad you could join us, sir," she said, her back ramrod straight as she helped the maids. "We were just saying—"

The door burst open and another young woman rushed in, then headed straight for Amelia. "I'm so sorry I'm late." She didn't even notice Lucas as he rose at the other end of the room. "I paid a visit to Lady Byrne. Her husband knows everything about everyone, so I thought he might have information about that American major Mrs. Harris said you—"

"Miss North," Amelia interrupted, then jerked her head toward Lucas. "Meet Major Lucas Winter."

Miss North stiffened, then slowly turned to see Lucas standing there, fighting a smile.

"Major Winter," Amelia murmured, "this is my good friend, Louisa North. She sometimes helps Mrs. Harris with our lessons."

"When she's not investigating your suitors," he added.

The women snickered. He wasn't worried. The few people who knew why he was really here weren't the kind to speak out of turn.

Unlike poor Miss North. Although a blush touched her cheeks, she met his gaze as boldly as Amelia. "Forgive me for my lack of tact, sir, but we don't usually have gentlemen at our little teas."

"No need to apologize." And he didn't want to antagonize Amelia's friends. He offered her his chair. "*I'm* the intruder here."

As Miss North seated herself, he walked over to the fireplace. On this fine June afternoon there was no fire in the hearth, so he leaned against the mantel, giving him a perfect view of the whole assembly.

Especially their bold leader, Lady Delilah—except today, she was as far from Delilah as a woman could get. With her lush hair bunched up tight atop her head and her frilly, flouncy gown, she looked too much like the other ladies for his taste. He wanted to march over, grab her up, and kiss that proper mouth until it softened into a smile.

That would give her friends something to talk about.

As if she read his thoughts, Amelia shot him a dark glance, then sat primly on the edge of a settee. "Actually, Louisa, the good major has agreed to give us his honest opinion about our usual topic."

Her tone put him further on guard. What had her so snippy today? Was she just nervous about her tea party? Whatever it was, he didn't like it. Especially when she gave him a smile so frigid it was like a blast of arctic air.

"You see, sir, we're all graduates of Mrs. Harris's school. Once a month, we meet to discuss what consumes our energies the rest of the time."

"And what might that be?"

"Men," one of the ladies said, then tittered.

Hellfire and damnation. "Seeing as how I am one, I suppose I qualify as an expert," Lucas drawled.

"Ah, but not *just* men," added the woman named Lady Venetia. "A certain sort of man."

"Scoundrels and fortune hunters, to be exact," Miss North put in.

"So tell us, Major Winter," Amelia said, "do you qualify as an expert on *that* topic?"

The room fell deadly quiet.

He glanced at the oddly hostile Miss North, then the inscrutable Lady Venetia, and finally Amelia, whose usually soft brown eyes held a steely glint.

Every battle instinct went up. He recognized an ambush when he saw one. And the last time he'd been ambushed by the English, he nearly hadn't survived.

This time would be different.

Crossing his arms over his chest, he cast them all a broad smile. "Depends on what you mean by 'qualify as an expert.' I've met a few fortune hunters and fought my share of scoundrels, but I don't believe I personally qualify as either." He narrowed his gaze on Amelia. "Not that you were trying to imply that, were you, ma'am?"

"Of course she wasn't," Mrs. Harris put in. When Amelia opened her mouth to retort, the widow added hastily, "Would you like some tea, Major? We were just about to pour when you were announced."

As Amelia sat seething, he shot her an insolent grin. "Thank you. A good cup of tea never hurt anybody."

Mrs. Harris motioned to the maids. One of them hurried over with a tray of plates containing cakes and such. Another wheeled a cart with a tea service over to where Amelia sat. She picked up the unusual-looking teapot and started to pour.

"I thought Americans didn't drink tea," said Miss Linley in a snooty voice that matched how she looked. "Amelia's stepmother said Americans only drink cider and small beer."

"She said no such thing, Sarah Linley." Amelia handed cups and saucers to the maids, who brought them round. "She merely said it was difficult to find good English tea there."

"In Boston?" he put in. "I don't see why." But it might be harder to find in Rhinebeck, where Dorothy Frier had been working as a housekeeper when Theodore Frier joined her after fleeing Baltimore. Even Dorothy's own employer hadn't known the real reason she'd run away with the man she'd introduced as her estranged husband. The same man she'd later introduced to the Canadian authorities as her "new" husband, Theo Smith. And who'd apparently become her "late husband, Obadiah Smith," once she'd arrived in England.

He eyed the vapid Miss Linley. "So what else does Lady Tovey say about America?"

"Not much, actually," Lady Venetia put in. "The woman's so timid, you have to pry information out of her."

Dorothy Frier, timid? The woman whose letters to her estranged husband had prompted a hardworking young man to steal a fortune from his employer and rush to her side? A woman who'd crossed a world, lying for her husband and spending stolen money? More likely, she kept quiet for fear of revealing too much.

"Dolly merely has a gentle disposition," Amelia said, strangely interested in her tea-pouring. "That's why elderly men love to dance with her at balls. She lets them drone on about their troubles because she's too sweet to interrupt."

"You're quite right," Mrs. Harris said. "How many ladies would allow a tea to be held in their homes when they could not be there to supervise? Yet Lady Tovey actually wrote to ask if she could supply anything else for the event."

So the woman was kind to old men and young ladies. That hardly proved anything. Since she thought herself and Frier safe, she could afford to be kind.

A maid brought Lucas his tea. He declined the milk she offered, but took the sugar. As he drank the aromatic brew, he listened avidly to what was said about the woman he'd known only on paper. Even her former employer hadn't told him much about her character.

"That sounds exactly like Lady Tovey," Miss North was saying. "She's such a giving soul. Despite being too timid to participate in a project like mine, she offered a generous donation."

Easy to be generous with somebody else's money.

As if she guessed his thoughts, which of course she couldn't have, Amelia glanced at Lucas, then said to Louisa, "I'm sure you also appreciate how Dolly supports your project behind the scenes, don't you?"

"I suppose." Miss North looked bewildered. "But I most appreciate the money. The Ladies Society needs the funds."

"I know that," Amelia said in a clipped tone. "I merely meant that her money isn't what matters to—"

"I think what Miss North is trying to say," Lucas interrupted, "is that money *always* matters to women." Not just Dorothy Frier, but his own mother. For all her gentility and fine manners, Mother had cared a whole lot about money.

When Amelia shot him a mutinous glare, he added, "If money didn't matter, you ladies wouldn't be here discussing how to keep from losing your fortunes to some man, would you?"

He'd swear the temperature in the room dropped several degrees, but he'd be damned if he'd take it back.

The ladies turned to Amelia, obviously waiting for her to defend them.

"Surely, Major," she said in a crisp, awful voice, "you're not implying that we ladies have no right to protect ourselves from scoundrels."

He drained his cup of tea. "I'm only pointing out that if you thought money was so unimportant, none of you would be here."

"So you think we're mercenary," Miss North retorted.

Yes, but he wasn't fool enough to say that. "I just don't understand why you ladies are so determined to hold on to it. If your fortune would keep you and some fellow happy, why balk at marrying him? I can understand a man being too proud to take his wife's money, but why would a woman be too proud to give it?"

"I quite agree, Major Winter," Miss Linley said.

"Oh, hush, Sarah," Miss North snapped. "You wouldn't be so quick to agree if the man you want didn't have a title." She scowled at him. "And I suppose *you* would have us marry whatever scoundrel we're fortunate enough to catch."

Mrs. Harris laid a hand on the woman's arm. "I'm sure he does not mean that, dear." Mrs. Harris fixed him with a pair of suddenly icy blue eyes. "But you have to understand, sir, that it's difficult for a woman to discern a man's motives for marriage when she has a fortune and he has none. As you once said, some men will do anything to get money. So how can we ever know their true character when money is involved?"

The words pricked his temper. Specters of his parents' arguments rose up to haunt him—endless discussions that twisted love and fortune so neatly, even his father couldn't separate them. They'd driven his father to work harder, faster, longer, trying to feed his mother's ambitions. At the heart of it, she was what had really brought his father to—

No, he wouldn't think of that now. Not here, among these young English copies of his mother. "A man doesn't assume a lady's looking only at his purse when she smiles at *him*, so why do you assume that a gentleman has sly motives when he smiles at *you*?"

"Perhaps because he so often does?" Amelia said, her eyes suddenly ablaze.

Damnation, now she was talking about *him*. That stoked his temper further, even knowing she had good reason to distrust him. "You can't really believe that, a pretty female like you." Ignoring the growing tension among the ladies, he set his cup on the mantel. "Believe me, Lady Amelia, a man's just as likely to be interested in you because he likes the look and the smell of you, or what you say or how you think, than because he hankers after your fortune."

A shocked silence followed his words. Too late, he realized they could be taken as a public declaration of his own interest in her. Which was how *she'd* taken them, judging from the blush that stained her cheeks a fiery red.

Lady Venetia broke the silence with a laugh. "Congratulations, Amelia. You've found the only man in creation who cares what a woman says and thinks."

That shattered the tension in the room. The other ladies laughed, and began to chatter about men and their antics.

Hell, he'd practically admitted publicly that he liked Amelia, and instead of being flattered, she seemed even angrier than before. What had riled her up?

Whatever it was had also kept her from responding to Kirkwood's dinner invitation, and he couldn't allow that. Time to get her alone.

He picked up his empty cup. "Lady Amelia, might I have more of your fine tea?"

"Certainly, Major." She held up the pot, but when he just stood waiting, cup in hand, she rose and approached him, scowling.

He held the cup close to his body, forcing her to lean in to pour, then murmured, "I need to talk to you privately."

"Not now," she answered, filling up his cup.

"Yes, now. I only want a few—"

She walked away without letting him finish.

Temper flaring, he rattled his cup in his saucer. "Don't I get any sugar with my tea?"

She took her seat. "I assumed you would prefer it black, sir." *Like your heart,* her glittering eyes said. She motioned to a maid, who hurried toward him with the sugar bowl.

Fine, if she wouldn't willingly speak to him in private, he'd provoke her into it. He let his gaze trail down the body he'd learned to know so well a few days past.

"Even a soldier can use something sweet from time to time."

A couple of the ladies nearest him tittered, and Amelia stiffened, but she kept her seat and turned deliberately to speak to a woman next to her.

As the maid offered him the sugar bowl, he noticed the design of it for the first time that afternoon. He glanced from it to the teapot, then burst into laughter.

When some ladies looked his way, he said, "Leave it to Lady Amelia to have tea dishes with crocodiles for handles."

Amelia tilted her chin up proudly. "The set is in the Egyptian style, sir, like everything else in the room."

"I suppose that shouldn't surprise me," he retorted, "given your penchant for the exotic—camels, xebecs . . . mamelukes."

"What's a mameluke?" Lady Venetia asked.

He kept his gaze fixed on Amelia. "A sword. Lady Amelia asked to see mine at the ball."

When a few girls giggled, and a few others whispered, his eyes narrowed. Some of the ladies seemed to be in on the private joke. They'd probably read the same harem book as Amelia, and judging from how she colored, there'd been some mention of "swords" in it, too.

Fighting back a laugh, he schooled his features to look innocent. "I was happy to oblige her. She was so admiring of my sword, she offered to do a rubbing of it."

Lady Venetia choked on her tea.

"I didn't even know English ladies did that kind of thing," he went on smoothly, "but I suppose when a lady wants amusement—"

"Major Winter!" Amelia abruptly rose. "May I speak to you in the hall?"

"Now?" he asked, unable to resist.

Her lips tightened into a line. "If you please."

With a nod, he set his cup and saucer on the mantel. She preceded him out the door, and he followed, pausing on the threshold to look back and wink at the ladies. As they erupted into laughter, he left and closed the door.

When he faced her, she looked fit to be tied. "You're the most arrogant, irritating—"

"Why didn't you accept Lady Kirkwood's invitation to dine?"

She blinked. "I did. I sent over my acceptance early this morning."

"It hadn't arrived when I left there less than an hour ago."

Frowning, she called for Hopkins. When he arrived, she asked what had happened to the message she'd sent to Lady Kirkwood.

"John, the new footman, took it over, my lady."

"It didn't get there," Lucas snapped.

"Begging your pardon, sir, but we needed the footmen here to prepare for the tea, so I only sent him off two hours ago. Then he was held up on the way."

That put Lucas on his guard. "Oh?"

"An elderly lady with a turned ankle, I believe. He helped her down the street. But John has returned, so if you wish to speak to him—"

"No, that's fine," Lucas said tersely. There was something odd about the incident, but damned if he could figure out what.

Amelia waited until the man left before asking, "There, are you satisfied?"

Shrugging off his unease, he nodded. He wasn't used to the ways of the English and their servants—these things probably happened every day.

"So tell me," she continued, "was that why you hurried over here to annoy my guests? Because I didn't answer your missive quickly enough?"

Her clipped tone rankled. He didn't like being made to look the fool. "I forgot all about your damned tea. And I sure didn't expect to be included. If I'd had any sense, I'd have followed Pomeroy's lead and run off as fast as I could."

"I wish you had." She turned back toward the drawing room door.

Seizing her by the arm, he bent close. "What's happened? Why are you so angry at me?"

She whipped her head around to glare at him. "We'll discuss it tonight."

"We'll discuss it now."

"Not with my friends here, probably listening at the keyhole."

He eyed the door, then tugged her across the hall into what turned out to be a study, probably her father's. "Then discuss it in here."

Jerking away from him, she faced him down like a redcoat defending a supply wagon. "We'll discuss it when I choose to discuss it, sir."

"Is this about my trying to run off Pomeroy? Because you only had to say the word, and I—"

"As I recall, I *did* say the word. But no, it's not about

that. I know that in your own arrogant, peculiarly annoying manner, you were trying to protect me."

"Then this is about the xebec. You've had time to think about it, and you're embarrassed that we—"

"Have you no shame?" With a furtive glance toward the open doorway, she approached him and lowered her voice. "I shan't have this discussion here, where my friends or Mrs. Harris may pop out any moment. It'll be easier tonight."

Turning her back on him, she headed for the hall, but he caught up to her in a few quick strides. He clasped her around the waist and pulled her out of sight of the open door.

As she began to struggle, he whispered against her ear, "Whoa, there, darlin', you and I aren't finished."

"For now, we are." She twisted to face him, spitting mad. "And if you think I'll stand here letting you manhandle me with my friends across the hall—"

"*Manhandle* you?" His temper erupted. "Maybe I should remind you that you enjoyed yourself very much the last time I 'manhandled' you."

Thrusting her against the wall, he kissed her hard, demanding a response and exulting when, after a moment of resistance, she gave it. And when she then slid her arms about his neck and pressed herself against him, he wanted to crow his triumph aloud.

Instead, he plundered her mouth with a fervency that alarmed him. Because it suddenly dawned on him that *this* was why he'd come here. Not to frighten off Pomeroy. Not to find out about the Friers.

He'd come for this. For *her*. Because after two days without her sparkling smile, her teasing comments, her lilting honeysuckle scent and luscious marvel of a mouth, he craved her like a prisoner craves release. Heedless of where they were, he ran his hands up her body—her tempting little hips, the waist that fit so neatly in his hands, and her breasts . . . oh, God, her breasts . . . that he stroked with his thumbs, wishing he could suck them, too . . .

Suddenly, her hands fisted in his hair. She tugged his head back to force him to break the kiss, then shoved him away from her. As she stared at him with reddened lips and quickening breath, a strange mix of emotions crossed her face—desire, anger, and oddly enough, regret.

Then a mask descended over her features. "I hope you enjoyed that, Lucas," she said in an ominous tone. "Because that's the last kiss you'll ever get from me."

Before he could react, she slipped from between him and the wall and left the room. With his cock hard as hell, he moved stiffly after her, reaching the hall just in time to watch her open the door to the drawing room.

She paused in the doorway to say, in a carrying voice, "I'm so sorry you have to leave, Major. I'll make your apologies to the other ladies."

As she disappeared inside, he had half a mind to walk in after her and make a liar out of her. But aside from the arousal that he'd have to banish before he could go in, the prospect of sitting through an awkward afternoon with her glaring and her friends snickering didn't exactly appeal. He'd rather take on ten armed redcoats than one of those damned Englishwomen.

Never mind. He would return to Kirkwood's and prepare for tonight's "discussion." As soon as he could bring his rampant erection under control.

He paced the hallway until he was presentable, then descended the stairs two at a time. Today's "adventure" had shown him one thing for sure: he had to have her. He had no idea in hell how to manage it—how to capture the Friers and take them back to America and at the same time gain Amelia.

But no matter what she'd said about it being the last kiss, that woman was going to end up in his bed. He'd do whatever he had to do to get her there.

Chapter Fourteen

Dear Charlotte,
Lord Pomeroy isn't as harmless as he appears. I heard
that he acquired a certain unwise obsession during the
war. Although I can't confirm the rumor, I'd advise you
and Lady Amelia to be on your guard with him.
Your concerned cousin,
Michael

You're being utterly ridiculous, Amelia told herself while changing her gown for the third time. *What you wear tonight doesn't matter one whit.*

After all, she needn't act the flirt anymore. She would be forthright with Lucas, demand evidence, then determine how to act. And yet . . .

As her long-suffering maid fastened her up, Amelia scowled at the mirror. She wanted to make him burn. And burn. And burn some more.

If ever a gown was meant for that, it was this rose-colored dinner dress of sprigged gossamer satin. The bodice alone would send the high sticklers into a swoon—it showed far too much bosom for a maiden. She twisted to the left and swallowed hard as the filmy fabric clung to her figure like wet muslin.

Which was precisely why she rarely wore the thing. Since she already had a reputation for being too unla-dylike, she avoided attire that might push the minor gossip about her manner into major rumors about her character.

But after what she'd found out about Lucas's purpose, then his behavior this afternoon—as if he really cared about her—she wanted to torture him.

His desire to marry her might be insincere, but his desire to seduce her clearly wasn't. She felt it every time he kissed her with that bold, consuming mouth or ran those clever, seeking hands over her waist, her hips . . . her breasts.

He wanted her. And she wouldn't let him have her. So why not show him what he threw away with his devious machinations?

Let him burn futilely, the way she had the past two nights, her hands fondling places a lady shouldn't fondle, delving into soft flesh a maiden should never explore. The worst had been knowing that *nothing* would ever come of it. She knew too little to pleasure herself, and she refused to let him pleasure her again.

He'd ruined her for the comfortable maiden life she lived, curse him.

"I shall wear this one. Definitely." She glanced at her maid. "And lace my corset tighter. I want my breasts so high I could eat my dinner off them."

Her maid looked shocked but did as her mistress demanded, unfastening the gown to tighten the corset laces. Only when the mounds of flesh rose to present themselves like beacons of impropriety did Amelia finally concede it was enough.

As her maid added the finishing touches—the heavy pearls that drew attention to her bosom and the matching Cambridge hat with its plume of ostrich feathers—Amelia prepared for her looming confrontation with Lucas.

Oh, if only she could talk to Mrs. Harris to calm her nerves. But the widow had left for her evening engagement an hour ago. By the time Amelia put on her pelerine cape and headed downstairs, she had only minutes to spare.

Hopkins met her at the bottom, looking rattled. "My lady, we have a problem. One of the carriage wheels has cracked, and we shall have to change it out. The stable master says it may require an hour or more. Perhaps we should send a note to Lord Kirkwood to have him provide—"

"No, please don't bother. Just summon a hackney. That will be fine."

"But my lady—"

"I'll have a footman with me. I'm sure it will be perfectly safe." Especially now that she'd rid herself of the Pomeroy Plague. "I'd rather not wait."

If she had to spend one more minute fretting over what she planned to say to Lucas, she might just explode.

"Very good, my lady," Hopkins said with a disapproving frown. Then he summoned John, who rushed off to get a hackney.

Within moments, John had returned to escort her down the stairs and hand her up into the big black carriage. She hadn't even sat down when it started up, throwing her off-balance. She landed on something decidedly too muscular for a carriage seat. Before she could even catch her breath, her hands were grabbed from behind and something silky wrapped around them to bind them.

She felt a moment's alarm, until she realized who it must be. "Lucas, stop that! I don't have the patience for your games tonight, and besides—"

"I see I'm saving you just in time," said a gravelly voice she knew only too well. "Especially if you already call that American by his Christian name."

Panic exploded in her chest. "Lord Pomeroy?" She tried unsuccessfully to scramble from his lap. "Release me at once! I shan't allow this!"

Ignoring her protests and struggles, he tightened her bonds, then tossed her onto the seat beside him with surprising strength. That knocked the wind out of her, with her excessively tight lacings, and while she struggled against dizziness, he lifted her feet into his lap to bind her legs.

As soon as she caught her breath, she screamed, "John, help me! Help!"

"No point to crying out for *him,* my dear lady." Lord Pomeroy wound the silken bonds around her ankles. "John has been in my employ since long before he answered your father's advertisement. Besides, these windows are very thick—you won't be heard above the horses. This rig was specially built for military purposes, to protect foreign dignitaries. It's as solid as the Rock of Gibraltar."

Fear settled like a lead weight in her belly. So he'd planned this. He'd probably arranged the broken wheel on her carriage, too. Lord help her.

She kicked at him, but her lovely satin gown, which had clung so nicely upstairs, twisted about her legs, and she could only produce a silly fluttering of her slippers. She might as well be a flounder. Not to mention that she could barely draw breath. A pity no one had told her to dress for a kidnapping.

He secured the bindings around her ankles as calmly as Lucas had, but the marquess wasn't pretending to capture her, and these were *real* knots, firmly tied.

"Speaking of Gibraltar," he said in a bizarrely conversational tone, "did you know I spent time there? With your love of the exotic, you would enjoy that place. We shall have to visit it once we're married."

She would *brain* him with the Rock of Gibraltar! How could he treat the kidnapping as a pleasure jaunt? "You won't get away with this!"

Setting her feet on the floor, he shifted to face her. "I already have." As the carriage turned onto a major thoroughfare, gaslight flooded his features, illuminating the determination carved there.

Her pulse started a mad stampede. Did he really think he could force her into marriage? She had to make him understand that he couldn't, before they left London where people were around to help her.

Before she'd been gone too long to salvage her reputation.

"My lord, this abduction will do you no good. If you drag me to Gretna Green and bring me before the parson, I'll simply refuse to marry you."

"Nonsense. You're a sensible woman. Given the choice between a respectable life with a war hero who adores you, and a future mired in scandal—"

"Yes, what about the scandal?" she said, preferring not to think of his disturbing claim that he adored her. "This will ruin your spotless reputation. Once people learn that you kidnapped a woman against her will, they'll despise you."

"The man who saved England from Boney?" He snorted. "Besides, we will be respectably married by the time anyone hears of it. It will merely be a romantic tale to be bandied about the card tables."

"Romantic! When I've said repeatedly that I don't want to marry you?"

He thrust out his bulldog's chin. "If I thought that you truly felt that way, I would not be doing this. But you welcomed my attentions when we first met—"

"Only because you were an interesting fellow with interesting stories!"

He shook his head vehemently. "I saw how you looked at me—you were animated, excited . . . eager for me. I have been the object of many a woman's affection, my angel. I can tell when a woman wants me."

"Wants to strangle you, you mean."

He ignored her. "Do not let my hoary locks fool you—I am as agile as any younger man." He waggled one hairy eyebrow, which made him look even more like a bulldog. "I know how to keep a woman happy in the bedchamber."

Oh, Lord. Now he fancied himself a Casanova. "I've no doubt of your ability to be a good husband," she said, attempting tact. "But despite what you think, I can't see you in that role, in the bedchamber or anywhere else."

He stared at her stony-faced. "It's only because those harpies at Mrs. Harris's school filled your head with false tales about me. If you knew how far that woman will go in trying to separate us forever, my angel, you'd be appalled. Why, only this morning—" He broke off with a frown. "I shall not speak of it until you are ready to hear the truth."

Oh dear, he thought Mrs. Harris responsible for the purgative. Should she set him straight? No, perhaps honesty wasn't all that wise under the circumstances.

"You would not think so ill of me," he went on, "if that woman had not indoctrinated you against men of a certain sort."

"Fortune hunters, you mean," she said dryly.

"I am not a fortune hunter!" he thundered, making her shrink back. He gave a shuddering breath. "Forgive me, but I thought you should know. While your dowry will be welcome—"

"If Papa lets you have it," she spat.

"He will, when he learns of the more than generous settlement I mean to give you. I intend to treat you as you deserve, my angel."

If he called her "my angel" one more time, she would treat *him* as he deserved and throw up all over his "specially built rig."

He patted her knee, and she jerked it away. He frowned. "Eventually," he said in a chilling voice, "you will recognize the wisdom of the match. Because we *will* be married. And you will not dispute it by the time we reach Scotland."

The fear in her belly twisted into terror. She could think of only one way he meant to ensure her compliance. "I'm *not* going to marry you! And if you plan to force my hand by stealing my virtue—"

"Certainly not!" He puffed up his chest. "I am not like your rude American friend, pushing my way into a woman's affairs after knowing her only a few days."

"No, you wait a reasonable length of time before kidnapping her," she said with heavy sarcasm. "At least Major Winter would never do that. And he won't stand for your doing it either." She hoped he wouldn't, anyway. "He'll hunt you down before we even reach Scotland. I'm expected for dinner at Lord Kirkwood's. When I don't arrive, he will investigate—"

"No, he won't, or at least not until it's too late. I have taken care of that."

The ominous words sent panic clawing at her throat. Frantically, she writhed against her bonds, but despite the silky fabric, they held very well.

Seeing her struggle, he turned solicitous. "Perhaps you would feel better with some refreshment, since you missed your dinner. I brought provisions. Would you like cheese and bread? Some wine perhaps?"

That might be a way to get him to free her. "Actually, I would. If you'll just untie my hands—"

"I'm sorry, but I cannot do that," he said in the indulgent tone of a father to his recalcitrant child. He unscrewed the top from a flask of wine. "You will have to settle for my help instead."

He held the wine to her lips, and she hesitated, remembering the purgative. As if guessing her thoughts, he gave her a patient smile and took a sip himself. "You see? Perfectly safe. I would never hurt you."

"These bonds say otherwise." She drank some of the wine, a sickly sweet port she didn't care for.

"If you would not struggle so, my angel, your bonds would not chafe you. I chose them carefully—soft fabric for a lady's soft skin."

He urged more wine on her, and she drank it eagerly. She hadn't realized how thirsty she was until now.

He smiled approvingly. "I thought you might like the wine. You ladies prefer sweet things."

Even a soldier can use something sweet from time to time.

Despair gripped her. How she wished she could take back the harsh words she'd thrown at Lucas that afternoon. He might be a scoundrel, but until then, he'd never forced his attentions on her. And even his courtship scheme was partly her fault. If she hadn't made him kiss her the night they'd met, he might never have tried to use kisses to get information out of her.

"Shall you have more wine?" Lord Pomeroy asked.

"No." The wine he'd already given her sat heavy in her belly. And why was he so sure Lucas wouldn't follow?

Screwing the cap back on the flask, the marquess turned to rummage through his provisions. "Some food then, some bread with butter."

"I only want you to release me!"

"I know this is vexing, but I'll do my best to make your trip comfortable."

"Comfortable! If you call being trussed like a pig for market comfortable—"

"It's only until the laudanum takes effect," he assured her.

She froze. "Laudanum?" When had he given her— Oh no, please, no . . . "The wine had laudanum? But I saw you drink it, too!"

"Indeed. But I am less susceptible to the effects of laudanum than some."

Panic made it hard for her to breathe. Or did the laudanum cause shortness of breath? She had never taken it—how did it work? Was it that unfamiliar warmth seeping into her blood? Or the way her eyelids began to feel heavy?

Suddenly she wanted so badly to sleep. "You have . . . poisoned me . . ."

"Certainly not. I gave you just enough to calm you. Do not fear, my angel. I'm very familiar with laudanum. I was given it to assuage my pain years ago, when wounded in battle. I have been something of a connoisseur ever since."

She blinked. "Y-You're . . . an opium eater?"

"If you prefer to call it that."

That almost made the man more interesting. No, what was she thinking? This cursed drug was fogging her reason. "I don't prefer to call it . . . anything . . ." She shook her head to clear it. "What was I saying?"

"Nothing, dear."

He caressed her cheek. Or was she merely remembering when Lucas . . .

She drew back, and nearly fell off the seat. "I don't want . . . I don't . . ."

He smiled. "Rest, my angel. You'll feel better later." His voice seemed to come from within a tunnel. Through a haze, she saw him lift her feet to his lap and begin to undo her bonds. "Now let's see about making you more comfortable . . ."

And sleep overtook her.

Chapter Fifteen

Dear Cousin,
The most awful thing has happened—we are keeping it
quiet until we learn more, but I know I can count on
your discretion. Lord Pomeroy has carried off my poor
charge! I wish I had listened to you—he's clearly a
monster! And now I am the most miserable of
chaperones for having neglected my duty so egregiously.
Your desperate friend,
Charlotte

"For God's sake, Winter, settle down."

Lucas stopped pacing the drawing room to shoot his cousin a foul glance. "She's late."

"Women often are," Kirkwood said. "Even Mother hasn't come down yet."

"Yes, but Amelia is generally on time."

"And you know this from a week's acquaintance?" His cousin snorted. "I take it your investigation is proceeding well."

"Not as well as I'd like." Lucas sat, then rose again, too agitated to stay still.

"Well enough you won't need me after tonight, I hope." Kirkwood set his feet up on the ottoman. "I'm getting married."

Lucas swung around to face his cousin. "What? When?"

"In a few days, I hope, depending on how long it takes me and Miss Linley to reach Gretna Green."

"What's Gretna Green?" Lucas asked.

"It's where a dastardly fortune hunter like me takes an underage heiress he can't marry in England without her father's permission. The town is just across the border in Scotland, where legal weddings are ridiculously easy to obtain. I've made arrangements for me and Miss Linley to head there tomorrow." He scowled. "Before I have pockets to let."

Lucas stared at him. "Do you even *like* Miss Linley?"

Kirkwood shrugged. "She's a bit of a goose, but I can put up with it if it means pulling my estate out of debt. Besides, she's too absorbed in her own affairs to worry about mine—so my life will be little different than it is now, as long as I let her have all the fripperies and jewels she wants." He grinned. "And I don't think consummating the marriage will be too much of a hardship, do you?"

Lucas didn't answer. He couldn't imagine bedding the snooty Miss Linley no matter how pretty she was. She'd probably worry about mussing her hair.

Unlike Amelia, who'd worry only about driving him crazy. Just the one kiss that afternoon had set fire to his blood. If he even imagined what she'd be like in his bed, he—

A footman entered the room to hand Lucas a folded sheet with his name on it. "Forgive me, sir, but we found this in the hall. Someone must have delivered it while the servants were otherwise occupied."

Not surprising, considering how Kirkwood had been forced to cut his staff after his late father had lost a fortune at the card tables.

Opening the note, Lucas read it swiftly. Anger gripped his chest. "I don't believe this. Mrs. Harris writes that Lady Amelia has a headache and won't be here for dinner." He frowned and read it again. Something about it bothered him. "I saw her a few hours ago, and she was fine. How can she now be so ill that Mrs. Harris has to make her apologies *for* her?"

With a shrug, Kirkwood settled back in his armchair. "You know ladies."

"Lady Amelia isn't the kind for vapors. And not tonight for sure. She insisted on having a chance to talk to me privately."

Kirkwood raised one eyebrow. "Perhaps she changed her mind."

"No, she'd never—" He stopped short. His kiss that afternoon had really angered her. Might she have decided not to see him because of one reckless kiss?

Damnation. He couldn't let her do that when he was getting so close. He started for the door. "I'm going to talk to her."

Kirkwood jumped to his feet. "The devil you are!"

Lucas strode out into the hall. "We argued this afternoon, and she gave me no chance to apologize. So now I'll make her listen." He called for his hat. "Tell your mother not to wait dinner for me."

"I'm going with you," Kirkwood snapped. As the footman brought him his hat, too, he told the man, "Inform my mother that Major Winter and I are off to fetch Lady Amelia."

"Very good, sir. Shall I call the carriage round?"

"We'll walk," Lucas said. Maybe that would settle the sudden queasy feeling in his gut.

But although Lucas set a punishing pace toward the Tovey town house, his unease didn't abate. Maybe it was ridiculous . . . but this just didn't feel right. And he'd learned years ago not to ignore his instincts.

When he spotted the town house, he saw no lights in the upper windows. If Amelia really had a headache, she might have gone to bed, but Mrs. Harris ought to still be up. It wasn't even seven yet.

The butler answered their knock at once. "Major Winter? Lord Kirkwood? What's wrong? Is my lady hurt? Did something happen?"

Lucas exchanged glances with his cousin. "Lady Amelia didn't stay home with a headache?"

Hopkins looked confused. "Certainly not. I put her in a hackney nearly an hour ago, headed for dinner with you gentlemen and Lady Kirkwood."

A chill shot down Lucas's spine. "She never arrived. But this did." He thrust the note at the butler.

The man read it, then paled. "This is not written in Mrs. Harris's hand. Besides, she left for an engagement with a friend nearly two hours ago." He lifted a distraught gaze to Lucas. "I told Lady Amelia not to take a hackney, but she said it would be all right since she had John with her—"

"The footman who delivered her acceptance this morning?" The acceptance had been waiting for Lucas when he'd returned from the tea. But John had taken his sweet time getting it there. Lucas had a sinking feeling he knew why.

"Yes, John handed her into the hackney himself."

"Why did Lady Amelia take a hackney?" Kirkwood put in.

"She insisted, sir. When our carriage proved to have a broken wheel, I offered to send for you, but she said not to bother."

This sounded worse and worse. A slow footman, a sudden need for a hackney, notes that lied. Something bad was afoot.

Lucas forced himself to stay calm and gather information; otherwise, he'd be no good to Amelia. "This hackney. Did you summon it?"

"No, John did."

Of course. "What did it look like?"

"I didn't see, sir, but surely we could find it if we head into the street—"

"It's probably on its way out of town by now. Pomeroy saw his chance to kidnap Lady Amelia and took it." Lucas cursed foully.

As the butler groaned, Kirkwood shot Lucas a skeptical glance. "How on earth did you come to *that* conclusion? And how would Pomeroy even know about our dinner—"

"The footman. This morning, he said he stopped to help a lady while delivering Amelia's note of acceptance. Something about that struck me wrong." He fought down the panic rising in his gorge. "Now I realize what: I should have run into the man on my way here. I didn't, because John lied. He was really bringing Amelia's note to Pomeroy to read. The man's probably been spying on her for a while."

"It might be someone other than Pomeroy," Kirkwood ventured.

Lucas shook his head grimly. "Pomeroy's carriage was leaving when I arrived here this morning. And this has been as well executed as any military operation. He didn't just carry her off—he left that note to allay suspicion until he could get well away. He didn't count on my temper sending me over here." His panic twisted into a raging anger. "But he chose a night when Mrs. Harris would be out. He probably hired John weeks ago—"

"That means John won't protect my lady." Dropping into the chair by the door, Hopkins buried his face in his hands. "This is my fault. I should have insisted that she wait until the carriage was fixed."

"It wouldn't have mattered." Lucas clenched his hands into fists. "Pomeroy was determined to have her. When I catch up to them, I'll tear him limb from limb."

He turned toward the door, but his cousin stayed him with one hand. "If you're right, then he's carrying her to Gretna Green."

"If that's what it takes to marry her, then probably so." Lucas shrugged off his cousin's grasp. "And unlike you, he doesn't care if she's willing."

"Even in Scotland, the woman must consent, or the ceremony isn't valid."

Lucas scowled at him. "You and I both know there's a thousand ways a man can force a woman to consent."

Kirkwood paled. "True. And, if she stays gone beyond tonight, she'll *have* to marry him to protect her reputation. It's difficult to hide this sort of thing, and in society's eyes, spending the night with a man is as good as sharing his bed."

Lucas's stomach roiled at the thought of Amelia having to marry that ass Pomeroy. He glanced at Hopkins. "Do you have a mount I can borrow to go after them?"

"You're better off with my carriage." Kirkwood led him toward the door. "You can travel faster and save your strength for when you confront Pomeroy."

"You'll need it yourself if you and Miss Linley—"

"I'll hire a rig." Kirkwood cast the butler a furtive glance, then waited until they were out the door before adding, "The viscount's crest that will serve *you* well will only help Miss Linley's father track *me*." They hurried down the steps. "Unless you want me to go with you."

"No need." Lucas broke into a brisk walk at the street. "Someone should stay to let Mrs. Harris and Amelia's parents know what's happened."

They fell silent as they raced down the street. But as they reached Kirkwood's town house and headed up the steps, his cousin said, "I'm surprised you want to do this. It's to your advantage to let Pomeroy have her; it will bring the Toveys back to London. You could take advantage of their crisis to interrogate Dorothy Frier."

Lucas glared at his cousin as they strode inside. "What kind of soldier would I be if I stood by while that ass Pomeroy ruined an innocent female?"

Kirkwood lifted one eyebrow. "She's English. Why do you care?"

"Because I'm partly responsible." If he hadn't pushed Pomeroy, if he hadn't challenged him—

"I'll have to take your word for that. But I suspect that's not your only reason for wanting to rescue her."

Ignoring his cousin, Lucas headed for the stairs. "I have to arm myself."

After ordering the carriage brought round, his cousin hurried up after him. "Be careful, Lucas. You can't murder an English war hero in cold blood."

"Don't worry, I'm not about to give your country-men reason to hang me." But neither would he let Pomeroy hurt Amelia.

As Kirkwood followed, Lucas entered his room to grab his pistol case, and then, as an after-thought, his sword and rifle.

"If you don't catch up to them until tomorrow—"

"I'll catch up to them tonight. I have to." Opening the pistol case, Lucas checked to be sure he had ade-quate ammunition.

"But if you don't?"

Lucas whirled on him. "I won't let her be ruined."

"That would mean—"

"I know," he ground out. "Someone would have to marry her." He strode out into the hall and down the stairs. "If I don't return by tomorrow, tell everyone she and I have eloped."

His cousin followed him in silence. As they reached the study, Kirkwood said, "Hold up, Winter. You'll need something else." He hurried into his study, and Lucas hurried in after him. Kirkwood took paper out of a drawer and began to write. "To escape being caught, most eloping couples post through the night and day until they get to Gretna Green, so you'll have to do the same. Since no one will want to give an American stranger information about a war hero like Pomeroy, here's a letter to smooth your way."

As he signed and marked it with his seal, he shot Lucas a rueful smile. "You'll have an easier time with a peer on your side. So throw my title around as much as you need to."

"Thank you." Lucas took the papers from Kirkwood and started for the door.

"Do you have money?" Kirkwood asked.

Lucas halted. "I have enough. Thanks to your family's generosity in letting me stay here, I haven't spent much of my pay since I've arrived." He glanced down at the papers Kirkwood had given him. "Cousin, I . . . I don't know how I can ever repay you for all you've—"

"Get Lady Amelia back. That's repayment enough." He added, eyes gleaming, "Besides, the more you use my title, the more it will mislead Miss Linley's father when he sets off after *me* tomorrow."

"Good luck."

"Be careful."

With those words ringing in his ears, Lucas rushed out to the carriage. As it set off at a quick pace through London's dark streets, his cousin's statement stuck with him.

Spending the night with a man is as good as sharing his bed.

If he brought Amelia back unmarried, she'd be ruined. She'd never marry, and she'd be a pariah in society, even if Pomeroy hadn't touched her. The parents of her former schoolmates would forbid their daughters to speak to her, as if scandal were catching, and her entire family would have to live with the shame.

He knew something about living with shame, and he sure as hell wouldn't wish that on his worst enemy. Maybe the adventure-loving Amelia wouldn't care, but she'd care a lot about having her family hurt. And about not having a choice in the matter. So he couldn't let her be ruined—not when he'd pushed Pomeroy into it.

But I suspect that's not your only reason for wanting to rescue her.

He tightened his hand into a fist on his knee. No, it wasn't. He just couldn't stand the thought of her in another man's arms when she was meant to be—

His. He scowled. He'd lost his mind if he thought Amelia could ever be his. His lover, his wife. Sharing his bed, his life, his future. Even if she agreed to it, once she found out what he was up to, she'd never forgive him. Then where would that leave him?

Without her.

The possibility made his chest ache. Staring out the window, he forced himself not to think about it. At the moment, he had to concentrate on rescuing her. Later, he could consider the ramifications of doing so.

He only prayed he got that far. Because if he caught up to them to find her married to Pomeroy, he might just have to kill the man.

Chapter Sixteen

Dear Charlotte,
I shall await further news with eager anticipation, but I
know that you, dear friend, could never be negligent.
Regardless of the circumstances, I stand ready to leap to
your aid in any way I can.
Your obedient servant,
Michael

Amelia felt like water coursing over rock, fluid, changeable, her stomach roiling with the motion, her eyelids so heavy . . . so very heavy. Was this another wild dream? Like the one with the camel who'd turned into a crocodile guarding a teapot? Or the xebec dream with Lucas at the helm and Dolly lashed to the mast?

No, this felt too . . . mundane to be a dream. She smelled stale oil and onions, overlaid by a stench of burning tallow and unwashed bodies.

The odors pierced the veil of sleep. It took her another second to realize she was being carried up stairs, with voices buzzing around her. Her mouth felt as dry as cotton. She swallowed, then opened her mouth to ask for water . . .

And closed it again. Drinking was dangerous. How did she know that?

A voice nearby hissed, "Can't you move any faster? I don't want her to wake before we reach the room."

She knew that voice. And she knew the one that answered so close to her head that it startled her. "Beg pardon, milord, but I'm moving fast as I can. Milady must weigh more than she looks."

If Amelia's head hadn't still been spinning, she would have given John a piece of her mind for that insult. And why was her footman carrying her, anyway?

Because he wasn't *her* footman anymore. He was Lord Pomeroy's. That was the other voice she knew.

"Damn these provinces," Lord Pomeroy grumbled behind them. "What can the owner mean—refusing to rent us a posting horse until morning?"

"The ostler told me the innkeeper won't risk them at night. That's why the inn is crowded. That fellow, the Scottish Scourge, has been riding the road near here."

"And I suppose you think I should have listened to you when we passed that other inn a few miles back. That we should have stopped there."

A tense silence was the answer.

As the fog in her head thinned to mere vapors, her memory solidified. She'd been carried off by the marquess. He was taking her to Gretna Green. And she had to get away!

But her limbs still felt so heavy. Yes, he'd given her laudanum. And bound her.

She didn't *feel* bound, though. Still, she dared not leap up and try to run, not in the stairway. Besides, she wouldn't get past John, much less Lord Pomeroy.

How long had she been asleep? What time was it? She cracked her eyelids open enough to see the lit candles puncturing the darkness of the stairwell. Thank goodness it was still night. If she could escape her captors, perhaps she could return to the town house before Mrs. Harris sounded the alarm.

They reached the top of the stairs. Through the slit between her eyelids, she saw that the innkeeper had preceded them and was already in the room, ordering maids this way and that.

"Here you are, sir," the man said, as John carried her into a room. "Your wife will be very comfortable here."

Wife! For half a second, she panicked, thinking she'd not only missed the trip while drugged but the ceremony as well. Then reason asserted itself. Lord Pomeroy wouldn't be fretting over their speed if he'd already married her.

John laid her on the bed, then turned away. She flexed her muscles. Her feet and her hands were definitely untied. And her cape was gone, leaving her scandalously low-cut gown exposed.

She had another moment of panic, remembering Lord Pomeroy's words about making her more comfortable. While she'd slept, he'd untied her and removed her cape. Had he done anything else? Touched her? Fondled her?

Deflowered her?

She didn't know, drat it! Her whole body felt different. Was that due to the drug? Or something else?

She forced herself to be calm. Right now all that mattered was getting away.

While the marquess and John dealt with the innkeeper and the maids, she stretched out her legs. They felt less heavy, more normal. And being unbound worked to her advantage. Lord Pomeroy had overpowered her the first time by surprising her, but never again. Not once they were alone.

She needed a weapon, though. Her slitted gaze scanned her immediate surroundings. She saw only a pillow—not much good unless the cursed idiot agreed to lie down and let her smother him with it.

She turned her head. A night table stood within inches of her, and on it sat a pewter pitcher. It wasn't much of a weapon, but it might do.

"I shall send your footman up with your dinner as soon as it's ready, my lord," the innkeeper was saying. "And some broth for your poor sick wife. I assure you, she will not suffer a moment's discomfort in our—"

"Yes, thank you." Impatiently, Lord Pomeroy ushered the man and the servants out of the room, including John.

She jerked her eyes shut, her heart sinking as she heard him latch the door. She'd just have to hit him hard enough to gain her time to unlatch it.

"Now, my angel," he murmured, "time for your refreshment. Can't have you waking up before the wedding, can we?"

Her heart pounded as she heard him rummage in his cursed bag of "provisions." It was now or never, before John returned. When Lord Pomeroy bent over her to make her drink his cursed potion, she would brain him with the pitcher.

She heard his footsteps near the bed. But as she braced herself for her one chance, a knock came at the door.

"Who is it?" Pomeroy snapped from very close.

"Dinner, milord," a muffled voice sounded from beyond the door.

No! she wanted to scream aloud. How could John be back so soon?

That was it—she'd had enough. She opened her eyes as Lord Pomeroy headed for the door. She would just have to do it anyway; she might not get another chance. The footman's hands would be occupied with holding the dinner tray, and Lord Pomeroy would be focused on opening the door.

Between that and the bloodcurdling scream she intended to let loose, she could gain her freedom. The marquess would have a hard time convincing the innkeeper she was ill when she stood over his prone body brandishing a pitcher and screaming bloody murder.

She used the sound of his flipping the latch to cover her slipping from the bed on the side farthest from him. As he opened the door, she picked up the pitcher and sidled to his right so the open door would block her from John's sight when he came in.

"You!" Lord Pomeroy growled, and she froze.

The marquess backed into the room, and then she saw why. Lucas was entering, sword drawn and aimed right at Lord Pomeroy's throat.

Her heart leaped. Lucas had come after her! Despite the risks, despite what it probably meant to his plan. He'd come to save her. She could kiss him!

"Where is she?" Lucas glanced beyond Lord Pomeroy to the empty bed.

"You're too late," Lord Pomeroy said, as Lucas forced him farther into the room and shut the door without taking his eyes off the man.

"Too late?" she whispered.

The marquess jerked his head around, then gave a start to see her standing a few feet away, pitcher in hand.

At the sound of her voice Lucas's hard expression shifted to blatant relief, yet he kept his gaze fixed on his quarry. "Are you all right, Amelia?"

"Yes. No . . . I-I don't know. He drugged me with laudanum, and I just now woke up. He could have done *anything* to me while I slept."

"I would never hurt you!" Lord Pomeroy made a motion as if to go to her until Lucas prodded him back with the sword. The marquess glared at Lucas. "And I would certainly never behave badly to a woman while she slept."

"Then why did you say he was too late?" she asked.

"Too late to save your reputation," he said hastily. "That's all I meant."

She thrust out her chin. "It's *not* too late." She glanced toward the window where night still held sway. "It's been only a few hours. If Lucas and I leave now, we can still get back to London before anyone discovers me gone."

A deafening silence fell on the room. Lord Pomeroy looked decidedly uncomfortable, and Lucas muttered a curse under his breath.

"I'm sorry, darlin'." Though Lucas still kept his gaze on Pomeroy, his voice held an aching remorse. "I tried to catch up to you sooner, but I don't know the road well, and I had to stop often to ask after Pomeroy—"

"What are you saying, drat it?" she demanded.

"It's been two days since you left."

"Two days!" She gaped at him. "That can't be! Surely I would have . . ." But now that her brain was pushing clear of the drug, she could sift the dreams from the hazy memories. Of someone coaxing her to drink more than once, of being led from a carriage to relieve herself, of dozing in a carriage too bright for it to have been night—

"You see?" Lord Pomeroy said, in a placating voice that further sparked her temper. "You'll be ruined if you return unwed. The only way to save your reputation is to marry me."

"Marry you!" She stalked toward him, brandishing the pitcher. Water sloshed out of it with her every step. "*Marry* you? *You're* the one who ruined me, drat it!" Her temper soaring, she whacked his arm with the pitcher. "How *dare* you keep me drugged for two days?" She whacked his other arm. "Lord only knows what you did to me while I was asleep!"

He held his arms up to block his head. "I did nothing, I swear!"

"Then why is my cape gone?" she spat.

"I removed it merely to allow you to sleep more comfortably, my angel—"

"Don't call me that!" She struck his crossed arms, tears welling in her eyes. "I was never your angel!" Half-blinded by tears, she hit him again. "I will never be your wife!" Her tears fell, and she swiped them away furiously. "How could you?" She punctuated each word with a blow. "You . . . had . . . no . . . right!"

"That's enough, darlin'." Lucas came up from behind to snag her around the waist with his free hand. "You've made your point."

As he dragged her off the marquess, she threw the pitcher at her captor. "I shall never forgive you for this, never!"

Lucas tightened his arm about her waist, pulling her up against him. With his sword arm now lowered to his side, he backed toward the door. "Time to go."

"No, wait, please," Lord Pomeroy begged. His hands slid down from his head to bare his reddened features and tufts of hair all askew. "I know you're angry now, Lady Amelia, but if you don't marry me, you'll never be able to hold your head up in society again."

"I don't care!" she cried. "I would sooner live the rest of my life a ruined spinster than marry *you*, my lord!"

"She won't be ruined," Lucas said firmly. "She's marrying *me*."

For a moment, her heart soared. He would marry her? Truly? Just to protect her from scandal? What a dear, dear man!

Then reality sank in. What if he wasn't doing it to protect her? What if he thought it would help him in his investigation somehow?

She swallowed. It didn't matter why. She could still use it to make sure Lord Pomeroy never attempted kidnapping her again.

"Yes," she said, "I'm marrying Lucas."

"An American?" Lord Pomeroy cried. "Think what you're doing!"

He started forward, but Lucas stayed him with his sword. "If you lay one finger on her, I'll make what she just did seem like child's play. You won't go unpunished for this, either. I'll see you dragged before the courts—"

"You'll do no such thing," Amelia said quickly, though his fierce words sent a thrill coursing through her. Perhaps he *did* care, after all. "No lawyer would take an American soldier's word over an English peer's about what happened. He has the weight of the public behind him. And even if you succeed in having him prosecuted, you'd have lost your appointment in your government. And my family would be shamed. So there's no point. Let's just go."

"You can't go off with him," Lord Pomeroy protested, casting her a glance of mute appeal. "He only wants your fortune, can't you see?"

"He can *have* my fortune if that's what he wants." She ignored how Lucas stiffened against her. "I'd rather marry anyone—*anyone*, do you hear?—than you."

Lord Pomeroy looked bewildered. "If you'd just give me a chance, I could make you happy. I know that in your heart you care for me."

"Then why did I send that purgative out to your carriage in London?" She had to put an end to his insanity right now. Kindness and evasion had clearly not worked. "I was the one who ordered that, not Mrs. Harris. I was that desperate to be rid of you."

When he looked stunned, she felt a moment's pang, but she reminded herself of what he'd just done to her, and her resolve hardened to ruthless intent. "I am *not* an angel. Did you really believe I'd choose a husband old enough to be my father over a virile young fellow like the major? That I'd willingly marry a man I'd soon have to nurse through his declining years? A man who has to eat opium just to—"

"Enough." Lord Pomeroy suddenly looked far older than his fifty-odd years. He drew himself up with a stiff dignity at odds with his mussed hair and rumpled coat. "It appears that you are correct—you are *not* the woman I took you for. I thought you had discernment and a kind heart. Apparently I was wrong."

"She's been kinder than you deserve," Lucas muttered under his breath.

Thankfully, Lord Pomeroy didn't hear him. "Do as you please then, my lady. Marry a scoundrel. I will not stop you."

"You'll have to do better than that." Lucas brandished the sword. "You'd best keep this whole matter to yourself, do you hear? As far as you're concerned, Lady Amelia and I eloped. My cousin is telling that story in London, and so help me, if you say something else—"

"I understand, sir," Lord Pomeroy said in the pompous tone she loathed. "I shall not gainsay you."

"Good." But Lucas didn't lower his sword. Instead, he released her. "Go open the door, darlin'. And make sure the way is clear, will you?"

She hurried to do as he bade, but when she swung open the door, it was to find a pistol pointed straight at her. John had returned.

The footman gestured to her to back up.

"Umm, Lucas?" she said as she did so. "We have a problem."

"Drop the sword and step away from his lordship, guv'nor," John said, then shifted his aim to the back of Lucas's head. "Unless you want to end your days right here."

"Put the pistol down, John," Lord Pomeroy ordered wearily. "The major and Lady Amelia were just leaving."

John blinked. "But, milord—"

"*Now*, John. Put it down."

When John did as the marquess said, Lucas sheathed his sword. "Thank you, General." He strode for the door, grabbing Amelia by the arm to tug her with him. "A wise decision."

Lord Pomeroy's lips twisted into a sneer. "I wish you joy of her. You will have a time of it, with that termagant for a wife."

"Don't I know it," Lucas muttered, as they hurried into the hall.

Wrenching her arm free of his grip, Amelia rushed down the stairs ahead of him. "Never fear, sir," she snapped. "I won't inflict my presence on you a moment longer than is necessary. As soon as we reach London—"

"Calm yourself, darlin'." They'd reached the ground floor and he slipped his arm about her waist again. "I was joking."

"But I'm not, Lucas. I know you only said you'd marry me to—"

"My lady, you're well!" cried a voice from the doorway. It was the innkeeper, looking astonished.

"Your inn has worked a miraculous cure." As Lucas hurried her through the door, she added under her breath, "Amazing how one's health improves once one removes the albatross from about one's neck."

A carriage drove up. She barely had time to register that it was Lord Kirkwood's before Lucas was hoisting her into it.

"To Gretna Green," he ordered the coachman, then climbed in after her.

As the coach set off, she slumped back against the seat. All she wanted right now was to find a nice

Pomeroy-less coaching inn, have a full meal and a hot bath, and spend a few minutes *not* thinking about her dismal future.

But clearly Lucas wouldn't allow that just yet. So she'd have to settle for laying her cards on the table, and hoping he would see sense once she did so.

"Going to Gretna Green is pointless, Lucas. Despite what I told Pomeroy, I'm not going to marry you."

With a scowl, he tossed his hat onto the seat. "Why not?"

"Because I know the real reason you want to marry me."

His face darkened. "If you think I give a damn about your fortune—"

"Not that. Because of Dolly." She took a steadying breath. "I know why you came to England. That's what I'd planned to discuss with you at the Kirkwoods' dinner. You came to find Dorothy and Theodore Frier."

As shock filled his features, she crossed her arms over her chest. "And ruin or no ruin, I refuse to let you marry me just so you can finish your investigation."

Chapter Seventeen

⌒⌘⌒

Dear Cousin,
I had to summon Lady Amelia's parents. No word has
come yet from the North. Then there is this latest
scandal with Miss Linley and Lord Kirkwood. I suppose
I should not be surprised, but I did think his lordship
had more sense than to elope so quickly after his cousin
ran off after Lady Amelia. What was he thinking?
Your very distraught friend,
Charlotte

As Lucas stared at Amelia's mutinous mouth and stubborn little chin and the glittering eyes he'd nearly despaired of ever seeing again, the rampant relief he'd felt upon finding her unharmed twisted rapidly into anger.

He didn't stop to question how she knew about the Friers or how long she'd known. He was too damned furious for that. "You think this is about Dolly."

She must have heard the edge to his voice, for she thrust out her chin even more. "Isn't it?"

He leaned forward to fix her with a hard glance. "You think I traveled two days, posting through the nights, unable to sleep, unable to eat, imagining that any minute I'd find you being ravished by that *ass*, because of your damned stepmother? Because I thought saving you would help my investigation?"

She blinked. "Well . . . yes." Her expression softened. "Don't mistake me, Lucas, I'm very grateful you came after me. But I know you were only 'courting' me in London to find out more about my stepmother. So there's no need to carry it as far as to marry me, for goodness sake."

That brought him up short. If she knew the courtship wasn't real, then she'd known about his investigation a while. Which meant that she, too, had been pretending an interest in him.

"What exactly do you think you know about the Friers?" he asked in a hollow voice. Clearly, they weren't getting any further in this little discussion until he could determine that. "And how long have you known?"

She sighed. "Ever since the moment we met."

He thought back, then cursed himself soundly. "So you *were* in my room the night of the ball." That's why she'd played the silly flirt—to keep him from figuring out that she'd been nosing around. And Dorothy and Theodore Frier were probably halfway to India or Jamaica by now.

"I saw your notes about all the Dorothys," she went on, "and recognized the name that Dolly bore before she married Papa. Some of the details seemed to fit her, and it looked like you were investigating her, so I decided to find out why."

His gaze shot to her. "You haven't told her? Or your father?"

"I didn't want to upset them until I knew more."

He released a long breath.

"But the day of the kidnapping, I found out from . . . a friend of Mrs. Harris's why you were looking for Dolly. Or rather, a woman like her."

"Oh? What did this 'friend' tell you?"

"That the American navy had charged you with capturing an embezzler named Theodore Frier. And since you're looking for a woman named Dorothy Frier, I assume that you think they're connected."

"They're married." Might as well tell her the truth—or most of it. He definitely didn't want her to know certain things. "Theodore Frier had been a trusted employee of a naval contractor for five years when he started to withdraw funds. To do it, he forged several documents, and no one at the bank or the company questioned his authority. Until he disappeared."

He glanced out at the bleak North England countryside, faintly illuminated by the coming dawn. He fought to keep his tone even. "Later I discovered that he'd received several letters from a 'Dorothy Frier' in the months before. The last one came on the day he fled. Apparently, it agitated him so much that he took the money and ran off to Rhinebeck. From there, he and Dorothy fled to Canada. She introduced him to everybody as her husband, Theodore Smith."

"But you see, that's where you're confused. My Dolly is the widow of Obadiah Smith."

He swung his gaze back to her. "So you say."

"Dolly isn't Dorothy Frier, I tell you. She would never live the sort of life you describe, and she would certainly never be party to an embezzlement—"

"No? She's been to Canada—you admitted that much yourself, though you tried to cover it up. The timing for her arrival in England is right, she has Dorothy's looks, and she came here with a fortune."

"How did you know about the fort—" She broke off

with a groan. "You didn't, did you? Until I just admitted it."

"I was pretty sure," he said.

She thrust out her chin. "She got that fortune from her merchant husband."

"In Boston, right? But I'll bet that if you ask her, she doesn't know a damned thing about Boston. And don't you think it's a mite strange that her husband happened to drag her to all the same places Theodore did his wife? A woman who fits the description of Dorothy Frier—"

"It's not Dolly, no matter what you say! She's the most timid creature. It's just an awful coincidence that she shares a name with your criminal's wife."

"Then convince me," he snapped. "Tell me the truth about her." Something finally dawned on him. "You've been feeding me lies up until now, haven't you? To throw me off the scent."

"No! Well . . . a few at first. Just to see how you reacted. So I could tell if she was really the woman you were interested in."

"So you could run off to Devon and warn her, help her escape."

"Only if I determined you were wrong. That's why I wanted to talk to you at the Kirkwoods' dinner, so I could settle once and for all that she wasn't the person you were after."

That's why she'd been so angry at the tea. Because she'd finally realized he was the enemy.

And he'd thought it was because of what they'd done on the xebec. He snorted. What a smitten idiot he was. Lady Delilah certainly lived up to her name, using her sweet little body to twist him this way and that while she tried to discover the truth. All the while, she hadn't meant any of her kisses and caresses.

Or had she? Amelia wasn't exactly a great liar. She hadn't kept up her silly flirt role past one day. And now that he considered it, once they'd started touching each other on the xebec, she hadn't talked one bit about Dolly.

Yes, what about that? "So all your flirting, the way you welcomed my attentions . . . they were just a pretense to get information from me. Is that what you're saying?"

"You did the same thing." Her voice was a hoarse whisper as she glanced out the window. "I did nothing you didn't do."

"Ah, but I *meant* my kisses, darlin'. Every single one."

"Liar." Her gaze shot to him, and the hurt he saw glittering there told him everything he needed to know. "You didn't mean any of it."

"I'm here, aren't I?" he drawled. "And contrary to whatever harebrained notion you've taken into your head, it's not because of Dolly. Trust me, if I'd wanted to help my investigation, I would've stayed in London until she and your daddy showed up and I could finally get her in my clutches. I came after you, instead. And you know why?"

Her lower lip trembled. "Why?"

He drew in a ragged breath. "Because I couldn't stand the idea of Pomeroy forcing you. Not when it's my fault he kidnapped you in the first place."

"Your fault?" She frowned. "Why do you think that?"

"If I hadn't sat out on your steps taunting him every day, he might not have taken such a drastic action."

A faint smile touched her pretty lips. "I rather think it was my purgative that did it."

"What *was* all that about the purgative?"

When she explained shamefacedly, he erupted into laughter. "So that's why he went racing off from your town house before the tea. I take it back, darlin', it *was* your fault."

"He deserved it!"

"He did. But remind me never to cross you. Between the way you handle a pitcher like a bludgeon and solve problems with purgatives, I don't want to be your enemy."

Apparently that reminded her that he might be her family's enemy, because she dropped her gaze to her hands. "So you really did come after me because you were worried about me?"

"No." When her head snapped up, he added fiercely, "I came because I was *sick* with worry about you. It had nothing to do with Dolly or Theo Frier." His gaze locked with hers. "And they sure as hell have nothing to do with why I'm taking you to Gretna Green. Marrying a woman to help an investigation goes beyond the call of duty even for me."

"So you're doing it because you feel guilty and think you should save me from ruin."

He shook his head. "I'm doing it because I want you."

She sucked in a harsh breath, her eyes widening.

"I've wanted you since the day I saw you standing in that hallway. I told myself that the kisses and caresses were just a means to an end, but when I had you alone on that xebec, my investigation was *not* in my mind, believe me. And that day at the tea, when you threatened never to kiss me again, all I wanted was to drag you back into that study, lay you down on the floor, and make love to you until you admitted that you want me, too."

He leaned forward to clasp her hands. "God help me if I'm wrong, Amelia, but I'm sure that you *do* want me. It wasn't all lies between us, was it?"

"No," she breathed.

"And if a man like me takes a highfalutin English lady to his bed without marrying her, it'll cause a big outcry. Hell, they might even hang me." He flashed her a rueful smile. "Doesn't leave me much choice, does it?"

"As usual, Lucas," she said bitterly, "you misunderstand English society entirely. Now that I'm ruined, no one will squawk about your taking a 'highfalutin English lady' to your bed. They'll assume that I'd leap at the chance to be your mistress."

"I don't want a mistress." When she tried to pull her hands free, he only held them tighter. "Marry me, Amelia."

"And what happens when you try to carry my stepmother off to America?"

"I thought you said she's innocent."

"She is!"

He shrugged. "Then there's no problem. I'll meet her, set this whole thing straight, and that'll be the end of it." He released Amelia's hands only to haul her onto his lap. When she lifted her startled gaze to him, he repeated, "Marry me, Amelia."

"You don't have to—"

He cut her off with a kiss, a long, hot, seeking one meant to trample her objections. Only when he had her trembling in his arms did he tear his lips free to murmur, "Marry me, darlin'."

When she stared at him uncertainly a long moment, he realized with a punch to the gut how much her answer mattered. Partly because he really did feel responsible for the kidnapping. Clearly the general was in love with her. If he hadn't felt threatened by Lucas, by a need to *save* her from Lucas, Pomeroy probably would have wooed her as long as it had taken to wear her down.

But guilt wasn't the only thing prompting Lucas's proposal. The truth was, no woman had ever gotten to him like she had in the past few days. He'd never felt so comfortable talking to a woman, being with a woman. And God knows he wasn't lying when he said he desired her.

Once she realized he was right about her stepmother, once she found out the whole truth about the embezzlement, there'd be rough sailing—but he'd deal with that later. Right now, he just had to get her to be his wife.

"Give me one good reason why I should marry you, Lucas," she finally said.

He'd already given her a handful, for God's sake. And if she was looking for a declaration of love, she could wait until doomsday. He wasn't about to hand her the key to controlling him.

But he knew what else would turn her up sweet. "Because, darlin', I can give you more adventures than any other man you're likely to meet."

He knew he had her when excitement flickered in

her eyes. "How do you know I still want adventures?" she said breathlessly. "After my latest one, I might have decided against them."

He laughed. "You? Swear off adventures? Never. You crave adventure like a Barbary pirate craves loot."

She arched one eyebrow. "You think you know me very well, don't you?"

Sliding his hand up to her neck, he caressed her pulse with his thumb as he bent his head to brush his lips against hers, toying with them but never quite kissing them.

When he had her pulse racing and could feel the eager breaths rushing from her mouth, he murmured, "I know how to excite you, and that's enough." He continued to toy with her lips. "So what's it to be, darlin'? Take a chance on marrying me and finding a world of adventure? Or be a coward and live a boring life as a ruined spinster in Torquay?"

"There *is* another choice, you know," she breathed against his lips. "I could become some explorer's mistress and—"

He blotted out that absurdity with a kiss as fierce as the jealousy she'd deliberately provoked. He made it very clear that the third choice was no choice at all. But just in case she didn't understand, he tore his lips from hers to growl, "We're getting married. You've run out of choices."

She gave him a self-satisfied smile that would put Delilah herself to shame. "Very well. But first I want a hot bath and a meal and a good night's sleep."

"You can have that after the wedding."

She eyed him askance. "If you think I'll go another day without—"

"Another hour, more like. Why do you think Pomeroy was so furious? He missed reaching Gretna Green by just a couple of hours."

She gaped at him.

"And I won't take the chance that he'll change his mind and come after you, so we'll be married first. There will be plenty of time for breakfast and bath and bed afterward."

Her expression softened as she reached up to caress his cheek, tears filling her eyes. "Thank you for coming after me. For whatever reason."

"You're welcome." He turned his lips into her hand to kiss it.

But when he then kissed her wrist and her arm, and headed further inland, she scrambled from his lap with a laugh and crossed to sit on the seat.

"Not until *after* we're married, sir. And definitely not until after I've had a bath and a meal. And I can remove this cursed corset."

He let his gaze drift down to where her breasts were pushed up so high. For the first time, he noticed just how provocative her gown was. "Is that what you were wearing when Pomeroy kidnapped you?"

Strangely enough, she blushed. "I had a cape to go over it while I was in the coach, but yes, I headed to the Kirkwoods' wearing this. Why?"

"Because if you'd shown up for dinner in that, darlin', I would never have made it through our private discussion without trying to ravish you."

"I know." She cast him a sultry smile. "That's precisely why I wore it. To make you burn."

Somehow that didn't surprise him. "Damnation, Delilah, you'll be the death of me yet."

With a grin, she tossed back her fallen hair and thrust out her fine, high breasts. And he burned. Every inch of the rest of the way to Gretna Green.

Chapter Eighteen

⁓

Dear Charlotte,
I doubt the rash of elopements will hurt the school's
reputation. I don't think anyone will protest the
Kirkwood wedding; he's of good blood and connections.
But the other might cause gossip—assuming that the
major can recapture Lady Amelia before the marquess
marries her.
Your concerned cousin,
Michael

They were wed in a marriage house beside a Gretna
Green inn, by one of the famous anvil priests. Amelia
tried not to think how she looked in her rumpled
evening gown and a corset so tight her breasts practically spilled out of it. She had to borrow pins to put up
her hair, since her own had vanished during her hours
of drugged sleep. But the parson didn't seem to care
about her appearance—no doubt he'd seen plenty of
travel-weary brides—and treated the wedding as if it
were an everyday occurrence.

Which it was, unfortunately. As adventures went,
Amelia found it more tame than expected. First, they had
to attest to their willingness to marry—she shuddered to
think how Lord Pomeroy had meant to accomplish that.

Then they spoke their vows. She hesitated after the
parson said, "Wilt thou have this man to thy wedded

husband, to live together after God's ordinance in the holy estate of matrimony? Wilt thou obey him, and serve him, love, honor, and keep him in sickness and in health; and, forsaking all other, keep thee only unto him, so long as ye both shall live?"

Was she mad to marry a man she barely knew?

Then Lucas said, "Darlin'?" in that low, sensuous drawl that made her toes curl, and she hesitated no more. "I will," she said firmly.

There were no long prayers, no taking of Holy Communion, nothing that resembled the usual nuptial service of the Church of England. Indeed, it hardly seemed like a real wedding at all.

Until the priest asked for the ring, and Lucas placed a ring of his upon her left hand. It was too big for her ring finger, so he put it on her middle one. The weight was a potent reminder of her new status.

Never again would she wonder about her future— pondering what country she might visit first and whether she would get there by packet boat or clipper ship or even camel. Her future had narrowed to the man standing beside her, and she hardly knew anything about him. Lord help her.

Yet he'd come to her rescue when no one would have expected it, when rescuing her affected his own plans. So surely he must feel something for her. Not love, since he'd made no mention of that. But a little affection?

And certainly a lot of . . . wanting. It was more than some women got from their husbands. Of course, none of them had to worry that their husbands meant to haul their stepmothers off to jail. But Lucas had made an excellent point earlier: if Dolly *was* Dorothy Frier and had taken part in the embezzlement, she deserved to be apprehended. If she wasn't, then Amelia had nothing to fear.

Besides, Dolly or no Dolly, she couldn't think of another man she'd rather marry. That thought got her through the rest of it with a measure of ease.

After the wedding, the anvil priest was in a jovial mood, introducing them to several people at the nearby inn as she and Lucas sat down to a substantial breakfast. Apparently, while runaway weddings were common, weddings between American soldiers and earl's daughters were rather rare.

Their hosts' festive glee was infectious, so despite her exhaustion, Amelia regaled them with tales of London. She even told them of her own Scottish friend, Venetia. To her surprise, they'd heard of Lord Duncannon and his mysterious tormentor, the Scottish Scourge. Unfortunately, she could tell them nothing about why the thief hated the lord.

After breakfast, Lucas rented a room there for the night. "We'll set out for London tomorrow," he told her. "We both need rest."

Rest, hah! They both knew it wasn't rest he had on his mind.

Yet when they went up to their room, he took one look at her weary motions and ordered her to sleep. She insisted upon writing Dolly and Papa to let them know what had happened, but by the time she was done, she couldn't even muster the energy for a bath. She swayed on her feet when Lucas began undressing her. As he stripped her down to her chemise and drawers, her eyes were closing of their own accord.

"Perhaps I'll have just a little nap," she murmured, as he bundled her into the bed with the impersonal efficiency of a servant. She was asleep before her head hit the pillow.

Hours later, she was awakened by the late-afternoon sun streaming in through the window. She'd slept so heavily that it took her a moment to remember where she was. But the man's coat slung over the nearby chair and the boots lined up with her evening slippers by the door reminded her only too well that she was no longer Lady Amelia. She was Mrs. Lucas Winter now.

But where was Lucas? She turned toward the fireplace to see her new husband half-sitting, half-lying in a large brass tub that hadn't been there before. His eyes were closed and his breathing even, but the water was steaming, so he must have just fallen asleep.

Good. Now she had to determine one thing: had Lord Pomeroy done anything to her while she was drugged?

She didn't think so. Oh, he might have caressed her, but her corset had still been awfully tight when Lucas had taken it off her. Pomeroy would have had to pry her breasts loose from it to fondle them, and he would have had trouble getting them back in.

She swallowed. Whether he'd fondled her breasts wasn't the problem. The slit in her drawers would have allowed him to thrust . . . whatever he liked inside.

Drugged or no, wouldn't she remember it if he'd actually done the deed? Wouldn't she feel different, sore or irritated or *something*?

There was only one way to be sure. She lifted her chemise stealthily so as not to awaken Lucas and examined her drawers in minute detail.

Then she sank back with a sigh of relief. No virgin's blood. He couldn't possibly have taken her innocence without getting blood on her drawers, so she was still chaste. Thank goodness. She would have hated to go to her new husband's bed unchaste, even if it wasn't her fault. Things like that seemed to bother men.

An odd sound filtered into her senses—a sort of rhythmic sloshing. Had Lucas awakened? She sat up and looked over at him. No, his eyes were still closed. But his breathing seemed to have changed, and that sound . . .

She slipped from the bed and crept near enough to see that his arm was moving. Rhythmically. Making the sloshing noise she was hearing.

Why, he wasn't asleep at all, the scoundrel! Instead he was . . . touching himself. In *that* way.

Though a blush stained her cheeks, she edged closer. She certainly didn't mean to miss *this*.

Sadly, she couldn't see beneath the surface of the soapy water. But she saw plenty above—shoulders broad enough to please the most discriminating female . . . well-muscled arms, one of which flexed deliciously with every stroke . . . and a nicely sculpted chest covered with little rivulets of black hair.

But it annoyed Amelia that she couldn't see the rest of him. Well, she'd have to remedy that situation.

"Enjoying your 'bath,' husband?" she teased.

Lucas started as violently as a footman caught napping. "Hellfire and damnation, Amelia!" To her amusement, he actually blushed as he jerked his gaze down to check that his "sword" was adequately hidden. "Don't creep up on a man like that, for God's sake!"

"Decided to start the wedding night without me, did you?"

"What are you doing up anyway?" he grumbled. "I expected you to sleep for hours more. Otherwise, I wouldn't have taken the bathwater. I figured it was better to use it before it cooled."

She burst into laughter. "Yes, I can see you were making good use of the bathwater."

It finally dawned on him what she'd seen. He groaned. "I only meant to . . . take the edge off my hunger. To make things easier on you later."

"Don't let me stop you," she said cheerily. "But sit up a little. I want to watch."

He blinked. "You want to *what*?"

"Watch you stroke your 'sword.' Why not? We're married now."

Glancing away, he raked his fingers through his wet hair. "Good point. Yes, a very good point." He was mumbling to himself as if thinking through some plan. "Might not be a bad idea."

"Lucas?" she prodded.

His gaze swung back to her. As he took in her state of dishabille, his eyes darkened to a smoky black. Then his lips curved in a smoldering smile that sent sensual shivers down her spine. "Fine, you can watch." Settling back against the tub, he rested his arms on either side. "But my sword will need 'encouragement' after being startled out of its wits by my wife."

"What sort of encouragement?" she breathed.

Scouring her with a glance hotter than the roaring fireplace beyond him, he rasped, "Untie your chemise."

"Oh. *That* sort of encouragement." She suddenly found it very hard to breathe. Now *this* was an adventure. She did as he bade, her fingers fumbling a little on the ties in her eagerness.

As soon as she had them undone, he said in a low rumble, "Take it off."

She needed no more prompting than that. Feeling devilishly wicked, she slid it off to bare her breasts and drawers. But the hungry glance he slid over her only made her impatient for more of *him*.

"You said I could watch you," she reminded him.

He rose abruptly from the water, and she sucked in a breath. Next time she saw Venetia, she'd have to answer her friend's question about whether the major had a sword worth worshipping. Oh, yes. Definitely yes.

His member jutted out from its nest of hair, as gloriously rampant as any sword raised in battle. She stared at it with unquenchable curiosity, marveling at how long and thick it was, and how much longer and thicker and more intimidating it grew beneath her avid gaze. And when he seized it and began to manipulate it as easily as if he were polishing his real sword, she added "sturdy" to its qualities.

"All right, Delilah," he growled, his breath coming faster, "your turn. The drawers. Take off . . . the drawers."

Casting him what she hoped was a provocative smile, she took her time about untying them.

"*Now*, darlin'," he said, with an officer's tone of command.

"Why, yes, Major. Whatever you say, Major. At once, Major." She dropped them to the floor.

His sudden silence would have alarmed her if it hadn't been matched by a sudden quickening of his hand on his "sword." "God have mercy," he said hoarsely, his gaze sweeping over her greedily, admiringly. "You sure are a fine piece of work."

Feeling suddenly shy, she gave a nervous laugh. "If you can say that when I haven't bathed in days and my hair is tangled beyond recognition, then you'll make a very good husband."

His hand stilled. "A very inconsiderate husband, to be rushing things. You should come bathe while the water's hot."

"There's room for us both, isn't there? Why don't we bathe together?"

A fleeting expression of alarm passed over his face before he nodded. "Whatever will make you more comfortable..."

He trailed off awkwardly, then sank down in the tub again. He was acting quite odd for a man on his wedding night. Of course, she really had no clue how men behaved then. Perhaps they were as nervous as women.

When she climbed in facing him, he said, "Turn around and sit between my legs."

She did as he said. The water was still blissfully warm, and with both of them in the tub, it rose almost to the top. Uttering a sigh of sheer pleasure, she sank down to immerse her head, sending some of the water sloshing over the edge. Then she slid back up to lean against his hair-roughened chest.

The rod of his arousal dug into her back, yet all he did was reach for the soap and lather her hair, his hands working soothingly through the tangles, scrub-

bing her scalp, turning her boneless beneath his ministrations. Once he dropped the soap, she snagged it to
lather her shoulders and under her arms.

But after she rinsed her hair, he took the soap from
her. "Let me," he murmured against her neck.

So she did. And it was wonderful, simply wonderful.

He started with her breasts, lathering her thoroughly.
As his long fingers worked magic over her rapidly hard-
ening nipples, he kissed her hair, her ear, her shoulder.
Soon his hands were everywhere, soaping her back and
then her belly. He lathered her legs while he trailed his
open mouth down her neck, kissing, sucking . . . heating
her blood until it was hotter than the bathwater.

She ran her own hands up his calves, past his knees
to his thighs, reveling in his sharp intake of breath
when she stroked the insides. "Delilah," he muttered,
pressing a hard kiss to her neck. "Tease me, will you?"

His soapy fingers slid between her legs to fondle her,
tenderly at first, then more boldly. She answered him
in kind by kneading his thighs as high as she could
reach, delighting to feel his flesh stiffen even more in
the small of her back. He retaliated by delving his finger inside her, rubbing her so deftly that she groaned.

Abruptly, he stopped. Planting his hands on either
side of the tub, he shoved himself up, then stepped out of
the tub. "Come, let's go to bed where I can do this right."

She laughed as she rinsed off the soap. "It seemed
pretty 'right' to me already."

He wouldn't look at her as he dried himself with the
towel. "It'll be more comfortable for you in the bed."

"Really? Have you found a miraculous solution for
eliminating pain from the process of deflowering?"

When he shot her a stricken glance, she realized something more was behind his odd behavior. And she was fairly certain she knew what it was.

Her throat felt tight and raw. "You think Pomeroy took my innocence, don't you? That's what's bothering you."

"No . . . yes . . . well, we don't really know what he did, do we?" Jerking his gaze from her, he wrapped the towel around his waist. "He could have done anything to you while you slept."

She shook her head no. "I would remember it."

He paced beside the tub. "For God's sake, Amelia, you didn't even remember that you'd been gone for two days."

"It wasn't my fault!" she protested.

He whirled on her, shock filling his face. "Of course it wasn't your fault. None of it was your fault. That has nothing to do with it!"

Heart aching, she rose and left the tub, then picked up the towel. She held it up to hide her body. "It has a great deal to do with it if you're disappointed because I might not be chaste—"

"Disappointed!" He gaped at her, then groaned. "Oh, Christ, I'm an idiot. That's not why . . ." He came up to gather her in his arms. "It's not whether you're chaste that matters to me." He kissed her temple, her brow, her hair. "I just don't want to hurt you."

A cautious relief bloomed in her chest. "That's unavoidable if I'm chaste. And if I'm not—"

"If you're not, I don't want to make it worse." He cupped her head in his hands, and the look he gave her was so tender it made her chest hurt. "He . . . he might have bruised you or caused you pain that I could aggravate when I—" Pure remorse filled his features. "I can't stand the thought that he drugged you, that he might have hurt you. I should have prevented it. You should never have had to endure such a thing."

"He didn't hurt me, Lucas." She brushed a kiss over his lips. "I think I'd know if he did." Leaving his embrace, she walked over to pick up her drawers. "There's no blood, you see?"

"Some women don't bleed at their deflowering."

"How do you know? Do you make a practice of deflowering virgins?"

"No!" He drew himself up at the insult. "I read it in a book, for God's sake."

"A book?" She felt better by the moment. Much better. Almost giddy. Dropping the towel, she came toward him, a slow smile curving up her lips. "You read a book to find out about women? Fancy that."

His eyes ravaged her, and the towel he'd wrapped about his waist started to lift of its own accord. "It was . . . a medical journal . . ." he choked out.

"A fine excuse," she teased as she reached him. Jerking his towel free of its knot, she dropped it to the floor. "But more likely it was some collection of tales cobbled together by an Englishman to titillate—"

His mouth crashed down on hers as his arms shot round her waist to pull her tightly, achingly, into his embrace. She swung her arms about his neck and held on as he plundered her mouth with glorious abandon. It seemed ages since they'd kissed, not just a few hours, and she meant to make the most of it.

Lucas also made that vow to himself as he thrust his tongue deep inside her mouth. He would make this good for her, even if it killed him. He still felt uncertain of how many liberties he should take, how much he should press her, but given her enthusiastic response to his kiss, maybe he wouldn't have to be as careful as he'd feared.

He kissed her lips, her eyelids, her hair. . . her lush, silky hair that he never could get enough of.

"Take me to bed," she breathed against his cheek. "Please. I've waited ages to find out what it's like to be with a man."

"Whatever my lady wishes," he said as he scooped her up and carried her to the bed.

He laid her down, then paused just to look at her, at the kittenish smile on her lips, at her swanlike neck with skin so delicate he just wanted to devour it, at the sweetly upthrust breasts that had driven him half-insane on the xebec. Climbing onto the bed, he parted her legs so he could kneel between them while he gazed at her slender belly and the smooth skin of her thighs. And what lay at their juncture, open, waiting. For him.

An instant's terror seized him. What an awesome responsibility this was—to make right whatever Pomeroy had done to her, while also easing her from maiden to wife. If he didn't handle it delicately—

"Lucas?" she said in that throaty voice that turned his knees to rubber.

And desire drove out the terror. He moved farther down toward the foot of the bed, then bent his head to where her pretty brown curls, still dewy from her bath, hid a second pair of pouty lips he just had to taste.

"What are you doing?" she cried, trying to draw her legs together.

He smiled at her. "Giving you an adventure, darlin'." Then he buried his mouth in her slick warmth.

She smelled of soap and musk, a scent guaranteed to drive any man crazy. It was all he could do not to just plunge his cock deep inside her.

But he couldn't. He wouldn't. After what she'd endured, she deserved better.

So he gave it to her, laving her with his tongue, using his teeth and lips to arouse her, glorying in how she wriggled and squirmed, how she rose to meet the thrusts of his tongue. The very taste of her brought him to painful heights of arousal, yet he went on and on.

Only after he felt the spasms of her climax against his mouth, heard her cry out his name, did he rise up on his knees and take advantage of her heightened state of pleasure to push his heavy cock slowly into her.

Her eyes flew open. "Well! That's ... oh ... you're so ..."

He came up hard against the barrier of her innocence and halted.

"What's wrong?" she murmured.

"As it turns out, darlin', you were right. You're a maiden still." A rush of relief hit him. Pomeroy hadn't harmed her.

And she was chaste. It shouldn't matter—it wasn't as if she'd done anything to invite that ass's attentions—but Lucas had to admit it did matter a little. He couldn't prevent the errant thrill of possession that went through him to realize that he was her first, her only.

"But you won't be a maiden for long." Giving her no time to think or worry about it, he broke through.

She gave a heart-wrenching cry, and he winced, wishing it didn't have to be this way. Wishing it didn't have to feel so damned good to be buried to the hilt inside her.

He pulled out a fraction, and her moan cut through him. "Tell me if it hurts too much, and I'll stop," he said hoarsely, praying that he actually could.

"Don't you dare." She grabbed his shoulders to hold him. "It hurts, yes, but I want to know the rest of it. Every bit."

He searched her face and could tell she meant what she said. "Thank God."

But when he continued pulling back, she frowned at him. "I told you not to stop," she said, almost petulantly.

"This is how it's done, darlin'. Out and in. Like the motion of a hand. Remember?"

Her eyes widened. "Oh. Right. I'm such a ninny."

He drove back in, then groaned. "A very tempting, very appealing ninny. God, woman, you feel so damned . . . good."

"Do I?" she said, with a Delilah smile of delight. "Tell me how it feels for you. That harem book didn't give nearly enough details."

He managed a rough laugh. "Leave it to you . . . to learn lovemaking from a . . . book." Holding himself off her with one hand, he caressed her breast with the other, wishing he'd taken the time to suck it earlier, too.

An anxious look crossed her now flushed face. "Lucas, the book . . . well . . . it didn't go beyond a certain point. I . . . I don't really know what to do . . . what *I* should be doing."

Bending to kiss her neck, her throat, her cheek, he increased his thrusts. "Do whatever pleases you, darlin'. Whatever feels good. What excites you."

"Oh." She wriggled a little beneath him. "L-Like that?"

"God, yes," he said hoarsely, his cock driving harder almost of its own accord. "Keep moving . . . like that . . ."

"And perhaps—" She licked and tugged at his nipple with that delicious mouth of hers, and he groaned. "Yes?" she asked, her sultry smile devastating him.

"Yes, my darlin' Delilah . . . oh, yes . . ."

After that, neither of them could manage speech. He was fighting too hard to delay his release, to wait until she could reach it with him. But it got more difficult by the minute, with her rubbing his shoulders, teasing his nipples, arching her pelvis up against him until he felt as if he drove into the very heart of her. With every thrust, he tried to pierce the part of her that was English and rich and noble, the part he ached to conquer . . . the part he feared he could never possess no matter how hard he struggled . . .

"You belong to me now, Delilah," he cried, determined to make it so. He pounded into her, feeling his release approaching, building. "You're my wife . . . forever . . ."

"My husband," she choked out, staring up at him with all the fierceness of a tigress laying claim to her mate. "Forever."

Feeling himself on the edge, he reached down and

fondled her slick little pleasure spot, until her body went taut and her fingers dug into his shoulders as she found her release.

Only then did he spill himself inside her. And in that brief, glorious moment, as he poured himself into her, he believed she could be his forever. That they could have a lasting marriage. That the empty loneliness of the past three years might actually be at an end.

He collapsed on top of her, his heart threatening to beat right out of his chest with the power of his satisfaction. The power of his intense joy.

After a while, he rolled off her to lie staring at the ceiling, savoring thoughts of their fine future as husband and wife, letting himself be seduced by hope.

It took them both several moments to regain their breath, several moments to settle their frantic pulses, as the sun set behind the inn room's lacy curtains, and the sounds of guests trooping down to dinner filtered in.

Then she stirred beside him. "It really did matter, didn't it?"

Her hesitant voice gave him pause. "What?"

"That I was a virgin. I saw your face. It mattered."

His heart twisting in his chest, he reached over and pulled her into his embrace. "What matters to a man isn't so much that his wife be chaste as that he be the one to teach her about pleasure. I won't lie to you. Every man wants that. But I would have had that either way." He managed a smile. "Because any woman who can't remember her deflowering is, for all intents and purposes, chaste as a nun."

She arched one eyebrow. "And you, sir? Were you chaste?"

He blinked. It wasn't a question he'd expected. "Sorry, darlin', but no."

"That's not fair," she pointed out.

"True, but it's the way of the world. And the world is pretty unfair."

"Don't I know it," she grumbled.

He couldn't help chuckling. She looked so adorably annoyed. "If it's any consolation, this was my first time to share a bed with someone who mattered to me, someone I cared about."

Brightening, she turned to search his face. "Really?"

"Really."

She snuggled close. "I'm glad. And I'm glad you were the one to take my innocence and not Pomeroy. Because there's another reason a man wants his wife to be chaste on their wedding night—so he can be sure his first child is his own."

He froze. Hellfire and damnation. He'd been so eager to do the honorable thing by Amelia that he hadn't thought once about children. But of course marriage—and the marital bed—led to children.

For a moment, he indulged in a pleasant vision of him and Amelia with laughing girls frolicking in the garden and sturdy lads sailing miniature ships in the pond. They would view his diplomatic career as an adventure, the same way their mother would.

Except that he couldn't start that career until he captured Frier and returned the money the man stole from the navy. Money that was giving Amelia's family their pleasant and comfortable life.

His enticing vision vanished. Amelia would never forgive him if he ruined her family while setting matters right. He'd convinced her to marry him despite her fears, but she'd done so believing that Dolly Smith was *not* Dorothy Frier. Once she heard the full story and learned otherwise, she wouldn't side with him.

Not that it mattered. They were married, and even if she hated him, he was responsible for her—responsible for their children.

So he'd simply have to lay down the law, make it clear how things stood, now that she'd thrown in her lot with him. She was his wife, and she had to support him even if she didn't like it. She would have to abide by the rules he dictated.

Ha—Amelia would never resign herself to anything anyone dictated. The woman had a mind of her own.

He groaned.

"Hmm?" Amelia asked sleepily, her head cradled against his shoulder.

"Nothing, darlin'," he murmured. "Go to sleep."

"Mmm."

As she fell back into a doze, he stared down at her damp hair, curling sweetly about her shoulders as it dried. When his cock stirred, he threw his head back against the pillow.

God, she had him panting after her like some half-wit hound. It was dangerous how much she affected him. He'd begun to crave her company, and not just in bed, either. That wouldn't do. No man could be master of his house when his wife had such power over him. God knows his father had proved that.

He stared bleakly up at the ceiling. Fine. He would teach himself not to crave her too much. He would enjoy what she had to offer—oh yes, he'd certainly do that—but he'd be careful. Because if he gave in to his need for her, if he showed any weakness, she'd have him twisted about her finger so quick he'd never unwind himself.

And that was something he definitely couldn't risk.

Chapter Nineteen

Dear Cousin,
Lord and Lady Tovey are both half-mad with worry, and
I am little better. I was tempted to tell them the
information you sent me about the major a few days ago,
but until we know which man Amelia has ended up
with, I did not think I should betray your confidence.
Your anxious cousin,
Charlotte

*S*ome impertinent servant was stroking Amelia's hair back from her face, pulling her slowly from sleep. She grabbed at the hand, then froze when she realized it was big and hairy and obviously male.

Her eyes flew open to find Lucas bent over her, already fully dressed. "Time to get up, darlin'," he murmured in a husky voice.

It came to her in a rush . . . why he was here, where they were, and what she was doing stark naked between the sheets.

She'd never slept naked before, and certainly never with a man. At any other time she would have found it wildly thrilling. But the window beyond Lucas showed it was still dark, and she felt limp as a dishcloth after their vigorous night.

Shutting her eyes, she snuggled back into her pillow. "Go away."

"Get up, Amelia," he said, his tone firmer.

"Not yet," she mumbled.

"You can sleep in the carriage."

She sighed. Major Crack-of-Dawn Winter wouldn't let her stay in bed unless she did something drastic. Opening her eyes, she propped herself up on one elbow so that the sheet drooped provocatively below her breast. "And *you* can come back to bed."

He froze. His black-as-Satan eyes raked down her with an ardent knowing that made her shiver. It reminded her he was now intimately acquainted with every line and hollow and curve of her body . . . that he'd kissed or fondled them all at some point during the long, very adventurous night.

His heavy-lidded gaze lifted to hers. "We can do *that* in the carriage, too, Delilah. Now get dressed. The inn is full, and we'll never get horses and a postboy if we don't leave early."

He tossed her a piece of linen that turned out to be her chemise. She vaguely remembered his washing it and her other undergarments in the bathwater sometime during the night and hanging them up to dry by the fire. It smelled clean, and the lingering warmth from the fire felt so good . . .

"No, you don't," he growled as he spotted her sinking back with the warm chemise clutched to her cheek as a child clutches a blanket. "We need to start out for London as soon as possible."

"Why?" she mumbled.

"We don't want to give Pomeroy time to spread nasty rumors. I don't trust him."

"He won't talk. He'll be too embarrassed."

"You didn't think he'd kidnap you either, did you?" When she frowned at him, he added, "Besides, your parents must be frantic with worry."

She sighed. *That* was a compelling argument. Sitting up, she rubbed the sleep from her eyes, then glanced around. The room was in perfect order, the tub and wet towels gone, her dirty gown and petticoat sitting folded on a dresser, and her drying drawers and stockings hung neatly over the backs of two wooden chairs before the fireplace. Clearly, life with a soldier would take some getting used to.

"You want tea?" he asked.

"Sounds wonderful." She watched as he poured her a cup from a steaming pot on the table near the window, then arranged it on a tray with several other items. "Is that breakfast?" she asked, incredulous. Living with a soldier might have its compensations after all.

"Breakfast for you." He set the tray down on her lap. There was toast and butter, a boiled egg, rashers— "I've already eaten."

She gazed up at him in astonishment. "For goodness sake, how long have you been up?"

"A couple of hours."

"It's not even dawn yet! Are you mad?"

A shuttered look passed over his face. "I don't sleep much these days."

"Obviously not." She sipped her tea. "I do hope you won't be waking me before dawn *every* morning."

"It depends on the circumstances," he said tersely. "But while we're traveling, you can count on it." As she began to eat, he walked over to a wardrobe and removed a muslin gown, a petticoat, and a wool cloak, which he came back to toss down on the bed. "You can wear these."

His matter-of-fact manner and cursory commands were beginning to annoy her. "Can I really?" she said sarcastically.

He misunderstood her comment. "It should fit. I told the innkeeper's wife I would pay her well if she could find a gown that would, and she said she had. But I couldn't get shoes to fit you, so you're stuck with your evening slippers."

"Where did you get the money for all this: the wedding, the inn room, the clothes?"

He looked insulted. "I receive a salary, like any other American officer."

Oh, dear, now she'd pricked his pride, and even she knew that a man's pride was a delicate thing. "I'm sorry, I didn't mean to—"

"I can afford to keep a wife, if that's what's worrying you."

"I'm sure you can." She paused, choosing her words carefully. "But the night we met, you said that the money you'd once possessed had vanished. So can you blame me for assuming that your funds are rather . . . restricted?"

A muscle worked in his jaw. "I only meant I didn't have a fortune. But I manage well enough."

Buttering her toast, she tried to appear casual as she broached what could prove a delicate subject. "There is always my fortune—"

"No." Anger flashed over his features. "We're not touching that."

"Whyever not?"

His gaze bore into her, black as obsidian and just as unrelenting. "Until I'm sure of how your stepmother came by her money, we're not taking your dowry. For all I know, every penny of it belongs to the navy."

"Only if Dolly's guilty," she protested, setting down her toast uneaten.

"If she isn't, and the money is a legitimate legacy from her previous husband, then we'll discuss it."

Pushing the tray aside, she left the bed and tugged on her chemise. "What do you mean, we'll discuss it?"

"Once this mess with the Friers is done, I may have a position waiting for me that pays well, certainly well enough for me to support a family. I don't need your money."

She sensed she was treading shaky ground, but it was probably best to discuss this immediately, while they could be rational about it, rather than later during some crisis when they couldn't.

She drew on her drawers. "Whether you need it or not, you have it, so it seems foolish not to use it." When he bristled, she added hastily, "I don't doubt, Lucas, that you can afford to keep a wife and family very comfortably—but what harm can there be in using my money to help pay for some niceties?"

"You'll learn to make do with my income, Amelia, and that's final." He went to a knapsack that he'd apparently brought with him and pulled out a knife, which he stuck inside his coat somewhere.

With quick, angry motions, she tied on her garters. "Why should I?"

He paused to glower at her. "Because I say so. I'm your husband, and I'll be master of my house. Or do they not teach that to you English ladies?"

"Oh, they teach it very well," she shot back. "Why do you think I haven't married until now?"

That seemed to bring him up short. Threading his fingers through his hair, he muttered a coarse oath. "I'm only saying it's better if you learn to live like you don't have the endless funds you're used to having at your disposal."

"Endless funds!" Her blood rising, she marched up to him and poked him in the chest. "I'll have you know, Lucas Winter, that until Dolly came along, my father and I barely had enough funds to put food on the table. When I was growing up and we lived in a cottage, he supported us by writing articles for gentlemen's magazines. When I was twelve, Grandpapa died, and Papa inherited the entailed estate. He did not inherit any money because there wasn't any. And while Papa spent his time reading about crops and struggling to improve the estate so it would support itself, I managed the household as frugally as a twelve-year-old can."

She poked his chest again. "So I know perfectly well how to pinch pennies. I know all about heating bricks in the fireplace to keep one's feet warm because one can't afford a fire going all night. I know a hundred ways to cook the fish freely available in our pond, and I can tell you exactly how to make rushes when even tallow candles are too dear. And furthermore—"

He caught her finger in midpoke. "Enough," he said gruffly as he engulfed her hand in his. "I take your point."

But she wasn't finished. "Was I happy when Dolly came along with her money and her generous kindness and made my life easier? When I could leave behind a life of drudgery and cheese-paring for the possibility of a real future in London? When instead of reading about adventures other people had, I could go to museums and exhibits and talk to a general like Lord Pomeroy personally? Yes, I confess it. I was delighted."

Her anger riding her, she snatched her hand free of his. "But I could return to living on pennies in a second if need be. Whatever you believe of me, I know how to survive very well on very little. And if you think I'll let you dictate how and when to spend whatever money comes to me through our marriage—"

"Pax, darlin'." Catching her head in his hands, he pressed a quick kiss to her lips. "Pax, I beg you. I didn't know your family troubles. I just assumed—"

"That I was a frivolous chit who cares only about jewelry and nice gowns and who will spend you into debt." She pushed him away, not the least mollified by his attempt to smooth over her temper with a kiss.

He frowned. "I didn't say that."

"Oh, yes, you did. At the tea. You said that money was the only thing that matters to a woman."

"Damn it, Amelia, I was angry at you that day because I thought you'd refused to have dinner with me. I didn't mean any of that." Leaving her side, he strode over to stuff a few things into his knapsack.

"It certainly sounded as if you did."

"We don't have time for this discussion now," he said irritably. "Get dressed, and we'll talk about it in the carriage as much as you please."

She wanted to discuss it this minute, but she knew he was right. "Fine." After shooting him a foul look, she hunted until she found her corset, then slipped it on. "Come tighten my laces, please."

He glanced at her. "Just leave the corset off. We've got a long trip ahead of us. You'll be more comfortable."

"I'll be more comfortable with it on," she countered. Then it dawned on her why he wanted it left off. "But comfort has nothing to do with it, does it?"

He snuffed the candle on the table. "I don't know what you mean."

"You want me to leave off my corset because you don't want anything hampering your lascivious enjoyments. But if you think I'll let you touch me after the things you've been saying—"

"Christ, woman!" He whirled on her, his eyes glittering like ice in the firelight. "This is exactly why *I* never married. Because I never hankered to have some female pestering me with her sharp tongue. God knows I heard enough of it from my mother growing up. I sure as hell don't need it from a wife!"

The harsh words hung in the air between them, and in that instant, everything made sense. Amelia should have seen it before, especially after Lady Kirkwood had told her about his family.

It explained so much. Why he was touchy on the subject of money. Why he'd shown contempt not only for the English but for society ladies. Why he'd never once mentioned his mother, though he'd talked about his father.

"Your mother was from a wealthy family, wasn't she?" she said softly. "She had connections and status, like me. Until she married your father."

Judging from how the blood drained from his face, she'd guessed the source of his agitation. "I don't want to discuss my mother right now," he bit out. "We have to get on the road."

"But Lucas, if you won't even tell me about your family—"

"Not *now*, Amelia." He picked up his pistol case. "Wear the corset or don't, I don't give a damn. I'm going downstairs to have the carriage brought around while you dress and pack." He gestured to the knapsack. "Put your clothes in there with mine. If you're not waiting at the inn door in fifteen minutes, I swear I'll come up and carry you down, no matter what your state of undress. Understood?"

Just that quickly, her anger returned. She thrust out her chin. "Yes, Major. Whatever you say, Major."

"Good," he snapped. "Fifteen minutes, Amelia."

And with that, he left.

As soon as the door closed behind him, she threw the corset at it. He'd effectively made the corset choice for her, hadn't he? She couldn't lace it herself. She'd have a hard time even getting the gown on without help.

Drat the arrogant devil! Hurrying over to where her dirty clothes were folded, she snatched them up and shoved them into the knapsack. If he thought he could order her about like one of his soldiers, he had another think coming. She would not stand for it!

Stalking over to the bed, she yanked the petticoat on and tied it. She should have known he'd turn into a tyrant the minute they were married. The man had been a beast from the day she'd met him at Lord Kirkwood's.

She shimmied into the gown, then froze. It opened in the front, making it easy for her to fasten. What's more, though it was tight in the bodice and pushed up her breasts a bit high, it fit very well. Papa had never bought her anything that wasn't either huge or too small for her, but in the space of a few hours at an inn in a tiny Scottish village, Lucas had managed to purchase a gown that fit her.

Tears welling in her eyes, she sank down onto the bed. Yes, what a tyrant and a beast he was. A tyrant who'd washed her virgin's blood away last night as tenderly as if she were a babe. A beast who'd had breakfast waiting for her when she rose, who'd bought her new clothing so she wouldn't have to wear a filthy gown. Who raced to the north of England to save her from a man anyone else would have expected her to marry gladly.

Lord, but he was a puzzle.

Dashing the tears from her eyes, she rose and set her shoulders. All right, so he was gruff and had a temper and a dictatorial manner that would try the patience of a saint. But sometimes beneath his belligerence, she glimpsed a man with a very troubled soul, a man who meant well but often went about it wrong. A man she even liked ... when he wasn't plaguing her to distraction.

Well, it was either learn to live with him or shoot him. And given the number of weapons he routinely carried on his person, she wouldn't get very far with the latter.

Her eyes narrowed. There was a third choice, one neither of them had considered. One she didn't particularly like. But since his honor had compelled him to marry her, *he* might prefer it. If Dolly proved to be a criminal, it would certainly make matters easier for them.

She'd just have to see how he reacted when she proposed it—because that would prove whether they could have a real marriage. And if he embraced the third choice, she'd simply have to go along. Even if it broke her heart.

Chapter Twenty

Dear Charlotte,
You must not fret over your charge. You will make
yourself ill. Lady Amelia strikes me as someone with a
great deal of good sense. She is not going to let any man
run roughshod over her.
Your obedient servant,
Michael

After the way he'd lost his temper in the inn, Lucas had prepared himself to endure a tongue-lashing, a fit of rage, or at least some sullen pouting from his new wife in the carriage.

But Amelia sat quietly across from him wrapped in the woolen cloak he'd bought her, staring thoughtfully out the window as the overcast sky lightened with dawn. With her feet tucked up beneath her she looked so incredibly young it made something twist painfully in his gut.

Not yet twenty-one, she'd been kidnapped, drugged, and dragged the length of England in the space of a few days. As if that weren't enough, she'd had to marry a man she barely knew just to save her honor. She'd had her innocence stripped from her, and her pride trampled. Yet she could still sit there pensively, like a little girl in a window seat waiting for her daddy to come home.

Or waiting for her husband to turn into something other than what he was—an American savage. A snarling brute. A man who lost his temper just because his wife offered him her fortune.

An idiot, who should apologize for being an idiot. And who had no clue how to do so without letting her think she could get round him anytime she liked.

"It's beautiful, don't you think?" she startled him by saying.

A lump lodged in his throat. "Yes. Beautiful." Achingly, hauntingly beautiful. Even in the dull gray light, her face bore the luminous glow of an alabaster angel, and it was all he could do not to pull her into his arms and beg her to forgive him.

But that was insanity. Do that, and he might as well open up his chest and direct her exactly where to place the skewer in his heart.

Still, he couldn't let her go on thinking him an ogre. He had to show her he could be sensible, reasonable. Not an idiot.

"Amelia, about the money—"

"I know, you don't want my fortune."

"It's not that I don't want it; it's that it doesn't belong to you."

She turned an unnervingly clear-eyed gaze on him. "So you say. But I think you're wrong."

"Time will tell," he said evasively. "So far you've told me nothing to prove me wrong."

"The truth will come out once we speak to Dolly." She drew the cloak closer about her. "And when you learn how wrong you are about her, we'll decide what to do about my fortune."

"Maybe we should just agree to save it for our children."

An uncertain expression crossed her face. "Do you even want children?"

He tensed. "Considering that my favorite pastime inevitably leads to them, I don't have a choice, do I?"

"That's not what I asked," she said softly.

No. What she'd asked was if he was prepared for *all* the responsibilities of marriage. With a sigh, he jerked his gaze to the window. "I've always assumed that marriage would include children, yes."

She was silent a long moment. "It occurred to me this morning, Lucas, that . . . well . . . we needn't have a traditional marriage if we don't want."

He froze, his heart pounding. "What do you mean?"

"We could always live separate lives. Couples do it occasionally. You could leave me here in England while you do as you please. It's not as if you chose this. You were only trying to do the right thing, and I appreciate that. But you don't have to take it so far as to actually . . . well . . . live with me and support me. You could just continue your bachelor's life without worrying about a wife or children."

A painful weight crushed his chest. They were barely married, yet she wanted to end it already. And in her typically English society way, she'd come up with a tidy solution that wouldn't offend any of her lofty friends.

Just him.

He strove to sound as calm as she did. "And what would you do?"

"I don't know. As a married woman, I'd have more freedom. I could travel. Or just live in London."

"I see." He stared out at the desolate mudflats that mirrored his sudden bleak mood. What she said made sense. It would sure simplify his situation. If he had to take Dorothy Frier into custody to capture Theodore Frier, he wouldn't have to be concerned about Amelia's feelings on the subject.

Yet the very thought of it made his stomach churn and his heart falter. Damn her. "I suppose that's what you'd prefer. Freedom to live as you like, to have as many adventures as you—"

"No." When his gaze shot to her, she thrust out her chin. "But it does seem to be what *you* want. You seem very uneasy with being a husband."

In other words, he'd behaved like an ogre, and she meant to make sure he didn't continue. "I'll adjust. I'm not going to give you my name, then abandon you. You're my wife, and that's the end of it."

He was sounding like an arrogant ass again, but he didn't care. The thought of her leaving struck him to the very heart, and he reacted as any man under siege would. He dug in.

"Lucas, I'm only saying—"

"I don't want to live separately, damn it!"

"And I don't want to endure a husband who despises me for forcing him into a marriage he didn't choose."

Now he could see the tears glimmering in her eyes, and the sight of them drove a fist into his gut. "I don't despise you, darlin'. And surely you know by now that nobody can force me to do anything I don't want. Not a stubborn ass like me."

She blinked back her tears, as if letting them fall would be an insult to her pride. He tried to imagine his mother holding back her tears and failed.

Forcing a smile, he searched for something to say that would reassure her. "A man can't live alone all his life, you know. As you pointed out the first night we met, I'm getting a little long in the tooth to be a bachelor."

"Practically doddering on the edge of the grave."

"Fortunately, I have a young thing like you to nurse me in my old age," he said, in an attempt at humor.

"If I don't kill you first," she snapped. But her eyes had dried, and her tone was more annoyed than anything.

He let out a relieved breath. She wasn't going to leave him. And he hadn't been forced to beg—or behave too badly—to accomplish it. Thank God.

"Of course," she went on, "if we're to have a real marriage, then I need to know some things."

"I rise early, I like my eggs fried, I prefer bacon to ham, and—"

"Not those sorts of things. I mean important things."

"Like what?"

"Tell me about your parents."

He stiffened. He should have known she'd never let him off so easily. "Do I have to?"

Settling back against the squabs, she gave him a small smile. "I told you about mine."

"You told me some about your father, but nothing about your mother."

She shrugged. "That's because I never knew her, never even knew her family. She was a squire's orphan when Papa met her. Shortly after they married, she died giving birth to me. Dolly is the closest thing I've ever had to a mother."

No wonder Amelia defended the woman so fiercely.

"But we're not talking about me. Tell me about *your* mother."

With a sigh, he laid his head back against the seat. "Not much to tell. She was raised in a fancy house in Virginia with plenty of money and strict Tory parents. My father was a gallant sailor fighting for America's freedom. She ran off with him to escape her rigid life. But too late, she realized she preferred a rigid life with rich parents to a free life with a poor husband."

Amelia cast him a solemn glance. "And you've decided that I'm like her."

"I thought so at first," he admitted, "when you were batting your eyelashes and calling me a 'strapping soldier' with every breath. Which, by the way, was a very clever way to distract me. You would have made a good spy."

"Do you really think so?" Her face lit up as if he'd said she would make a good queen. Then the light died. "You're only saying that because you don't want to talk about your parents."

At that moment, he wanted so badly to soothe her pride that he would speak any lie. "I'm saying it because it's true."

She snorted. "You saw through my flibbertigibbet role, remember?"

"Not right away. And I *am* a man who does investigations. I'm harder to fool than most."

"So am I." She gazed at him with steadfast intent. "Tell me the truth, Lucas. You still think I'm like your mother."

"Not exactly." He smiled faintly. "Somehow I can't imagine Mother beating up a marquess with a pitcher.

But . . ." He trailed off, not sure if honesty was such a good idea right now.

"But?"

He hesitated, but she wouldn't let him rest until he told her *something*. "Once she was settled in a house half the size of the one she'd grown up in, having to raise a child by herself while Father spent most of his time establishing his business, the adventure of her marriage lost its appeal."

"No doubt. I wouldn't fancy raising a child virtually alone, either. If I understand you correctly, she gave up everything for your father, then he was never there."

"Because he was working his fingers to the bone trying to please her," Lucas bit out. "From the day they married, she wanted more money, more gowns, a better house in a finer part of town, prettier dishes—all the things a fancy female craves."

"I do hope you're not implying that *I'm* a fancy female."

On the edge of retorting, he paused to gaze at her stubborn mouth, her lifted chin, her unadorned neck. Yes, she'd indulged in that Egyptian stuff, but he'd never once heard her speak of anything else she wanted to buy. Her jewelry had never seemed extravagant; her gowns were more unusual than costly. Her drawers and her stockings were plain cotton. Though he hadn't known her long, she'd spent that time in charitable meetings and a tea for her friends, not shopping.

"No," he admitted. "I'm not."

That seemed to mollify her, though she drew her cloak even more tightly about her. "You see, Lucas? It's not so hard to be reasonable, is it?"

Yet she still sat there remote from him, like a cornered raccoon ready to snap his hand off, and suddenly he couldn't bear to have her annoyed at him another minute. All right, he probably wasn't the easiest man to live with, but they'd married each other for more than just practical reasons. Maybe it was time he reminded her of that.

Shifting to sit next to her on the other side of the carriage, he caught her face in his hands. "I can be a very reasonable man, darlin', given the right incentive." As she gazed up at him, startled, he kissed her. Threading his fingers through her hair, he shook it free of its pins and kissed her as if his life depended on it.

When he slid one hand inside her cloak to caress her breast, he was surprised to find fewer layers of clothing than usual. He drew back to grin at her. "You didn't wear the corset."

"I couldn't put it on by myself," she said peevishly, "as you know very well."

"I'm sorry, darlin'," he drawled.

"No, you're not. If you had your way, I'd be traveling naked."

"Now that you mention it . . ." Eyes gleaming, he opened her cloak and reached for her buttons.

But this time she shoved his hands away. "Oh no, you don't. We'll stop to change horses soon, and I don't intend to be lying naked beneath you when we do."

"Fine. We can keep our clothes on."

"No," she said, staying his hand as he reached for his trouser buttons.

"Had enough of my 'manly form' already?" he grumbled.

"No, but you haven't finished telling me about your parents."

With a groan, he sat back against the seat. "What else is there to tell, for God's sake?"

"I don't know how or why they died."

That was the *last* thing he wanted to discuss with her. Still, as his wife, she had the right to know.

When he continued to hesitate, she went on, " Lady Kirkwood said it was tragic, but she didn't elaborate—"

"My father hanged himself." The minute the bald statement was out of his mouth, he wished it back. "He threw a rope over a rafter in one of the Baltimore Maritime buildings and kicked away the chair he stood on."

She sucked in a breath. "Good Lord. I'm so sorry, Lucas, I had no idea. Lady Kirkwood didn't even hint at that."

"Of course not," he said tersely. "It's the shameful family secret. Except it wasn't that secret—he was found by a company clerk when the man came in to work." Bile rose in his throat. "The Baltimore newspapers discussed it at length."

He stared blindly ahead. "Not that I got to read them. Oh no, I wasn't there. And by the time I even learned of it, Mother was dying, too, so I only have the little bit she was able to tell me in her last hours."

His throat ached as he remembered his anxious return to Baltimore. How he'd burst into his house to find strangers living in it, who'd bought it from his father before his suicide. They'd kindly directed him to the hospital, which was swarming with his mother's kin, whom he'd never even met until that day. Surrounded by those vultures, she'd barely been sensible enough to speak.

"What did she die of?" Amelia said softly.

"Shame," he snapped. Then he sighed. "Or it might as well have been. After Father's death, Mother moved into a lodging house and then . . . just languished there. When there was no word from me, no answer to her urgent letters begging me to return, she assumed I was dead, too, and I think she just gave up. She didn't have me—or Father—to take care of her anymore, so she willed herself to die. By the time she learned I was alive, it was too late."

"But Lady Kirkwood said she died three years ago. Wasn't the war over by then? So why were you not—"

"There? A very good question." He took a shuddering breath. She'd have to know about Dartmoor eventually. But could he tell her without revealing the full truth about his father's death?

He had to. Because he damned well couldn't tell her the whole truth until the mess with her stepmother was done.

He turned to look out the window, trying to figure out where to begin.

Then, as he stared unseeing at the heather, lost in thought, what he was looking at registered. Something looked strange. The clouds had lifted, and now he could see the sun rising . . . in the wrong place.

"What is it, Lucas?" Amelia asked.

His blood began to pound. "We're going west, deeper into Scotland. That can't be right."

"Perhaps the postboy misunderstood—"

Somehow Lucas doubted it. Thrusting his head out the window, he called up, "Boy, we're supposed to be headed to Carlisle!"

"Aye, sir," the boy responded. "This is the shorter way."

"That can't be—"

The coach lurched suddenly, throwing him across the carriage. By the time he caught his balance and got back to the window, he couldn't make himself heard over the thundering hooves.

This was bad. Very, very bad. Knowing he might have little time, he dragged the pistol case from under the seat and began to load his pistol.

"What are you going to do?" she asked breathlessly.

"Climb up onto the perch and get the damned post-boy's attention."

"Are you mad? You'll kill yourself!"

"But it will be quite an adventure, won't it?" he quipped as he shoved the loaded pistol into the band of his trousers.

"That's not funny," she said hoarsely.

Bending over, he brushed a kiss to her lips. "I'll be fine. I've done this kind of thing before." He handed her his sheathed knife. "Hide this somewhere on your person just in case."

He reached for the door just as the carriage slowed. They barely had time to brace themselves before it came to an abrupt halt.

Shouts from nearby and the sounds of men surrounding them alarmed him. Amelia leaned toward the other window, and he jerked her back. "Don't let them see you until we know who it is," he growled.

The carriage door swung open. "Come on out, then," said a voice in a heavy Scottish brogue. "And if you want to live, don't be doin' nothin' foolish, ye ken?"

Lucas climbed out slowly to gain time to assess the situation. Three masked men in motley garb faced him—one on horseback brandishing a pistol and two on the ground aiming blunderbusses at him. The traitorous postboy held the horses.

"Your lady, too," the fellow on horseback said with a more cultured voice than the first man.

Lucas wished he could shoot them both right there. But his pistol contained only one shot and he'd be dead before he could reload, leaving Amelia at their mercy. Fighting to remain calm for her sake, he turned and lifted her down.

Thankfully, he'd gained her enough time to hide the knife under her cloak. But not enough to put up her hair. It fell about her shoulders like a rich velvet cape, lustrous and rippling and bursting with vitality. She looked as if she'd just been bedded, and the thought of these asses seeing her like that made him want to slaughter them all.

Steady, man, steady. This is no time to unleash your temper.

The man nearest them said, "Here's a right fine lady for the laddies."

"We're not here for that, Robbie," said the leader. "So you'd best be putting your eyes back in your head."

Heart thundering, Lucas slid his arm about Amelia's waist and pulled her close. "You're welcome to our money if you'll just release us unharmed."

Robbie thrust the blunderbuss in his face. "Let go of the lady and keep your mouth shut."

Gritting his teeth, Lucas did as he was bade.

The Scot on horseback gestured to Amelia. "You're the lady who's friend to Lady Venetia Campbell, aren't you?"

"How did you—" She broke off with an accusing glance at the postboy. "You must have heard what I said at the inn."

The boy shrugged. "Word gets round."

Her gaze swung to the leader. "I suppose you're the one they call the Scottish Scourge."

"Aye." He smiled. "And you, my lady, are going to be my guest for a while."

Lucas went cold. "Now see here, you damned Scot, you can't take—" He broke off when Robbie thrust the blunderbuss against his chest.

"In these parts, I do as I please," the scoundrel said. "And in case you decide to get brave after we leave . . ." He jerked his head toward Robbie. "Make sure he has no weapons in his pockets. And search the carriage, too."

Lucas groaned as the Scots found not only the pistol on him, but the sword and rifle under the carriage seat. He could only pray they didn't search Amelia.

Robbie scowled up at the Scourge. "He's got plenty of weapons."

The Scourge looked none too happy. "Why are you so heavily armed?" he demanded.

"I'm a major in the American Marine Guard."

"Holy Christ, Jamie," the man grumbled at the postboy. "You didn't say the lady's husband was a Yankee officer. What the devil am I to do with *him*? If I leave him, he won't rest until he gets the girl back. He isn't some English lord who'll wring his hands and wait for the authorities to act."

"I say we kill him," Robbie said, thrusting his blunderbuss right in Lucas's face. "He isn't worth the trouble he'll cause—"

"No killing." The Scourge muttered a curse. "Looks like we'll have to take him, too." He turned to the postboy. "Ride the coach over to the French Horn Inn in Carlisle. I'll be along presently to give you instructions."

"Now see here," Amelia cried, "what do you mean to do with us?"

The Scourge eyed her coldly. "You'd best pray that Lady Venetia is as good a friend to you as you claim. Because her father is the one who'll be paying your ransom."

Chapter Twenty-One

Dear Cousin,
We have still heard nothing of Amelia and her new
husband, whoever he may be. Lord Tovey torments Lady
Kirkwood daily for information, but her ladyship has
been most unhelpful. She seems more concerned that her
son's carriage be returned unharmed than she does about
whether Major Winter was able to stop Lord Pomeroy.
Have none of your connections learned anything?
Your anxious friend,
Charlotte

Amelia couldn't believe that merely mentioning Venetia at the inn had gotten them taken prisoner. Thanks to her, the Scots now prodded Lucas up a hill at the end of a blunderbuss while Amelia traveled astride a horse before the Scottish Scourge himself.

The next time she prayed for more adventure, she'd be sure to specify what sort. This being kidnapped grew exceedingly tedious.

"It's absurd to hold someone for ransom and ask her friends to pay it," Amelia grumbled at her captor. "What possible quarrel could you have with Lord Duncannon that's bad enough to warrant kidnapping people?"

"Quiet! I don't need your tongue just now."

She sat there seething, biding her time, hoping she and Lucas could escape later. At least she still had his knife. She'd shoved it in the only hiding place she could think of—her bodice.

They crested the top of the hill, and she spotted a ruined castle in the little valley below them. "Is that where we're going? To that ruin?"

"Hardly. The boys claim it's haunted, so they won't go near it. A lot of rot, I say, but you can't tell them that." He paused. "And since you insist on chattering, tell me something of use: Is Lady Venetia as beautiful as the London papers claim?"

A Scottish kidnapper who read the London papers. How extraordinary. "Why do you ask?"

"No reason."

But she could sense his irritation. Perhaps she should encourage him to reveal something that might help her unmask him if they ever escaped. "Venetia is the most beautiful woman I know. Men trip over themselves trying to marry her."

He tensed. "Then why does she remain a maid?"

"I suppose she hasn't yet found a man she likes."

"Or a man her father will approve," he said dryly.

"So you know her father personally?"

He growled, "That's enough chatter. You'd be better off preparing yourself for a long stay in Scotland than trying to get the truth out of me."

She sighed. Her spying skills clearly still needed work. It was most annoying.

As they rode down the steep hill, she saw beyond the castle a stand of beech and firs surrounded on all sides by oat fields. They passed through the half-grown oats, then entered the little island of forest, picking their way through the trees until they reached the center. They stopped by a burned-out fire where the brigands had apparently spent the night.

After sliding off the back of the horse, her captor helped her dismount, then gestured to Lucas. "Bind the Yankee's ankles and tie him to a tree." He mounted his horse again. "I'm headed off to instruct Jamie and set up a place more permanent for our guests."

"And the woman?" Robbie asked. "Bind her, too?"

"She's not going anywhere without him—not a fine English lady like her. But if you're worried, tie her hands. In front of her, ye ken?" He scowled at the men. "Don't be getting ideas about touching her. She's worth more to me unharmed."

Amelia watched with a sinking heart as their leader rode off across the field, leaving his accomplices eyeing her and Lucas as they'd eye a couple of plump chickens ready for the plucking.

The younger fellow held his blunderbuss on her while Robbie forced Lucas to sit, then bound Lucas's hands together around the tree and his legs in front.

Robbie rose to face her. "Your turn."

She thrust her hands out, swearing that when this was over, she would make Lucas teach her how to use a weapon. She'd be damned if she'd ever let some scoundrel tie her hands again.

"Sit," Robbie barked when he was done.

After she did, he went to the other side of the spent fire to set down his blunderbuss. Sweeping aside some leaves, he drew a jug out of a hole in the ground, then sat and drank. His friend walked over to join him on the ground, laying aside his own weapon to seize the jug and swig from it.

Lucas called out, "Damned inhospitable of you not to offer *me* any."

"This is good Scotch whiskey," Robbie said. "I'm not wasting it on a Yankee."

"I dunno," the other man said. "He might be easier to handle if he's foxed. And God knows no Yankee could hold much of our whiskey."

Robbie laughed cruelly. "True. Well then, give the man a snort." As his friend rose, he said, "No, wait—he just wants you away from the weapons so he can attack you. Send the girl."

With her heart thundering in her ears, Amelia waited. She mustn't look too eager. This was her chance to slip Lucas the knife.

Robbie sneered at her. "Well, girl, didn't you hear me? Come take the jug. You can manage that, can't you, even if you are a fine lady?"

Trying to look offended, she rose and went to clasp the jug in her bound hands. As she walked toward Lucas, she used the jug's mouth to push the cloak back over her shoulders, then maneuver the sheathed knife up between her breasts. By the time she bent over to offer Lucas the jug, the hilt was thrust up very nicely.

"Interesting hiding place," Lucas murmured.

With her hands bound, she couldn't hold the jug and also extricate the knife, so she whispered, "Pull it out, will you?" She thrust the hilt close to his mouth.

He caught it with his teeth and slid it free, his eyes

gleaming up at her. She wanted to brain him. How could he think of *that* in a situation like this?

As soon as it was out, she moved the jug closer so she could tuck the sheathed knife under her fingers.

"Drop it by my hands," Lucas whispered.

"Hey!" Robbie cried from where he was sprawled. "Do you mean to give him the whole damned thing, for God's sake?"

"He's thirsty, that's all," she threw back over her shoulder.

Her pulse pounded furiously as she dropped the knife. While Lucas sank lower so he could run his bound hands over it, she shrugged her cloak back into place.

"Come on then, that's enough," Robbie said.

"Got it," Lucas whispered. "Now distract them."

She straightened, turned, and walked toward the men. When she'd gone far enough past so they were forced to turn away from Lucas to look at her, she lifted the jug to her lips. "I do hope you gentlemen won't begrudge *me* any of this."

Robbie laughed. "Not a bit. But if you can get that down your throat without choking, I'll eat my hat."

"Fine." Never one to resist a challenge, she took a swallow—then sputtered and spat. Lord, what would ever possess a man to drink that?

As Robbie laughed, an idea struck her, and making sure both men watched, she "accidentally" spilled it down her front.

"Zounds, what a clumsy wench," Robbie snapped as he leaped up and took the jug from her.

She glanced behind him. Lucas's hands were free,

and he sawed at the ropes around his ankles with grim purpose.

She batted her eyelashes at Robbie. "It's seeping into the fabric." Loosening the ties of her cloak with her bound hands, she shrugged it off. "This nasty whiskey will destroy my delicate skin."

Robbie's eyes scoured her, taking in her now damp and clinging gown. Thank goodness for breasts and tight bodices.

His friend said, "Remember what the laird ordered—"

"I'm just looking, is all. Can't hurt to look, can it?"

The laird? The Scottish Scourge was a man of property?

"Then let me have a look, too." The younger one stood and came toward her.

"If one of you would just wipe off the whiskey," she said in a plaintive voice, "I would be ever so grateful . . ."

"*I'll* do it," Robbie said, whipping out a handkerchief.

Suppressing a shiver, she glanced behind them. Lucas was on his feet, creeping toward the other fellow with knife raised.

Then everything happened quickly. Whether it was her glance or the other Scot's instincts, as Lucas brought his knife down, the other fellow turned, and the knife caught him in the shoulder.

As he let out a roar and Robbie's head jerked around, she grabbed the jug from him and brought it down on his head so hard it shattered. But although he dropped to his knees wailing, he was already reaching for the pistol.

Lucas yelled, "Run, damn it, run!"

She rushed toward where Lucas and the other Scot struggled for control of the knife. Lucas punched the man in his wounded shoulder and broke free, then seized her by the arm and set off at a run.

Terror hounding her, she raced along with him, though her dainty slippers were little protection for her feet. Behind them a pistol sounded, but they kept running, weaving through the trees, pounding across the forest floor. Ahead of them she saw sunlight. They were coming to the end of the grove.

Between them and the ruined castle lay a field, but Lucas didn't even break stride as he dragged her across. The waist-high oats wouldn't hide them, and she ran harder, knowing that their assailants might soon reach the field behind them.

Just as she and Lucas reached the castle, she heard a noise to their right and saw the Scourge galloping down the hill, headed for the grove. Probably drawn back by the pistol shot, he thankfully hadn't seen them. Yet.

Despair gripped her as she and Lucas darted into the castle ruin. Around them, high, crumbling walls stretched up to the sky. There was no roof, and as they scanned the space, they realized it was little better than an open pile of rubble.

"Do you still have your knife?" she asked, thrusting out her bound hands.

"Yes." He cut the ropes. "For all the good it does against blunderbusses and pistols."

She peeked around the edge of the wall and groaned as she saw the man on horseback abruptly wheel round and head toward his men, who'd broken free of the forest. The man Lucas had stabbed was cradling his bleeding arm, but it didn't seem to slow him much.

"We have to do something," she hissed. "If they take us again, that Robbie will kill you for sure."

He glanced around the side of the wall, too, then jerked back with a grimace. "You run for help. I can hold them off long enough to buy you time—"

"I'm not leaving you! They'll kill you, Lucas!"

"If you get free, you can bring soldiers back for me."

"And by the time they reach here, you'll be dead, and those murdering Scots will be long gone." She left the wall to roam the enclosure, being sure to stay out of sight of the Scots. "There must be a place to hide here somewhere."

"Damn it, Amelia!" He came after her and jerked her around to face him. "You have to go! We don't have time for this."

"If anyone stays behind, it should be me. I'm the one worth something to them alive."

"You're *not* staying." Turning her around, he pushed her toward the gap in the wall that led to open fields.

Instead, she headed for a still-standing chimney. "Perhaps we could crawl up into the chimney."

"You wouldn't fit." He stalked toward her. "And I damned sure wouldn't."

She knelt to look up in it, bracing her hand against the stone mantelpiece. A creaking noise made her jump back. Perhaps the castle *was* haunted.

Then she realized that the side piece of mantel had moved. She gazed at it uncomprehendingly a moment, then pulled on it. The slab moved toward her. It was blocked by debris at the foot, but when she gazed around the edge, she saw an enclosure about six feet by four feet.

"It's a priest's hole!" She began shoving the debris aside.

"What's a priest's hole?" Dropping to his knees, he scooped away handfuls of rubble.

She rose, and this time was able to pull the slab out enough to squeeze through. "A priest's hole, my dear husband," she said triumphantly, "is where we're going to hide."

Chapter Twenty-Two

❧

Dear Charlotte,
Forgive me for taking so long to answer, but I can learn
nothing of the whereabouts of any parties involved. I've
spoken to Lord Kirkwood's friends and to the American
consul, but no one knows anything. It is most vexing.
Your baffled cousin,
Michael

Lucas stared into the yawning hole and shook his head. "I'm not going in there. Not now, not ever."

Having already slipped behind the slab, Amelia turned back to glare at him. "Yes, you are. It's the only chance for escape."

"Fine. You hide, and I'll hold them off so they'll think that you've gone on. I'm not taking the chance that we'll both be trapped inside—"

"We won't. There's an iron handle on the inside to close it, and a little latch that you press to open it."

"Do as I say, Amelia. Stay inside, and I'll hold them off."

Already his vision had narrowed to a pinpoint, and his breath caught in his throat. If she didn't close that maw of hell soon, she'd see him clawing for breath.

He set his shoulder to the slab, but as she realized he meant to close it, she thrust her arm out to grab him by the coat. "Absolutely not, Lucas Winter."

"Move your arm," he ordered.

She shook her head. "You'll have to break it. Because I'm not hiding in here while they murder you within my hearing."

Damn her and her stubbornness! "I can't," he gritted out. "I'd rather be out here in the open with a chance of fighting than be shut up in there."

"Then we'll face them together, because I'm not moving."

Now he could hear the sounds of their pursuers crunching across the gravel surrounding the place. If he didn't act fast, she'd be discovered. And considering how that damned Robbie had spoken of her and leered at her . . .

Closing his eyes, he slid through the crack into hell.

He heard rather than saw her pull the slab shut. He was already starting to sweat, his heart to pound. Keeping his eyes closed didn't help. There couldn't be enough air in here to breathe. They would die in this damned hole, smothering the way he'd nearly smothered those last few hours in the tunnel. . . .

"Shh," she breathed against his ear.

Only then did he realize he must have made some sound—a groan, a moan, something. And that wasn't acceptable.

With a sheer act of will, he forced the fear back. He didn't have the luxury of falling to pieces. If they were discovered, he'd have to come out fighting, giving Amelia a chance to run. And he couldn't do that if he was huddled in a quivering mass on the floor.

Voices very near arrested him. "Devil take it, they can't have just vanished."

As he recognized the voice of the Scots' leader, his eyes shot open. To utter darkness. Panic rose in him again, choking his throat, clogging his lungs.

Then Amelia pressed against him, shaking in her fear of being caught. For her sake, he had to stay in control.

"I told you the place was haunted," Robbie muttered outside their cell. "They were carried off by the ghosts."

"They weren't carried off by any damned ghosts," their leader snapped. "They've got to be here somewhere." He paused. "Sean!" he barked, making Amelia and Lucas jerk. "Are they in the fields?"

They could barely hear the voice that answered. "I don't see them. P'raps they're hiding close to the ground."

"Spread out! We'll search the fields around the castle!"

The voices stopped, but that was worse, because now Lucas could hear the rasp of boots along stone, like the rasp of bodies being dragged across the floor above the tunnel. Like the bodies of his men, whom he should have been with, should have saved. The horror rose up in him again, and each breath grew more labored—

Damn it, man, you can't let the fear conquer you— not with Amelia's life at stake. Think about something else. Anything else.

He made himself listen for the world beyond the cell, keep track of where the men were. If he and Amelia stayed in here until sunset, they could probably escape. Three men couldn't possibly watch the whole area at night, and they might not even try—if they couldn't find their quarry quickly, they might just decamp.

But the idea of spending hours in this godforsaken cell made his terror return, his heart pound, his throat close up. Hellfire and damnation, how would he make it? He didn't even know how much time he and Amelia had before the air petered out.

But the air didn't seem stale. Forcing himself to concentrate on something other than the close space, he gradually realized he felt a draft from somewhere.

Abruptly, he released Amelia to move along the perimeter of their cell, running his hands systematically from top to bottom. When he found an iron grate set into the stone with air coming through it, he sagged against the wall with relief. At least he and Amelia wouldn't have to worry about suffocating.

But that almost made it worse, knowing that they could be trapped in here for weeks without food or water. He needed to test the mechanism, make sure the door would open again.

No, not yet. "They won't stay gone long," he whispered, as the darkness weighed heavily on him.

"Shh, my darling," Amelia murmured. "They might hear you."

Only then did he realize he'd spoken the words aloud. "Either I talk or I scream," he rasped. "You choose."

Damnation, he wished he hadn't said that. It mortified him to think of her knowing the full extent of his weakness.

"I have a better idea," she whispered. She pressed against him, then cradled his face in her hands, stroking him, caressing him . . . kissing him.

Damn her. She was dangling a lifeline before a drowning man, and he wanted desperately to grab for it, to lose himself inside her warmth. But the only thing terrifying him more than this hellish darkness was the violence of his need for her. If he gave in to it here, he'd never be able to resist her.

"No," he breathed against her lips. "I'm all right, I swear. It'll pass. And we have to stay alert in case—"

"They find us? You're trembling all over, and your skin is clammy. You won't endure five minutes more unless you let me take your mind off the darkness."

"I can handle it," he choked out.

She cupped him between the legs, where his traitorous cock leaped to her touch. Stretching up to press her mouth to his ear, she added, "And I can handle this. You needn't do anything. Just let me worship it."

Worship it? What the hell was she talking about?

Then he felt her hands on the buttons of his trousers, and he knew. Or he thought he knew. But as usual, he didn't know a damned thing about his wife, for after opening both his trousers and his drawers, she didn't put her hand inside, as he expected. No, she sank to her knees and kissed his cock.

God have mercy. He'd definitely never taught her *that*. So either she'd been pretty wild with some other man before coming to his bed, or she'd learned another skill from those damned harem tales.

Odds were on the latter, since she was kissing and licking his shaft instead of taking it into her mouth. That was probably her idea of "worshipping" a man's cock, but it was driving him crazy.

"Suck it," he hissed, then cursed himself for speaking aloud. He hadn't heard the boot steps for a while, but that didn't mean the men were out of earshot.

Luckily, he didn't have to say anything else. Her mouth enclosed his cock, warm and silky and wet, and he thought he'd leap right out of his skin. He thrust his hands out into the blackness to grip her head, then urged it closer.

Having her mouth surround his cock felt too damned good to resist. Her tongue . . . oh, God, her tongue was laving him, stroking him, making him squirm and fist his hands in her hair. Her mouth worked along his shaft with such sweet uncertainty that his chest ached. Knowing that she would do this . . . for him . . . to soothe him . . . was more arousing than even the hot silk of her tongue twisting around his cock as she sucked and sucked and . . .

Dragging himself free of her mouth, he bent and grabbed her by the shoulders to haul her up into his arms.

"Lucas?" she breathed against his mouth.

Pride be damned. "I need to be inside you. But I can't take it slow."

"Then don't," she answered, looping her arms about his neck.

He shoved her against the wall and lifted her skirts. Catching her legs up to straddle his waist, he found the sweet, melting center of her and thrust his cock through the opening of her drawers to impale her on it.

She swallowed his heartfelt groan with her lips, kissing him as she'd never kissed him before, fiercely, blatantly. Drowning himself in her whiskey-scented mouth, he let the taste and feel of her blot out the terror that still held him in its grip.

He drove inside her, and the terror receded. He thrust deeply again, and it receded more. With every thrust, he drove it back, and with every honeyed kiss of hers she shoved it back more until they moved in perfect rhythm, swept up in a conspiracy to beat back the nightmare plaguing him.

And when he found his release inside her and buried his cries in the lush warmth of her mouth, the sweet contentment that stole over him banished the rest of his fear.

They stood there panting, kissing, touching. In the intimacy of complete darkness, he discovered that her earlobes were amazingly sensitive, that one careless stroke of his forefinger over the inside of her wrist could send her pulse beating wildly, that she seemed to enjoy the rasp of his whiskers against the delicate skin of her neck.

She smoothed the hair back from his ear, to whisper, "I haven't heard anything in some time, have you?"

"No." He paused to listen, concentrating on what a soldier notices—the break in natural rhythms like wind and birdsong and ground vibration. "They're not nearby. But they won't have gone far."

"Then I guess we can't leave yet," she murmured.

"Not until after sunset."

She was silent a long moment, her breath hot against his cheek. "How will we know when sunset comes?"

"I'll know. Sounds change. And the temperature of this breeze coming through the grate will drop."

"Oh. I'm certainly glad one of us notices things like that."

"You'd be surprised how much you learn to notice when you're trapped underground—" He broke off as he realized what he'd revealed.

"Tell me," she murmured. "Please. If you think it won't . . . well . . ."

"Make me crazy again?" He paused, then realized that he didn't feel so panicked anymore. He still didn't like the close space and the darkness, but the breeze helped, and having her in his arms almost made it bearable.

Almost.

He slid down to the floor, urging her down, too, then sat with his back to the wall and pulled her onto his lap. When she laid her cheek against his, he steeled himself to relate his tale. "My ship was captured by the English toward the end of the war. I was taken prisoner and sent to Dartmoor Prison."

"In Devon? That's not terribly far from where I live. It's a ghastly place."

"Trust me, I know. It's why I wasn't in Baltimore when my father hanged himself. Apparently my parents didn't even know I'd been taken prisoner. They never got any of my letters. Father went to his grave believing me dead."

"That's why he killed himself."

He hesitated before speaking the lie. "Yes." The old bitterness swelled in him. "Then Mother heard from one of the earliest released prisoners that I might be at Dartmoor, so in desperation she wrote to Kirkwood. He's the one who tracked me down, then persuaded the British to release me." He gritted his teeth. "The treaty was signed at Ghent in March, yet I wasn't released until May. Some were held until as late as July."

"Which means you were there in April."

"Yes." He let out a shuddering breath.

"Oh, Lucas," she murmured, her voice achingly soft. "You were there during the massacre."

Chapter Twenty-Three

Dear Cousin,
Lady Kirkwood has finally admitted to the Toveys the
most astonishing thing—Major Winter was imprisoned
at Dartmoor during our late war. Given the horrible
events taking place during that time, Lord Tovey is now
even more worried to learn that his daughter may have
married a vengeful man.
Your concerned cousin,
Charlotte

Amelia didn't have to hear Lucas's answer; she knew. With a sinking in the pit of her stomach, she knew.

Still, when he said, "Yes, I was there during the massacre," she couldn't prevent the tears from coursing down her cheeks.

Because she finally understood why he hated the English so much. And why it would be so hard for him ever to accept her and her countrymen.

She struggled to keep the pity out of her voice, knowing he would loathe it. "Did you . . . see it happen?"

"I heard it, which was nearly as bad." He clutched her so tightly she could hardly draw breath. "When the firing began, I was taking my turn in the escape tunnel. The other prisoners hastily moved the flagstone over the shaft to hide it, not realizing I was still inside." His tone grew bitter, cold. "The redcoats were above me, killing seven of my fellow Americans and maiming over sixty others, some of whom died later. All I could do was listen to the screams."

"Good Lord." She kissed his cheek. "They said nothing about tunnels in the newspaper accounts."

"The British papers kept silent about half the things that happened at Dartmoor. About how many of us died from the cold and damp. About the outbreaks of smallpox; the starving prisoners scavenging food from offal piles—" He halted abruptly. "It's not a tale for a lady."

"I don't care—I want to hear it." Even if every bitter word broke her heart. "The way the papers told it, the prisoners were attempting to escape over the walls when the soldiers fired on them."

"And if that were true, what would it have mattered, for God's sake? The war was over and the treaty ratified. Only a damned administrative matter kept us at Dartmoor, yet Shortland, governor of the prison, still had us slaughtered! That damned haughty English—"

He halted, breathing heavily. Then his voice turned grim. "The bastard claimed at the inquiry that we were planning to wreak havoc on the countryside, but that was pure claptrap. He was just frustrated by our determined opposition."

"He did say in the papers that he'd rather have charge of two thousand French prisoners than two hundred Americans."

"We hated him, and he hated us." His body shook with outrage beneath her. "No matter what Shortland claimed, *he* was the one who ordered the soldiers to fire. Some redcoats discharged their muskets over the heads of the crowd, but the rest were animals, cutting the prisoners down like dogs. One of the dead was a man from my own ship who—"

His voice broke. When he spoke again, his tone was as hard and cold as the stone walls of the priest's hole. "I'm told he begged for his life, but the redcoats said, 'No mercy here,' and put a bullet in his brain."

Her throat ached with pain for him. "And while this was going on, you were trapped in the tunnel?"

"For two days."

A shiver swept her. "How on earth could that happen?"

When he shrugged, she felt the motion against her shoulder. "Everything was chaos the evening of the massacre. Then it took the guards the whole next morning to clean up the mess—half a day to wash away the blood of men it took only three minutes to murder and maim. And once the thousands of prisoners *were* let out of their quarters, it took hours for an accurate count to be made."

"And they forgot you still."

"Until one of my fellow prisoners, fueled by anger over the massacre, decided to go back to work in the tunnel. He found me insensible—thirsty, half-starved, and very near death."

"Oh, my darling." She threw her arms about his neck. "How awful for you!"

A shudder wracked him. "I tried to move the stone, but it normally took two men to move it from above— I couldn't move it alone from below. Soon I was forced to blow out the lantern for fear of its burning too much of the breathable air. I spent both days in the dark, wondering if I was to die gasping for breath, or if they'd come for me only to riddle me with holes like the men whose screams I—"

When he broke off raggedly, she laid her head against his and cried. She cried for him and the cruelties he'd suffered, for the soldiers he'd known, for his father who'd died believing he was dead, and even for his poor mother.

She cried because she knew he couldn't, because even now, after pouring out his soul in this dark cell, he sat rigidly, no dampness on his cheeks, no sobs erupting from his throat. He sat like a soldier and suffered in the dark, as all soldiers suffer defending their country.

"Shh, darlin', it happened long ago," he murmured. He brushed his lips over her cheek. "Shh, don't go on so."

That he could comfort *her* in such a situation made her want to cry even more. But the hoarse pain in his voice told her that her tears unsettled him, and she certainly didn't want to do that.

As she fought to restrain her turbulent emotions, he stroked her hair. "It's all right, you know," he said soothingly. "It's all right now."

"No, it's not all right," she choked out. "You can't go belowdecks on a ship, you have no family left, and you hate the English—how is that possibly 'all right'?"

He cradled her close. "I don't care if I ever go belowdecks again, you're my family now, and I don't hate all the English. Just the ones in red coats." Nuzzling her cheek, he added in a low rumble, "I could never hate you."

"You'd better not," she whispered. But there was still so much bitterness and anger left in him. She'd heard it in his voice, felt it in his taut muscles when he'd told his story. It would be many years before he could forget.

Could he ever really live contentedly with an Englishwoman? If he couldn't—

No, she wouldn't think of that. He'd said he wanted a real marriage, and she would take him at his word. Somehow she would drive the past from his mind. Somehow she would make him love her.

Tears burned her eyes. Love. Oh, what an elusive dream. Would he ever love her? *Could* he?

Because she now realized that she loved him. It had been stealing over her gradually for days, but now she knew. She loved him so much that it ached to think of it. And it would break her heart if he couldn't love her in return.

Fighting back tears, she rested her head against his shoulder. In the meantime, she would take what she could have of him. What else could she do?

"Listen, darlin'," he murmured, "we should probably try to sleep while we have the chance. When we're able to leave this damned hole, we'll have a long night ahead of us."

"I don't know if I can relax enough to sleep."

"Try." Parting his thighs, he settled her between his legs, then pressed her head to his chest. "But first, tell me—what exactly *is* a priest's hole?"

"When the Scottish Parliament made it a crime to be Catholic, and wild-eyed Protestants roamed the land seeking Papists to imprison, devout Catholic families hid their priests in specially built rooms like this.

There are priest's holes in England, too, from the days of Elizabeth, believe it or not."

"I believe it. You English love to force your enemies to hide in the dark." But the rancor in his voice had lessened, and his body was no longer stiff.

With a sigh, she settled into his arms, letting herself be lulled by his soothing warmth, his comforting embrace. And as the companionable silence stretched on, she fell asleep at last.

Lucas wasn't so lucky. Speaking about the tunnel had drawn off some of his poisonous terror, but he could never be completely easy in the total darkness of the close room.

Worse yet, speaking of the massacre had dredged up painful memories of the days after it. The British government's formal inquiry had absolved Shortland of any responsibility. Nobody had held the individual soldiers to account, because nobody had known who'd fired and who hadn't. The whole thing had been termed a tragic misjudgment, with both sides partly at fault.

Right. Unarmed men responsible for being murdered in cold blood. Not in the heat of battle, not even in the interests of war. In cold blood. And for nothing.

The injustice of it still rankled.

Amelia shifted in his arms, mumbling something, and he pushed the dark memories from his mind. Other, more important things must concern him now. He had to figure out the best strategy for escape. Should they return the way they'd come or cut across the fields and pick up the road farther down? Which would the Scots anticipate?

Such thoughts absorbed him, lulled him. After a while, the exhaustion of several sleepless days and nights on the road overtook him, and he lapsed into a fitful doze.

The dream began as always. Wearing only his prison rags, he was trapped in the tunnel, listening to the screams, choking for air, desperately groping for his knife, with the blackness always surrounding him—

He woke gasping and trembling, but this time Amelia was there, too, running her hands over him, murmuring soothing words in his ear, kissing his cheeks, his jaw, his throat. She settled him as a groom settles a fitful stallion, and beneath her tender ministrations, he finally relaxed.

This time when he slept, it was a deep and dreamless slumber.

When he next awoke, he was sprawled across the cold stone floor. And Amelia was gone.

He shot up, panic seizing him until he saw—*saw*, damn it—her faint silhouette in the open doorway with the moon rising above her head. "What are you doing?" he hissed as he rose up on his knees to jerk her back inside.

"It's after sunset. And you were right. If you really listen, you *can* tell when the sun goes down."

He stared at her dumbfounded. He'd slept all day in this hellish spot? Amazing.

Rising to his feet, he moved to the opened slab and cautiously scanned the ruin beyond. Then he slipped outside. When she started to join him, he shook his head. "Stay here. If you hear *anything* alarming, shut the slab and wait until you can escape on your own."

He left to prowl the ruin on silent feet. At the edge, he paused to stare at the woods. He saw no sign of a fire, though that didn't reassure him. They might have fled for fear that Lucas and Amelia would bring back soldiers. . . or they might be hunkered down waiting somewhere outside the ruin.

He had to take that chance. He and Amelia might not get another.

After scanning the night sky to orient himself and determine which direction they should go, he returned to the priest's hole, amazed that he could enter the cell without gasping for air. "We're leaving. But I have some instructions for you first."

"Why doesn't that surprise me?" she said, with a soft laugh.

"I didn't see any sign of the Scots, but that doesn't mean they're gone. So once we leave this chamber, we don't speak until we reach the road. Sound carries at night, and we'll have a hard enough time passing unnoticed across the fields."

"All right."

Removing his coat, he put it on her. "Hold on to my hand and don't let go unless I say. If I tell you to run, you do it and don't look back, understand?"

"Yes, Major. Whatever you say, Major."

"I mean it." He caught her face between his hands. "Don't stop to quarrel with me or try to help me. I can take care of myself. But no matter what happens, I won't rest unless you're safe."

She sighed. "Yes, Lucas."

He pressed a swift kiss to her lips, then tugged her out into the night.

Moving silently across the fields and up the ridge, they reached the road without incident and began the long walk back to Gretna Green. The moon gave them enough light to see by, though the road seemed deserted. No wonder the Scots had chosen to haunt this route.

They walked nearly a mile in silence before he felt it safe to speak. "Are you all right?" he asked softly.

"I'll live," she grumbled.

That's when he noticed her limping. "Something wrong with your foot?" he asked in alarm.

"Nothing that a decent pair of shoes wouldn't fix. These are nearly worn through. I'm afraid dinner slippers aren't designed for tramping across Scotland."

Cursing himself for not thinking of it sooner, he stopped and made her remove them. He unlaced one of his boots halfway, used his knife to slice off the top, cut the wide strip in half, and stuffed the pieces of leather inside her slippers. Maybe with the extra leather, they could hold out a while longer.

When she put the slippers back on and took a few steps, he asked, "Better?"

"*Much* better. Thank you." As they continued down the road, she threaded her arm through his. "Aren't you a handy fellow to have around for escapes from brigands and kidnappings? Since I seem to attract adventure wherever I go, I'll need a companion like you."

He groaned. "I sure hope you're joking, because many more adventures like this will be the death of me." He shot her a glance. "And I can't believe you can laugh about it."

"It's either laugh or scream, to paraphrase a certain major."

He covered her hand with his. "Had enough of adventure, have you?"

"Bite your tongue! No one can ever have enough of adventure."

He shook his head. "I swear, darlin', you're nothing like any woman I've ever met, English or otherwise."

"I do hope you mean that as a compliment, Major."

"Absolutely. You did a fine job with those Scots, slipping me the knife and keeping them distracted and the rest of it. I wish I had more soldiers like you under my command."

She beamed at him. "So I'm not much like your mother, after all?"

"Darlin', if my mother had ever been taken prisoner by Scottish brigands, she'd have fainted dead away. Or asked them to increase the ransom demand so *she* could have some of the money." He stroked her hand. "Trust me, you're nothing like my mother."

They walked a while longer in silence. Then she squeezed his arm. "Don't you even miss her?"

He thought a moment. "Sometimes, I guess. She had this habit of crooning to herself whenever she cooked. She couldn't cook worth a damn, but her singing . . ." He sighed. "She had the voice of a nightingale. Even a dinner of corn mush and lumpy gravy was good enough as a boy if I got to hear Mother sing."

"My father hums," she said. "Only he can't carry a tune, so his humming sounds more like cats mating."

"With my father, it was whistling . . ."

For the rest of their trek back to town, they spoke of their families. To his shock, talking about his parents eased some of the grief buried in him for three long years. And it made it easier to hold his tongue when Amelia told him about Dolly.

By the time they reached sleepy little Gretna Green, most of the lights were out. Despite the hour, Lucas returned to the same inn they'd left from to confront the innkeeper about his "postboy."

The innkeeper swore up and down that he'd had nothing to do with the robbery, that Jamie the postboy had only been hired the week before. Lucas was on the verge of slamming the man's head against the wall to knock some truth out of him, when a familiar voice behind him said, "What the devil is going on here? My wife and I are trying to— Winter? Is that you?"

Lucas turned to find his cousin coming down the inn stairs and gaped at him . . . until he remembered that Kirkwood had said he meant to elope with Miss Linley. Apparently he'd succeeded.

Now Kirkwood was looking from Lucas to Amelia, shock suffusing his face. "For God's sake, what happened to you two?" Then he glanced beyond them through the inn door to the empty inn yard, his shock darkening to a frown. "And what the bloody hell have you done with my bloody carriage?"

Chapter Twenty-Four

❦

Dear Cousin,
I have news! Lord Tovey received a letter saying that his
daughter and Major Winter are on their way to London,
now married. I wish I could witness the joyful reunion.
However, matters at the school have called me back
there. But as soon as I can return to London, I shall. I'm
eager to hear how dear Amelia is enjoying married life.
Your much relieved friend,
Charlotte

As it turned out, Lord Kirkwood's "bloody carriage" was in Carlisle at the very inn where the Scottish Scourge had ordered it taken. It still contained Lucas's and Amelia's belongings, but his mameluke sword had been driven into the interior's back wall, pinning in place a note:

> Tell Lord Duncannon he cannot escape the Scottish Scourge forever. One day I will come for what he owes me, and when I do, he will rue the day he denied me what is rightfully mine.

Young Jamie had vanished; apparently, the Scourge had warned the boy to flee when he'd ridden to Carlisle to leave his note. So Lucas and Lord Kirkwood spent a full day dealing with the authorities on both sides of

the border before the two couples could set off for
London in Kirkwood's carriage.

While sharing the carriage seemed a godsend to
Amelia and Lucas at first, it rapidly became a tribula-
tion. Sarah's constant chatter sent Lucas into a brooding silence. Amelia tried to steer the subject away from
how many varieties of jewels Sarah meant to buy, but
that soon proved impossible.

Even Lord Kirkwood began to show signs of strain
after the first day, and Amelia didn't know whether to
pity him or berate him. After all, he should have realized what he was agreeing to when he married Silly
Sarah for her fortune. While Amelia understood the
circumstances, it was his own fault that he'd chosen
such a flighty woman.

But if Amelia's days in the coach were vexing, her
evenings in the coaching inns were glorious. There was
no posting through the nights on their return trip, oh
no. They traveled like civilized people, at a leisurely pace.
So every evening, after dining with Lord Kirkwood and
Sarah, she and Lucas retired to their room—and their
bed—as soon as possible. As if by tacit agreement, they
didn't speak of Dolly or the Friers; indeed, they didn't
speak much at all.

They spoke with their bodies, and their bodies were
downright talkative. Amelia had never dreamed a man
could pleasure a woman so many ways, or a woman
discover so many secrets in a man's flesh. And if Lucas's
lovemaking sometimes seemed almost desperate, she
ignored that. She knew the situation with her stepmother worried him, but he would learn soon enough

that Dolly was innocent. Then the cloud over their heads would dissipate.

Still, on their last night on the road, they could no longer avoid the subject. As she and Lucas lay sated in their bed, naked bodies entwined, he stared off with that distracted gaze he had more and more of late. She brushed a kiss to his bare chest, and with a start he cast her a smile. But she could feel the tension in him as he took her left hand, then rubbed his ring.

"I'll buy you a real wedding band in the city," he said.

"I rather like this one, actually."

"It belonged to my father. My mother gave it to him in the early years of their marriage, and he wore it all his life."

She digested that a moment, thinking of how devoted her own father was to Dolly. "Lucas?"

"Hmm?" He stroked her hair. "God, I love your hair, the silky weight of it, the way it smells, everything. You've got the most beautiful hair I've ever seen."

It was such an oddly intimate thing for her taciturn husband to say that she nearly lost her nerve. But she pressed on. "I know you're eager to have this situation with the Friers resolved. But promise me you'll discuss it with Dolly privately, without Papa present. I don't want him . . . I don't think he—"

"Would approve of a wife who's a criminal?" Lucas bit out.

"Should be hurt by your baseless accusations," she countered.

A weary sigh escaped him. "I'll keep it private if I can. But only if *you* promise not to speak to her about it until I confront her. I don't want you warning her off; I want to watch her face when she hears the name Theodore Frier for the first time. You owe me that, Amelia."

She did indeed, especially after he'd put aside his own plans so gallantly for her by marrying her. "All right, as long as you keep it private."

Later that night, he had one of his dreams. When he woke her with his cries, she soothed him as best she could, but she couldn't help noticing that he hadn't had a nightmare since they'd been shut up in the priest's hole. Had talk of Dolly set it off? And if so, why?

As they neared London the next day, Amelia grew nervous. Lucas was as solemn as a priest, Lord Kirkwood seemed agitated, and even Sarah held her tongue. Between Sarah's furious parents and Amelia's wary ones, they all knew this would not be the joyous homecoming most married couples could expect.

It was nearly dinnertime when the Kirkwoods left Amelia and Lucas on the doorstep of the Tovey town house, eager to get their own homecoming over with. As Amelia reached for the massive knocker, Lucas caught her hand, a sudden heat flaring in his dark eyes. "Whatever happens, remember that we're married now. You're my wife, and that should count for something."

She tipped up her chin. "I should hope it counts for *more* than something, with you as well as me."

He sucked in a harsh breath, then pulled her close to kiss her with a passionate abandon that curled her toes. She forgot they were standing on her doorstep with probably half her neighbors looking on from behind their curtains. She forgot that her father and stepmother were inside impatiently awaiting their arrival. She forgot that she hadn't exactly *meant* to marry this stubborn, arrogant man.

When Lucas kissed her with the ardent sweetness of a lover, she remembered only that she loved him. So she kissed him back, putting her whole heart into it and praying that one day he could love her, too.

Amelia wasn't the only one putting her whole heart into it. Now that the moment of truth was near, Lucas wanted to lay claim to her before all hell broke loose. Because if he was right about Dolly being Dorothy Frier, then Amelia's affection for him would be sorely tested. And when that happened, he meant to have her firmly in *his* camp.

So he didn't exactly mind when her butler opened the door to find them in a passionate embrace. Might as well give them notice that Amelia belonged to *him*.

As Lucas slowly released her, Hopkins stammered, "Oh, I-I beg your pardon, milady, I heard voices and—"

"It's all right, Hopkins." With a strained laugh, Amelia took Lucas's hand. "And I'm not 'milady' anymore, for I've taken my husband's name. Would you please tell Papa and Dolly that we've arrived?"

There was no need. The second Amelia and Lucas crossed the threshold, two people hurried out of the dining room and rushed to grab Amelia in their arms. As the three hugged and laughed and cried, Lucas stood back watching. So this gaunt gentleman was Amelia's father. Which meant that the petite, delicate-featured female must be Amelia's stepmother.

Amelia's father looked more like a scholar than a lord, with his spectacles and his ink-stained fingertips.

Unlike Pomeroy and even Kirkwood, Lord Tovey didn't seem too concerned about appearances—his thinning brown hair stuck out in all directions, and his coat, cravat, and breeches were as rumpled as Lucas's after days of travel.

But Lucas could see the family resemblance in his eyes and wavy hair, both the same chocolate brown that he found so appealing on Amelia.

Then there was Lady Tovey. During these months of searching, he'd envisioned a sultry, auburn-haired seductress, not a freckle-faced pixie with hair that was almost orange.

It unnerved him to see his quarry in the flesh—if indeed she was his quarry. She didn't act like a deceitful woman. In fact, she was the first to pull free and include him in the reunion.

"And is this your young man, sweetheart?" she asked, her affection for Amelia apparent in every soft word.

"Yes!" Amelia exclaimed, blushing when she realized she'd abandoned him. She left her father to stand beside Lucas, sliding her hand in the crook of his arm. "Papa, Dolly, this is my husband, Major Lucas—"

"We know who he is." Lord Tovey's wary gaze assessed Lucas. "He's the man who stole my daughter from me."

Lucas narrowed his eyes at the unexpected attack. "Lord Pomeroy stole your daughter, sir. I only stole her back. And if you didn't want her stolen, you shouldn't have left her alone in London to be preyed upon by the likes of that damned fortune hunter."

Lord Tovey bristled. "I did as my daughter requested."

"A request you shouldn't have indulged, with Pomeroy sniffing around her."

Giving Lucas's arm a warning squeeze, Amelia said lightly, "Forgive my husband's harsh words, Papa. As a soldier, he tends to be overprotective of me."

"And we're very grateful for it, Major." Lady Tovey stepped forward to seize her own husband's arm. "I should have hated to see our sweet Amelia married to that awful man."

When she cast Lucas an anxious glance, he understood instantly why Amelia defended the woman so fiercely. She looked like a little lost waif, not the full-grown temptress of thirty-two that he'd thought Dorothy Frier to be.

"Yes, Papa," Amelia added. "Remember that if not for Lucas, I'd either be ruined or married to Lord Pomeroy."

"Believe me, daughter, that's the only thing keeping me civil just now. That, and the good report I've had of the major from Mrs. Harris."

"And where is Mrs. Harris?" Amelia asked blithely, smoothing over her father's gruff words.

"She was needed at the school," Lady Tovey explained. "But she urged me to have you and Major Winter ride out to visit sometime tomorrow."

"They can't do that," Lord Tovey said. "We've got to consult the lawyer about the marriage settlement. In fact, your husband and I should go back to my study right now—"

"Not yet, George," Lady Tovey protested. "We're just sitting down to dinner. Poor Amelia and her fellow probably haven't eaten yet either, although they may wish to change clothes first." She smiled at Lucas. "Lady Kirkwood had your things brought over here when she heard you were on your way, so everything is upstairs in the room adjoining Amelia's, if you wish to freshen up."

"I doubt he can wait that long," Amelia put in. "I know I can't. We're famished."

"Starving my daughter, are you?" Lord Tovey grumbled at Lucas.

"She eats whenever she wants," Lucas snapped.

"Then why is she famished?"

"Enough, Papa," Amelia said with a forced laugh. "I swear, if you continue like this, my husband will want to head back to America within the week."

That silenced her father, sobered her stepmother, and set Lucas's stomach to roiling. When he headed back to America with her stepmother in tow, would his wife be going, too? Or would she send him off with curses?

Right now she was chattering as they headed for the dining room. Lucas had noticed that Amelia tended to babble when she was nervous, and tonight was no exception. After they entered and took their seats, she launched into an amended tale of how Lucas had saved her from Lord Pomeroy.

She made her account entertaining enough to elicit a smile from her sober father. While the soup was served, she related Pomeroy's self-serving excuses for kidnapping her. During the fish course, she glossed over the drugging part to leap ahead to how Lucas had rescued her, which seemed to soften her father toward him considerably.

So Lucas, of course, reciprocated by describing the beating she gave Pomeroy with the pitcher, which actually made her father laugh and her stepmother smile. Apparently, Amelia's Amazonian side hadn't escaped their notice.

But when Amelia began to describe their wedding, Lady Tovey burst into tears.

"Dolly!" Amelia exclaimed. "What's wrong?"

"I so wanted to see your wedding," the woman wailed. "I'm sure you made a glorious bride!"

"She sure did," Lucas put in hastily, unnerved by the pixie's sobs.

"Nonsense," Amelia said, laughing. "My hair was down, and my gown was filthy. I looked like an émigré from the French Revolution."

"Not to me," Lucas answered. "You looked beautiful. You always look beautiful." As soon as the words were out of his mouth, he wished them back—they made him sound like a smitten fool.

But at least Lady Tovey had stopped crying, and Lord Tovey's frown had softened. And the dazzling smile Amelia shot Lucas made him want to leap across the table and kiss her senseless.

Damnation, this was killing him. All he wanted right now was to take his wife and flee England, forget about Dorothy and Theodore Frier, forget about his duty, forget about justice.

No, he couldn't. And if he let his wife's smiles tempt him into ignoring what he'd come here for, he wasn't any kind of man at all.

Time to start his investigation. He'd promised Amelia not to say anything that might alarm Lord Tovey, but that didn't mean he couldn't ask Lady Tovey some sly questions. "I understand that you're originally from Boston, Lady Tovey," he said in a conversational tone, watching Dolly's face.

Her gaze shot to his, suddenly wary. "I . . . well . . . my late husband was from Boston, you see." She picked up a glass of wine with a shaky hand. "I lived there while we were married." She took a swallow of wine as if to steady herself, then smiled at him. "Have you ever been to Boston, Major?"

"No, ma'am. The closest I've ever been to Massachusetts was when I visited Rhinebeck, New York."

When her face went pale, his stomach sank. He wasn't the only one to notice Dolly's reaction, for Amelia looked equally stricken.

"What were you doing in Rhinebeck?" Lady Tovey ventured.

He hesitated, wondering how far he dared go without breaking his promise to Amelia. "I was there on an assignment for the navy."

"What sort of assignment?" the woman whispered, her eyes huge in her face.

He drank deeply of his wine, more shaken than he'd expected. It was one thing to trap a brazen hussy who'd driven her lover/husband to steal a fortune from the navy and quite another to torture a defenseless pixie.

"An assignment, you say?" Lord Tovey put in. "Is this the same assignment Mrs. Harris mentioned? The investigation of some disappearance of a criminal?"

As Lucas stared at him dumbfounded, Lady Tovey whispered, "What are you talking about, dear? Mrs. Harris said nothing to me about any criminals."

Lord Tovey cast his wife an indulgent look. "I know, my love. She told me this morning before she left. She explained about Major Winter's real work here. You were so busy preparing for Amelia's arrival that I didn't bother you with it."

"How did Mrs. Harris know?" Lucas shot his wife a dark glance.

"Don't you remember, Lucas?" Amelia said hastily. "Mrs. Harris's cousin found out the information from his connection in the navy."

Right—he'd forgotten about that. And, of course, the good Widow Harris had passed the information on. Clearly Lord Tovey had no clue of its significance, which meant he was completely unaware of his wife's activities. But judging from Dolly's bloodless features, *she* was beginning to guess why Lucas was here. Apparently even pixies could have dark secrets.

"Well, Major Winter?" Lord Tovey picked at his roast beef. "Is it the same investigation? The one regarding that embezzlement from a shipping company?"

Lucas searched Dolly's face. "Yes." As she stared at him with growing confusion in her eyes, he added deliberately, "I'm hunting a man named Theodore Frier. And his female companion."

"Companion?" Lord Tovey said, completely oblivious to Dolly's distress. "There were two of these criminals?"

Lady Tovey rose abruptly. "Pardon me. I shall return shortly."

As she hurried to the door, Lord Tovey served himself more roast beef. "My wife means no rudeness, Major Winter," the man explained, "but in her condition, the smell of food sometimes upsets her stomach."

She was upset, all right. Lucas rose. "As it happens, I need to . . . er . . . use the necessary myself. Pardon me."

It was a clumsy exit, but he didn't care. He wasn't about to let Dorothy Frier flee now, if that was what she had in mind.

To his shock, however, Lady Tovey was pacing the hall when he came out. Though she looked startled to see him, she put a finger to her lips and gestured to the parlor across the way. He followed her there, his blood pounding.

She closed the door, then turned to face him, her eyes alight with anger. "I know what you want, Major Winter. If indeed you are a major."

That flummoxed him. "I assure you I am. Why would I lie about it?"

"Because you've lied about so many other things," she said hotly. "I know this tale about an embezzlement is a sham. You're here for the money." Wringing her hands, she paced to the fire. "Well, I can give you some of it. I have five thousand dollars' worth of jewels, at least." She turned to him, tears shining in her eyes. "I'm sure I can get the rest if you give me time."

He gaped at her, shocked that this had been so easy. Though she denied the embezzlement, that was probably just an attempt to save her pride. "So you admit that you're Dorothy Frier."

"Of course I admit it. I'm no fool; I know what's going on here. You married my stepdaughter to get at her fortune, since you probably thought you couldn't get your money any other way." She blinked back hot tears. "You should have come to me first. I would have given you anything to keep you quiet about my past. I still will, but only if you swear to return to America and leave my poor dear Amelia out of it. Anybody can see she's already half in love with you, so you must leave while she can still recover from her broken heart."

"I did not marry Amelia for money, damn it!" he growled.

She thrust out her chin, though it trembled violently. "Pretending to care about her won't get you any more. It's bad enough that she has no clue what a filthy blackmailer you are, but—"

"Amelia knows everything—why I'm here, who you are, and what you've done."

"Done!" Dorothy gaped at him. "I've done nothing!"

"Then why are you offering me money, why are you hiding your past—"

The parlor door swung open to reveal Amelia standing there with her father. "I'm sorry, Dolly," she said softly. "I-I tried to keep him in the dining room, but when Lucas left, he got suspicious."

"What the devil is going on here?" Lord Tovey snapped. "Major Winter, what is the meaning of this?"

For a moment, they all just stood there. Lucas was perfectly willing to tell the man, but he'd promised Amelia he wouldn't. And Dorothy was clearly torn.

Then she shifted her gaze to Amelia, and her expression changed, became almost pleading. "What exactly did your husband tell you about me, sweetheart?"

"About Dorothy Frier, you mean?" Amelia said in a whisper.

Dorothy flinched. "Yes. About me."

When Amelia's expression shattered, Dorothy turned to glare at Lucas. "What lies did you tell her? What does she think I've done?"

"She never thought you did anything," Lucas snapped as he saw the last of Amelia's hope drain from her. "You're the one who's broken her heart, damn you. I knew you were Dorothy Frier from the beginning, but she kept insisting you couldn't be the wife of Theodore Frier—"

"Wife!" Shock filled Dorothy's face. "I was not Theo's wife."

"Common law wife, lover . . ."

"I was none of those things, you horrible man!" Lady Tovey drew herself up. "I was Theodore Frier's sister!"

Sister? For a moment, Lucas's entire world tilted on its axis.

Then he reminded himself what a liar the woman was. "The hell you were—are. No one in Baltimore mentioned his having a sister, and your employer in Rhinebeck described you as Theo's estranged wife."

"That's because when I applied for the position of housekeeper, the Webbs said they wanted a married woman. So I showed them a miniature of Theo and me and said we were estranged. That part was true—I hadn't seen Theo in years. Then one day he showed up in Rhinebeck to tell me he'd given up the gambling and gotten a good job in Baltimore. I could hardly tell the Webbs I'd lied."

"Yet you expect us to believe you're telling the truth now."

"I know she is," Lord Tovey said in a hoarse voice. "She was an innocent when she came to my bed."

"George!" Dorothy said with a blush. "You shouldn't tell him such an intimate—"

"To keep this scoundrel from accusing you of God knows what, I'll tell him whatever I must." Lord Tovey glared at Lucas. "On my honor, my wife was chaste when we married. She told me Obadiah Smith was too old to consummate the marriage, and I believed her." He stepped to his wife's side. "As I believe her now when she says that this Theodore Frier is her brother."

"We'll see what Theo says when I talk to him." Lucas fixed Dorothy with a dark frown. "Where is he?"

Shakily, she slipped her hand into her husband's. "He's in Lisieux, France. But I'm afraid you won't be able to speak to him."

"Why not?"

"Because he's dead."

Chapter Twenty-Five

Dear Charlotte,
I have heard that both pairs of newlyweds have
returned to town. Rumor has it that Lord Kirkwood's
new father-in-law grudgingly agreed to the terms of the
settlement his lordship demanded. As for Major Winter,
no one has said what reaction his new father-in-law
has had to him.
Your gossiping cousin,
Michael

*D*ead?

Amelia gaped at her stepmother, as shocked as Lucas. And hurt, too, not to mention confused. Was Dolly guilty of anything? Were her claims even true?

Suspicion clouded Lucas's brow. "Frier's dead," he repeated.

"Of pneumonia." The words poured out of Dolly. "He fell into a river while drunk one winter night. He caught pneumonia and never recovered."

Lucas scowled at her. "How very convenient."

Dolly stared at him, clear-eyed. "It's the truth, no matter what you believe."

"I tracked him over half of France, and never found anyone to testify that he'd died. The last place you were together was Rouen—"

"No, it was Lisieux. We left Rouen while we still had

the lease on a cottage. He was always doing that—moving on to evade his pursuers."

"Me and the United States Navy."

"No! Those gamblers from Baltimore. The ones who got so angry when he won money in a card game that they accused him of cheating." Her eyes narrowed on Lucas. "The ones you clearly work for."

As Papa drew Dolly into the protective lee of his arm, Amelia groaned. Dolly was just the sort to believe some trumped-up tale given her by someone she loved.

"Dolly," Amelia interjected before Lucas could rage at the poor woman, "Lucas is most assuredly working for the United States Navy. He has letters of introduction describing him as a naval representative. And I know the Kirkwoods would confirm his story."

Lucas scowled at Amelia. "She knows I'm telling the truth. She's just trying to cover Frier's tracks." When he shifted his gaze to Dolly, he again became Major Winter, military investigator. "If you thought Theo had gained the money honestly, you wouldn't have let him pass you off as his wife. You wouldn't have changed your name, fled to Canada—"

"Theo told me that the gamblers would hound him to the ends of the earth for their money. And to be honest . . ." She stared down at her hands.

"Yes," Lucas snapped, "let's have some honesty for a change."

Dolly began to cry, and although Amelia knew why, she also knew Lucas would see it as the sort of tactic his mother had used to get her way.

"Leave her be," Papa snarled, enfolding Dolly in his arms. "She's told you what she knows."

"She hasn't told me half of what she knows," Lucas retorted. "All she's told me is a pack of lies."

"Lucas, please," Amelia said softly.

"You believe she was duped, too, don't you?" he ground out. "She cries, and all logic vanishes. But think, Amelia—if Frier really is dead, and your step-mother really believed he'd won his fortune in a card game, why lie about where she got it? Why invent the late Obadiah Smith? Why lie to you, to your father—"

"Because I was afraid Theo really *had* cheated!" Dolly burst out, tears coursing down her cheeks. "I couldn't bear to tell George . . ." She stared up at her husband. "I knew you'd be appalled if I told you my fortune might have come from such a thing. And I really wasn't sure if it had."

"Because it didn't, damn it!" Lucas shouted.

"I didn't *know* that, did I?" Dolly cried. "I wanted to believe Theo so badly. I was at my wit's end. Mr. Webb's wife had fallen ill, and he'd started drinking and . . . and making lewd advances. When I tried to give notice, he refused to give me a reference if I left his employ, and I had nowhere else to go. The town was small—he said he'd make sure I never worked again." She shook violently. "I wrote Theo to ask if I could come live with him, and he said yes. But Mr. Webb threatened to report me as a thief if I left, so I wrote again to tell Theo that I couldn't come—"

"And he stole a fortune." Lucas sneered at her. "For *you*. Instead of just marching up there and jerking you out. Is that what you're claiming?"

She sighed. "No. If he really did steal the money, it was for him. I'm sure he told himself he was doing it for me, but more likely he took his chance to enrich himself. That was the cause of our original estrangement. He fell into a bad way of life after our parents died, so I became a housekeeper and had nothing to do with him, until he claimed he'd reformed and wanted us to be family again. When he took that job, I believed him. But Theo had a fondness for fine things—"

"As do you," Lucas growled.

Amelia's heart sank as she watched her husband. To Lucas, Dolly was just another example of his mother.

"You begged Frier to come rescue you, didn't you?" Lucas said bitterly. "You begged him to give you a better life, and he complied."

"Enough, Major Winter," Amelia's father said, tightening his arm about Dolly's waist. "My wife is no grasping witch. Most of her money went to my estate and Amelia's dowry. I'll turn over as much of the funds as I can—providing you can prove your claims. My estate is entailed and cannot be sold, but if I auction off some things—"

"George, I won't let you sell everything you care about—" Dolly began.

"Hush, love, it doesn't matter." Her father brushed a kiss on Dolly's forehead. "I care about nothing but you and the child. And Amelia, of course, though I do hope her new husband still means to support her." He shot Lucas a disdainful glance. "Given that he married her as part of his investigation—"

"I married her to save her from ruin," Lucas snapped, clearly uneasy at the sight of her parents' visible affection. "Besides, the money doesn't matter. I

want . . . *we* want justice: Theodore Frier, tried, con-
victed, and executed for his crimes."

As Dolly flinched from the word "executed," Amelia
wondered at the vitriol in Lucas's voice. Why was he
still so determined to capture Frier?

Papa said, "My wife has already told you—he's
dead."

"Forgive me for being skeptical, sir. Your wife has
told so many lies that only solid proof of the man's
death will convince me. And I doubt she has that."

Every eye turned to Dolly, who trembled. "I-I have a
death certificate."

"Your husband . . . oh, excuse me, your *brother*,"
Lucas said snidely, "is a forger, ma'am. Forging a death
certificate wouldn't take him much effort."

"If you won't believe *me*, then go see his grave in
Lisieux," Dolly said.

"Anyone can erect a gravestone," Lucas retorted.

"There was a local man who prepared his body. His
name is Lebeau. I'm sure if you go there and speak to
him—"

"Right. Then when I can't find him, you'll tell me he
must have moved away. Or died. You have an answer
for everything, don't you, Dorothy?"

"Don't call my wife that!" Papa put in. "She's Lady
Tovey now, and you will address her with the proper
respect."

Amelia groaned. *Oh, Papa, that is the last thing you
should say to my arrogant husband if you want to save
Dolly.*

The look of icy disdain crossing Lucas's face would
have shamed even a duke. "I'll be sure to remember that

advice when I arrest her and take her back to America so she can tell her lies to my government in person."

"Lucas, no . . ." Amelia began.

"She's done nothing wrong!" her father protested.

"Except lie about Frier's whereabouts. And if I have to take her into custody to bring her brother out of hiding, I sure as hell will."

"You're not taking my wife anywhere, damn you. She's carrying a child, and she's fragile. I won't risk losing another wife in childbirth. Especially when she has told you everything she knows!"

Eyes glittering, Lucas crossed his arms over his chest. "Can you prove that?"

Papa didn't answer, because he couldn't. Neither could Amelia. Yet she knew in her heart Dolly was guilty of nothing but blindly trusting her brother, the way she blindly trusted everyone she loved.

"Lucas," Amelia said, "be reasonable."

His gaze swung to her, so icily distant it froze her blood. "I'm not letting Frier escape justice on the strength of his sister's word."

Why did it matter so? Because Frier was born English? "At least investigate Dolly's tale before you take such drastic action as to take her back to America. Go to France—see if her brother's grave is there."

"And then I'd return to find you all decamped, wouldn't I? You'd be somewhere I couldn't find you, while she'd be off meeting with her brother wherever he's hiding now."

"How could you think I'd consent to such a deception?" Amelia's heart broke to see him regard her with such distrust after what they'd been through.

"What if I were to travel to France with you, Major Winter?" her father put in. "Dolly and Amelia could remain here while you and I gather proof of my wife's claims. I'd be your surety for Dolly." He added in as snide a tone as any Lucas had used, "That way, if my pregnant wife did happen to run off, you could haul *me* to America. Would that arrangement satisfy your demand for justice?"

Lucas went rigid. "That wouldn't keep her from writing to alert him. For all I know, he's hiding in the next county—"

"I won't let you take my wife. I'll fight you in the courts first."

"Don't try to bluff me, sir," Lucas said coldly. "Going to court would mean having this all come out in the papers, and you'd never risk the scandal."

"The scandal is nothing to me. What I won't risk is losing my wife or child to your dubious justice." His gaze narrowed on Lucas. "And before we go any further, I expect you to prove your claims about my wife's brother."

"Yes, Major Winter," Dolly put in, desperation in her voice. "You claim that Theo stole the money, but my husband said at dinner that it was embezzled from some company called Jones Shipping. So my brother couldn't possibly have stolen it."

Lucas released a low curse.

"Why not?" Amelia asked, suddenly very afraid that she knew the answer.

"Because the company Theo worked for wasn't Jones Shipping," Dolly explained. "It was Baltimore Maritime."

Chapter Twenty-Six

~∞~

Dear Cousin,
I do hope Amelia will adjust well to her new situation.
The major can be a difficult man, I suspect. But if any
woman can weather his temper, it is Amelia.
Your devoted friend,
Charlotte

Hellfire and damnation. Lucas had nearly gotten through this without Amelia's learning the whole truth. But he should have known her stepmother would seal his doom.

He dragged in a breath. Maybe Amelia wouldn't remember the name of his father's company. Had he even told her?

When he swung his gaze to her to find her frozen, her eyes accusing him, his gut twisted. She remembered.

"You lied to me," she whispered, her eyes huge in her face.

"No," he said. "I just didn't tell you everything."

She stepped forward, her eyes glittering. "It's a rather important thing to leave out, don't you think? That your father hanged himself not only because he thought you were dead, but because Frier's embezzlement destroyed his company." Her eyes widened. "That's why your family fortune 'vanished' a few years ago, isn't it?"

Slowly, he nodded. "I couldn't tell you. It was part of my investigation—"

"Balderdash!" Her pretty cheeks flushed with her anger. "You couldn't tell me because then you'd have to admit this isn't just about doing your duty or capturing a criminal. It's about revenge for your father."

"It's about justice, damn it!" His temper flared. "And that's exactly why I didn't tell you. Because I knew you'd assume that I wasn't being fair, that I was trumping up the charges for personal reasons."

"Aren't you? The navy spoke of Jones Shipping, so how—"

"Jones Shipping *was* involved," Lucas clipped out. "So were the navy and my father's company." He sucked in a heavy breath. "Jones Shipping contracted with the navy to provide several ships and refit others. That included thousands of cannon, which Baltimore Maritime contracted to Jones Shipping to provide."

"An endeavor that Theodore Frier oversaw, I take it?" she whispered.

"An endeavor that Theodore Frier methodically drained of all funds."

"And your father was blamed," she said, with her usual uncanny insight.

"Of course he was," Lucas said hollowly. "Frier forged Father's signature week after week, siphoning money out of the Jones Shipping account, then shifting the stolen funds to a bank in another county."

"Theo was always good with numbers," Dolly put in.

Furious, Lucas cast her a cold glance. "That's why Father hired him. And because my mother was taken with the man, with his English background and his fine manners." He ignored the clear remorse on her face as the ancient wound festered in his gut. "So the cannon were cast and the employees paid, while the bills for materials mounted unseen and unpaid."

He glared at Dorothy. "Then your brother fled, leaving behind a mountain of financial obligations and my father's signature on the bank documents. So the navy and Jones Shipping went after my father, believing he and Frier were in the plot together. They hounded him until he gave Jones Shipping his own precious company to make up the losses. He auctioned off everything he loved, and once he'd done all he could to make it right, he . . . he . . ."

"Hanged himself," Amelia said softly.

Lucas faced his wife. "Yes. By then Mother despised him for letting the embezzlement happen, and Father thought I was dead anyway. He had nothing left to live for. Nothing."

Lord Tovey looked stricken. "You would have inherited your father's company if not for my wife's brother. So it's not the American navy to whom the money is owed, or even this Jones Shipping. It's you."

"I don't care about the money," Lucas growled. "I don't want a damned thing for myself."

"Except Theodore Frier," Amelia said.

"Oh yes. *That* I do want. I want Frier to hang like my father. I want justice, and after what he did to my family, I *deserve* justice."

"Of course you do," Amelia said. "You even deserve revenge. But against *him*—not Dolly. You can't hang a dead man, Lucas."

"I have only your stepmother's word that the man is dead." Lucas didn't want Frier to be dead. He couldn't stand that the bastard might have escaped the humiliation of a trial, the torment of a public hanging. It wasn't right, damn it!

Amelia gestured to her stepmother. "Come now, Lucas, you can't really think she's capable of engineering some plot to hide her brother—"

"She's shown herself capable of lying to protect him, hasn't she?" It infuriated him that his wife continued to take her stepmother's side. "So if I have to cart her off to America to prove she's lying, then I will."

"You just want to torment her because you can't torment *him*. The only thing she's guilty of is being foolish enough to trust her wicked brother."

"And you're foolish enough to trust *her*, Amelia," Lucas bit out, even though her words held a certain truth. "Even you must admit you aren't the best judge of character. You thought Pomeroy was harmless."

She fixed him with a haunted look. "You're right—I *am* a poor judge of character." Her voice lowered to an aching whisper. "After all, I was foolish enough to trust *you*. But no more. No more."

When she turned on her heel and stalked from the room, he stared after her. No more? What the hell did *that* mean? What did she mean to do?

He headed after her, then paused to tell his new father-in-law, "We can discuss this further in the morning. I'll have my evidence ready for you then, and I'll expect to see this 'death certificate' your wife claims to have." When Lord Tovey nodded in consent, Lucas added, "If your wife goes missing before then, sir, or makes any attempt to reach her brother, I will hold *you* accountable, do you hear?"

"We'll both be here in the morning, I assure you," the earl said stiffly.

Lucas went after his wife.

He found her swiftly climbing the stairs and stalked up after her. "Where are you going?"

"To my room."

"Our room, you mean."

"I mean *my* room. I'll have a servant move my things."

"No, you won't." He had to quicken his pace to keep up with her; she was racing up the stairs like bloodhounds were after her. "This changes nothing between us."

"It changes everything. I'm not sharing a bed with you until you come to your senses."

"Until I agree with *you*, you mean." He followed her down the long hall to a door at the far end. "Until I pat your stepmother on the head, and say, 'Thanks for the information, ma'am, and sorry I interrupted your cozy life.'"

"If I thought you were merely doing your duty, Lucas, I wouldn't interfere." When he snorted, she cast him a heartbreaking glance. "But you're not merely doing your duty, and we both know it."

She entered the room and turned to close the door in his face, but he thrust his foot forward to block it. His temper erupting, he forced his way in, then turned and shut the door behind him.

"Please leave," she whispered.

"Not until we settle this. When we married, you agreed that if your stepmother proved to be Dorothy Frier, you'd let me deal with her as I saw fit."

"That's not what I said. I said that if she'd played a part in the embezzlement, she deserved to be captured. But she didn't. And she doesn't."

"The point is, she traveled with Frier spending the money, so she's the only one who can lead me to the man."

"He's dead, and you know it!" Her hands curled into fists. "In your heart, you know it." As he glared at her, struggling to ignore the niggling fear that she was right, she softened her voice. "But if you admit he's dead, you have no justice at all. So you've let your desire for revenge blind you to the truth."

"And you've let the spurious claims of a sweet-faced female blind you to the facts," he ground out.

"What facts? Have you any evidence that Frier is *alive?*"

He clenched his jaw. He didn't. His evidence actually supported Dorothy's story, because he'd found no trace of the man after Rouen. But only because Frier must have realized someone was pursuing him and decided to separate from his sister to throw off their pursuers.

Unless Dorothy wasn't lying, after all.

"Just as I thought," she said softly. "You have no facts."

"Damn it, I can't simply close this investigation on the word of a woman who's admitted to multiple untruths—"

"Exactly: she's admitted to them. The only thing she won't admit to is what *you* don't want to hear. Even her own husband believes her—"

"Because it's either that or accept that his wife could be shielding a criminal, and he's not going to accept the latter."

"Yet you can readily accept that your own wife is a fool. Or worse yet, that she'd actively seek to deceive you if you turned your back."

"This isn't about us, Amelia," he said sharply.

"Isn't it?" She strode up to him. "I married you when every instinct told me I was mad to do so, and do you know why?"

"Because you didn't want to live as a ruined spinster in Torquay?" he bit out.

"If that were why, I'd have married Pomeroy, who wasn't seeking to destroy my family." She faced him squarely. "I married you because I trusted you. Because you were honorable and just, and I knew you'd do the right thing by Dolly."

Her lower lip trembled. "But that was before I realized that the hatred burning in your heart was so powerful, it could overwhelm your more rational impulses."

"Rational! You think it's rational to take the word of a liar?"

"No one's asking you to do that. *I'm* not asking you to do that. I'm asking you to give her story a chance. Go to France. See if you can determine the truth by independent means. Then if you can't, and you still want to drag my family through the courts—"

"You'll accept my decision," he said sarcastically.

"Yes. Because then I'll know you aren't just trying to strike back at us because you can't strike back at Theodore Frier."

He sucked in a breath, disturbed that his wife could read his emotions so well. The truth was, he was already leaning toward doing as her father had asked, if only to satisfy his conviction that her stepmother's claims were false.

But having his pretty little wife demand it sparked his temper. He'd sworn not to let her lead him about by the nose, and now she was testing that. "And if I don't go to France? How long will you punish me by refusing me your bed?"

She cast him a look of weary regret. "If you don't at least confirm her story, then I won't be refusing you my bed, Lucas. I'll be refusing you everything. You can do whatever you want, but *I* will be living with Papa and Dolly, helping them through the scandal *you* set into motion to flush out a dead man."

The words crashed over him like waves battering a ship's hull. She meant to leave him. After all they'd endured together, she would still—

"The hell you will." The panic squeezing his chest was worse than any he'd endured in the priest's hole. "Have your fit of temper if you must, but you're my wife, and I won't let you force my hand with idle threats."

"It's not an idle threat," she said. "I can't live with a man I can't trust."

He fought to hide the terror that her assertion roused in his chest. "As I recall, darlin'," he said, struggling to keep his tone unaffected, "our marriage vows didn't include the word 'trust.' But I do remember something about you obeying me."

"And that's what you want? A wife who will obey you blindly, like the soldiers under your command? Who will never voice her own opinion, never make demands on you?"

What he wanted was for her not to leave him. But he'd be damned if he'd admit that. "It doesn't matter what I want, because I won't get it, will I? You couldn't be an 'obedient wife' if your life depended on it."

"And you don't *want* blind obedience in a wife, no matter what you think."

He suddenly saw his chance to get what he *did* want—his pride preserved, and his wife where he wanted her.

"Why don't we find out, darlin'? If you'll be my obedient wife for one night, I'll go to France. But you have to do exactly what I say. Because if you fail, if you show your usual willfulness, then I'll do as I please with your stepmother, and there will be no more talk of living apart. Agreed?"

What an excellent strategy! His wife had failed at playing a half-wit when they first met; she'd never manage "blind obedience" for a whole night. So when she failed this, too, he'd win what he wanted.

Then, when he magnanimously agreed to go to France in the morning, it wouldn't look as if he'd given in to her demands, but was being generous. And once he'd determined in France that he was right about Theo Frier, she wouldn't object when he used her stepmother to flush the man out of hiding.

It was a brilliant plan—if she accepted the challenge.

For a moment, he feared she wouldn't. Her eyes narrowed as she searched his face. Then she flashed him a suspiciously bright smile. "As you wish, my husband. When do we start?"

Chapter Twenty-Seven

Dear Charlotte,
You have good cause to worry about Lady Amelia and
her husband. An American marine officer is unlikely to
tolerate impudence in a wife, and of all your pupils,
Lady Amelia seems the most capable of impudence.
Your equally impudent cousin,
Michael

Now is as good a time as any," Lucas said.

Amelia nodded. Not for nothing had she spent the past few nights warming her husband's bed. She knew what he liked, and she'd begun to learn what he expected of her. An obedient wife wasn't it, no matter what he told himself.

But it was time that *he* learned it. Whenever Amelia tried to reason with him, he balked at the challenge to his authority. She didn't mean to have that battle every time some matter arose that they couldn't agree upon. Nor did she intend to watch him destroy their future—and her family's—because he couldn't put his past behind him. If being obedient was what it took to get him to go to France, she'd do it. Because once he was there looking at a grave, once he'd talked to the people in Lisieux, how could he possibly ignore the facts?

So she would be obedient tonight if it killed her. And judging from the gleam in her devilish husband's eyes, he meant to make sure that it did.

He strode over to her favorite armchair and settled himself in it, then gestured to the bags that had been brought over from Lord Kirkwood's house. "You can begin, wife, by unpacking those and stowing everything away." As she nodded and headed for the bags, he said, "And I want everything neatly folded. None of your messy habits, do you hear?"

She gritted her teeth.

For the next two hours, he barked orders like a general at the front lines, until she started to wonder if she'd been daft to marry a military man. After the unpacking came more intimate duties. He ordered her to remove his coat, waistcoat, cravat, and boots, which she did with the same cool efficiency *he* always showed.

When he commanded her to clean and polish his boots, she had to forcibly hold her tongue. He was giving her a servant's duties when they both knew that officer's wives didn't do such menial tasks. He was trying to bend her to his will as an officer bends a soldier to his.

Very well, let him do his best. He'd soon learn the depths of a woman's will.

By the time she was done with his boots and they shone to a high gloss, Lucas didn't look quite as smug as when they'd begun. No doubt he'd expected her to give up being "obedient" before she got to this point.

He eyed her for a long while, and finally pointed to the door. "Your stepmother cut short my dinner, wife. Go downstairs and assemble a tray of food suitable to assuage my hunger, then bring it up."

"Yes, husband," she said in the same mousy voice she'd used all evening.

This time it made him arch one eyebrow. "And no purgatives."

"Certainly not," she said as she turned for the door, though the idea grew more appealing by the moment.

She took the backstairs to avoid running into her parents, but then dawdled in the kitchen. He hadn't said to hurry, after all.

In fact, there were a number of things he hadn't been specific about. Perhaps it was time she took this obedience game to the extreme.

When she returned to the room some time later with a tray containing black bread, sausage, and stewed apples, her frowning husband had moved to her bed. He was sitting propped against the headboard with his legs stretched out, his stocking feet crossed at the ankles, and his shirt unbuttoned.

"You took your sweet time, didn't you?" he grumbled.

"The kitchen staff has retired for the night," she said, as if that explained everything.

Despite his obvious displeasure, she didn't approach him with the tray after pushing the door shut behind her. Instead, she stood there perfectly still.

"Well?" he said. "What are you waiting for?"

She hid a smile. "Your orders. I don't know where you want the tray."

With a scowl, he tapped the bedside table beside him. Giving him a servantlike nod, she walked over and placed it there, making sure to give him a thorough glimpse of bosom when she bent over. His sharp intake of breath afforded her some satisfaction.

That satisfaction only increased when he hauled her onto his lap. She sat there primly, regarding him with the expressionless gaze of a soldier as he studied her. Then he glanced over at the food, and his scowl deepened. "You know I don't like sausage or black bread."

"You said food. You didn't specify what you wanted."

"Wouldn't an *obedient* wife bring what her husband likes?"

"Blind obedience is what you demanded. Since you didn't say what meal to bring you, I gathered what was ready to hand." She smiled sweetly. "I brought you apples, and you like those."

"I sure do. So why don't you feed me some?"

His husky voice sent desire curling in her belly. Drat him. If he turned her ploy into a sensual game, she'd never be able to make her point.

Then again, perhaps she could use even that to her advantage. "All right," she murmured, wriggling her bottom as she reached forward for the fork.

"Not with that," he said. "With your fingers."

No doubt he was waiting for her to protest that stewed apples didn't lend themselves to that manner of eating, or complain about his eating on her bed.

She wouldn't give him the satisfaction. Forcing a smile, she picked up a slice of apple, dredged it heavily in juice, then carried it dripping to his mouth.

With the juice trickling down his chin, he ate the apple, then pointed to his jaw. "Clean this up."

"I'll fetch a rag." She started to leave his lap.

"No," he drawled. "Use your mouth."

Her mouth? Oh, he was devious. If she licked his chin, matters would progress naturally.

So she'd have to thwart him. "As you wish, husband," she murmured, then leaned forward and scraped the juice from his jaw with her teeth.

"Ow!" He jerked back to scowl at her. "What are you doing?"

"You said use your mouth."

"You know very well what part of the mouth I meant."

She cocked her head. "I would never dare to assume—"

He cut off her words with a kiss and she nearly responded, seduced by the taste and touch and scent of him. But she caught herself and forced herself to sit unmoving while his mouth caressed hers and his tongue pressed against her closed lips.

"Kiss me back," he growled.

So she did, but only with her mouth. She kept her body still as a stone, her hands folded in her lap.

At first, he didn't seem to notice. He plundered her lips as ardently as ever, his tongue driving deep as his hands swept knowingly over her hips, her belly, her breasts. But when she continued just to sit there, he drew back to glare at her. "I said, kiss me back."

"I am."

"But you're not touching me."

"I'll be happy to touch you as soon as you tell me what to touch. And how. And when."

"So that's your game. If I don't give the exact command, you don't act."

"I'm merely being an obedient—"

"The hell you are." He stared at her a long moment. "Fine. I'm more than happy to command you in even the smallest detail because sooner or later you'll rebel. You can't help yourself."

She just stared at him, more determined than ever to continue her campaign of passive resistance.

"Stand up and take off your clothes," he demanded. "Oh, and in case you mean to misinterpret the word 'clothes,' I want you naked. Understand?"

"Perfectly," she said, and rose to her feet.

She started out slowly, but within seconds her husband anticipated that teasing tactic, and murmured, "Quickly, darlin'. You have one minute."

To unhook and unsnap and unlace *everything*? Drat him, he was determined to tax her patience. It took her the full time, so only when she was done and standing there while he looked her over did she realize how unnerving it was to be fully naked before a clothed man. The last time she'd stood naked before him, he'd been naked, too. That had felt far, far different.

This felt more like their encounter on the xebec, when she was his "captive." But that had been a game, with stakes smaller than these. Because theirs wasn't a game. It was a war. And it remained to be seen who'd win it.

He took his time about looking her over, letting his intimate gaze linger on her unbound breasts, her trembling belly, the rapidly dampening curls at the juncture of her thighs.

She had to dig her fingers into her palms to keep from covering herself. When at last he lifted his eyes to hers, she could read in them a determination to conquer her that mirrored her own.

"Do you remember our wedding night," he asked, "when you wanted to watch me pleasure myself?"

Warily, she nodded.

He smiled with all the sly charm of a born seducer. "Now it's your turn. I want to watch you pleasure yourself."

Lord help her. A blush spread over her cheeks as she realized what he meant.

But she could never . . . had never . . . well, she *had*, but not like this. She'd touched herself in the secrecy of her own bed, under the sheets, furtively. This would be utterly mortifying.

And he knew it, too, the wretch, for his smile broadened. "*Now,* wife. Put your hand between your legs and caress your tender parts for my enjoyment."

She searched frantically for a way to misconstrue his request, but she was too flustered to think of one. Blushing from head to toe, she did as he demanded.

Her flesh was already damp and aroused, but now it seemed to pulse against her fingers, so violently that she was sure he could see it. She wouldn't know, however, because she couldn't bear to watch him watch her.

He realized that at once. "Look at me, darlin'," he said, in that sensuous drawl that always sent delicious shivers down her spine.

She lifted her gaze to find him staring not at her busy hand, but at her flushed face.

"Use your other hand to caress your breasts," he ordered.

When she did so, however, he didn't watch that; he just kept watching her face.

Then she realized what he was doing. It was her reaction that mattered to him, her embarrassment that he wanted. And perhaps he also wanted to see her lose herself in pleasure and give up the control that he wanted to gain for himself.

Hah! Now she knew how to thwart him.

So she did exactly as he said, caressing the slick petals of flesh, rubbing her finger over the tight, aching little nodule. But she steeled herself against any reaction, though it took every ounce of her will. She forced herself to caress her body mechanically, as if she were grooming herself or brushing her teeth.

It wasn't easy with him watching her, searching her face, hoping for signs of a break in her control. But having his heated gaze on her sparked her temper, making it easier for her to be cool and distant as she worked her fingers over her private parts.

The longer she did it, the deeper his scowl became until his eyes were blazing at her, not just with desire but with anger. "Come here, damn you."

"As you wish, husband." She approached the bed, ruthlessly suppressing her smile of triumph. He could command her to do many things, but he couldn't command her to feel pleasure, and he was finally beginning to realize that.

"Undress me," he ordered.

"As you wish, husband," she repeated blithely.

"And stop saying that," he growled.

"All right."

She set about undressing him, but it was more diffi-

cult than she expected. Not so much because of the
awkwardness of getting trousers off a seated man—an
aroused, seated man—but because she could smell him
and feel his breath quick and hot against her cheeks.

After she'd stripped him down to his drawers, he
launched into a new torment. He began to kiss and
touch her. As she worked the buttons free, he kissed her
cheek, her brow, her ear. He took down her hair, caressing it, rubbing it . . . twining it over her breasts over
and over.

And then, when he had her nipples taut and aching,
eager for a firmer caress, he stroked them . . . but with a
feathery touch that could only arouse, not satisfy, until
it was all she could do not to shove her breasts in his
mouth and beg him to suck them.

Which was exactly what he wanted.

Beast. Devil. She wouldn't let him win. She would *not*.

She worked his drawers off, fighting to ignore his
caresses. But it was not so easy to ignore the rampant
erection that reared up before her very eyes, demanding her attention.

When he caught her staring at it, he said hoarsely,
"Touch me."

Her gaze swung to his, and the savage intensity of
those dark eyes nearly banished her resolve.

But her will was stronger. Holding his gaze with a
perfectly cool one of her own, she very deliberately
fondled . . . his ankle.

A foul oath erupted from him. "You know damn
well that I want you to touch my—" He caught himself. "Never mind, I have a better idea. Get up on the
bed astride me."

She blinked, not quite certain what he meant, but when she climbed up over his legs, he caught her by the waist, then positioned her so that she sat straddling his thighs just below his erection.

"Put my cock inside you where your fingers just were," he rasped, leaving no room for misinterpretation.

So *that's* what he wanted. How very intriguing and different . . . and adventurous. Of course. The devious scoundrel knew exactly how to tempt her to lower her guard.

Could she do what he asked without succumbing to him?

She could. She must. Tonight she was fighting for their future.

Casting him a curt nod that deepened his scowl but didn't seem to dampen his arousal, she maneuvered herself onto his rigid staff, which took some doing since he still sat with his back against the headboard. But when she sank down fully, fitting herself firmly against his groin, he slid his eyes shut with a look of pure ecstasy.

"Yes, darlin', like that." His fingers dug her into hips. "Damnation, you feel good."

He felt good, too, so good that the urge to move against him was nearly irresistible. But resist the urge she did. She sat there immobile, careful not to touch him except where they were joined.

After a moment, his eyes shot open. "Move, damn it."

"All right." She placed her hands on her thighs and stroked in circles.

The glare he cast her would have set fire to a glacier. "Up and down, Amelia."

Struggling not to smile, she ran her hands up and down her thighs.

"Amelia . . ." he said in a warning tone.

"Isn't that what you want?" she said innocently.

"You know damned well it's not. I want you to make love to me."

"Then you'll have to be more specific in your requests," she chirped, enjoying herself. "How exactly do I make love to you? What part should I move first? Where? How often? When do—"

"Damn you." Seizing her head in his hands, he kissed her with a desperation that resonated deeply in her loins. Still she sat there, not touching him, not moving.

He ripped his mouth from hers to growl, "An obedient wife would know what I want of her."

"She'd be able to read your mind? How extraordinary. I didn't realize that such a talent came along with obedience." She cast him a mischievous smile. "And you know perfectly well that any mealymouthed, blindly obedient wife wouldn't be sitting atop your lap unless you demanded it. She'd be too embarrassed. And too busy groveling at your feet. In fact, if I were to be a truly obedient wife—"

She started to lift up off his cock, and he caught her to him. "Enough," he growled against her ear. "Enough, you teasing, impudent plague of a woman. Give me what I want, Amelia."

"An obedient wife?" she whispered, as he skated his mouth over the pulse beating furiously in her throat.

He hesitated, then let out a heartfelt groan. "No. You. Just you. You're the only one I want."

She sucked in a breath, not daring to believe that she'd won. "And in the morning? What then?"

His hands slid down to cup her breasts, to rub the nipples erect once more, and his mouth was warm and tender as it laved her ear. "I'll go to France, all right? Just give me my Delilah back." He pumped his hips beneath her as his hands feverishly caressed her breasts. "Please, darlin' . . . be my Delilah tonight . . . because in the morning we begin a very long dry spell . . ."

That was all it took to make her move, to have her throwing her arms about his neck and showering his face with kisses. She undulated against him, sliding up and down on his cock, pumping it fervently.

They'd never made love this way before, but she felt as if she'd been born to do it. It was the most exquisite sensation yet, having him deep inside her while at the same time having control, being able to press herself hard against him exactly where she wanted to *feel* him hard against her.

"Yes . . ." he rasped as she rode his cock in a fever of need. "Yes, Delilah, yes . . . faster, darlin' . . . God have mercy . . . faster, faster . . ."

She did exactly as he asked. Since she'd won, she could afford to be generous. And he responded to it with all the fervency she could desire, his fingers plucking her nipples, his mouth plundering hers and giving her such rich pleasure, she thought she would die of it.

As she ground down upon his cock over and over, the tension building inside her, she tore her lips from his. "Is this what you want?" she demanded, feeling her own release just beyond her, out of her reach. "Is this what my big, strapping soldier of a husband wants?"

"You know it is," he said, his voice raw, guttural. He nipped her lip, then soothed it with his tongue. "I want you, darlin' . . . just you . . ."

She fisted her hands in his hair, her legs aching from the force of her motions. "But only . . . if I do as you say."

"Do as you want." His eyes slid shut. "Do as you please . . . just don't . . . leave me."

Her throat tightened. "I won't," she vowed.

"If you try, I'll hunt you . . . to the ends of the earth."

The fierce words sent a thrill coursing through her. It was the closest Lucas had ever come to a declaration of love, and she cradled it to her heart. "No need for that." She brushed a kiss to his lips, his closed eyelids. "I'll never leave you, my love."

At the word "love," his eyes shot open to search her face. "You won't rest . . . until you . . . have me broken and bleeding at your feet . . . will you?"

Leave it to Lucas to see "love" as defeat. Even as she ground her hips more urgently, feeling the rush to release seize her, she fixed him with a fiery glance. "I won't rest . . . until you love me . . . as I love you . . ."

The look of yearning that came over his dark features was so powerful even his scowl couldn't disguise it. "God have mercy on me," he groaned. "Because it's damned certain . . . that *you* won't."

Then they were straining together, pounding, thrusting, lost to anything but each other, to their mutual need and desire and . . . dare she hope . . . love.

As he spilled his seed inside her and cried out her name with all the fervency of a vow, all the desperation of a prayer, she clutched him close and let her love wash over them both, hoping it was enough, swearing she would make it enough.

And long after she collapsed atop him, long after their hearts had settled into a more normal rhythm, and she lay spent and sated across his powerful body, she repeated the vow to herself. She loved him. And somehow she'd teach him to love her.

He stretched out and dragged her into his embrace, pressing her head to his chest and brushing her hair with his lips.

It was only later, after his breath had grown even and she was certain that he slept, that she roused the courage to say again, in a furtive whisper, "I love you, Lucas." Then she gave herself up to the sweet exhaustion tugging her own eyelids closed.

When next she awakened, he was gone, and the sun was streaming through her filmy curtains. She jerked upright in a panic, cursing her tendency to sleep like the dead. Surely he wouldn't have left without telling her good-bye!

But a cursory examination of the room showed that his knapsack was gone, along with his boots and some of his clothes. An unnamed fear gripping her, she dragged a nightrail and a wrapper over her body, then hurried down the stairs.

She found Dolly sitting in the breakfast room, staring vacantly out the window.

"Where's Lucas?" Amelia asked.

When Dolly turned to Amelia, her eyes were red. "Gone to France with your father. Didn't you know?"

"I did, but . . ." She sank into a chair. She'd hoped he

might say *something* before he left, something to give her hope for their future.

"George suggested that you and I return to Torquay to await their return. The season is ending anyway, and if you stay here, you'll have to deal with gossip about the elopement." She stared down at her hands. "This way, we can start the tale that you and Lucas are on your honeymoon. No one need know that you're in Torquay. Besides, if George has to make arrangements to sell the town house upon his return—" She broke off with a little sob.

"Oh, Dolly," Amelia said, forcing her own troubles to the back of her mind. She hurried to sit beside her stepmother and put her arm about her shoulders. "Everything will be fine, I promise. Lucas will never demand money of Papa, you'll see. And in France he'll find proof that your brother is dead, and that will be an end to it."

"*You* believe me about Theo, don't you?" Dolly said in a plaintive whisper. "You believe I never set out to deceive you?"

"Of course, dearest. Of course."

Tears slid down her cheeks once more. "I wouldn't blame you if you didn't, you know. I saw your husband's evidence this morning, all the banking documents and newspaper reports and—" She broke off with a choked cry. "Theo was every bit as bad as your husband claimed—a bounder, a scoundrel, a thief."

"You didn't know," Amelia said softly.

"I did," Dolly protested. "Deep down, I suppose I knew. I just didn't want to face it."

When she burst into sobs, Amelia drew her into her arms and murmured soothing nonsense, wondering what she would have done in Dolly's place. Probably brained Theo Frier with a pitcher. And that wicked fellow in Rhinebeck, too.

But that wasn't Dolly's way. She always wanted to believe the best of people, and when she couldn't, she retreated. Or, in the case of those she loved, avoided the truth. Dolly had spent a lifetime hiding from things, and Theo Frier had taken advantage of that.

After a while, when her sobs lessened, Dolly pulled away. "Listen to me, sweetheart. You mustn't let any of this come between you and your husband."

"It's all right, I—"

"No, I mean it." A soft smile touched her lips. "I won't have you lose him over me. Anyone with eyes can see that Major Winter adores you."

Amelia's heart tightened in her chest. If he did, he had an odd way of showing it, running off to France without even so much as a kiss good-bye. "Do you really think so?"

Dolly nodded. "Of course, your father feels differently. He's too angry to see it." She gave a small smile through her tears. "He spent half the night vowing to thrash the major."

Amelia gave a bitter laugh. "That's not a surprise. I spend half my days vowing to thrash the major."

"And the other half? How do you spend *them*?"

Her throat tightened. "Wanting to hold him so close, he can never doubt that I love him."

Dolly beamed at her. "I'm sure he knows, sweetheart. And I'm sure he loves you, too."

Lord, she hoped so. Because she didn't know how she'd survive if he didn't.

Chapter Twenty-Eight

❦

Dear Cousin,
Amelia's husband and father have gone to France on an
errand neither she nor her stepmother will divulge. It
has made my dear pupil very melancholy, which tells
me that poor Amelia is in love with the major. I can
only hope for her sake that he feels the same. As I
learned very well from my marriage, loving a man who
does not love you leads to nothing but disappointment.
Your anxious cousin,
Charlotte

I love you, Lucas.

Lucas had expected those words to eventually lose their power over him. Yet after a week spent crossing the Channel, then trudging across the same French countryside he'd traversed barely a month ago, they only consumed him more. They glittered in every morning dawn, they beat through every step he took, they swirled maddeningly through his dreams at night.

They succored him after every chilling nightmare.

At first he'd tried to convince himself that Amelia had spoken them only to manipulate him. But after days reliving every moment he'd spent with his wife, he'd given up believing that. If he ever had.

Amelia wasn't his mother. If she had been, she would have said she loved him the first time she'd thought it might gain her something, like when she was first ruined. She'd have thrown the words at him when she'd begged him to show her stepmother mercy.

She wouldn't have said them after she'd made her point. She wouldn't have burst out with them in the midst of their lovemaking. She certainly wouldn't have whispered them when she'd thought him asleep.

So he had to accept them as truth: she loved him. His bewitching Delilah of a wife loved him. And instead of racing back to England to swear his undying devotion, he was standing in a graveyard in Lisieux with his gruff father-in-law.

Throughout their long trip, Lucas and Lord Tovey had discussed Lucas's military career, his prospects as a consul, even his imprisonment at Dartmoor. Lucas had heard about the progress of Lord Tovey's apple orchards, how many sheep had lambed the past spring, and which tenants had done well. The one thing they hadn't talked about was what absorbed them most—their wives. It was as if they feared that talking about the situation would make it real.

But now they were staring at a gravestone neither of them could ignore. It read, in English:

Here lies Theodore Frier
Beloved brother and friend
May he find the peace in death
Denied to him in life

Lucas read it with a sinking in his chest. Amelia had been right when she'd said it was revenge that drove him. Because now that he saw the words carved in stone, his disappointment was so overpowering that he realized just how badly he'd wanted Dorothy to be lying.

"It looks authentic," Lord Tovey said beside him.

"Yes." But they both knew that didn't mean much.

"What shall you do now? We could hunt down that fellow Lebeau, who prepared the body for burial. The man maintaining the parish register may not have known where he went, but surely someone does."

The desperation in Lord Tovey's voice struck a powerful chord with Lucas. The man was in a terror that he'd lose his wife, and Lucas knew exactly what that was like.

"We could also speak to the local apothecary," Lord Tovey went on. "Those fellows at the inn said he would return by evening. He might know something more about the death recorded in the parish register."

Lucas sighed. If the apothecary didn't know anything about the death, there would be another trek to find this Lebeau. And for what? So Lucas could prove that Frier was alive? So that he could make sure his revenge hadn't been snatched out from beneath his nose by a twist of fate?

In the end, all he'd probably learn is what he'd learned here—nothing solid. A lot of little things, but no real proof.

When Lucas still didn't answer, his father-in-law growled, "Tell me what to do, Major. Give me some task, or I shall go mad with worrying what you will do to my Dolly."

Lucas tensed, shaken to the soul by such desperation. He understood it only too well. There were some things worth lowering one's pride and begging for—redemption, mercy . . . one's wife.

Lucas stared at the drawn face he'd come to know well in the past days, at the graying temples and the anguished brown eyes that reminded him so much of Amelia's. "You believe Frier is dead, don't you?"

The sudden hope in Lord Tovey's eyes was so poignant, Lucas had to look away. "I do. But whether I believe it is not the question. It's what *you* believe that counts. And what proof your government will accept."

Lucas was silent a long moment, then finally admitted what he hadn't dared to before. "As long as they get their money, my government will accept what I tell them. If I make a rubbing of the gravestone, report what I found out here, and give them the death certificate, they'll probably accept my word. For them, the money is what matters."

"Are you sure?" Lord Tovey said hoarsely.

"Yes. The one who cared most about seeing Frier dragged back to stand trial was me. If I proclaim him dead, they'll accept that he is since they know how fiercely I wanted him captured."

"Ah," Lord Tovey replied, a wealth of meaning in that word. Clearly, he understood after a week what Amelia had recognized that night in London—that Lucas was driven by far more than the embezzlement. Lucas wanted justice, for his father and for himself. And he could finally acknowledge that he wasn't likely to get it—at least from Frier.

He'd had plenty of time over this trip to review his evidence in light of Lady Tovey's claims. Things he had ignored before now loomed larger in his memory. Like the evasive manner of Dorothy's former employer when Lucas had asked why the woman left. Or the trail of good reports she'd left behind her wherever they lived.

He'd been so determined to see her as a manipulative seductress that he'd made the evidence fit. Because it suited him. Because it suited his hate.

Because his search had given him something to live for, when his whole life had been one long measure of grief.

But finally he had a chance at something other than grief—a wife who suited him, who wanted to bear his children and have a life with him . . . who loved him.

He gave a shuddering breath as he faced his wife's father. "So you would stake your honor, everything you stand for, on the belief that your wife is telling the truth?"

Lord Tovey stared him down. "I would be a fool not to. I've spent two years learning her moods, finding out what will bring tears to her eyes, and what will make her laugh. Two years of breakfasts and dinners together, two years of memorizing every freckle on her dear face . . . two years of knowing when she is lying and when she is telling the truth."

Lucas lifted an eyebrow. "You didn't know she had a brother."

"No, but I knew she had a past."

Lucas blinked. Apparently he hadn't been the only one hiding things.

"Despite what you think," Lord Tovey continued, "my wife is not particularly adept at deception. I guessed after a week of marriage that Obadiah Smith was a clear invention, for no woman who'd ever been married could have been as continuously surprised by the intimacies of marriage as my shy wife. After a month, I realized that she had some dark secret plaguing her. But I never pressed her because I knew she'd tell me when she was no longer afraid of losing me if she did." His voice shook. "When she could finally accept that I loved her too much ever to let anything separate us."

A lump lodged in Lucas's throat. "You're as much a romantic as Amelia. Who, by the way, never realized any of what you realized about your wife. She believed Dolly was innocent from the very first, no matter what I said."

"That's because Amelia desperately wanted a mother, and Dolly gave her that. And because my daughter couldn't imagine that anyone she loved would ever deceive her in anything but the most superficial manner. When she gives her trust, she gives it with her whole heart, and it would take a powerful effort for anyone she loved to destroy that trust."

I can't live with a man I can't trust.

And could she trust him now? Would she be able to trust him in the future?

She'd said that as long as he went to France and confirmed Dorothy's story, she would live with his decision about what to do after that. But he was no fool. If he dragged her family's name through the mud in some vain attempt to draw out a man who might very well be dead, she would never recover from it.

It would chip away at her trust of him as surely as his evasions had done. He would lose her. And suddenly, that was just one sacrifice too many in his life.

"Well then," he said, turning toward the entrance to the cemetery, "we're done here. I think it's time to go home."

Two weeks had passed since Amelia's father and husband had gone off to France, and she was fit to be tied. Torquay wasn't a lively town in the best of times, but in her current state it was excruciating. With little to occupy her, she had far too much time to worry about Lucas.

The one bright spot was that she and Dolly spent a great deal of time together. That's when Amelia realized how difficult it must have been for Dolly to deceive them all—because now that she could speak freely, she couldn't stop talking. She told Amelia about her parents, her childhood in New England, her awful time as a housekeeper in Rhinebeck. She seemed so relieved that her mood was lighter than it had ever been, despite the worry about the future hanging over both their heads. Clearly the secrets of her past had plagued her for some time, and it took an enormous weight off her to have them out in the open. So perhaps Lucas had done some good, after all.

As long as he didn't cart Dolly off to America.

After a suitable time of pretending to be on her honeymoon, Amelia resumed her correspondence with Venetia. Desperate for news, she wrote her friend daily, claiming that she and Lucas were spending time in the country before returning to London.

From Mrs. Harris, who knew about Lucas's trip to France, she learned that Lord Pomeroy had come to town and spoken nary a word about her or Lucas. But word had leaked out about his perfidy, and while some dismissed it as rumor, others were giving him the cut direct at parties. More importantly, parents were more careful with their daughters around him, which relieved Amelia enormously.

From Venetia, however, she heard nothing. She found that odd, given that her first letter had been a lengthy account of her and Lucas's encounter with the Scottish Scourge. Of course, the London papers had already covered it, quoting the Kirkwoods' description of the affair and lauding Major Winter and his wife for their successful escape. But Amelia wanted to hear what Venetia might tell her privately about the Scottish Scourge.

So when a letter finally arrived from her early one morning, Amelia seized on it eagerly. But it merely raised more questions:

Now, dearest friend, regarding your bizarre experience on the roads in Scotland, I confess I had no idea when I read the newspapers that I had some part in your abduction. How appalling! But I don't know what it means. I still have no idea why this Scottish Scourge fellow is plaguing Papa, and Papa says he doesn't, either. Unfortunately he's had another of his painful spells, which is why I've taken so long to answer your letter. And in his present condition, I fear to press him on the matter. But you can be sure that as soon as he is better, I will do so.

The letter went on to beg information about what married life was like. Amelia didn't know whether to smile or weep as she read it. Or how she could answer.

But even as she pondered it, a servant rushed into the drawing room. "The master's home, milady! He's home!"

Her heart pounding, Amelia raced into the hall, arriving at the same moment as Dolly, who threw herself into her husband's arms with a cry of joy. Lucas was nowhere to be seen.

"Papa?" Amelia asked. "Where is my husband?"

Her father was too busy hugging his wife to even spare Amelia a glance. "He'll be along this evening," he said. "He had something to attend to first."

Her heart sank. "Something regarding Dolly?"

Her father's gaze shot to her. "No, dear, no. I see I have arrived before the letter I sent from France. But everything is fine." He stared tenderly down at Dolly. "Major Winter has decided not to pursue the matter further. He's going to make a full report on your brother's death to his government. We'll arrange to have the rest of the stolen money repaid, and that will be an end to it."

A rush of relief hit Amelia, so profound that her knees went weak. "So where is he?"

"He went to Dartmoor Prison. Said he wanted to see it now that it's empty."

"And you let him go alone?" Amelia cried. "Are you mad? That will set him to thinking about all his wrongs again, for heaven's sake." She ordered the footman to fetch her pelisse and hat.

Her father watched her in clear alarm. "Now see here, he'll be fine. There are some things a man should do alone."

"That may be," she snapped as the footman helped her on with her pelisse. "But this is not one of them."

"Amelia—" her father began.

"Let her be, George," Dolly shocked her by saying. "It's not more than a few hours by coach, and if it will ease her mind, she should go." She laid her head on his chest. "It has been a long wait for both of us, you know."

Amelia's father softened. He never could resist Dolly. "Whatever you wish, dear heart." He glanced at his daughter. "We docked in Plymouth, but he was still trying to find someone willing to drive him the thirty miles to Princetown when I left. So if you leave now and take my carriage, you might arrive there shortly after he does. Take a footman with you."

"Of course." She kissed her father on the cheek. "Thank you, Papa."

A short while later, she headed for Princetown. Although Dartmoor Prison was in Devon, she'd never been there. And two hours later, as the coach climbed higher and higher, she realized why. Because no one with any sense would come willingly to such a desolate spot.

Still a wilderness part of England, the rocky outcroppings and impassable bogs and mires of the barren moor were legendary. She'd heard that it was often plagued by fog, but today it was clear, affording her a grim view of Dartmoor Prison's distant granite walls. Ugly and remote, the prison was flanked on one end by Princetown, a town there only to serve the prison. As her coach drove through it, she saw few signs of life. Now that all the prisoners were gone, the town seemed to be languishing.

As her carriage approached the prison proper, her heart sank to think of Lucas locked up in that inhospitable place, plagued continually by damp and cold, with nothing but a bleak vista as far as the eye could see. As she imagined him forced to obey the dictates of men as arrogant as himself, to endure the many petty humiliations inflicted upon prisoners of war, her heart sank further. Even if he'd resigned himself to giving up on his revenge before, seeing this place would surely renew it. How could it not?

She had no trouble finding Lucas, for as she drove up, he was standing in front of the stone arch entrance. Apparently he'd walked up from the town, for there was no carriage nearby.

If he heard the approach of her carriage, he made no sign, for he didn't alter his military stance. His arms remained folded behind his back and his feet set slightly apart as he gazed at the locked wooden gates.

He wore his uniform—not the one she'd seen at the ball but a different one, without the red sash. It hung on him, and with wifely concern she wondered how well he'd been eating. Or sleeping, since passage to France had probably required his going belowdecks.

He looked so lost in thought that she was careful to warn him of her approach by speaking his name before she reached him.

He hesitated a second, then swung around, his face mirroring his surprise. "Amelia! What are you doing here?"

She managed a smile, though his drawn features made her want to weep. "I didn't think this was the sort of place you should come to alone."

To her relief, he returned her smile with a faint one of his own. "Afraid I'd run mad over the moor, were you?"

"Afraid you'd forgotten you had a wife, more like," she said lightly, though her heart was in her throat.

He held out his arms, and she went into them eagerly, not even resisting when he hugged her so tightly she could scarcely breathe. "I missed you," he murmured into her hair. "I missed you every moment I was away."

"I see how much you missed me," she teased, choking back tears. "Instead of coming home to me, you came to this nasty old prison."

With a chuckle, he drew back but didn't release her, just turned to face the prison gates with one arm looped about her waist. "I was saying good-bye," he said.

"To what?"

"To everything. The war. My parents." He dragged in a breath. "My revenge. You were right, you know. My pursuit of Frier wasn't about justice—it was mostly about revenge. But not just against him." His fingers dug into her. "Against the English, for this . . . *travesty*. For men held beyond the rightful time, men kept from returning to their families. Men murdered in cold blood."

"Men locked in tunnels beneath the ground, gasping for breath."

He nodded. "In my mind, Dartmoor marked the beginning of my troubles. I was convinced that if it hadn't been for the prison, I would have been home and able to help my family. Frier wouldn't have been able to embezzle the money, or if he had, I would have caught up to him before he could spend it, while he was still able to exonerate my father."

A thoughtful expression crossed his face. "But the truth is, I could still have been elsewhere after the war ended. The marines returned to Algiers in 1815. And other events might have kept me from home, especially since I was never eager to be around my parents' constant bickering. Dartmoor didn't mark the beginning of my troubles—it was just another tragedy of war."

A shuddering breath shook him. "That's the hardest part to face. That there's no one to blame, no one to punish."

"Not even Theodore Frier?" she asked hesitantly.

He cast her a thin smile. "Not even him. He's dead, you know."

She sagged against him, her relief so profound it made her knees weak.

"He's dead, and so is this place." He regarded the rusty padlock on the gate with a pensive look. "I expected to find it the same as it was when I was here—redcoats marching and prisoners in ill-fitting yellow jackets. But of course it isn't. Because life goes on." He gestured to the weeds growing in cracks of the abandoned prison's walls. "Time erodes everything eventually, doesn't it?"

"Not everything," she murmured, then gathered her heart in her hands and offered it. "Not love."

He sucked in a breath. "No, not love." Turning her toward him, he cupped her cheek. "That's really why I came here today—to be sure I could put it behind me, to see if I could be the man you need."

"And what did you decide?" she asked in an aching whisper.

"I have no choice. I love you, Amelia." His eyes burned into hers, tender, tortured. "I can't bear to live even one day more without you. So if keeping you means forgetting my past, then I will try."

Her heart filled with joy. "I'm not asking you to forget your past, my love. I'm just asking that you not let it ruin your present." She slid her arms about his neck. "Or our future."

"I won't," he vowed, then kissed her with all the love she could ever want.

The cough of her father's coachman reminded her they weren't alone, and she drew back with a blush. "We should probably retire to a more private place."

"Like a consulate in Morocco?" he asked.

She gazed at him, startled.

"Among the mail waiting for me when we returned from Scotland was a letter offering me the position of an American consul. I read it the morning your father and I left for France."

"You mean, the morning you left me without a good-bye?" she said archly.

He cast her a rueful grin. "I was afraid to wake you, afraid that seeing you in all your naked glory might dim my resolve." His grin faded. "I should've realized my resolve was dimmed the second I found you lurking outside my room, plotting to thwart me by fluttering your eyelashes and calling me 'a big, strapping soldier.'"

She ran her hands over his shoulders. "You *are* a big, strapping soldier. *My* big, strapping soldier."

"Soon to be your big, strapping consul." A mischievous glint appeared in his eye. "*If* the pesky wife I've acquired, the one who gets annoyed when I make decisions without asking her, agrees to it. That's why I haven't answered the letter yet."

Sobering, he searched her face. "I know you like adventures, darlin', but after everything we've been through since we met, life abroad might have lost some of its appeal. The conditions may be primitive, and since your dowry will help repay what Frier stole, our income will be pretty modest. We won't be able to afford—"

"Lucas . . ." she began in a warning tone.

"I'm just saying that the only crocodile crockery we'll be buying is whatever you find in the cheap bazaars in Tangier."

Tangier! The very word conjured up delightful images of mosaics and houris and dangerous desert expeditions. "Will I get to ride a camel?"

He broke into a smile. "If you want. Hell, darlin', if you agree to live with me in Morocco, I'll make sure you even get to *eat* a camel."

"Riding one will be quite sufficient, thank you. Very well, I consent to your accepting the position. But under one condition."

"And what is that?" he asked with a lift of one thick eyebrow.

"That you don't expect me to be an obedient wife."

With a laugh, he took her arm and led her toward the carriage. "I don't think I could live with you if you were. The last time nearly killed me."

"Really?" Her mind raced ahead to their next sensual encounter. "In that case—"

"Oh, no you don't," he growled as he lifted her into the carriage. "You were right about that, too, darlin'. I don't want an obedient wife." As he joined her on the seat inside, he took her in his arms. "What I want is a loving wife."

"Thank goodness. Because *that*, my dear husband, you already have."

Epilogue

Dear Cousin,
I received the loveliest gift from dear Amelia Winter last
week—a teapot in the shape of a camel! She also sent
news that she is once more expecting a child. She says
that Major Winter is delighted . . . and does not try to
restrict her movements too terribly much. But knowing
our Amelia, no matter what he tries, she will prevail.
Your friend,
Charlotte

The sun was setting west of Tangier when a noise in the hall of the American Legation Building made Lucas turn from the open French doors of his new study. Seconds later his wife and brown-eyed daughter Isabel burst into the room, followed closely by the young Moroccan nursemaid they'd hired to care for her once Amelia had learned she was expecting another child.

"And where have you been, young lady?" Lucas made himself look stern, though his minx of a daughter was already giggling hard enough to shake her chestnut curls. "Don't tell me you've been off getting into trouble."

"Not trouble, Daddy," Isabel cried. "Adventure!"

He didn't know whether to laugh or groan. His little sweetie wasn't quite three yet, and she could already lisp the word *adventure*. He glanced at his smirking wife, and lifted one eyebrow. "This is all your fault. Just imagine—if our daughter is eager for 'adventure' at this age, our son will probably leave the womb brandishing a pistol."

"You do realize we might not have a boy," Amelia said, eyes twinkling as she rubbed her thickening belly. "Dolly said that she felt her quickening at five months for young Thomas, but some time later for baby Georgiana. I'm already at five months and haven't felt it. So the baby may be a girl."

"God have mercy on me if it is," he teased. "I can hardly handle the two females I already have." He smiled at his daughter. "Well, sweetie? What do you think will happen if Mama gives you a little sister?"

"More adventure, Daddy!" she crowed.

He chuckled. "Probably." Tucking his thumbs in his trouser pockets, he gazed down at her. "So what sort of adventure did you and Mama have this afternoon, while Daddy was at an audience with the sultan? Did you herd fish in the bay? Write messages for pirates? Beat a brigand?"

Isabel laughed, the sweet sound warming him to the soul. "Daddy silly," she said, holding out her arms.

He scooped her up with a mock growl. "Silly, am I? I'll show you silly, you little wiggle-worm . . ." And he pretended to eat her ear as she giggled and squirmed.

"We toured all the rooms and made a list of what will be needed," his wife said. "This place is amazing. Does your government have any idea how valuable this property is?"

"If they don't, I'll make sure I tell them." He jiggled Isabel on his hip. "So you like it, do you?"

"Like it!" Amelia beamed at him. "It's magnificent! There are enough rooms for us to have as many children as we please, and we're right in the heart of the city. There are courtyards and fountains and—"

"And this." He gestured out the French doors. "Come see."

With Isabel in his arms, he took Amelia out onto the fourth-floor terrace, then pointed. "When it's clear, as it is now, you can see Gibraltar from here."

"Goodness gracious," Amelia whispered, as they took in the vista before them—the bustling harbor, the shining blue Straits of Gibraltar, and even the old city itself.

As the three of them stood gazing out across the straits, the peace of pure contentment stole over Lucas. He'd never expected to have this heaven of a life, to have an adoring wife, a lively daughter, and the expectation of other children. Dartmoor was a distant memory, and so were his nightmares. He hadn't had one since he'd left France three years ago. He could even, when necessary, tolerate going belowdecks on a ship.

Not that he wanted to. He enjoyed being a consul, enjoyed the periods of quiet punctured by moments of sheer surprise. And his income had proved more than adequate for their needs. They actually lived very well. They hadn't touched the money his father-in-law insisted upon sending them monthly in an attempt to repay what his wife's brother had stolen. And Amelia even got to have her exotic dishes, not to mention exotic berber rugs, exotic visits to the sultan's palace, and an exotic ride on a camel.

And now this. After three years of living in modest lodgings, they'd been shocked when the sultan had taken it into his head to give the American legation a consulate that amounted to a palace. They'd moved in today, and Amelia had already set herself to making it into a home.

Isabel wriggled in his arms, having lost interest in the view. "Daddy, down!"

Laughing, Amelia took the child and went back inside to give her to the nursemaid with instructions to feed her supper and prepare her for bed.

When Amelia came back, Lucas wrapped his arm about her waist, and they returned to admiring the view. After a moment, she laughed. "I should write Lord Pomeroy and tell him that I can see Gibraltar whenever I please."

Pomeroy—he hadn't thought of that scoundrel in a long time. "What's the general doing these days? Do any of your many correspondents ever say?"

"He finally found a wife—can you believe it? Some Italian countess worth a fortune. I'm sure they'll be very happy together, as long as she doesn't mind polishing his opium pipe from time to time."

At the tart comment, he glanced down to find her gazing at him with eyes agleam. She wore one of her brightly hued Moroccan gowns, the ones that always heated his blood and set his pulse racing. Judging from her sultry smile, his temptress of a wife knew just what effect the gown had on him, too.

"Speaking of polishing," he said as he drew her back inside, "we've been so busy preparing for the move these past few days that my sword has grown a mite rusty. It could use some attention."

"Really?" She cast him a teasing glance. "I shall fetch a rag at once."

"You don't need a rag," he growled as he dragged her into his arms. "Your hand will be good enough."

"For a sword as fine as yours? Hardly. I'll need a rag and polish and—"

He cut her off with a kiss that was hotter than the desert sun. When she pulled back sometime later, she was smiling as only his Lady Delilah could.

"Very well, I suppose we can make do with my hand." Her gaze turned seductive. "Or my mouth. Or any number of things suitable for worshipping a man's fine weaponry."

"Craving a little adventure, are you?" he murmured as his "fine weaponry" made an instant response.

"Always." She tugged him toward their new bed-chamber. "When it comes to the man she loves, a woman can never have too much adventure."

Author's Note

$\mathcal{D}$oing research for this book made me realize how significant the War of 1812 was in making America feel like a nation and not just a rebellious British colony. When I read firsthand accounts of how American sailors who suffered impressment by the British laid down their arms at the declaration of war, refusing to fight against their countrymen, I was moved to tears. They preferred being prisoners of war to serving in the British Navy against their will. Many of them ended up at Dartmoor Prison, where they had the British tearing their hair out with their constant attempts to escape. Freedom has always been important to us, hasn't it?

The Dartmoor Prison Massacre is an actual historical event—the only change I made to the story was in having someone trapped in a tunnel during it. But the rest of the tale of Dartmoor, including the fact that the massacre took place long *after* the war ended, is true. To this day, no one can agree on whom to blame—it was the senselessness of it that broke my heart and made me include it.

And although the local militias fled before the British at the Battle of Bladensburg, the Marine Guard fought until they were forced to retreat, many of them taken prisoner or killed. Also, it was the march on Derna that gave us the lines of the marine hymn, "From the halls of Montezuma to the shores of Tripoli." And yes, they really did eat a camel!

Pocket Books
proudly presents a preview of

Don't Bargain with the Devil

The fifth novel in Sabrina Jeffries's
New York Times bestselling
The School for Heiresses series

Available in June 2009 from Pocket Books

And look for Charlotte and Cousin Michael's
book

Wed Him Before You Bed Him

Available in July 2009 from
Pocket Books

Lucy headed to the blooming cherry orchard that separated the school from its neighboring estate, Rockhurst. According to the headmistress, Mrs. Harris, Mr. Pritchard had been trying to sell it, but no one would meet his exorbitant price since the house was nearly beyond repair. So Rockhurst had lain vacant for the past three months, which was why Lucy felt free to wander onto its orchard.

As she entered the trees, a breeze sent blossoms tumbling about her like snowflakes and her heart lightened. Unable to resist the enticement, she kicked off her kidskin slippers and began to twirl amidst the falling blossoms as she'd done when she was a girl. The more she twirled, the less her heart ached. Her hair pulled loose from its pins to fall about her, twirling with her.

For the first time in days she felt free to be herself, without Peter's nasty words about her being a hot-blooded hoyden taking her to task. When she was gasping and too light-headed to make another turn, she threw herself to the ground. Tucking her hands beneath her head, she stared up at the branches and lifted her face to the blossoms drifting gently onto her gown.

If only life could always be like this, just cherry blossoms and spring. Or even as it was during her blissful student days here, when she and the other girls learned geography and the waltz and how men could deceive you—

A sigh escaped her. She should have heeded those lessons. Instead she'd let her imagination run away with her, soaking up the nonsense in that scandalous book of harem's tales she and the girls had read in secret. She'd convinced herself that one day she and Peter would marry and try—she yawned—all those . . . naughty . . . things. . . .

The previous night's tear-torn sleep caught up with her, and she fell into a doze. She was dreaming of a harem where the women were in charge, and the sultan had to do *their* bidding, when a deep male voice penetrated her haze.

"What have we here? A local lady come to welcome me to the neighborhood? Or a goddess descended from Mount Olympus to sport with a mere mortal?"

Lucy's eyes shot open. Was she still dreaming? The devilishly handsome man standing at her feet could easily be a sultan, with his olive skin and eyes the color of roasted almonds. He'd clearly just come from a bath, for his glossy black hair lay damp upon his neck. Shockingly, he wore only a white shirt tucked into black pantaloons tucked into a pair of top boots, with no waistcoat, coat, or cravat.

She *must* be dreaming. No man hereabouts would leave his house in shirtsleeves. Or leave his shirt open at the throat to reveal a smattering of chest hair, or wear pantaloons so tight they showed every well-defined muscle in his thighs. He was such a delicious specimen of manliness that he fairly took her breath away.

Meanwhile, *his* gaze slid down her body in an intimate and decidedly wicked perusal. It paused at her breasts before moving to where her gown dipped between her parted legs. After casting her stocking feet a pointed look, he smiled, his thin black mustache quirking up.

"A goddess, most assuredly," he said in faintly accented English. "No local señorita would walk about without her shoes."

Señorita? Oh no. He wasn't her dream sultan. He was very much real. And foreign. And a complete stranger.

Belatedly, she scrambled to a sitting position. Lord, what must he think of her? Before she could struggle to a stand, he held out his hand. She hesitated half a second before taking it, and the moment she was on her feet, she snatched her hand free.

A chuckle escaped him. "I should beg your pardon for disturbing your siesta, but I do not regret it. You make an enchanting picture lying in the cherry blossoms."

His amusement sparked her temper. "Who *are* you, sir, and why are you on private property?"

He arched one finely groomed black brow. "I could ask the same of you."

"I'm a teacher at the school that adjoins this orchard." She smoothed her skirt, trying to make herself look more teacherly. It was woefully hard to do with her hair tumbled down about her waist.

"Ah yes, the girls' academy." He cast her a speculative glance. "But that is *what* you are, not who. What is your name?"

Oh dear, she wasn't supposed to be here, and if he were to mention it to Mrs. Harris . . . "I shan't give my name to a stranger. Especially when you haven't given me yours. *You* are the intruder here."

"Intruder! What a suspicious little thing you are," he

said without rancor. "As it happens, you already know my name. It's on my calling card."

The comment threw her into confusion. "I-I . . . haven't seen your calling card. If you left it with our schoolmistress—"

"No need to dissemble, señorita. You have it right there." He reached up to pull something from behind her ear, then held it out with a flourish.

Caught off guard, she took the gilt-edged calling card from him. "How did you . . ." She trailed off as she read the printed card.

Diego Javier Montalvo, Master of Mystery.

Master of Mystery? She lifted her gaze to him, seeing nothing in his half-smile to enlighten her. It didn't sound like anything a normal person would put on a card. It almost sounded like . . .

The truth dawned. "Oh, Lord, you're a magician."

"Indeed I am." He gave her a mock frown. "You don't seem very pleased to hear it."

Hardly! She had a weakness for magicians—their swirling black capes, their intriguing smiles, their astonishing ability to surprise at every turn. Coupled with her weakness for devastatingly handsome continental gentlemen, Diego Javier Montalvo was the perfect temptation. But Peter would *never* eat his words if he learned she'd been flirting with a stranger.

"So why is a magician wandering around Rockhurst?" she demanded. As a teacher, she would be most irresponsible if she didn't find out.

"Are you worried I have come to steal your neighbor's valuables?"

"Have you?" she asked archly.

That made him grin. "I would hardly tell you the truth

if I have." The words rolled off his tongue melodically, turning her knees to butter.

None of that! she chided herself as she glanced about for her shoes, which were nowhere to be seen. *You must be responsible. Mature. Not swayed by good-looking men. Not the sort of woman a man only dallies with.*

"Perhaps I am here to steal something else." His voice had turned calculating. "The heart of a beautiful lady like you, for example."

She burst into laughter. *That* sort of nonsense she could handle perfectly well. "Do you rehearse such compliments when you rehearse your tricks? Or do flatteries simply come naturally to you?"

He looked genuinely surprised. "You are very jaded for one so young."

"Young! I'll have you know I'm over twenty years old."

His eyes seemed to mock her. "Ah, then you are clearly a woman of the world. My mistake."

She crossed her arms over her chest. "I'm certainly worldly enough to tell when a man is trying to turn me up sweet for his own purposes."

Some unreadable emotion swept his angular features. "And what purposes would those be?"

"I have no clue." She blew out an exasperated breath. "You still haven't told me what you're doing here."

"Very well, if you must know, I am the new tenant at Rockhurst."

Pure shock kept her motionless. "Oh, dear," she murmured, mortified anew.

Laughter glinted in his gaze. "So you see, Señorita Schoolteacher, *you* are the intruder. I saw you from the window upstairs as I was dressing, and came down to learn who was invading my property." He reached up to pluck a leaf from her disordered hair. "*Now* will you allow me the pleasure of your name?"

Definitely not. For one thing, just the brush of his fingers had already quickened her pulse most dangerously. For another, it would be a great deal easier for him to complain to Mrs. Harris if he knew her name. "I-I didn't think the house was even habitable."

"It will suffice until I decide if I want to buy the estate."

But weren't conjurers nomads, living in inns and lodging houses? He was too young to retire, and surely even London theaters didn't pay well enough for him to afford a property the size of Rockhurst. "What would you do with it?"

His gaze grew shuttered. "It depends."

Something in his evasive manner sparked her concern. "On what?"

"Whether it and its environs meet my stringent requirements."

Its environs? Did he mean the school? "What sort of requirements? Surely once it is put into shape, Rockhurst would be sufficient for your family."

"I am not married." He cocked his head, dropping one raven lock over his eye, then smoothed it back with the nonchalance of a man sure of his exotic appeal. "And you? Does your position as a teacher mean you have no husband?"

She caught herself before answering. "Why are you avoiding my question?"

"For the same reason you are avoiding mine, I would imagine." His eyes gleamed with mischief. "To prolong this intriguing conversation."

A laugh bubbled up inside her that she struggled

to tamp down. "Actually, I find it less intriguing than frustrating. You are purposely being mysterious."

"As are you, Señorita Schoolteacher. Indeed, your reluctance to divulge your identity fascinates me." He bent his head close enough that she caught a whiff of soap and hair oil. "You stand in my orchard and interrogate me bold as brass, yet you will not tell me something as small as your name. Are you hiding a secret? Acting as a spy?" Seeing the smile rise to her lips despite her struggle to prevent it, he lowered his voice to a throaty murmur. "Waiting for a lover, perhaps?"

She jerked back as an unfamiliar heat rose in her cheeks. Good Lord, did she give off some scent that led people to make assumptions about her character?

Then again, he *had* found her shamelessly lolling about in his orchard. She would have to set him straight.

"That's a very impertinent suggestion, sir," she answered in her loftiest tone. "Especially when we haven't been properly introduced."

A slow smile curved up his finely carved lips. "And do such trivialities matter to you, *cariño?*"

Cariño? Oh, but that was too wicked of him. Her Spanish was rusty, but she did remember that *cariño* was an endearment. A trill of pleasure skirled along her nerves. He should never have used it with her, whether he thought she understood it or not. And she certainly shouldn't let it do funny things to her insides.

She answered sharply, "This is not the Continent, sir. 'Such trivialities' matter to everyone in England. So if you hope for success in your ventures here, you'd best start showing some concern for propriety yourself."

Her remark darkened his gaze to a dangerous glitter. "I forgot how obsessed you English are with propriety," he bit out. "Except, of course, when you are invading other people's property."

He was right to chide her for that. And she'd been rude indeed to point out his improprieties when she'd been the one trespassing. Though she couldn't fathom why it angered him now, when he hadn't seemed to care earlier.

"Forgive me for intruding," she said, wanting to escape with her dignity—and identity—intact. "I must go."

She whirled toward the school, but had taken only two steps before he called out, "Aren't you forgetting something?"

When she looked back he was dangling her slippers from two fingers, his features smoothed into a charming mask once more.

"Thank you, sir," she murmured, but when she reached for the shoes, he held them out of reach, easy enough for him to do with his great height.

"Your name, señorita," he said softly, a smug smile playing over his lips.

She hesitated, weighing her choices. But there were none.

"Keep the shoes," she retorted, then ran.

Better to lose her slippers than have him inform Mrs. Harris of her shameless behavior. If Peter should hear how she'd reclined on the ground like a "hot-blooded hoyden" while some stranger looked her over, she'd simply die. As long as Señor Montalvo didn't know her name, this incident need never reach anyone. Their paths weren't likely to cross again.

Still, she wanted to warn Mrs. Harris about the man. It wouldn't do to have the girls trailing after him like lovesick puppies. Besides, something wasn't right. Why would a magician rent an estate the size of Rockhurst just for himself?

If she hadn't been so busy reacting to his flirtations, she might have pressed him for more information. But when he'd cast his hot gaze down her body and had spoken Spanish endearments in a voice of warm honey . . .

Lord help her. Continental gentlemen were the worst. Or the best, depending on how one looked at it. They knew exactly how to warm a woman's blood.

Perhaps Peter was right about her after all.

She frowned. All right, so she found the foreigner appealing, but he was a performer, for pity's sake. He made love to the audience every night—he'd honed his abilities for years. Of course she was tempted. What living, breathing female wouldn't be, when a man that sinfully attractive looked at her like that?

Peter's new love wouldn't. Lady Judith would be appalled.

Gritting her teeth, Lucy cut through the garden while twisting her hair up in a knot. She'd best pray she never saw him again. She was much too susceptible to his charms.

She'd nearly reached the steps to the entrance when a female voice asked, "Feel better now, dear?"

Startled, she whirled to find Mrs. Harris sitting at a table, reading the paper. "What do you mean?" Lucy asked guiltily.

"A good walk always cheers one, doesn't it?" she said without looking up.

"Oh." Lucy relaxed. "Yes."

Itching to get inside before Mrs. Harris noticed her missing shoes and disordered hair, she hurried forward. But the schoolmistress's cry of alarm stopped her short.

"What is it?" Lucy hastened back, all thought of her own disarray banished by the woman's stricken expression.

Shaking her head, Mrs. Harris finished scanning an article in the paper. When she threw down the paper with an unladylike oath, Lucy grabbed it up. Front and center was the headline, *Magician to Build Pleasure Garden in Richmond.*

Blast it—she'd *known* that smooth scoundrel was up to something!

Delve *into* a **passion** *from* the **past** *with* a **romance**
from Pocket Books!

LIZ CARLYLE
Never Romance a Rake

Love is always a gamble....But never romance a rake!

JULIA LONDON
The Book of Scandal

Will royal gossip reignite her husband's passion for her?

KARIN TABKE
Master of Surrender
The Blood Sword Legacy

A mercenary knight is bound by a blood oath to reclaim his legacy—and the body of the one woman he desires.

KATHLEEN GIVENS
Rivals for the Crown

The fierce struggle for Scotland's throne leads
two women to courageous new destinies...

**Available wherever books are sold
or at www.simonandschuster.com.**

Delve into a timeless passion...
Pick up a bestselling historical romance from Pocket Books!

Karen Hawkins
To Catch a Highlander
In this game of hearts, love is the only prize.

Johanna Lindsey
The Devil Who Tamed Her
He loves a challenge...and she is an irresistible one.

Jane Feather
To Wed a Wicked Prince
This prince has more than marriage on his mind...

Sabrina Jeffries
Let Sleeping Rogues Lie
Enroll in the School for Heiresses, and discover that desire
has its own rules...and temptations its own rewards.

Meredith Duran
The Duke of Shadows
Born an outcast. Raised to nobility. Only one dangerous
passion can unlock his heart.

Ana Leigh
One Night With a Sweet-Talking Man
He talked his way into her heart.
Can he do the same with her bed?

Available wherever books are sold or at www.simonandschuster.com.

Available wherever books are sold
or at www.simonsayslove.com.

18158

Catch up with love...
Catch up with passion...
Catch up with danger....

Catch a bestseller from Pocket Books!

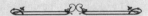

Delve into the past with *New York Times* bestselling author
Julia London
The Dangers of Deceiving a Viscount
Beware! A lady's secrets will always be revealed...

Barbara Delinksy
Lake News

New York Times bestseller!

Sometimes you have to get away to find everything.

Fern Michaels
The Marriage Game
New York Times bestseller!

It's all fun and games—until someone falls in love.

Hester Browne
The Little Lady Agency
New York Times bestseller!

Why trade up if you can fix him up?

Laura Griffin
One Last Breath
Don't move. Don't breathe. Don't say a word...